# The KO Artist

by
Maurice Kamhi

PublishAmerica
Baltimore

First printing

ISBN: 1-4137-2543-0
PUBLISHED BY PUBLISHAMERICA, LLLP
www.publishamerica.com
Baltimore

Printed in the United States of America

I dedicate this to Morshia who, among the myriad wonderful things she's done, found the right publisher; to PublishAmerica for being the right publisher; and to Barbara, Jay, Adam, and Katherine who, for years, put up with my scribbling and other things and, despite them, continued to love me.

$A$rt is the communication of ecstasy.

-Peter Demianovich Ouspensky

# CHAPTER ONE

The first time I realized I was different from other children was when I developed the practice early of placing a wooden stick the size of a pencil—and sometimes an actual pencil—between my forefinger and middle finger, making of it a horse, my forefinger and middle finger jointly being the rider. Sometimes the stick turned into a sword or a revolver and various other weapons in stories I made up in a corner where I secluded myself to play this game of creating adventures that made me feel wonderful in a way that caused everyone and everything else, except for the stick, to be unnecessary to me.

Can you picture what it means to discover you can be the cause of your own joy and happiness?

Not that I didn't like playing with other kids and participating in the kinds of games children play, but I could do those other things or not do them and it didn't matter much either way. I always had the stick and my two digits, which made me happier than anything.

You can imagine what it did for my mother. Until a child has reached the age of—well, at least adolescence—a mother's life verily revolves around the needs of that child. Think of what it means for a mother to have a child who loves sitting in a corner, playing by himself with his little stick in his little hand for hours on end.

Did that come out wrong?

The other difference between me and other children was I found myself with an urge for baby sitters to sit on me.

How did this come about?

I don't remember. One of them probably, while I was lying on my stomach on the couch, must have sat on my rear end playfully or accidentally, and it must have given me a thrill. I remember I nagged every sitter (they were all women) to sit on me and would not relent until they did.

They didn't have to do anything other than sit on me. I would lie on the couch, sometimes on my back, sometimes on my stomach, and they would sit on me. They could read, knit, watch television, talk on the phone—as long as they sat on me. They could be young, middle aged, old, they could be pretty or pretty homely, it made no difference—I loved them to sit on me. The heavier they were, the better I liked it. And the way I remember it, they seemed to like it too. I don't think any of the sitters ever told my parents. *Cosa Nostra*, as the Italians might say—our thing. At least, the subject was never mentioned to me. Else my parents decided it would be wiser to skip it.

At some point around the age of six, I remember playing with a girl my age. She had somehow wrestled me to the floor and, to mark her advantage, sat on my face. She wore black panties and the bottom part of them was on my mouth and nose. I loved the smell—and the feeling. I think this might've served as my graduation from the baby-sitters-sitting-on-me phase.

I mention these things to foreshadow what was to come.

Might as well mention something else. This, too, in retrospect, seems foreshadowy. At some point between the ages of ten and eleven I was riding my bicycle, and I suddenly had a revelation: one day I would form an army. It would be an international army that would mete out justice to the world. I'm not sure I worked it out how exactly this was going to be accomplished. I envisioned—it *would* be.

*You, who have dreams—*

# CHAPTER TWO

Something happened during my last high school semester that turned my life—one might say—outside in. It was the point at which the airplane of my life took off.

The irony was, though the world witnessed its results, I could not tell a soul the story behind it for fear I would be locked up.

So I just sat back as in a canoe without a paddle, heading toward what I knew to be a monster waterfall. Now add to it there are beautiful women in the canoe and the tastiest desserts you can imagine and I could either worry I'd be shattered to smithereens in the oncoming fall, or I could savor the goodies in the canoe and go out in style.

Which would *you* choose? Heh-heh.

It happened in—of all places—gym class. Seward Park High School on New York's Lower East Side. You can imagine the mix of humanity.

The school was named after an erstwhile Secretary of State who bought Alaska for us from the Russians for a pittance. It stood on the corner of Broome and Grand Streets, a square, dirty white building with graffiti on all walls and windows reachable from the street and some places you would've thought unreachable. *To reach the unreachable star.*

Seward Park was in a neighborhood that had for decades been populated by Jewish immigrants—*If I were a rich man, ya-da, da-da*—and become famous for its bargains on just about anything you could think of. In the fifties, sixties, and seventies the Jewish population was replaced by the Hispanic one but the numerous stores with terrific bargains still do a bang-up business.

The smell in every classroom bore the unerasable imprint of too much sweat seeping into too many walls and floors over too many years. This was especially true of the gym, a cavernous, gloomy space with benches that had more curse words sliced in them than a stand-up comic's monologue.

The gym was a place where Shamaz, a Mike Tyson clone, and his gang brought guys who, in Shamaz's judgment, deserved a beating and young women who, in Shamaz's judgment again, deserved raping. The talk was that Shamaz's gang was armed to the teeth and the school authorities were unwilling to find out whether the stories about what happened in the gym at night were true.

There was a new gym teacher, a sturdy looking African-American in his late forties or possibly early fifties, with gray at the sides of black, curly hair and a casual scattering of silver throughout his thick but short-cut mane, very gentle eyes, square-ish, set jaw-line and a vocal tone in the middle register with the tiniest hint of a nasal twang. He had a decency to his presence that gave you a good feeling, something akin to what you get when you see Morgan Freeman on the screen.

I might as well confess I am an out-and-out sucker for decency. If I came across a woman who liked me and who happened to be the homeliest hag in the world—if she were full of goodness—I would be full of love for her. I suspect it must be an aberration. So I have to watch out.

If it *is* an aberration, I must share it with a lot of people. Because, when you come down to it, look at the greatest stars Hollywood produced in the olden days—still untouched by the stars of today in terms of how much the audiences loved them—Gary Cooper, Henry Fonda, Clark Gable, John Wayne—what was their essence? Integrity, decency, honesty, courage. Today's stars even approaching that magnitude you could count on the fingers of one hand and still not use up all the digits.

You could not be a male star being a bad guy. If a man made a tremendous splash in a movie being the bad guy, they immediately turned him into a good guy and he turned into nothing. Think of

Richard Widmark, Jack Palance, Robert De Niro, Joe Pesci; when they were bad, they were glorious. When they were good, they were blah.

This was not the case with women stars. The women stars were not known for their decency and integrity. Rather, they were known for their femme-fatality. Their quintessence said, "I will seduce you and then destroy you; the Carmen/Delilah syndrome. And men were drawn to them like nerds to computers. Sure enough, the men got destroyed. They might've been left standing when the movie ended, but they'd been gutted. There were a few among the women stars whose quintessence *was* decency and integrity but it's hard to remember those. The ones you remember—Bette Davis, Hedy Lamarr, Barbara Stanwyck, Vivien Leigh—were the ones who enticed, castrated, tortured, then terminated.

Now this teacher. The word was he had been a boxer and a pretty good one at that—a number of his bouts had been televised.

It was the beginning of my senior term. I was going to go to college so I was feeling happy. I loved studying. I loved anything that improved me. If I found something was bad for me, I immediately hated it. Except for tomatoes and olives. I knew tomatoes were supposed to be good for you, and possibly olives, but I hated them anyway. No idea why. Up to that day this had been the only mystery of my life.

Was I in for a surprise.

This new teacher, Mr. Johnson, didn't do any of the things other gym teachers had done, like having us jump up and down or do sit-ups or run or play basketball or dodge ball—you know, where you have two teams and throw the ball at somebody on the other team and try to hit them, eliminating them from the game, until whoever's left is the winner? No, this guy brought out a carton full of boxing gloves, handing out a pair to each of us until the supply ran out and then those who got gloves were paired off as opponents while the next group waited its turn.

I was paired off with, of all people, Shamaz, who not only looked like Mike Tyson but was built like him and was one of those tough guys whom I had successfully avoided throughout my high school career. And now, just when I thought it was safe and I was on my way to a higher learning institution where I wouldn't have to worry about tough guys—this new gym teacher pairs me off with him.

You know, I've always had the feeling that, no matter how good and kind an African-American person was, any day could turn out to be hate-whitey day. And it certainly seemed that way with this decent-seeming teacher. Give a guy like Shamaz boxing gloves and you're giving him license to send you to never-never land. Jesus, I thought, I could lose teeth, get a concussion, I could be a vegetable for the rest of my life. Boy, oh, boy, I thought, in a million different ways, for centuries to come, we're going to be paying for the slavery thing. I wouldn't be surprised if the debt eventually got paid way after the monetary national debt and with a hell of a lot of interest to boot. Man, if the Native Americans hadn't been for all practical purposes annihilated, we'd be having the same problem with them rather than simply having it on our conscience.

Mister Johnson gave us some pointers on how to defend ourselves, how to jab, how to duck, how to throw a hook, an uppercut, how to move our feet, how and where to throw a knockout punch— I really needed for Shamaz to know how to throw a knockout punch.

What I did like about it—and this was the only thing and in spite of myself—was he made us go through each motion until we had it right. Went around correcting us and making us do it over and over till we really had it down. You don't get that in the rest of the educational system. They lecture you and give you incomprehensible stuff to read and then they give you an exam and if you memorized the stuff, you could pass with flying colors. And what practical good did it do you in terms of being able to apply it? Except for the education of doctors, lawyers, accountants, and engineers, I didn't see it did any good at all. It felt good to really learn something and know how to *do* it.

And—and then it appeared we were ready for battle.

"Now when I blow this whistle," Mister Johnson said, "start boxin'. When I blow it again, stop. Don't hit below the belt and, once the guy's goin' down, don't keep hittin'm. No head butts and no elbows. Everybody got that?" He looked around, getting acknowledgement from each pair of opponents. "Okay, get your guards up. Ready?" He blew the whistle.

The opponents all began to circle one another.

Except for Shamaz and me.

Why not us two?
Whether I can describe adequately what happened—I doubt.
Too weird. Much too weird. Way—way—*WAY*—too weird.

*Shamaz—before my eyes—changed from a seventeen-year old African-American built like Mike Tyson to a white guy in his thirties with a hawkish nose, a white sheet draped about his body and, from one of the folds of the sheet, his right hand stuck out, holding a big knife with a crossbar, the part of the pommel I could see etched with all kinds of unfamiliar decorations.*

*He held the knife shoulder-high, like the mother in Psycho in the I'm-about-to-plunge-it-into-your-chest position, coming right at me.*

*I had the hopeful thought I might already have been knocked out and was having* eine kleine *nightmare but, really, this was no time for hopeful thoughts. It was a time when you did something—*toute de suite*—or died.*

*As this guy in sheets moved toward me, bringing the massive Roman-looking knife along, I bent down and, screaming in guttural, animal-like sounds, "You, ugly one," lunged diagonally, crossing over with my left leg while feinting with my left fist, and brought my right leg forward and right fist over his left arm, parabola-style, impacting his left temple with what felt like unnatural abandon.*

After my fist had made contact, I fell to the floor. Just lay there. It was cold and hard and smooth and smelled of piss. Let him stab me now, at least I got a blow in.

Like Sinatra—I did it my way.

Everything was very still. Faintly I heard a piece of a song going through my head:

*Sweet illusion*
*Sweet as a face in a dream*
*Only to dreamers you seem*
*A clear ray of sunlight*

# CHAPTER THREE

I felt the cold, dusty wooden floor against my cheek. I saw a body—and knees by the body. I looked up. Mister Johnson was kneeling by Shamaz's body. Gently slapping his face. It was so peaceful on the floor. The whispering and talk going on above me was like a babbling brook. I felt like lying there and lying there. Kids were gathering around, staring.

Someone said, "What about Dan?"

Mister Johnson looked over in my direction. "He's all right. Somebody get me some water."

One of the kids ran out. I continued lying there. It was nice to lie there. You didn't have to think. What was there to think about? It was too weird to think about. It was like *Alice in Wonderland*; the more you thought, the nuttier it became.

The water was brought in a paper cup and Mister Johnson raised Shamaz's head, bringing the cup to his lips. After a while, Shamaz opened his eyes and sipped some of the water. Blood was coming out of his nose. I guessed he had fallen on it when he went down. He closed his eyes again.

I sat up and stared at him.

"What happened?" I asked Mister Johnson.

He stared at me. Everybody stared at me. Very intently. Too intently.

I asked, "Why're you all staring at me?"

"You knocked him out," a boy said.

"Yeah, right," I said.

"You don't know you knocked'm out?" another boy asked.

Mister Johnson was looking at me under contiguous eyebrows.

"I never hit anybody in my life," I said.

"You sure fuckin' hit him."

"Are you telling us," Mister Johnson asked, "that you don't know you hit him?"

Uh-oh, I thought. Careful now. Men working. Proceed with caution.

"Oh, I know I hit him," I said, Mister Cavalier in person.

Lying through my teeth. I really didn't know. I hit an older white guy dressed in a sheet who was trying to stab me with a big knife and now this guy was gone and here was Shamaz lying there and people were telling me I hit him. So I had to go along with them. I sure as hell wasn't going to tell them what had *really* happened. It was like with people who have the little stroke and a certain period of time when they're unaware of what's happening. A very unsettling thing, you can see that.

"Somebody help me carry this guy," Mister Johnson said.

Mister Johnson grabbed Shamaz by the armpits, a couple of boys each grabbed a leg and they carried Shamaz into the little room where the cot was.

The others stood there and stared at me.

"Why're you staring at me?" I asked again—a little impatiently maybe.

And then I saw something I'd never seen in people talking to me—fear.

"Never saw anybody knock anybody out in person before," a fat, curly-haired kid who liked to pick his nose said.

Mister Johnson came out of the little room. "You can all go to the library till next period. Class dismissed. You," he said to me, "you stay."

"Shamaz gonna be okay?" the fat kid asked.

"Shamaz gonna be fine," Mister Johnson said. "Just got knocked out. Go and do some jogging, lose some weight. Everybody the hell out, all except the KO artist."

In filing out, they all looked at me in wonder. I had never been looked at in wonder before.

*And I had done a hellish thing;*
*And it would work'em woe*
*For all averred I had killed the bird*
*That made the breeze to blow*
*"Ah, wretch!" said they, "the bird to slay*
*That made the breeze to blow!"*

Mister Johnson came over and extended his hand. "Bill," he said. I extended mine. "Dan Kahn."

"Yeah, well, I got the roster here."

I managed a thwarted smile. We shook. He had big, strong, hard, rough hands and a firm grip. Very firm.

"Ever box before, Dan?"

"Never even got into a fight."

"Jesus, where *you* been living?"

I rattled off a line about right here in River City from *The Music Man*.

"Like musicals, huh? Not exactly the portent for a fighter. How you manage to grow up without a fight?"

"Guess something there is that doesn't love a fight."

"Paraphrase of the Sandburg poem?"

"Robert Frost."

"See you like poetry too. Like musicals — like poetry — and nobody ever beat the shit out of you?"

"Nope."

"You know, ever' boxin' promoter, ever' manager, ever' trainer in the world would give twenty years of his life to find a fighter with a knockout punch." He was looking at me like one might look at a lottery ticket suspected of being a multi-million-dollar winner.

"I'm not a fighter."

"Who knows?"

"Don't *I*?"

"Don't know shit. We find things out as we go along. You find as you go along you happen to have a talent in a certain area — hell, if it was writin' poetry or sword fightin', I say forget about it, won't make a cent. But you happen to find out it was baseball, football or basketball — tennis — boxin' — hell, you crazy not to pursue it."

"I'd consider myself crazy to pursue boxing."

"Why's that?"

"Trying to beat somebody up who's trying to beat me up? What is that?"

"You like poetry, right?"

"Some poetry."

"Don't be jerkin' mah chain, boy, why in hell would I be talkin' about *bad* poetry?"

"Okay."

"Boxin' can be like great poetry. In boxin' a man can rise to undreamed heights—heights he can reach in no other way. Could Ali have been Ali any other way except through boxin'?"

"Who knows?"

"You know. You—*know*. And Tyson. Think he could've given the world the kinds of thrills any other way?"

"Biting his opponent's ears? Roman gladiators would've been proud of him."

"And the other side of the coin. All those guys who've committed rapes and murders and cheated and stole. If they'd found something they were supremely talented at and if the world was thrilled by those talents—would they've resorted to killing, raping, cheating, stealing?"

"Didn't stop Tyson."

"Nothing compared to what it would've been had he not been in boxing."

"You may have a point."

"Oh, I have a point."

"What *is* your point?

"When you have a true, God-given talent—when it's evident you're born for something—like could you picture Brando not having been an actor? Or Agassi not having been a tennis player? Or Albert Einstein having been a philosopher instead of a physicist? Or anybody great not having done what they were great at?"

"I'm sure it's happened."

"I'm sure it's happened a lot. And it's tragic it did and does. Because the world can use all the greatness it can get—in any field. Because spiritually—emotionally—the world, its material riches notwithstanding, is a very, very poverty-stricken place."

"The world didn't lose a thing when it didn't get Einstein as a philosopher—it's got you."

"Jerkin mah chain again, boy?"

"Why should I do that? All you did was try to get me killed. Which brings us to the subject of *your* goals."

His brows took another meeting.

"I'm not jerking your chain," I said. "I really want to know. What are *your* goals?"

It's always fascinating when you ask people about their goals. We're the only living beings we know of with the capacity to have goals. Yet, when you ask people about their goals—let us say their dreams, their visions regarding what they want to achieve in life—they act about the way they would with a surprise question on their SAT's. And it becomes obvious, as far as most are concerned, that their goals consist of little more than eating, fucking, seeking entertainment, and finding shelter and rations for the winter—of their discontent.

"Well, now, that's a very interesting question," Bill Johnson said. "I guess I used to wanna be a great fighter. Looking back, though, I can see it wasn't because I really had greatness in me as a fighter, but because I wanted the kind of attention great fighters get. When I found out I was a pretty good fighter—not a great one—I kept doing it as long as I could, kind of vainly hoping I might someday pass for a great one, the way many try to do. When I quit and got into teaching, I suppose my goals became pretty much like everybody else's, to make a living and work up enough of a pension to supplement my Social Security. Today—at this moment—something else occurs to me. What if I could play a part in bringing greatness to the world—in the person of someone else?"

"Uh-oh."

"Don't have to be you. Most likely that was a freaky punch you could never repeat. Talkin' 'bout the idea. There's this Russian writer, Dostoyevsky—he believed you had to have a big idea, a big goal—not unreachable, but big. You had that, he said, life would become this big, fluffy cushion. Not the way he put it—actually, he said you could fly—but anyway, life would be like a wonderful dream and the petty things of everyday life would no longer annoy you. And, lookin' back, when I had the dream of bein' a great fighter—life *was* a dream. And I just realized when you have a wonderful dream, life becomes a wonderful dream."

"Are you saying you'll discover other guys who can be great and bring them to the world?"

"Why not? Here we are in a little old high school in New York City and here you are, a not particularly muscular white guy—likes poetry and musicals—nobody in the world would suspect you could have a punch to knock out somebody built like Mike Tyson—and yet—"

"You said yourself it was a freaky accident."

"Still— 'A SPECK, A MIST, A SHAPE, I WIST!'"

"If, as you say, every manager, promoter, trainer dreams of finding a fighter with a knockout punch—aren't the odds somewhere in the realm of winning the lottery?"

"And I'm telling you," he went on, a glow in his eyes I hadn't seen there before, "there is no equivalent of it like in the ring. *The fair breeze blew, the white foam flew, the furrow followed free; we were the first that ever burst into that silent sea.* When it's done the way it *can* be done, it's no longer about money or fame or even competition. It's about heights the human spirit can reach."

"And depths."

"For depths, all you have to do is pick up a paper or turn on the news."

And now I wanted to go. Not because I would not have liked to stay and continue the discussion; I like discussions like the one we were having. Discussions that I felt enriched and titillated the mind. But there was a group of us met in the library whenever we had free time. Several of them were girls—Stella, her best friend Maria, and Anna, who had come from Italy recently. Sicily, to be more precise. Stella, a black haired beauty with charcoal blazing eyes I had promptly fallen in love with. I had just as promptly, then, enrolled in an intensive Italian language course, working at it assiduously till, within three months, I could carry on a fairly fluent conversation. *Cherchez la femme.* Or in Italian, if you'd care to test me, *"Si cerca la donna."*

I said to Bill Johnson, "I'll come back later to find out how Tyson's feeling," turning to leave.

"Aren't we being a little cavalier, considering Shamaz may not be feeling exactly pleased at the idea the whole school's gonna know he was knocked out by someone he ought to be able to kick the shit out of with one hand tied behind his back?"

I stopped. "First you put me up against Tyson's clone and now you're trying to make me feel good, right?"

"Would it be realistic to think he'd let the matter drop?" Johnson asked.

" 'Hm, let's see,' as Kevin Spacey might say, 'that's a tough one.' "

"It's called consequences."

"The consequences of making the wrong individuals put on gloves?"

"Come out of that pussy you better put on gloves—else don't come out."

"Or skip gym."

"Can't skip things, man. Gonna have to confront what's waitin' fer ya either on this corner or the next. Everybody got his World Trade Center waitin' somewheres."

"You're full of optimism. What do you advise?"

"We each create our problems, we each have to resolve them."

"You aware of how helpful you're being?"

"There *is* something I could suggest for you to *look* at. Not advising you to do it—just to look at and decide whether it indicates to you as being something that makes sense—to *you*."

"I'm wide open."

"Fight'm again."

"What?"

"We'll arrange another bout. With me as the referee and the entire school watching. It would be a great activity. Like instead of assembly."

"I don't suppose you're aware of how much your suggestion sucks."

"Why?"

"First of all, didn't I say I don't want to have anything to do with fighting?"

"'Less you plannin' to leave the school and the neighborhood, Shamaz gonna continue hanging over your head."

Matter of fact, my mother *had* found an apartment for us on the Upper East Side. Yorkville, where there were still some walk-ups that were not totally beyond financial reach. She had been working overtime in the garment district for years and taking in extra sewing at home to save for the move and finally we were making it. She had saved enough for money under the table, for the security deposit, a month's rent and, within weeks, *We were movin' on up—to the East Side* so all I would have to do was make it safely home from school and to school from home for a few weeks and be careful where I went in the neighborhood and then, after we moved, gravitate safely from subway to school every morning and from school to the subway in the afternoon—for less than one measly school term. It was a doable proposition.

"Secondly," I said, "you *are* new. You really think the principal would let you hold a bout under school auspices so he could get sued if somebody gets hurt—especially since somebody already got knocked out?"

"We hold it in the park and spread the word for kids to come watch it."

"Now we're back to where your idea sucks because I don't want to have anything to do with fighting."

"You can't say we're not makin' progress. 'Cause now, the only thing you have to consider is how Shamaz gonna waylay you outside the school someplace and there ain't gonna *be* no gloves. Matter of fact, you lucky if there ain't knives and a baseball bat or two around."

I took a deep breath.

"Are you aware of the fact," I said, "that if you had had us play the kinds of games in gym that other teachers have the kids play and didn't make us put on boxing gloves, we wouldn't have to be having this conversation?"

"If you wanna play the buck-passing game, how about this? How about, if you had played the rope-a-dope game with the guy?"

"Rope-a-dope? Rope-a-dope?"

"All right, forget that. How about this? You could've refused to put on gloves and say, 'I refuse to fight.' "

"That would've made me look real good."

"How come you could say it to me now?"

"I don't have a bunch of peers standing around now."

"That's what I'm sayin'. You makin' a choice. We always makin' a choice. Thing is to take responsibility for our choices."

"I can see, by hook or crook, you're determined to be right. The bottom line—fighting, as far as I'm concerned, is not a choice."

"Fine. Then you got Shamaz to deal with."

As if on cue, Shamaz, fists primed for jaw breaking, came running out of the little room, glaring at me, heading for me.

Oh, shit, I thought, I can't outrun this guy, he's gonna pound me into the walls.

# CHAPTER FOUR

Unfortunately for Shamaz, some of the effects of the knockout must've still been lingering. For, though looking at me and obviously believing he was running toward me, he was actually running diagonally at full speed toward the one column in the gym that, for some reason, did not have padding on it.

When he hit the column the sound, though not loud, was so definitive—and communicative— a shudder went through me.

"Boy seems to be havin' a real bad day," Bill Johnson said as we both looked at the prostrate figure by the column.

Shamaz was bleeding fluently from the forehead and nose. I remembered a passage from *A Farewell to Arms* in which the wounded protagonist is being transported in an ambulance where, through the stretcher above his, another wounded soldier's blood is dripping on him. And then it stops dripping. And the protagonist knows the man above him has died. When a person dies, he does not bleed.

Also something not quite right about the way Shamaz's nose was bending.

We walked over.

Bill Johnson went to one knee and examined the nose. "One of the best breaks I seen, I'll give you that."

"What do you mean, you'll give me that—don't give me that. That was the column did that, not me."

"Think Shamaz gonna make that fine distinction?"

"You don't let up, do you?"

"Just the facts, ma'am."

Neither of us could take our eyes off Shamaz's nose.

"Wouldn't they have to reset that?" I asked.

"If one is vain. It'll heal. All fighters get their noses broken—time and again. Sooner or later you remove that damn bone in there an' then it don't matter no more."

"Shamaz boxes?"

"Amateur stuff, locals."

"That's who you paired me off with? A guy who not only looks like Tyson but who has actual experience boxing? Is it because I'm white or you just like to see people who are not physically oriented severely damaged?"

"Let's say I like playing the odds."

"You know I hate fighting, but I must tell you—it would give me pleasure at this moment to see *your* nose broken."

"Had my nose broken lots of times."

"I think I could even do it myself."

"See? A minute ago you didn't wanna have nothin' to do with fightin'. You makin' progress, baby-cakes."

I looked at Shamaz's peaceful figure lying on the floor. "Does this mean I don't have to worry about him for a while?"

"He'll heal fast; Shamaz a tough young man."

"Do I have till the end of the term?"

If I could make it to the end of the term, he'd never find me on the Upper East Side. That was the thing about New York. You could live in it for years and never see the same person twice. You could even go for years without seeing the person lives on the same floor with you.

"He'll heal before the term is over."

"Will his friends take it upon themselves to revenge him in the meantime?"

"His pride wouldn't allow it. Plus when they see him with bandages all over, he's either gotta tell'em he ran into a column or let them believe you the one did it to'm. Either way, it's the result of your doing. No, it's gonna be a point of pride to take care of this himself."

"You've been a gift horse full of—something."

"Help me carry'm back to the little room."

Most of the crowd I hung with was in the school library when I got there. I could see they'd heard about the incident. It's a thing that fascinates me about humanity. The moment people know you've done something unusual—something that's considered "news"—they don't look at you like you're you any more. They get a glazed look in their eyes and gape. They do it with famous people and now they were doing it with me. Gaping at me. All except Stella who knew I had a crush on her so she had that power over me, she wasn't gonna gape. And after they'd seen Shamaz walking around with bandages all over his face, it was going to get worse.

Kind' a nice, though. People pretending they were acting normal except everything about them was heightened. Their enthusiasm, admiration, quickness, brightness, communicativeness—aliveness—like a flourishing stock market. Nice to be in a position where you knew you were causing this.

Put me in mind of Walt Disney when he was asked how it felt to be a celebrity. He said it felt fine when it helped him get a good seat for a football game but it never helped him make a good film or a good shot in a polo game, or to get his daughter to listen to him. It didn't even keep fleas off his dogs and if being a celebrity didn't give one the advantage over a couple of fleas, then he thought there couldn't be much to being a celebrity after all.

For me there wasn't *really* anything to be famous about anyway, except in Seward Park High where people knew how tough and strong Shamaz was.

For the person toward whom this star-gazing is directed, it's irresistible. When it first happens, you think, *What the hell is this, it's only me; why're they—? And then you think, Well, there's no harm in enjoying it while it lasts. Hell, it's fun.* And then, in a very short time, you figure you deserve it, it's your due. And you get to the point where you walk around as if you're supposed to be this famous person rather than—well, you.

So we kidded around in the library, like we always did, but there was this different atmosphere about it. They had a famous person in their midst. Kids would walk by and make comments how they'd heard what had happened and they'd ask questions and I'd say, "Just an accident, a lucky punch," but I was making a thing of being humble and modest, which just made it more convincing and impressive.

And even Stella, while teasing and flirting the way she always did—it's the Italian way, after all—kept glancing at me as if thinking, *Hmm, more to this guy than I thought*—only in Italian. *C'e in questo ragazzo piu di quello che credevo.*

It went on like that the rest of the day. I had become a star—for the day, anyway. School is like life that way—you get fifteen minutes. I felt like hanging out in school as long as it'd take for the fame to fade. Outside the school, they had no idea I was a star.

At the end of the day all of us usually waited for each other in the library and then the guys walked the girls home, dropping them off and then walking to our own homes. It had been going on for a year now and I'd had thoughts about things working out in such a way that I could have some time alone with Stella and then maybe tell her how I felt about her. Though she must've known. Women know these things. I guess men do too. Who doesn't know when he/she's admired?

But there was always a bunch of us and it never seemed to work that I'd see her alone. I remembered my mother singing a forties' song she said had been a hit by Louis Prima about his girl Maggie's father, mother, sister and brother always being there and, oh, he never saw Maggie alone.

There *was* something exciting in it. The flirtation, the teasing, the enjoyment of one another. On my part there was also the feeling that if I made a move and it didn't work, it would all be gone. The anticipation was—ecstasy-producing. But the consequences of rejection were—forbidding.

On the other hand, this term was the last one and if I didn't make a move before its close—we'd be scattered in different directions and to paraphrase Louis Prima,

*Oh, I never see Stella again*

My mother was sitting alone in her room in the dark.

We lived in a sixth-floor-railroad-style-apartment-walk-up at 299 Broome Street. The stairs were steep and the space between the railing and the rough, paint-chipped wall up those stairs, or down them if you wish, was enough for a person and a quarter so whoever was climbing up or down from the opposite direction had to wait on a landing for the other person to reach it so they could get past one another. It wasn't an ideal apartment or neighborhood but after my father died, things were rough and it was the best my mother could do. And it was pretty good exercise, climbing those stairs.

"What's the matter?" I asked.

She began to cry. It pierced my soul. My mother was a strong woman who worked her heart out sewing in the garment district to support my grandmother and me. To see her cry was a heavy blow to my guts. Whatever joy I might have felt in having freakily been catapulted to school fame and from my ongoing crush on Stella went out the window.

"What is it?" I asked, sitting alongside her on the couch-bed.

She shook her head and continued crying.

"Please tell me," I said.

She cried. I waited, my arm about her shoulder.

Finally, she said, "Something is growing."

"What do you mean?"

Perhaps before the bizarre apparition during my encounter with Shamaz I might've been able to accurately guess what might be growing in a woman that would upset her, but once you experienced something as illogical as what had occurred to me, anything could be growing anywhere.

"My breast," she said. "Something is growing on my breast."

And then I suddenly wasn't devastated anymore. I have this conviction—about me—about those around me—about the world—that, once the problem is identified—everything—is going to be—okay. The drama unfolds—but that's exactly what it feels like—like—a play on the stage and after everyone does what he/she has to do—everything'll be—okay.

I understand I could be wrong. Dead wrong. But—so what? I plan and take precautions, thinking in terms of the worst-case scenario. But I have the conviction everything'll turn out fine. Sue me.

"You have to go to the doctor," I said.

"I'm afraid."

My mother had an almost superstitious fear of doctors and hospitals. I say, "almost" only because it was so obsessive, not because there isn't a valid reason for such a fear, considering that over 60 percent of fatalities taking place in hospitals are due to mistakes by the medical staff. They even have a name for complications resulting from medical blunders. "Iatrogenic: caused by a physician's comments or treatment." You could see how they put that "comments" in the definition to mitigate the "treatment" part. Hell, it's hardly ever comments. It's always some kind of blunder connected with treatment. One of my mother's friends who was a medical assistant was in the hospital for some kind of illness and this young doctor comes into her room and he's about to give her a shot and she says, "What're you giving me?"

"It's your medicine, dear," he told her. "Now be a good girl and give me your arm."

"Don't give me that God attitude," she said, "tell me what's in the shot." This woman knew her medications.

So the young doctor told her and she told him, "I'm not supposed to be getting that."

"You're not? What room is this?"

He'd come into the wrong damn room.

Another story this friend told my mother was how, when the doctor she worked for first started working at this hospital in Brooklyn, he was scheduled to assist in a mastectomy and, in preparation, read the woman's medical file. When he finished reading it, he went to the surgeon who was to do the operation and said, "Listen, there's some kind of a mistake here; this woman doesn't need a complete mastectomy. A partial should be perfectly satisfactory."

The chief surgeon stared at the young doctor. For quite a while. "Do you want to continue working in this hospital?"

"Of course."

"Then, if I were you, I would learn quickly what to say and what not to say. Do we understand one another?"

"Of course."

*I sent for Radcliffe; was so ill,*
 *The other doctors gave me over:*
 *He felt my pulse, prescribed his pill,*
 *And I was likely to recover.*

*But when the wit began to wheeze*
*And wine had warmed the politician,*
*Cured yesterday of my disease,*
*I died last night of my physician*

In ancient China they had a different way of dealing with doctors. A doctor got paid only if and when he healed a patient. If a patient died, a lantern was lit and hung outside the doctor's house, signifying one of his patients had gone to join his ancestors. People could walk by the doctor's house and see how many lanterns had been lit.

In our society, the more serious the illness, the more the doctor gets paid and the longer the illness lasts, the longer the doctor's income from it lasts. Hmm, which is the better method — ours or the ancient Chinese? A tough one.

Not that in other areas of society things aren't going to hell as well. Years ago there was a very popular book on the subject: *Zen and the Art of Motorcycle Maintenance*. It dealt with the phenomenon of people giving only a fraction of their attention to any given task they were performing at any given time and for that reason there were a hell of a lot of mistakes being made not only in hospitals but everywhere. Under Jimmy Carter's administration, for instance, U.S. Forces tried to pull off the same kind of rescue mission the Israelis had pulled off a few years back in Africa and, though the Israeli mission had been successful, our version was a disaster that only Laurel and Hardy could have done justice to. Our helicopters crashed into each other and our men were killed right and left without a shot fired by the enemy. And think of how many of our boys have died through friendly fire. Think of how much weaponry was smuggled onto the airplanes that were crashed against the World Trade Center. Think of how we had prior warning that the attacks were *going* to take place.

I don't see that the *Motorcycle Maintenance* book did much good. Though there have been great technological advances in the passing years, conscientiousness, integrity, and responsibility have all been falling off at a dizzying rate. Things are breaking down in proportion to the steep lessening of care on the part of those who are in charge of them. A tragedy like the World Trade Center disaster is the tip of the iceberg.

"If there's something growing," I told my mother, "there's no choice."

"I'm afraid."

I stared at her, trying to fill the stare with all the intention I could muster. "You *have* to—see—the doctor."

Without blinking or dropping my gaze I glared at her.

After a while she said, "After we move."

"You have to make me a promise."

After another pause she said, "After we move."

I would have to keep an eye on her. I was dealing with a woman here who, when my pacifier mysteriously disappeared at the age of four, took me to five different stores that, I was unaware at the time, sold anything *but* pacifiers, and made a show of asking the sales staff if they had pacifiers, undoubtedly winking away at them to let them in on the scam and when they all made a show of telling her, no, they most absolutely did *not* have pacifiers, took me home again and promised we would try finding a pacifier again the following day.

The following day we went to three more stores that stocked no pacifiers. It was far beyond what a child's attention span can support. By the third day, I was on to new adventures. That might have been the time I took up the little stick for entertainment. So you see, all is for the best in this best of all possible worlds.

I realized it wasn't only her fear of doctors and hospitals but her consideration regarding the man she was seeing and their intended marriage. She had been a long time finding someone who wanted to marry her. I did not have any special liking for the man and I'm not too sure my mother did—he was not a likeable man—but she wanted to get married. She was one of those women who did not consider it normal to be unmarried but she knew that with a son and a mother to support, finding a man who would be willing to share those responsibilities was a challenging task.

Though he was a government clerk with not much money coming in, he had agreed there would be a marriage within a few months and she would no longer have to shoulder the responsibilities alone.

We were moving to a better neighborhood, a larger apartment, I was going to go to college, and my mother had found someone who would share her burdens on the journey to old age; everything was getting better.

But now there was this.

So she did what Scarlet O'Hara had done: she would think about it tomorrow

I knew this was the most I could get from her at this time.

But I would keep my eye on her.

# CHAPTER FIVE

Shamaz didn't show up in school the next day. Nor the day after. I was walking around, as they say in the army, ready on the left, ready on the right, ready on the firing line.

A great baseball player, Satchel Paige, had said, "Don't look behind—something might be gaining on you."

I didn't know but that Shamaz's friends might "waylay" me despite what Bill Johnson had said.

When Shamaz didn't show up for a second week, I spoke to Bill Johnson after gym.

"Nobody knows where he is," he said. "Mother's on welfare, eight other kids. She doesn't know where he is. Doesn't live at home any more. Drops by once in a while. His buddies won't tell me. They give me hints. That he'll be back. They try to do it in an Austrian accent— you know—'I'll be back.' Then, you know, 'Hasta la vista, baby.' "

Call me Mary Sunshine but I like to look for the good in the worst of situations. And the good here was his friends were going to wait for him, they were not going to beat me up and possibly make a vegetable or a dead person of me. It was going to be like *High Noon*. His friends hanging out at the railroad station, waiting for Frank Miller to come in on the noon train. *Git along, li'l doggie.*

And then I drifted into thinking, what about my mother? If something happened to me—what would it do to her? This was the first time in our life together that she needed me. After the death of my father, she had fought so hard and suffered so much and now, if something happened to me, it would completely destroy her.

Funny—it was the first time I was considering matters in terms of how something that happened to me would affect someone else. Everything till now had been how anything and everything would affect ME.

I remembered how, when I was thirteen, my mother had the flu and one night I'd come home and hadn't done something I was supposed to do that day and she yelled at me and ended up by saying, "Everything with you is ME, ME, ME!"

I'd lost my temper, put my fist through a pane of glass in the kitchen cabinet, and rushed out, leaving my mother in tears. I walked around the city for a long time, the blood steadily trickling from the skin around my knuckles. Eventually, I calmed down and felt so bad about what I'd done that I called and when my mother answered the phone, I paused because my throat was tight and when she said, "Who is it?" I said, "It's ME, ME ME!" and then we both laughed. There's nothing like making up with someone whom you hate being mad at.

But, of course, nothing *would* happen to me. Wasn't it all a play and weren't we all actors, acting out our parts according to the script? Shakespeare had written that and had there ever existed a greater philosopher? On the other hand, who had written the script for *my* life and what did He/She have in mind?

"Is there anything to be done?" I asked.

"Like what?"

"Oh, I don't know—some little thing—going to the POLICE maybe?"

"What you figure they gonna do?"

"Isn't it part of their job description to protect the citizens?"

"Has Shamaz threatened you personally?"

"You said his friends told you what he intends to do."

"It's called hearsay. And even if he'd threatened you, the most could be done is issue what's called an order of protection. But an order of protection never stopped anybody who intended to harm somebody."

"Doesn't seem right."

"Oh, you lookin' for right? Let's see—I know an Ed Wright—an Amy Wright. Let's see—any others? Nope, those are the only Wrights I know."

"Nothing quite like someone attempting to be witty when you're looking into the muzzle of a loaded gun. So I'm supposed to just wait around to get beaten up? Maybe crippled or paralyzed?"

"You could go to the gym and let me train you."

"There he goes."

"Wonderful opportunity for you to find out whether it was a freaky punch or—"

"What's the point?"

How could I tell him the punch had come because it was the only thing that could keep me from getting stabbed and its force had been generated purely from my desire to stay alive?

"The point is," he said, almost as if fathoming my thoughts, "you hit the jackpot. One way or another, you were able to muster the elements that knocked somebody very tough out. I've been watching Shamaz fight in these local contests. I've seen him hit and get hit. He can punch and he can take a punch. Let me tell you something about boxing. Since it began, it's the one dream every boxer has had and trained for. To develop the knockout punch. Freaky or not, training or not, most fighters don't have it. Those who do are worshipped like gods—in and out of the fight game. Why do you think people pay millions to watch certain fighters and others, no matter how much they win, the public just never gets too excited about? It's the knockout punch, that's what people want to see. What I'm tellin' you here is that 99-point-nine percent of the people on the entire globe— no matter what they do—can't come up with the knockout punch. You, somehow, managed to come up with it—while the other guy was defending himself and defending himself well. Could you walk away, knowing you might have the two-hundred-million-dollar lottery ticket right in your fist?"

"And that's supposed to be reason enough for me to go in there and try to beat up somebody who's trying to beat me up?"

"Since you don't seem to be impressed by two hundred million bucks, let me put it to you this way. It's an art. The art of boxing, a way for certain individuals—the only way—to express not only their artistry but their supreme greatness."

"At the expense of battering other individuals—who may not be either artists or great—into brain damage and broken bones—not to mention broken hearts."

"Hey—nobody forces anybody to get into that ring."

"Society's obsession with money and fame forces them—when they're young and stupid—to go into something that will get their brains pulverized. It's no more civilized than what they used to do in Rome when they had gladiators slaughter each other and fed people to the animals."

"Maybe you're right. Maybe you *are* too intelligent and too literate for this game. On the other hand, Jack Dempsey was pretty literate. They say he read a lot of Shakespeare—and he was a great fighter at the same time. I just think it'd be a pity not to at least want to find out if it's something you could repeat. *Then* you could make an *informed* decision."

The truth of the matter was the phenomenon I had experienced in my encounter with Shamaz was so frightening I did not want to go anywhere near it even in thought, let alone deed. But I could not tell Bill Johnson that. I could not tell anybody. Not even my mother. More and more I was feeling the ever-escalating effects of being burdened with something I could neither control nor reveal.

The only thing I could do was click onto what my belief about boxing might be if I did not have a "two-hundred-million-dollar lottery ticket" in my pocket.

"I *am* making an informed decision. The decision to live in a world where I'm not being a destruction whore."

"Whoa—gonna strain my neck lookin' up at you. Nice ideal for them ancient Greeks who used to sit around readin' all day an' occasionally promenadin' peripatetically about the square, carryin' on their philosophical discussions while their slaves did their work for them. But you'll find in this world you gonna have to *do* some whorin' if you intend to survive—and then you might ask yourself— 'Hell, what's the difference between *some* whorin'—and a whole *lot* of whorin'?' And another thing you gonna find out, my dear idealistic friend—every situation in life comes down to some kind of force. A .38 always beats aces. The force might be money, fame, violence—but there's some kind of force dictating every aspect of life. And whether you like it or not—at some point or other you either gonna cooperate with it or you gonna butt heads. Like right now, for example. You can talk idealism till black is white. It comes down to what you're gonna do when Shamaz, fists cocked, catches up with you."

"And you—knowing Shamaz was a boxer, a good one by your own account and built like Mike Tyson, and seeing I am obviously not—have nothing to say about the fact you put us together?"

"You stickin' to somethin' that's come and gone like it was glue. How about looking at it another way? How about considering the possibility—no, the probability—that had you fought somebody who looked to be in *your* league you probably would've done a hell of a lot more damage? And the school might've gotten sued to boot?"

"You're some piece of work, Bill Johnson."

"Every coin has two sides, that's a fact."

"My heart bleeds over the possibility the school might've gotten sued."

"But the kid might've gotten hurt. I mean really hurt. That's what a knockout punch does. Its devastation and its rarity are what makes it so valuable."

"Valuable? Valuable?"

"Anything the public is willing to pay millions of dollars for is valuable. Is it any less logical than the value of diamonds?"

"You figure you're being a help?"

"Hey, listen: when Shamaz came runnin' out of that room the other day, headin' fer ya—or thinkin' he was headin' fer ya—I was ready to clock'm. But the chances are I ain't gonna be there when you next see the beast."

"So what it comes down to is, when trouble comes, you're gonna be nowhere around."

"That's what I been tryin' to tell you, Dan Kahn. It all comes down to the man leavin' his cave with nothin' but his stick in his hand with all kinds of dangerous beasts all over the place, and he got nothin' but himself—and that stick. It's what life keeps tryin' to convey to you at every corner. You got nothin' and no one—but yourself. If you lucky enough to have a weapon—you better sure as shootin' be willin' to use it."

# CHAPTER SIX

**W**e moved to a three-bedroom apartment of an elevator building on 84th Street between First and Second Avenues. It was on the seventh floor and from the master bedroom, which my mother occupied, we could see the seventh floor apartment of the building across the street where a Puerto Rican family lived. My grandmother would look out the window every day and tell us she thought the young man in that apartment across the street was signaling someone by shining his shoes and leaving them out on the ledge.

"Who do you think he's signaling?" I asked her.

"His accomplices," she said.

"What do you think he's signaling them to do?"

"Rob somebody."

I nodded. "Interesting."

"You'll see. You'll see."

The Upper East Side was like a different world. No—it *was* a different world. But the main difference is in how you view things. As far as my grandmother was concerned, the difference between the Upper East Side and the Lower East Side was that the prices on the Upper East Side were higher. And that, for her, was intolerable. So she took the subway twice a week to the Lower East Side to shop for things that were needed in the house.

After a while, I put my fear of Shamaz on the shelf. We have a way, I found, of avoiding looking at unpleasantness that isn't in our face. Jewish refugees in WWII Europe would tell Jews of whatever country they'd been able to escape to what Hitler was doing to Jews back where they'd come from. No one believed them till the Germans had occupied *their* country, when it no longer mattered whether they believed it or not. Experts had been telling us for years what terrorists were going to do to our country. They had done it in other countries; there was no reason for them not to do it here. Yet we acted as if it were out of the question.

I began to think it would take a while for Shamaz's broken nose to heal and, by the time he was ready to "waylay" me, I would have moved to another school and then good luck, just try to find someone in New York City.

*They've gone about as fur as they could go — in New York City*

Another fantastic thing happened to me: I discovered acting.

Just for kicks, I had taken a drama class and, unexpectedly, it opened a new world. A world better than any dream I'd ever had. It was even better than the world I'd experienced when, as a child, I sat in a corner, playing with my little stick. Came out wrong again, didn't it?

The teacher, Mrs. Hopper, who fancied herself a latter day Bette Davis, lectured resonantly and definitively, ultra sure of herself in everything she did. One might think of her as a caricature throwback to the forties except, when she assigned each of us to rehearse and perform a monologue, something happened that changed my world and drew Mrs. Hopper and me closer together.

I chose to do the Mark Antony oration from *Julius Caesar*.

Why that particular speech in that particular play? I don't know. Later — much later — I would find out.

As I rehearsed the monologue in the privacy of my room, I found myself experiencing so much feeling and passion for what had happened to Caesar that I kept doing it over and over. It moved me much and, ironically, gave me a high. Very high. I kept running the speech over and over in my mind wherever I went. I went to sleep reciting it and woke up doing it as I prepared for the day.

When I finally did it in class, something overtook me that I had never experienced before. I had gone beyond acting the part of Mark Antony. I *was* Mark Antony — feeling so much empathy for Julius Caesar that I became Julius Caesar. Munch on that one, Konstantin Sergeyevich Alexeyev Stanislavsky.

Friends, Romans, countrymen, lend me your ears;
I come to bury Caesar, not to praise him.
The evil that men do lives after them;
The good is oft interred with their bones;
So let it be with Caesar. The noble Brutus
Hath told you Caesar was ambitious:
If it were so, it was a grievous fault;
And grievously hath Caesar answer'd it.
Here, under leave of Brutus and the rest–
For Brutus is an honorable man;
So are they all, all honorable men–
Come I to speak in Caesar's funeral.
He was my friend, faithful and just to me:
But Brutus says he was ambitious;
And Brutus is an honorable man.
He (Caesar) hath brought many captives home to Rome,
Whose ransoms did the general coffers fill:
Did this in Caesar seem ambitious?
When that the poor have cried, Ceasar hath wept:
Ambition should be made of sterner stuff:
Yet Brutus says he was ambitious;
And, sure, he is an honorable man.
You all did see that on the Lupercal
I thrice presented him a kingly crown,
Which he did thrice refuse: Was this ambition?
Yet Brutus says he was ambitious;
And, sure, he is an honorable man.
I speak not to disprove what Brutus spoke,
But here I am to speak what I do know.
You all did love him once–not without cause:
What cause withholds you, then, to mourn for him?
O judgment, thou art fled to brutish beasts,
And men have lost their reason; bear with me;
My heart is in the coffin there with Caesar,
And I must pause till it come back to me.

At this point the citizens of Rome who are listening are beginning to be swayed by his speech and feeling some emotion in regard to Caesar. Antony continues to drive the point home:

> But yesterday the word of Caesar might
> Have stood against the world: Now lies he there,
> And none so poor to do him reverence
> O masters, if I were disposed to stir
> Your hearts and minds to mutiny and rage,
> I should do Brutus wrong, and Cassius wrong,
> Who, you all know, are honorable men:
> I will not do them wrong; I rather choose
> To wrong the dead, to wrong myself and you,
> Than I will wrong such honorable men.

Antony, then tells the Roman citizens he found Caesar's last will and testament in his closet and will read it to them. But first he makes his way to Caesar's body and kneels by it.

> If you have tears, prepare to shed them now.
> You all do know this mantle: I remember
> The first time ever Caesar put it on;
> 'Twas on a summer's evening, in his tent,
> That day he overcame the Nervii
> Look! In this place ran Cassius' dagger through:
> See what a rent the envious casca made;
> Through this the well beloved Brutus stabbed;
> And as he plucked his cursed steel away,
> Mark how the blood of Caesar followed it,
> As rushing out of doors, to be resolv'd
> If Brutus so unkindly knock'd or no;
> For Brutus, as you know, was Caesar's angel:
> Judge, O you gods how dearly Caesar loved him!
> This was the most unkindest cut of all;
> For when the noble Caesar saw him stab
> Ingratitude, more strong than traitors' arms,
> Quite vanquished him: Then burst his mighty heart;
> And his mantle muffling up his face,

Even at the base of Pompey's statua,
Which all the while ran blood, great Caesar fell.
O, what a fall was there, my countrymen!
Then I, and you, and all of us fell down,
Whilst bloody treason flourish'd over us.

By the time I was done, I was crying—and so was everyone in the class. So was Mrs. Hopper. I didn't care. Nobody else did either.

When it was over, everyone remained silent. Finally, the bell rang. My fellow students came over to where I still stood and , one by one, shook my hand, as they might've had someone very near and dear to me died, and filed out in silence.

When they'd left, Mrs. Hopper came over, hugged me and kissed me on the forehead.

In my English class, the teacher, Mrs. Engels, a heavyset woman in her forties, one of those rare teachers whose enthusiasm and knowledge of her subject had the capacity to inspire, assigned each of us to write a play, cast it, and direct it.

"It's one thing to put it on paper," she said. "It's another to make it live. That's probably why some of the best and worst things you'll ever see have been written and directed by the same person."

"Why?" I asked.

"I was hoping someone would ask." And she looked at me as if she and I understood one another. It was one of those looks that said, *Yes, you are a male but perhaps not so bad as most males*. "Writers have certain ideas they want to express about life. It's imperative for them those ideas get out there." She took a tiny pause, looking at the students. "Who knows what 'imperative' means?"

I raised my hand.

"And the rest of you?" she said. "You were going to let me go on without knowing what a key word in my sentence means? How would you know what I said if you don't know what a key word means? Goodness. Yes, Dan."

" 'Imperative' means something that must be done. Comes from the Latin, 'imperare,' 'to command.' "

"Excellent."

Teacher's pet. But since I'd knocked out Shamaz and caused him to disappear, what might've been a bad quality—being a teacher's pet, for instance—was now a good quality. Practically anything I was to do would be a good quality. Had Bill Johnson had a point about force being the ultimate determining factor?

"Writers who direct their own pieces in the movies," she continued, "either adjust their ideas to the reality of life—in which case the work can be superb—or insist on bulling their ideas through despite their not working for the audience. It's the equivalent of living in denial—which, of course, is the *modus operandi* for so many of us."

Yes, she was pontificating, which teachers, judges, and bosses often do because of their position and, when you are in their domain, you have no choice but to make like you like it. In her case, though, I really did like it. I loved getting bits of information that made me think. Give me practical stuff about how to fix something, figure something out mathematically, or memorize dates, places, and facts, and I get sleepy. But give me something for my thoughts, emotions, and spirit—and I'm a sow in mud.

I remembered another bit of information Mrs. Engels had come out with. It was in regard to a poem she had assigned us to read and which she afterwards analyzed. She'd been full of passionate contempt for a line in the poem that said:

*I could not love thee, dear, so much*
*Loved I not honor more*

"She should've bopped him one," Mrs. Engels said. "You think that's what a woman wants? For a man to love honor so much he'll leave her, go into battle, and die? Ridiculous."

At the time I thought it fascinating she would refute the work of Richard Lovelace. I didn't have any thoughts as to whether she was right or wrong. I went along with her on the basis of her having the boldness to put her beliefs up against a classic poet.

Later, years later, I did give thought to it and decided it was the poet who had been right, though by then you would be hard put to find anyone in the country or world who would not have agreed with Mrs. Engels on the matter. Honor had slid from the days of chivalry to become not only a worthless but also a pejorative term. Then, after the World Trade Center attack, I think we all began to think of such valueless characteristics like honor, courage, sacrifice as perhaps not so valueless. But that lasted only a short time because, six months after the WTC attack, we had Tanya Harding fighting Paula Jones and it made headlines in the papers, it was all over the news.

Stella happened to be in that class with me. I wrote a play in which there was a girl, coincidentally named Stella, on whom this boy had a crush. This boy, another boy, and another couple of girls all hang out together, close friends. The two boys vie for Stella's affections and the first boy declares his love for her. She, however, turns him down. He remains alone on the stage where he plays "Jealous Heart" on the harmonica and then starts to cry. That's how the play ends.

I cast the play, with Stella playing Stella. I happen to play the harmonica, which made me perfect for the role. So, after auditioning several boys in the class for the part of the boy, I squeaked through and won the role. Lucky I was also the director.

When we performed the playlet for the class, my tears at the end so moved the class the same thing happened that had happened in Mrs. Hopper's class—only Mrs. Engels did not kiss me on the forehead as Mrs. Hopper had. Mrs. Engels did not have the same flair for the dramatic gesture.

Once again it felt wonderful to act. At the time I gave no thought as to why. Later, though, I did think about it and wondered if performing for people and having their attention was what made me feel good. I think a lot of people probably do it for that reason but I didn't think I was one of those. For me, it had something to do with becoming a different character and experiencing different emotions. Why would that make me feel good? Maybe when we're being ourselves we're carrying all the garbage we've accumulated during our travels through time. When we're being someone else, we have the luxury of adopting only those aspects of a persona we want— without the secret baggage we all carry when we're being ourselves.

Never mind. The point is acting made me feel great. Feeling great with the end of the term drawing nigh, I decided this was to be the day I would unburden my heart to Stella. And, as often happens when you make up your mind to do something, events work out in such a way as to either help you or hurt you. In this case they helped me.

The other people in our little crowd went ahead and Stella and I were left by ourselves. And so I walked her home alone.

My heart behaved as if it were desperately struggling to break all the connections holding it in its designated place.

It was strange when you associated with someone for a year in certain circumstances, others always around, suddenly to be alone with that person and relating to her in a completely different way. She felt it, of course. There was something awkward about it. When the others had gone ahead and I was left alone with her, I thought maybe it was a sign everything was going to go well and she would be my girlfriend. Now, in the dark vestibule of her apartment building, it didn't feel that way. It felt unreal and gloomy. The portents seemed awry.

But it was my one chance. We were less than four weeks to the end of the term. Our crowd would not be getting together any more. I would be in one world and she would be in another. If she were my girlfriend, my dream would come true and we could go on being together.

I suddenly had the feeling that all I wanted out of life was for Stella to be my girlfriend. My dream and my desire were so intense I felt it could never happen. It was too good to become reality.

It was like lovemaking. There was such an aura of ecstasy about it that, though I knew other people did it, it felt as if it were much too good for it to ever happen to me—if for no other reason than that I wanted it to so much.

But the sexual act itself was not in my thoughts as far as Stella was concerned. My thoughts about her were wrapped in the aura of romance, excitement, and beautiful, joyful feelings. At the moment, it did not feel I was on the threshold of such wonders.

But I went ahead and said it anyway. In Italian.

"Ti voglio bene." (I like you a lot) "Vuoi essere mia ragazza?" (Will you be my girl?)

They say there are a thousand ways to say "no," but only one way to say "yes."

I see no point in duplicating her reply here because—well, it's like that old song about accentuating the positive, eliminating the negative, and not messing with Mister In-Between.

I went home, locked myself in my room, and cried. My mother kept knocking on my door, asking me what was the matter, was I all right. She did no more than that because she probably knew it had to do with teen love. My mother had flashes of extra-sensory perception, especially when it came to me.

I went to sleep crying.

In the morning I woke up feeling I had stepped into a different world. It's interesting how there are certain things in life that seem to put you in another dimension.

I felt cleansed. At peace. Without anxiety. Even the thought of Shamaz wasn't stressful.

I also felt ravenous from not having had dinner the night before.

In the kitchen my grandmother sat with her feet on another chair, looking out the window. Her legs always seemed swollen and I think she had the idea that if she kept her legs up, there would be less fluid and pressure going to that area. I never asked her about it. Kids accept things.

Neither did she ask me how I was or what had been the matter that I'd locked myself in my room the night before. She acted natural, asked me if she could fix me something to eat. She was of the generation of women who expressed themselves through fixing something to eat.

"I'll just have some Grape Nuts," I said.

We both had Grape Nuts. It was something my grandmother had gotten from me. I had stumbled onto the cereal, loving the crunchiness, and she tried it one time and not only liked the crunchiness but got the idea there was something especially healthful about it. From that point, she imbibed Grape Nuts as one might a medicine—with regularity and ever-renewable gusto.

The phone rang. I picked it up. In those days I was eager to find out what wondrous thing was going to happen next. Actually, I still am. Also, I thought it might be Stella to tell me she was sorry, that she had thought it over and I could be her boyfriend after all. But the thought didn't move me one way or the other. I had somehow gotten to the other side. The side where you're not fixated on thinking you couldn't do without a particular person—or a thing—or an activity.

"Hello," I said.

"*Perche non sei venuto a scuola?*" It was Maria, Stella's best friend, asking me why I hadn't come to school. It didn't occur to me to wonder how she'd gotten my number.

Obviously, Stella had told her what happened. But why had Maria called? It didn't occur to me to wonder about that, either. I think now that maybe the reason I didn't wonder about so many things is I was still operating under the child's fundamental law that everything is a game and you don't ask questions about how or why a game started or why it's being played. If there's a game, you just play it. These days I know the most important part of a game is getting a bead on what the other person is thinking and feeling, what their motivations are.

Maria was one of those *zaftig* Italian girls whose weight sags even when they're in their teens and who are going to end up marrying the butcher, the baker, or the neighborhood undertaker, and who are going to get fatter and fatter as the years go by. And, of course, there would be many children.

At this point she was still just a year or two too young to know that. She knew enough to know she wanted to find a guy and she, too, was still in the mode of liking to play games and Italian women are really experts in that area so she was making conversation, joking, flirting— playing a game. And, I realized soon during the conversation, it was a way of going after a guy.

The concept of any kind of romantic relationship with Maria hadn't crossed my mind. But I can't tell you how good it felt, after the rejection by Stella, to have a girl convey through her tones she liked me. Not only that, but my connection to Stella could continue through my connection with Maria. And, though I wasn't acquainted at the time with the law of "must have, can't have," there was the thought that Stella might get jealous and a desire on her part to take me away from Maria might be lighted.

*Oh, the games that people play*

I had never had a girlfriend. There had been flirtations and crushes but never an actual girl friend. And, as you might have gathered, I'd never had sex.

Considering boys younger than I by several years were impregnating their teachers, I often wondered if I was challenged in that area. Don't answer that.

Maria and I began going out on dates. We would go to the movies (mostly movies that had been made out of operas), picnics, walks in the park. She told me about her family, how they'd gotten to the U.S. There was a cousin who was connected. He was the one who had arranged for her and her family to come over. Not only to come over, but to become citizens. It appeared guys who were connected could do anything. His name was Joey Mangiacavallo (Mangiacavallo in Italian means "eats horse"). I remembered hearing his name pop up in the news sometimes. It was kind of interesting knowing someone who was related to a bona fide gangster.

She would prepare these hot baked sandwiches. There would be ham and cheese and sausages and homemade sauces in them and she would wrap them up in tin foil and then a towel so they would stay warm and she would bring them to the movies and we would eat them while the movie was playing. Some of these would be dessert sandwiches that had fruit and homemade jam in them. They were like pies, only baked in dough—like a calzone. Soft, moist, warm, and sweet—to die for. Had I had a love for food that some people have, I would have fallen head over heels in love with her just on the strength of those sandwiches. One could only imagine what her spaghetti and meatballs tasted like. Made me think of a great number by a big, fat African-American mama in *One Mo' Time*: "Oh, How I Miss My Sausage Man."

A couple of weeks later I was pretty much over Stella, finding out in the process I was one of those fortunates who, the moment they learn someone doesn't want them, don't want that someone either. I found out I am the kind of person who moves on and doesn't dwell on what's done.

But now I had this thing with Maria. I had started going out with her because of Stella but here she was and here I was and I was in it. There was an obligatory sense to continue.

One Saturday night, after the movie, we took a walk. We sat on a bench by the East River and, at a certain point, I leaned over and kissed her. It wasn't that I'd particularly wanted to; it was I knew she expected me to. And, yes, there was a certain amount of curiosity. Coming, perhaps, from those forties' movies—and even some of the current ones—where a couple kiss and find out during the kiss that they are in love. Oh, happy day.

Her lips felt flabby. It made me think of one of those fish they catch in the movies where it's really dead but they're shaking it to make it appear it's alive and struggling. Looking back, I probably got out of it what I'd put in. Believe it or not, up to that point the only girl I'd kissed was one I'd had a crush on when I was twelve and it was at the movies. Just a quick kiss, really. And, as I had no romantic feelings in regard to Maria, what had I expected to feel? A pair of lips—without feeling—is just a pair of lips

### The fundamental truths apply

Well, Sicilian women are not—and have never been—nearly as modern as American women. There *are* no women as modern as American women. Many in the world try to emulate what they believe are the free, glamorous, and wild ways of American women—but none can touch the original.

I doubt Maria had had much experience in the area either. They still maim and kill for stuff like that in Sicily. But she *had* seen soap operas. And had evidently gone to them for inspiration.

"*Non lo dovevi fare,*" she said. (You ought not to have done that.)

Do you find there are things that happen—or are said—that are definitive in terms of causing you to decide what needs to be done, and you feel very good about it because now there is not the slightest doubt about what your next step is to be?

With that one sentence Maria had freed me from any question of whether I should continue seeing her. I found the concept of a woman coming out with a line like that too funny. Right then and there I knew it was over with us forever and ever.

When I walked her home, I was very pleasant and cheerful, feeling a great big stone had been lifted from my chest. It was a case of you know you don't really want to be going with somebody but they haven't done anything wrong. And then they do something that sets you free. That's a great, great relief.

I gave no consideration whatsoever to the matter of how she was going to feel when I didn't ask her out again or when I didn't return her phone calls. I wish I could say it was because I was very young and that, when you are very young, you have a tendency to think pretty much only of yourself.

Unfortunately, in this, as in so many other things, getting older doesn't necessarily change so many things about being wiser and more considerate that really ought to change.

When I went to school the following Monday for my final week, I felt better than I had in my entire life. I saw Maria and Stella and the rest of our crowd in the library and we kidded around and I had no feelings of longing for Stella and Maria had no idea she and I would never be going out again. I felt I would be going to college with a clean slate and I had the feeling there would be big and wonderful things ahead of me.

Maria's first call to me had been at the point when I was in grief over being rejected by Stella. It was as if she'd been sent by Providence at just the right moment to see me through my transition. And when that mission had been accomplished, she set me free with the killer line after the kiss.

I had the feeling that was what my life was going to be. When I needed something—it would appear. Akin to what was said about America: when there was a crisis, the kind of leader America needed was always at hand. It had been like that from George Washington on.

I was flying. I remembered Bill Johnson mentioning Dostoyevsky, how, if you had a big idea, a big purpose, a big goal, you would be flying and the petty everyday cares would seem minuscule. My idea had to do with writing, acting, and directing. That was a big idea. There was no limit to where you could go, no one was as famous as those who became successful in the fields of acting, directing, and writing.

Walking on Allen Street after school, our little crowd suddenly found itself surrounded by eight African-American bruisers. I had not seen them approach and I don't know from which direction they'd come, nor how they'd managed to suddenly be all around us.

My fear was so great that, had Stella not been there, I might well have made ka-ka in my pants.

# CHAPTER SEVEN

Shamaz, I eventually noticed, was one of those eight, no sign on his jaw or forehead or anywhere else that there was anything physically wrong with him. There *was* a slight crookedness to his nose that hadn't been there before and a tiny smirk on his face and that, too, reminded me of Tyson. The way Tyson looked when he said things like his intention being to drive his opponent's nose through his brain or eating his opponent's children or how the amount of time it would take him to finish a fight was the amount of time it took to kill a man, stuff like that.

Ah, what heroes America was breeding these days.

There was no question in my mind at this point that Bill Johnson had been on the money when he said, "A .38 always beats aces." Ultimately, it always comes down to force.

Though still scared beyond anything that could be conveyed with words, because of Stella I decided to go to Humphrey Bogart for my attitude.

"How's it hangin', Shamaz?" I said.

"Bigger'n yours, mothuh-fuckuh," he said.

I noticed, when he spoke, there *was* something crooked about his jaw.

"That clearly makes you the better man, doesn't it?"

"Got some unfinished bidniss."

"Gonna beat me up?" I asked.

"Gonna drive yo nose up yo brain."

Hadn't someone said "Imitation is the sincerest form of flattery"?

"Bring your friends so they could help you?"

"Nobody gotta help me squash a li'l worm."

"What'd you bring them for?"

"They gonna help me escort all you faggots to someplace special."

"Think we're stupid enough to go anywhere with you all?"

Three of the eight immediately pulled out .38's and held them chest high, pointing them with the weapons' sides facing the ground, as was so fashionable in the movies and TV these days.

"We blow yo brains right here, right now, mothuh fuckuh," one of the three weapon-wielders said.

"Anybody know any sentences without 'mothuh-fuckuh' in them?" I asked, Humphrey still talking for me.

"All I gotta do is nod my head," Shamaz said, "and all you white mothuh-fuckuhs cease to exist."

"I said a sentence *without* 'mother-fucker' and that includes the plural form."

"One mo' minute, we fuck you up in prural fohm right here, right now."

"If it's me you want," I said, "what do you want my friends for?"

Now it was Sidney Carter from *A Tale of Two Cities*. *"Tis a far better thing I do now—"*

"They gonna see what happen mothuh-fuckuh fuck wid me, den go 'roun' braggin' he de man."

"Bragging?" I said. "Nobody's bragging. It was a freaky accident, who's giving it any thought?"

"Thass what *you* say, mothuh-fuckuh. Word is *you* knock me out, *you* broke mah nose. So now dey gonna see whass what. Now move yo' mothuh-fuckin' asses, all'a y'all, or it's all over right now."

So with the eight bruisers semi-encircling us, we began to walk. The three weapon-wielders put their pieces in their pockets but their hands were in there, holding on to them in case we tried something.

Funny thing was I had often thought, what would prevent someone, anyone, from approaching you in broad daylight, pointing a gun at you, and taking your money? By the time anything significant happened, presuming someone called 911, the perp would be in the subway. Now these guys were marching us, taking us somewhere, but they could do anything they wanted to us right here and they could disappear without a trace and no one would ever find them. It was the Big Apple. You could do anything in the Big Apple and the chances of your getting caught were infinitesimal

West of the Allen Street Playground was Third Avenue, formerly known as The Bowery. The Bowery had been famous as the home of alcoholics. If people wanted to see alkies sprawling on the sidewalks and in the gutters, they would go to the Bowery. But why would they want to see alkies sprawling on the sidewalks or gutters—or anywhere? They could see them in the movie *The Lost Weekend,* with Ray Milland. Anyway, the Bowery was where the alcoholics, or better known in those days as drunken bums, used to be. Now, of course, they were all over town. All over the country, as a matter of fact. Only, as with everything, it was no longer politically correct to call them alkies or drunken bums. Now they were called the homeless. There was even a newspaper put out on their behalf. But the newspaper didn't do very well. People didn't want to buy the paper and read about the homeless.

East of the playground was Allen Street. The playground itself was like a buffer zone between avenues that strove toward some kind of respectability and streets that had questionable denizens.

The Allen Street Playground was the playground we came to.

There were mothers and children and other kinds of people there. As we approached, I noticed these others who filled the playground were mostly teens. Standing among them was Bill Johnson.

I had not thought it would be possible to be that happy about seeing anybody, let alone a gym teacher who had put me in this predicament in the first place.

The tom-tom inside my chest stopped pounding and settled into a strong punk-rock beat. Bill Johnson was holding two pairs of boxing gloves, a pair over each shoulder.

I gave vent to my relief with a sigh. *Beautiful dreamer, wake unto me.*

Then I remembered a lot of people had been killed by boxing gloves, not to mention consequences that might arguably be worse than death. Look at Ali, Meldrick Taylor, et al.

I walked toward Bill Johnson while my friends remained behind. Shamaz and his gang walked to the opposite side from where Johnson stood. A number of them, I also noticed, made circling motions to the people who were standing around. These people then began fanning out to form a circle. When I looked at them a little more closely, I realized they were from Seward Park. I remembered Bill Johnson had suggested Shamaz and I might hold a rematch in the playground with school kids attending.

"Did you arrange this?" I asked Bill Johnson.

"Somewhat," he said.

"What does that mean?"

"I finally located Shamaz a few weeks ago and asked him what his intentions were toward you."

"And he said...?"

"Bad. The intentions were bad."

"And you said...?"

"I said, like I told you, instead of waylaying you somewhere on the street, it would do his rep more good to have a quorum of kids from the school witness the rematch with the situation that took place in the gym being duplicated in the playground. That way, nobody could accuse him of maybe having been unfair or maybe his friends helping him or that, had you all used boxing gloves, you still might've knocked him out. There would be plenty of witnesses to his fighting fair *and* using boxing gloves. As you can see, this logic appealed to him. He also agreed to my acting as referee."

"I often go to the mountain top, cup my hands at the sides of my mouth and shout—'What would I do without Bill Johnson?' "

"And what does the echo answer?"

" Says," and here I cupped my palms at the sides of my lips, " 'without Bill Johnson, without Bill Johnson.' "

"Cute. Paraphrasing *The Raven* there, I get it. 'Without Bill Johnson.' You know, I think my wife asked herself that very question before she took me to the cleaners."

"Love these philosophical discussions of ours. Wish this one could go on and on."

"I hear ya, buddy."

He took the gloves that hung over his left shoulder and handed them to me. Then he walked over to where Shamaz stood and gave him the pair that had hung over his right shoulder.

I untied the cords that connected the gloves he'd given me and put the right one on. Bill Johnson came over to help me with the left one. I looked over and saw Shamaz already had his on. Bill Johnson assigned one of my friends to act as my second and one of Shamaz's gang to act as his. Then he took his place in the center between us and motioned us both over. In my mind's ear I could hear Michael Buffer's voice shouting, "Let's get ready to rumble," rousing the rabble's roar.

Bill Johnson gave us the same instructions he'd given us at the gym, then sent us back to our corners. One of the kids in the crowd must've had the same thought about Michael Buffer because he shouted, "Let's get ready to rumble," doing a pretty good Buffer, and the other kids all roared the way crowds do at these fights. We had an event on our hands. Calls for a standing ovation, what?

What had Bill Johnson said about rope-a-dope? I remembered seeing tapes of Ali doing it with Foreman and Foreman pounding him to the body and on the fists and arms that covered Ali's upper chest and face. Those had to be very painful and if you had not been blessed with a body that could take that kind of punishment and if you were not in top condition, trained for that kind of stuff, there would be ribs broken and you would have to lower those protecting arms—and *then* you would get knocked out.

Any way you looked at it, I was in for a hell of a beating, if not a concussion. What if I took a fall like Liston had in the second fight with Ali via the "phantom" punch? Stella was there along with everyone else, watching.

*I could not love thee, dear, so much*
*Loved I not honor more*

I remembered the scene in Hemingway's *The Sun Also Rises,* in which Robert Cohn beats up the bull fighter Romero and keeps knocking him down again and again but the young matador just won't stay down. A manifestation of Hemingway's theme, "grace under pressure."

I believed in grace under pressure. But when the chips were down, it was a hell of an item to live up to. And the only time it counted was when the chips were down.

Bill Johnson pointed his forefinger and somebody rang a bell. It was one of those little hand-bells—the kind Ralph Kramden used in a *Honeymooners* episode to call the maid. The kid who had been assigned as my second pushed me out toward the center of what had become the ring. I turned to look at him. Thanks, pal.

*When I turned again to face Shamaz, he was nowhere to be seen.*

*Instead, I was looking at the man with the Roman nose, wearing sheets and carrying that same massive dagger with the decorated pommel and crossbar.*

*Dear lord. It's one thing when it happens once. It's another when it happens again.*

*A look of calm intention in his eyes, he was heading for me, the big knife above his head at a 45-degree angle, once again just like the momma from Psycho.*

*It did no good for me to tell myself this was nothing but an illusion and, when I woke up, I would see it was really only Shamaz wearing boxing gloves and pants that hung down to the crack of his ass, looking to drive my nose into my brain.*

*As bad as that might sound, it rarely ends up as anything more than a knockout, which is nothing compared to getting a knife big enough to chop wood sunk into your chest.*

*Consider, when you're having a nightmare, you're not saying to yourself,* Oh, this is just a nightmare, I'll wake up soon and everything'll be fine. *The man with the knife moving toward me was more real than anything around. It was like one of those movies where one actor is in focus and everything else is fuzzy.*

*Running away was no good. When you are in a static position and someone is moving toward you, he has already gathered momentum and, by the time you've garnered yours, he's overtaken you and you'll get it in the back.*

*In such circumstances, some individuals will go into apathy—like in the moment you witness an animal attacked by a lion finally give up and succumb. Others—like the mother who lifted the back end of a car to save her baby—will perform super-human deeds.*

*My reaction on this occasion was similar to the one I'd had the first time this happened. Only I added something.*

*A flash thought came to me. Something I'd read that the French statesman Clemenceau had said: "L'audace, l'audace, toujours l'audace." (Audacity, audacity, always audacity.)*

*It made sense. Do something audacious that your opponent didn't expect and you had a good chance of success. It was the reason the German* blitzkrieg *had worked so well.*

*I began running full speed at my opponent.*

*For the shortest moment—he hesitated*

*During that moment I lunged with my left leg, extending my left fist toward his solar plexus. This caused him to lower his left arm in protection of that part of his body while trying to zero in on some meaty part of my body with his right, knife-wielding hand.*

*Meanwhile, I threw an overhand right hook to the left side of his face, hearing myself roar, "You ugly one!"*

*The instant after my gloved fist made contact with his jaw, I did a belly flop on the pavement.*

I lay there peacefully. The pavement was raspy and rough against my cheek. I could feel blood seeping from the spot where my right cheekbone was. It didn't hurt, though. It would hurt later. The sounds of kids playing and teenagers talking again sounded like a babbling brook. Probably because it was so peaceful. An ant was moving toward my face. It stopped just before it reached my nostrils. It stood there for a while as if inspecting them to see whether there was anything in there it could take to its hill. Or, as I didn't see any hills around, to wherever its home was. Weren't ants supposed to be able to carry something like a hundred or five hundred times their weight?

It was so peaceful.

*Sweet illusion,*
*You who will stay till the foggy, foggy dawn*
*Hastens your dreams to a dreary dawn,*
*Still dreaming of you*

# CHAPTER EIGHT

I saw feet and legs gathering and there was the prostrate body of someone, who I quickly figured out to be Shamaz, lying on the pavement at a 45-degree angle to me, face down. He must've fallen forward.

"Don't crowd them, goddamn it," I heard Bill Johnson say, "give'em room to breathe. Move back—move *back*!"

Feet began to shuffle backwards. I pushed myself up and sprang to my own feet as Bill Johnson turned Shamaz over so he lay on his back.

Then I saw Shamaz's face and, caught unawares by the strange way his nose was twisted and the freely flowing blood, I began throwing up, managing to turn away after the first spray. Now everybody seriously backed up.

Bill Johnson kneeled by Shamaz and kept putting tissues against the nostrils where the blood flowed, making sure the mouth wasn't covered.

"Man, that looks like a better nose-break than the first one," he said, then called 911 on his cell.

Everybody else stood around, staring, mesmerized.

Then another unexpected thing occurred. I felt empathy for Shamaz. Here was this guy lying there, bleeding with a terribly broken nose and I remembered Bill Johnson saying the guy's mother was on welfare with nine kids. Joe and Rose Kennedy had had nine kids. How much care and attention could Shamaz have had during *his* upbringing? Not graduated from high school, without a father, and already on his own, rummaging for a living, existing from hand to mouth. How is a person who is treated badly all his life going to treat others? We have the animal's instinct to beget children but, once we beget them, most of us don't have a clue as to how we should raise them so they are able and happy. And we rationalize it by believing you *could* be able—after all, it's hard to deny *that*—but you couldn't be happy, thus handily removing responsibility for having or creating happiness in yourself or anyone else.

Bill Johnson was staring at me.

"What?" I asked him. "What?"

"Once could be a freaky accident," he said. "Twice? No."

I crouched by Shamaz's body and gazed at him. I remembered a long time before, when I was very little and my father was alive, we'd been driving on a highway and a dog ran out and our car hit the dog and the dog got bounced off to the side on the shoulder of the road. My father pulled up ahead of it and got out and we all went to look at the dog. The dog was all bloody and broken and unmoving and—dead. We stared at it and my father crouched by it and tears were flowing down his face. Seeing him cry, I began to cry as well.

I looked at Bill Johnson.

"I know what you're thinking," he said. "Remember, though—he's been doing this to other people in local clubs, and he didn't have to go after you and box you again. Also, it's just another broken nose. Maybe a little worse than the first time but noses break and they're okay again. He'll be fine. He may have second thoughts about going into boxing as a career—you know, for a strong, muscular black guy to be beaten by whitey is no small thing—but he'll be okay, that's the important thing."

I've noticed often there's a tendency to get carried away by some happening of secondary importance and maybe that was why Dostoyevsky talked about big ideas and big goals. They give you perspective. If people were able to keep their perspective when they got into arguments over parking spaces or even over a romantic break-up, they would not stab or shoot each other. I could get into a funk over the fact Shamaz had grown up disadvantaged and there were many millions in the world who were growing up disadvantaged and, if I felt strongly enough about it, I could become some kind of a social worker or a missionary or join the peace corps, and dedicate my life to helping disadvantaged people but the thing was to find out what my true goals were and get out of falling into funks over secondary singular incidents and use them instead as a springboard toward discovering the road *I* was to travel.

The ambulance came and they carted Shamaz away and everybody again looked at me as if I were the Elephant Man—except there was a hell of a lot of admiration in the looks and it occurred to me that this might mean a lot of women in my future. The magic of Stella was dissipating with awesome speed.

# CHAPTER NINE

I walked that day. I walked to the East Village. I walked to the West Village. I walked all over Greenwich Village. I walked uptown. I looked at the people. I looked at the traffic. I looked at the tall buildings. I looked at the garbage containers. I looked at the litter on the streets. I looked at people's faces. They looked tired and worn and not happy and not friendly.

How had all this come about? These people, these buildings, the air we breathed, the millions of cells in us? All these mysteries. The people did not look at one another. No one said hello to anyone. When you went to a little town, people said hello, how are you, nice to see you. I walked to Harlem. People stared at me in Harlem. They were not friendly stares. On Third Avenue between 122nd and 123rd Streets there was a Scientology Mission. Two African-American women, one in her fifties, one in her thirties handed out leaflets. People took them. Downtown, very few people took leaflets. It was communication. People didn't want communication.

On 125th Street I walked west to Broadway and started walking downtown. Different neighborhoods had different kinds of people in them. None of them looked very happy. On 86th Street I turned east and walked across Central Park to the East Side.

When I turned the lights on in the living room at midnight, my mother was sitting on the couch. I flinched in surprise and not only because I'd expected her to be asleep in her room. I had become jumpy. From this point on, I would never know when the guy in white sheets, carrying the knife, would show up. It was, I imagined, like having had a heart attack or having been mugged. You never knew when it might happen again. It was not a good way to go through life. Except you could tell people about heart attacks and muggings. About this I had to keep still. Not a good way to go through life.

"What now?" I asked irritably and was immediately sorry for my tone.

My mother started to cry. Anything I'd felt about being beset by the apparition problem got dissolved in a flash. It was a horrible thing to see my mother crying, my entire world split apart.

I sat by her and put my arm about her shoulder. "Is it what's growing?" I had bugged her a number of times about going to the doctor and she'd finally gone and I'd forgotten about it.

"He cut a little piece and sent it to be examined and now he says he'll have to cut my breast off." She burst into a new gush of tears.

"See another doctor."

"I can't afford to keep going to doctors. They give you drugs or they cut. But mainly they charge. And this whole health insurance business. You still have to pay out of pocket, the only thing health insurance does is enable the doctors to raise their prices. Anyway, it was examined in the laboratory."

"What're you going to do?"

"I'm not going to let them cut my breast off."

"What're you going to do?"

"Nothing. It's going to go away by itself."

"You've had it for months. You have to do something about it."

"I'm afraid."

"Thousands of women have had this done and they're all walking around alive and well."

"I'm afraid."

"You have to do it."

"I'm afraid."

"You *have* to do it."

"No."

"You have to do it."

"I have a right to do what I want with my body. I won't do it."

"You don't have a right to make Grandma and me watch you kill yourself."

"No one's going to make me go in there and let them cut my breast off."

"Are you telling me you're going to let this thing grow and do nothing about it?"

She began to cry again. "I don't understand why, after I worked so hard, after we moved to a nice apartment in a good neighborhood and everything's going so well—"

"That's not going to help us now."

"It'll go away by itself."

"You have to do something."

"No. No, no, and that's it."

I walked out into the hallway, pulled an empty suitcase out of the closet, and brought it back to the living room, placing it on the couch and opening it.

"What's this?" she asked.

I went into my room, opened one of my drawers, pulled out a bunch of clothes, and carried them back to the living room, throwing them into the open suitcase.

"What're you doing?" she asked.

I went back to my room, got another bunch of clothes, and came back to the living room, throwing them into the suitcase as well.

"What're you *doing*?" she asked again.

"If you don't do what they tell you, I'm going to go away and you'll never see me again."

"You wouldn't do that."

"We're on the fourth floor. Rather than watch you do this to yourself, I would open the window right now and jump out. Leaving is the lesser evil. So that's what I'm going to do."

I went back to my room and got another bunch of clothes. I could've laid out the suitcase on my bed in my room, it would've been more efficient, but I wanted her to watch me pack. Where I was going I had no idea. Vaguely I thought of Bill Johnson. He might let me stay with him a few days. I would have to find out where he lived.

But it didn't come to that. Two more trips to my room and she said, "All right. I'll do it."

"You have to make the appointment tomorrow and have it done as soon as possible."

"I have to see what arrangements I can make at my job."

"No. All you have to do is tell them you're having an operation and you'll be back when it's over."

"I have dresses I have to finish altering at home."

"No. They can all wait. If they can't wait, let them come and pick up their dresses when they want."

"I'll lose customers."

"To hell with them."

"Don't talk like that. They're my customers."

"Fine. But they can't have their dresses done till you're well."

"I could finish the work before."

"You want me to leave?" I put a batch of my clothes I had thrown on the couch into the suitcase.

"All right. All *right!*"

I called the school the next day and told them I could not come to graduation and asked when could I pick up my diploma.

I stayed by my mother's side through the phone calls to the doctor. I went with her to the hospital two days later and stayed with her till visiting hours were over. Next day I came and sat in the waiting room while they operated. After work, her fiancé came and waited with me.

Talking to this man my mother was going to marry was something I had to do but not something I liked. It was talk about solid happenings, news events, the stock market, gossip but not analyzing anything or gleaning something. It did absolutely nothing for my spirit.

I hadn't had more than a few minutes with him at any given time previously, just during moments when he'd come to pick up my mother and they'd go somewhere. Now, talking to him and thinking about someone like Don Quixote or Sidney Carter from *A Tale of Two Cities* enabled me to have a full cognition on the difference between a small spirit and a large one. It was an irony that I lived in an age when the concept of small spiritedness ruled the day.

The man did visit my mother every day during her hospital stay and that was good. It set her mind at ease about losing him and not being able to get married again.

I started going to Hunter and evolved into a whole new life. It felt wonderful. Acting, writing, and directing gave me the feeling life was wonderful. I directed a scene from *Of Mice and Men* for the drama club and in another production I played a laborer in *Waiting for Lefty* who rallied other workers to go on strike. It was a powerful scene and I did it on the auditorium stage with a full audience, which I used as if they were other workers. I spoke directly to them and the experience of being able to move them to the point where the entire audience was yelling, "STRIKE! STRIKE! STRIKE," and stamping their feet gave me a hell of a high.

I'd begun doing a lot of bicycle riding and realized vigorous physical activity made me feel good. I kept it up. In school I got into not only studying and the dramatic society but physical movement classes, speech classes—I was all over the place.

But life always seems to be throwing hand grenades in your path and, in each case, if you didn't pick them up and throw them back or get the hell away from them far enough so they didn't blow you up, you were going to be up the proverbial creek without a paddle.

One night I came home from school and there was my mother crying again. Seeing my mother cry did not get easier with repetition.

I got that sick feeling in my stomach. There must be something primordial in us that brings horror to our souls when there is the slightest signal something is going wrong because I wasn't even thinking of anything connected to her operation, I wasn't thinking of anything specific at all, yet I was in the throes of horror.

"What? What?" I asked, running to her.

It took her a while to answer me, she was crying so hard.

"He—he—he—doesn't—doesn't—want to." She kept repeating it.

"What?" I asked. "Who doesn't want to? What?"

"Marry—marry—marry—me." There were these spasmodic sobs coming out of her that broke my heart.

"He doesn't want to marry you?"

"No—no—no—nnno." She was a little child swept by sorrow.

I was about to ask why but quickly stopped myself. I put my arm around her instead and we sat like that for a while.

I felt I should hate the guy for causing my mother so much sorrow and misery, for ruining her life. But I didn't. I didn't hate him, I wasn't mad at him. Why? There was something in me from early childhood that had stayed on and on and seems to be a part of me. I accept things and don't get into a frazzle of how it shouldn't've happened or what might've been. I can grieve over something—but not because there are regrets or feelings it should've happened another way. I grieve over things because it's part of the experience in the same way I laugh when something is funny. But I don't hold on to it. I know it sounds like I'm making myself out to be such a wonderful guy but I can be a prick in other ways so don't worry about it.

I held her for a while.

"He'll change his mind," I said.

"No," she said. "He won't."

After a while, I said, "I never liked him much."

"Really?"

"Never liked him."

"Why?"

"Something about him made me feel like dry, smelly skin, and rot—and dandruff."

"Better than not having a husband at all."

I didn't agree with her but if that was what she thought, then, for her, that was how it was. You try to show somebody they're wrong, they're not going to applaud you for it.

"Somebody better'll come along," I said.

"Nobody better came along when I had two breasts. Now there'll be nobody. Men want young women with two breasts and without extra people to support."

She was right.

Why, though? One breast, two breasts, why should it make such a difference? If there were something useful missing like a limb, I could see it. But a breast was something you used on only two occasions and, for each, one would do as well as two. Why would men care so much?

Did it have something to do with our obsession for normalcy? In the olden days, if you were other than normal, you were punished. Then, in the sixties, there had been the great revolt against normalcy.

But even in that instance, you were rejected if you did not conform to the anti-establishment dress code and ways of doing things that became the uniform in the fight *against* normalcy.

Then came the revolution against treating gays as if they were inferior to the "normal." In fact, they claimed, they *were* normal. Just different. Yet, despite the fact there was a lot of PR about gays being equal but different, society just didn't take to it. Most people would simply dread their son or daughter becoming one and the moment a movie or TV star was discovered to be one, the star's popularity plummeted with alarming speed and permanency. Witness Ellen DeGeneris and Anne Heche. On top of the world one day—out of the closet the next—down the chute the day after.

My mother continued to be sad, cried frequently. I had a hard time seeing her like that. She was a woman who had a great deal of vitality and *joie de vivre* and it's dispiriting to see such an individual in the doldrums, especially when it's your mother.

Finally, I contacted one of her friends to find out where this man who had broken her heart lived. My mother's friend was one of those busybodies who knew where everybody was and she told me he was living with another woman in a residential hotel on 86th and Broadway. I went there to see him one evening. They announced me from the desk and he told them to send me up.

It was raining and I wore rubber boots over my shoes. My feet felt very heavy in them. My entire body felt heavy and clumsy and out of place. I walked through the hall toward the room I had been directed to and felt like *The Graduate* in the underwater scene without the slightest idea of what I was going to say or do to the man.

Did I have it in me to do something violent to him? Would that guy with the knife show up and would I, then, go and break the man's nose as I'd done to Shamaz? They would arrest me and put me in jail and the man would have no compunctions about pressing charges. It would be a way of confirming he was right to disconnect from my mother and her family. But did I have any control over the appearance of the apparition or what I did when it showed up?

Having opened the door, the man asked me in. It was one room with a double bed and the woman he was living with was sitting on the bed, her hands in her lap. She was elderly—when you're nineteen, most of the world is elderly—slightly overweight, as is the wont of many elderly people, and sad looking; not from anything particular necessarily, just a general malaise from an accumulation of things that had piled up over the years. There were a table and a couple of chairs, a portable electric hot plate on the table, a little fridge, a closet, and a bathroom.

I stood there in the middle of the room still without an idea of what I would say to him and still fearful the guy with the knife would suddenly turn up. They both looked at me and waited, she with an openly hostile look, he with a guilty one he tried to make seem neutrally benevolent. I had never seen any signs of benevolence in him before.

I had a feeling she had been against my coming up but, out of guilt, he had prevailed and she wasn't liking it.

After a pause that seemed to stretch into eternity, I spoke.

"My mother is very sad."

The man nodded. "What can one do?"

The woman glared. As if she were saying, *I found this guy and I'm keeping him*. She looked to be in her forties, flabby, weighed down, and miserable.

This man did not deserve my mother, not only because he was small spirited (could you sense I'm at war with the small spirited?) but because he had chosen such a petty, miserable woman when he could've had my mother—because of one measly breast.

"I was thinking," I said, "if you were to go to her and ask her to forgive you and tell her you changed your mind and could she take you back—"

I could see as I was talking he thought it was a terrible idea but I plowed on. Very little so disheartening as to be communicating an idea that so obviously stank.

"—she wouldn't take you back," I said. "It would just make her feel better to think you came back and she turned *you* down."

"What if she didn't turn me down?"

"She would, though, I know she would. Her heart's been broken, you hurt her too much, she wouldn't take you back; I know her."

"I appreciate your trying to help your mother. I wish I could help her too, she's a good, good woman. But I can't. I really can't."

"Why can't you? It's just cross-town, it would take less than half an hour and then you wouldn't have to see her again."

"It's not something I can do. I'm sorry."

"All right. All right."

I was thanking God the man in sheets with the knife hadn't shown up. If he had, there might've been a tragedy. With me not wearing gloves, the man might've gotten killed. I guessed that was what they meant when they talked about taking the gloves off.

I went out in the hallway again. The door had remained open while I was in the room. That had probably been his hedge in case I got physical. The fact he'd let me come up showed he knew me, knew I would not get violent. I still could not find it in me to be angry with him. Or with the woman. They were two elderly unhappy people who lived in a little hotel room and who were trying to hold on to what was slipping away: life.

Never occurred to me I might one day be an elderly person myself. Does it occur to anyone?

I felt better for having tried. Not much better. Good enough so I could say to myself, *I did what I could.*

I remember in later years going with a young woman and running across a list she'd noted down of things that had to be done. At the end of the list, as if fearing she wouldn't get to any of the items, she had written, "Do SOMETHING!"

I guess it's better to do something than nothing.

Is it better to compromise in something than risk ending up with nothing?

# CHAPTER TEN

Life went on. It always does. Stella had broken my heart and life had gone on. Something you'd planned and counted on you didn't get—or you lost something you had—and you went into the doldrums. And then things kept on happening—and you were out of the doldrums. Life went on.

There are people who stay in the doldrums longer than others. They are afraid of going out and getting battered again. But that was not my mother. Her life force was much too strong. She got back to working hard, continuing to support me and my grandmother and that got her back to her usual vitality. *Elan vital, monsieur.*

My life, too, was full. Acting became my main driving force. Everything I did was fueled by my desire to be an actor, writer, and director. The apparition that had caused me to break Shamaz's nose receded further into the chasm time creates.

My enthusiasm waxed as my involvement with acting grew deeper and more rooted. In the dramatic club I joined, scenes were rehearsed and performed by various members at weekly meetings for the rest of the membership to enjoy. I reached the point where I was in demand by directors who staged scenes for the dramatic society and for their drama classes.

When rehearsing and acting, I was in a state of ecstasy. I was not acting; I *was* the character, experiencing the situations in the most intense way—as myself.

Hearing talk about summer stock (summer theatres in various vacation spots), I got the idea of writing a letter to 50 summer stock companies in different parts of the country, asking if they had any kind of a position in which I could work to earn some money and also gain some experience in acting and theatre.

I didn't know at the time that the odds against my finding a position where I could have all the things I was requesting were about ten thousand to one. A perfect example of ignorance being bliss. If I'd asked for such a position without pay, the odds would have dropped to about fifty-to-one. If I had asked for such a position and volunteered to pay for the privilege, the odds would have dropped to about three-to-one.

Does that give some notion of how many aspiring actors and actresses there are in this country? Yes, many theatres throughout the land actually charge money to have young people work, building their scenery, doing props, and various other tasks connected with putting on a play. This is justified by the rationale they are teaching these young people about theatre and one can charge money for teaching.

Because I was ignorant of this, I had no idea that, in writing the letter, I was wasting my time.

Ignorance, however, often reaps unexpected benefits.

One theatre did respond. The reason behind the occurrence of this miracle I was to discover later. But it was the Cape Playhouse in Dennis on Cape Cod. Its letterhead said it was the biggest summer theatre in the country. In the interview with the manager, a man in his forties with rather pasty, flaccid looking features and limpid blue eyes behind black-framed glasses, I was informed I would be cleaning the Star Cottage, where the star of each week's show stayed. Another of my jobs would be picking up litter from theatre grounds, helping to build scenery, parking cars for people who came to eat at the theatre restaurant and saw the show each night, after which I would be acting as traffic cop when they drove off the lot. If extras were needed for various shows or if there was a bit part I was right for, I would be considered.

It was a great summer. Seeing in the flesh stars you'd seen on the screen. It felt strange. It was a little like the sensation I'd experienced watching a three-dimensional feature on Imac. Where on regular screens you saw these stars looming like some giants with super-lives, in 3-D they seemed so tiny. And, of course, in person, when you heard the tenor of their conversations, their teensiness was more than confirmed. Forgive me, that's a nasty way to look at it. They were nice people for the limited extent to which we were relating to one another. And they created magic on the screen and I was feeling wonderful being around them, looking forward to the day when I would be working alongside them. Well, I was working alongside them now but doing mainly menial stuff, which is like being a zero. Knowing, however, I would one day be in their position, I felt very good about my time there.

With one exception. The theatre manager who had interviewed me and given me the job made a play for me one night at his cottage and I got my answer as to why he had chosen me for a job he could have given to thousands of others. There must have been something in my letter that gave him a sense I might be a viable seduction prospect. What was it about my letter that had given him such an idea? Did I show some kind of sensitivity or some kind of flair that made him think I might be gay? I suppose heterosexuals aren't supposed to be sensitive or show flair. C'est la vie.

He was quite taken aback when I ran out of the cottage and straight to the assistant manager's quarters with the horrible news. I could see, though the assistant manager himself was a hetero, he was neither moved nor about to empathize with my naïve stupidity. There was an upside to my crybaby-assistant manager-visit. Much as the manager might've wished to get back at me for turning him down and find somebody more amenable for the job, at least after that he didn't dare fire me. We live in a time where you can get sued for practically giving somebody a dirty look, forget about sexual harassment. I thought it somewhat ironic I got the job because he thought I was gay and kept the job because I was a hetero who'd rejected his advances.

And I did get to do the things I'd set out to do; met some TV and movie stars, got some experience, and got cast in an upcoming Broadway show. It looked as if my acting career were going to take off like a rocket.

In New York that fall, the Broadway show got terrible reviews and closed in a week. I found myself on the street without a notion of what to do. The obvious thing was to make rounds like other would-be actors. I had pictures taken, attaching my resume, which consisted of one season of stock and a failed Broadway show.

I soon discovered the amount of time you wasted on seeking auditions added to upwards of ninety-nine-point-nine percent. Hundreds upon hundreds of people competed for each available part and they all had to be sent by agents.

Getting an agent was perhaps even harder than getting cast in a show. Added to this was the widespread, almost routine practice of casting entire shows and films through the agency from which the star of the show or film was booked. In other words, the big agency that delivers the star says, "We would prefer you cast the other parts from our roster." All the other actors sent by other agencies at that point audition purely on the chance the casting people were unable to find what they wanted from the agency that had delivered the star.

Suddenly, what had seemed so promising on the Cape turned in New York to a ring-a-round-the-rosey. Did you know it is said that ring-around-the-rosey came about during the bubonic plague in which "rosey" was the rash and "all fall down" was all these people dying as a result of the plague?

The other thing was I valued my time too much to waste 99.999 percent of it indulging in activities and meetings which would bear no fruit whatsoever except for creating an ever growing sense of rejection.

Also, I reasoned people reflected the nature of their jobs. Cops were a certain way, teachers another, doctors another—actors another. Except I would not be assuming the personality of an actor. It would be the personality of someone who wanted to be an actor but was being rejected right and left. I didn't want to be such a person.

I didn't want to be a person who has, in hopes of getting a part, kissed ass so often it has become his nature to kiss one wherever he sees it. Mister Propitiation.

I wanted to find a plan that would get me to where I wanted to be—where I could act, write and direct—but not with the current system that would instill in me the psyche of a reject.

I needed a plan. Some bright idea that would cut through all the counter-productive effort. Something along the lines of what I'd done in writing all those letters to summer theatres. But what? In a market where thousands upon thousands of young men and women strove to become stars, how in hell did you go about building a better mouse trap?

There had to be a way. It was a moment when I realized this was the foundation upon which my life stood. To dream the impossible dream—and then to turn it into reality.

The apparition. That was why the apparition had appeared. The apparition had something to do with where I was going.

It occurred to me that—

*When you see the truth of something, you can come up with a plan to achieve anything.*

# CHAPTER ELEVEN

Once I make a decision that affects my life and resolves something that's bothered me, a kind of euphoria and serenity overtake me. I get a new appreciation of things. Like walking on the street. The people on the streets. The buildings. The weather, no matter what kind. On this day it happened to be sunny so I appreciated the sun. I looked at the sky. It was clear except for a few cloud wisps floating by that seemed more like cotton candy than clouds.

I climbed the five steps that led to the landing where the outer door of the apartment building in which I lived stood and walked through the lobby to the elevator. I stepped into the elevator, feeling the slight bounce from my weight. I pressed seven and the door closed. It began climbing upward slowly with something between a hum and a rumble. It had a mirror on the ceiling so when you looked up you could see your face and the verticality of your body. The inside was painted a deep glazed brown; one of the elevator walls had a mirror so you could inspect yourself from above and the side. There were brass handrails running around the walls except for where the door was.

When the elevator stopped on the seventh floor, the inertia caused it four up-and-down bounces before it settled even with the landing. The landing was made of cement with an iron railing that wound along the floor and up and down the stairway. Chips of the metal that had been scraped away through the years left the railing scarred, the white lines and markings jumping out of the iron's blackness.

Stepping into the apartment, I looked to the left where my mother's bedroom was. The door made up of glass squares over which my mother had put curtains was open. There was no one there. The sun's rays streamed into the room. I walked down the long hall to my room which was on the right just before you hit the living room. I left my backpack in my room, then walked through the living room to my grandmother's room, which was really a maid's room located just off the kitchen. There was no one in my grandmother's room either. She must be downtown, getting bargains on Orchard Street.

I went back into the living room, picked up the phone from its cradle on the little table between the two chairs against the wall, pulled out the White Pages from the lower shelf of the table, and flopped on the couch. I flipped through the pages till I found the number and pressed the buttons. Heard the phone ring on the other end. Pick up.

"Bill Johnson here."

"Mr. Johnson, it's Dan Kahn."

"How's the college boy?"

"College-ing away. How about yourself?"

"Same old, same old—you know."

"How's—everybody?"

"Well, let's see. Mrs. Hopper's out with the gout, Mr. Arnstein broke his leg, Ms Chambers quit and went to teach in a private school. Otherwise, same old, same old."

"What about Shamaz?"

"Shamaz is taking some remedial courses in English and math, gonna try to get into CCNY."

"Wow! Shamaz going to college?"

"Ain't life somethin'?"

"How's his nose?"

"Little more crooked than it used to be and he talks a little more gutturally, you know, but he's okay."

"He still boxing?"

"Gave it up."

"Had he been serious about it?"

"Hell, yeah. But like I told you, when a black fighter gets knocked out by whitey, time to take stock. When it happens twice, 'bye-'bye blackbird."

"You said Shamaz was good."

"Yeah, he was good. But you get knocked out by whitey—"

"You talk like there's never been a Marciano or a Zale or Graziano or—"

"That was all before blacks came on the scene. Hasn't been a white fighter in decades can challenge a good black fighter. 'Less you count Hispanics and the whites don't count Hispanics. But that's beside the point. Fact is, you get knocked out that early in your career, it's a sign. Like those ice-skating contests in the Olympics. Fall or slip during one of those, you can forget about a medal. Except when the judging is even more crooked than usual."

"What about you, run into any prospects?"

"What do you mean?"

"Remember, you talked about finding somebody and making him a great boxer? Somebody who'll create art and poetry in boxing? Excite the world?"

"Oh—pipe-dreaming."

"You don't strike me as an individual who pipe-dreams."

"You beginnin' to sound like you goading me. What's on your mind?"

"If you were pipe-dreaming, nothing."

"What's on your mind?"

"Nothing if you were pipe-dreaming."

"Okay."

A beat or two. "What made you change your mind?"

"Don't run into potential greatness in Seward Park. Don't run into it no matter who or where you are, okay? If you're Don King, you can buy greatness so you can use it up and destroy it. You wanna discover it and nurture it so the world can experience the ecstasy of it, it's not so easy."

"Do I hear bitterness?"

"You hear what you hear. Let me repeat my question. What's on your mind, baby cakes?"

"You said knocking Shamaz out once can be a freak accident. But twice it couldn't."

"So?"

"What does that mean?"

"Means just what it says; you possess the power to knock

somebody out, I told you that. What else you wanna know?"

"You think I could be a professional?"

"Professional what?"

"Who's goading whom now?"

"You askin' if you can be a professional fighter? That what you askin'?"

If you answer sarcasm, you participate in it. I didn't say anything.

"Could you picture in your wildest dreams there was ever a fighter or there could ever *be* a fighter who would say, 'Who's goading *whom*'?"

"Didn't you say Jack Dempsey was a literate guy?"

"He was pretty literate, yeah, but even he, formidable as he was, would never have said 'whom.'"

"So we got a deal breaker in 'whom'?"

"Deal breaker, listen to that. What kind of deal we talkin' about?"

"About you maybe training me and arranging for me to fight in some of those clubs that Shamaz fought in and see if I got the stuff."

Now that it had come out of my mouth, I couldn't believe I'd said it. Was I actually proposing I train to get into a ring and hit people and have them hit me? When the idea for the plan came to me, it had seemed viable and there had seemed to be some sensible reasoning behind it: the idea of a shortcut to show business. Make a name in the fighting game and get a part, on the strength of the name, in movies and shows. Lots of sports people had been given that opportunity and how many had been prepared for it?

But now I'd said it, it seemed as sensible as if I'd planned to become President of the United States by robbing a bank and becoming a rich, influential citizen first. Jean Valjean.

"Now who's pipe-dreaming?" Bill Johnson asked, echoing the ridiculousness of it.

"All you have to do is answer yes or no."

"What're we, in a courtroom here? Have you given *any* thought to what you're sayin' here?"

"I'm willing to do whatever it takes."

I had been ready to change my mind but, once you put your foot in your mouth, it's almost impossible to take it out. The only course remaining is to keep hopping on one foot and develop a taste for toe-jam.

"What of all that stuff about wanting to be creative and not being a, what'd you call it—destroyer whore? Was all that pipe-dreams too?"

"I thought about what you said. Having a God-given talent that's rare. Maybe it *can* be an art, boxing."

Funny how, when you want something, you will bullshit your head off. You'll do so many things you despise—in others.

"You have any idea at all what you'd be letting yourself in for? You have any idea what it is to take punches from very strong guys born and built for fighting and who've had access to the most modern, scientific, and rigorous methods on how to deliver punches that'll scramble your brains and who love doing it, who are hungry to do it, who dedicate their entire lives to doing it?"

"No, I don't."

"Yet you call me out of the blue and tell me, 'Let's do this'?"

"Excuse me, but aren't you the one who talked to me about having a rematch with Shamaz so we could see if I really had the knockout punch? What was that?"

"Foolishness, that's what. Pipe-dreams, that's pipe-dreams right there. Anybody can se you're no boxer; you a college boy. Like to read, get educated, like using your mind, you said so yourself, that's what you been pursuin'. For a moment back there a few months ago I had this notion that—oh, hell, it was ridiculous. I see clearly now it was ridiculous and you were right in what you said then and you're full of shit in what you proposin' now. See, Shamaz, with his background, his build, his desire to be somebody—he was the logical candidate for this. Frankly, I thought he had the potential to really get up there. I didn't wanna tell you this back there but I put my heart and soul into trainin'm. I really thought he had a future."

"Amazing the way certain information slowly seeps through bit by bit. You were training him—were you managing him too?"

"Well, yeah."

"And so in a gym class you taught in a public high school, you paired him off against a white boy who you are now implying is the furthest thing from a boxer you can imagine."

"Won't let go, will you?"

"Look what the consequences have been. Shamaz, who you say had a promising future as a boxer, had his jaw broken once and his nose twice, he quit the idea of boxing and is taking steps to go to college and I, who love studying and creating and hate boxing, am on the telephone, asking you to train and manage me as a boxer. All because you did something, the reason for which still eludes me. There were quite a few boys in that gym class who would have been much more appropriate as Shamaz's opponents than me just as there was a number of boys it would have been more appropriate for me to box than Shamaz. Whenever I've brought it up and asked you about it, you've danced around it and come up with some kind of, quote unquote "witty remark" as a retort. I would really like to know what prompted you to make such an illogical choice so fraught with danger."

"There you go again. How could you even think of being a fighter, using words like 'fraught'?"

"Wasn't Bobby Chyz a college graduate with an IQ of about 150 and didn't he become a champion and isn't he one of the most intelligent and articulate fight commentators who's ever been on the scene?"

"How do you *know* all this stuff?"

"You're still dancing."

"Yeah, Bobby Chyz was a champion all right but he was also built like a bull and could take and deliver a hell of a punch."

"The Golden Boy isn't built like a bull and neither was Caesar Chavez, and they were great champions who could take a punch."

"Jesus, you're a goddamn encyclopedia."

"Doesn't it all add up to how strong your intention is, how much you want something?"

"So why do you suddenly want *this* so much?"

"You still haven't answered why you chose to pit Shamaz against me."

There was a pause.

"You really wanna know?" he asked.

"I really do."

"I'll tell you. I don't know. After having lived for decades, I mostly don't have the slightest idea of why I do most things, why other people do most things, what makes somebody happy—or sad—or great or small or benevolent or mean."

"I'm only asking why you did something so glaringly illogical as to put two opposites like Shamaz and me against one another."

"I just got through telling you I don't know. May have something to do with destiny. Or it may have something to do with wanting a nice looking white boy to get his brains beat out by one of my own and you know where *that* comes from. Or maybe it was a way of fucking my future up the way most of us do. All I know is it was what I felt like doing at the time. No more than you probably know why you suddenly decided to go into fighting. Or do you?"

"Actually, I do."

"Why?"

"If the only reason you can come up with for pitting Shamaz and me against one another is because it was what you felt like doing at the time, then you're going to have to be satisfied with the same answer from me."

"You don't wanna tell me?"

"The only thing on the table is whether you're going to help me or not."

"You askin' me to train and manage you?"

"Right."

"What about college?"

"What I'm proposing is that we train after school."

"When you gonna study?"

"Free periods during the day and when I come home at night after training."

"You gotta get at least eight hours' sleep."

"I'll manage it."

There was a pause.

"Be a hell of a thing," Bill Johnson said.

"What?"

"A white guy—a Jewish white guy—who has a KO punch. The public would go nuts. Be more than with Ali or Tyson or anybody. Be like—Fantasy Island."

"You're dating yourself, Bill."

"What happened to Mr. Johnson?"

"I figure since we're gonna be—"

"To you that means dissing me?"

"All right. Mr. Johnson, then."

"Just yankin' your chain, boy. Bill's fine. Now, aside from the extremely rigorous methods bein' used today for training athletes, especially fighters, there's one other thing we haven't talked about that, comparatively speaking, is even more important than a KO punch and/or having a good technique."

"What's that?"

"Being able to take a punch. Those guys you talked about—Golden Boy, Frazier, Marciano, Graziano, Zale, all those guys, Ali, Tyson—they could all take a punch. It may have scrambled their brains but they could take a punch. Most guys have glass jaws. Hit'em and down they go like a sack of potatoes. Now the chances of your being one of those guys who could give a punch *and take* a punch are extremely—extremely—let me say that again—extremely rare. So next thing you and I are going to do when we get together—I'm going to test your ability to take a punch. You willin' to be tested?"

"You wouldn't perchance be talking about me standing there with my hands at my sides and you hauling off and hitting me as hard as you can?"

"No, I'm talking about us two getting in the ring, putting on gloves and then fighting—just like you and Shamaz did. Only I'm not Shamaz. I got some world class experience behind me. I may be in my forties but for three or four rounds I could go in and mix it up with the best. So I'm gonna find the opening and I'm gonna hit you. I'm gonna hit you hard, the way a world class fighter would hit you. Because, even with the best training in the world, at some point in the fight somebody's gonna nail you. I wanna see what your jaw is like."

"By hitting me before I've even gotten trained?"

"As I say—even with the best of training—sooner or later you're gonna get nailed. When *I* nail you, I will know the potential of your jaw. The fact I'm gonna knock you out—and I *will* knock you out, you can count on it—will not necessarily be an indication you have a glass jaw. But, in that respect, I'm like the specialist your doctor has referred you to. He can look at something, touch something and know what's goin' on. When my glove comes in contact with your jaw—I will know the potential of your jaw."

"I get to defend myself, though."

"You can defend yourself all you want—I *will* knock you out. You have to understand that if I don't feel any potential in your jaw, I'd be wasting my time and yours by training you. Are you willing to submit yourself to that test?"

"Well, of course."

"Well, good."

# CHAPTER TWELVE

In bungee jumping there are precautions. You don't hear of bungee jumpers smashing their heads against the pavement. You do hear of fighters getting brain damage. But the feeling when you're standing that high up must be the same. I don't know what the feeling is of looking down when you know you're about to jump but I do know what it is to be up high somewhere and look down. Then just add to it the concept of having to jump and you got it. I would not want to do that. And now I felt as if I had committed myself to something worse.

Why is it, when you're dreaming something up, it seems like such a great idea and then, when you are faced with the reality of doing it, it's quite another matter?

When I was little, my father took me to a wrestling club. That was the first time I encountered the smell of sweat from men who work out. It's different from the smells of other kinds of sweat. And, because at that time I was excited and happy about learning how to wrestle, the smell, rather than being offensive, was pleasant and part of the general thrill.

Well—I was a child; I was excited and happy about everything except when they tried to make me sleep. I fought against that, very hard, as most children do, because it seemed I was missing so much. I didn't want any of my days to end.

How interesting that, with the passing of years, you get less and less excited and happy about things and look forward more and more to sleeping. Wouldn't it be something if, as George Carlin had suggested in one of his monologues, we could start our life in a nursing home or recovering from a heart attack and get stronger and younger as the years go by, going on to drink milk from a woman's breast and moving on to end up as a gigantic orgasm?

When I walked into this little hole in the wall on Lower East Side's Henry Street where a number of young guys and three women were in various phases of working out and got a whiff of that sweat smell I remembered from long ago, I thought, *By God, how could I ever have liked this stench,* and *What am I doing among these ruffians for whom this activity is the be-all-end-all of life.* It was as if I'd arrived at the very opposite of the place in which I belonged.

Then Bill Johnson walked up, shook my hand, and took me to the locker room. As instructed, I had brought gym shorts, sweat socks, sneakers, towel, and a combination lock. After changing, I went back to the workout room. Bill Johnson was standing by the ring and motioned for me to come over. He had a pair of boxing gloves, which he gave me, then took a pair for himself from a big carton by the ring. It was the same carton he'd had in the gym when he paired me off with Shamaz. He held the ropes apart for me to get into the ring, then I held them for him. I remembered how Charlie Chaplin had held them for his corner men in *City Lights.*

The moment Bill Johnson got into the ring, a crowd started gathering. People in clubs who had been fighters and the young ones who were training to become fighters knew about Bill Johnson. They had all heard about him and many had seen tapes of his fights on the Sports Classics cable channel. Very likely, though, not many had seen him fight in person, judging from the way they stopped what they were doing and came to watch.

Now I really felt foolish. I was in the ring with this semi-legend who had earned the respect of his peers and who had said he was going to flatten me. Yes, he was in his forties and, at one time, that might have been considered old but more and more it wasn't so any more. George Foreman had regained the heavyweight crown when he was in his forties. What was I? Nothing and no one. I knew absolutely nothing about fighting and they would see it the moment we began and they would all wonder why Bill Johnson had gotten into the ring to beat up this kid who knew nothing about boxing when there were so many guys in the club who were seriously training to become fighters and could gain from the experience of being in the ring with Bill Johnson.

But there were times when you had to proceed with something even though you knew it was going to make you feel and look like a jackass.

The moment the bell rang to begin the round, it happened.

*Taking Bill Johnson's spot, the man in sheets, holding the knife in the ready-to-plunge position was moving toward me.*

*For some reason—maybe because I'd associated the man with Shamaz—I'd forgotten about him. I had somehow skipped him and had it in my mind I possessed a legitimate knockout punch and was going to be trained into a bona fide fighter.*

*But now he'd appeared, a neuron pattern that had cut out its path seemed to become activated. I ran at him full speed. I could see the surprise on his features. "L'audace, l'audace, toujours l'audace."*

*This time I did not simply do a cross-over lunge with my left leg as I had done during my last encounter with Shamaz; I dove at the man the way a football player might execute a tackle except I aimed for the middle part of his sheeted body rather than the legs. And, instead of encircling his mid-section, I threw my right over his left that had slipped slightly down to meet my body coming at him like a heat-seeking missile—and again out of my mouth came the animal growl, "You ugly one!"*

*Where had this marvel of timing, co-ordination, foxiness, speed ,and strength come from? It was like finding yourself speaking in tongues, only it was in boxing. And why was I saying, "You ugly one"? Neither Bill Johnson nor this apparition that had taken his place was ugly.*

*The moment my fist made contact with his head, I plopped onto the mat—somewhat the way the dodo bird lands when it's taking its clumsy break from the miracle of flying.*

*Sweet illusion*
*Sweet as a face in a dream*

Everything was very, very quiet. I opened my eyes. To my right I could see Bill Johnson lying on the canvas. Others were all outside the ring, staring. No one had moved, no one had come up into the ring. What had all these people been doing when the guy holding the knife was there?

It all had the elements of a nightmare—only each time it happened, the consequences of this nightmare spilled over into reality you then had to deal with.

What would happen if I didn't succeed in disabling the person with the knife? Would I be the one on the floor—with a bleeding hole in my chest?

Slowly I raised myself to my knees. Crawled over to Bill and propped up his head. His eyes were closed but he was breathing. There are some people who frown or are sad when their eyes are closed. Bill Johnson had the same expression of decency he had when awake. Then other people started coming into the ring. Somebody sprinkled water on his face, a very old man gently slapped Bill Johnson's cheek but without waking him up.

Someone had called 911 and an ambulance came and they carted Bill Johnson away. Everyone looked at me as if I were something from outer space. It's one thing to know how to box and knock your opponent out. It's another to be diving at your opponent as if you were playing in the Super Bowl.

I changed into my clothes and, walking through the gym, received not a word, not a glance from anyone.

*And I had done a hellish thing*
*and it would work'em woe*
*for all averred I had killed the bird*
*that made the breeze to blow*
*'Ah, wretch,' said they, 'the bird to slay,*
*that made the breeze to blow.'*

I took the F train to West Fourth, then walked to St. Vincent's, where they had taken Bill. When I got there they told me he was coming to on one of the rolling stretchers.

"Could I see him?" I asked.

"Wait here," the woman behind the partition said, "he'll be out in a little while."

I sat in the waiting room with people who were waiting to be seen and others who had come with them. People in an ER may be the embodiment of life's essential question: What's it all about—Alfie? Why are these people sitting here, in pain and suffering? What is the point? Is there some progress to be made from it, some lesson to be learned? We have somehow accepted it's part of life just as we've accepted death as a part of life—but it is a forced acceptance. As Nixon had said, "Grab'em by the balls and their hearts and minds will follow."

Would we not be able to have joy and fun without the flip side of the coin on which you have pain? Yet, children who are unacquainted with pain can have all kinds of joy and fun and, suddenly, the kid gets hurt and is in pain. Why? The kid was having a perfectly good time without knowing what pain is. Suddenly, there is pain.

I'm not satisfied that's how it's supposed to be and remain. I don't think it's the truth. It is reality—but it is not the truth. Truth is what sets you free. And truth is beauty. This is not it.

Bill Johnson was escorted into the waiting room by a young black nurse in a very close fitting uniform.

There is something ass-kicking about well fitted clothes. Her buttocks and legs looked formidable as they do with many black women. The advertising industry had conditioned us to think of beauty being represented by a small, compact ass.

After I'd read that in the old African culture it had been considered a mark of beauty for a woman to possess a big ass my attitude regarding big buttocks and legs slowly began to shift—until it evolved to where I thought big buttocks and legs were a hell of a lot sexier than compact ones.

This, however, can work only if the person who possesses them thinks so too. How can you possibly watch Mae West in an old movie and, buxom as she was, think of her as anything but sexy when it's so obvious she thinks of herself as the sexiest thing ever created?

The nurse gave Bill Johnson a folded slip of paper, said goodbye, and went back inside. I approached as he unfolded the paper, looked at what was written on it, and smiled.

"Hi, Bill," I said.

He looked up, and, deducing I had taken in the scene, re-folded the paper and put it in his back pocket

"She used to watch my fights on TV with her daddy when she was a little girl," he said.

"And now she wants to do some wrestling?" I said.

"One can only hope."

"From the old movies I watch and from what I read, it used to be a girl gave a guy her number and it meant they would date for a while and there would be kissing and what they called necking but it would be a long time, if ever, without an engagement or marriage, that she would 'go all the way.' Now, when a girl gives you her number, it's like she's saying, 'Let's fuck,' and a long courtship is when it happens on the third date instead of the first or second."

"Somewhat bluntly put," Bill Johnson said, "but not inaccurate. The sixties and the women's movement have been a great boon to us men in that department. Let's get the hell out of here, hospitals give me the creeps." He led the way out. "Nurses, however, I like — especially when they wearin' those tight uniforms and walkin' all smooth'n soft in those white stockings and rubber-soled shoes that squeak on those tile floors."

It always gave me a kick about Bill Johnson, the way he would switch from showing his intelligence and education to street talk. Indulging in a bit of that street talk seemed *au courant* in the African-American community, no matter the amount of education, culture, or intelligence.

He stood on the sidewalk and took a deep breath, looking around.

"Nothin' like bein' released from a hospital," he said, "to make you really appreciate life. Let's walk."

We headed toward Sixth Avenue — or Avenue of the Americas, if you want to be technical.

There is a special feeling about Greenwich Village. And it's the one the media have created. Tourists come to see what they've heard about on the media. The starving artists who used to live in the Village moved out a long time ago due to how expensive it had become. But the tourists keep on coming, thinking of it as where the artists are.

The media dictate our feelings far more effectively than any dictatorship can ever hope to. Someone on TV comes up with something that appears clever and original and others in the media start copying it and the public starts copying it and pretty soon people all over the place are doing or saying that thing, one a copy of the other. We don't realize we're conforming—but, hell, we're conforming. Take this business of guys shaving their heads, for instance. Started with guys who wanted to mitigate their hair loss and turn it into a macho tough look and it gets on TV and then guys all over the place are going around with bald heads, looking like they came out of an assembly line, wimps thinking they look cool and tough.

"Say," Bill Johnson said, "I've never been hit like that in my life. You dove on me, though, usin' your flyin' body to give the punch—well—body. Where'd you get that?"

Should I tell him? I flirted with the idea. Hell, no. Maybe they would not go so far as to lock me up—if they thought I was harmless—but there would be no one who would not think me crazy.

"Just came to me," I said.

"Well, I'll tell you—if you still wanna train, I'll train you, and manage you."

"I thought you wanted to see how well I could take a punch."

"Didn't get to punch you, did I? And if I didn't get to punch you, you're not an easy guy to punch, are you? The important thing, however, is that you *have* a punch—and you delivered it three times in a row, the last one against somebody who can take a punch, never been down, duck a punch and deliver a punch—and I wasn't able to do any of those things. Now, there've been some great fighters in the history of boxing who had some unorthodox ways of keeping from being punched while they themselves delivered the punch. Roy Jones was one—Naseem was another—for a while. What you did with Shamaz and me was the most unorthodox thing I ever seen. Good training builds on those qualities rather than trying to eradicate them. Doubtlessly, someone you fight at some point or other *will* be able to both avoid and deliver a punch. Then we'll see if you can take one or not. And even then, if you have enough presence of mind, you'll see to it by tying him up it's only one punch and not a one-two. It's the one-two that's the killer. Usually, unless a fighter can follow up that one disarming punch with another and then another, the opponent will recover. What's unusual in fighting is what *you* did — and what very few others have been able to do — one punch and the opponent is out. That's better than gold in boxing. So — if you wanna be trained, I'll train you, and manage you."

Just then, we heard a scream.

It's a strange thing about that kind of a scream. It transforms everything. You're walking around and think everything's okay with the world and suddenly you are shoved into the realization — it's not. Before the World Trade attack, everything seemed so civilized, so pleasant. Even the dramas you watched on TV — there was an order to them, a logic that brought justice to badness. The things you did from morning till night were pretty predictable. Think about the Stone Age when all kinds of wild and mysterious animals roamed the earth. You left your cave and could run into anything. Things were more or less unexpected. We've come a long way since then. And then the WTC, and we were right back to the most primitive of times — some wild animal pouncing on someone. When that scream belongs to a woman — as this one did — well, it tears at your heart. You remember men and women jumping from great heights into the abyss — and it's not a movie.

We were a few yards from Sixth Avenue on Eleventh Street by now and saw a mid-sized, slim swarthy man run uptown on the west side of the street. Bill Johnson and I both took off after him.

It was what I did ever since I was little whenever I saw any kind of conflict anywhere. My mother kept telling me over and over, "Don't get involved," but there was something that drove me. I think that was why, when I read *Don Quixote*, I was in tune with him. Once, when I was seventeen, I saw two very husky men about to start fighting on the street in front of a bar. Just as they started going at each other, I lunged between them, trying to separate them. Some other guys who had been standing around, watching, then decided to help and we got them separated. Later, when I was home, I noticed the back of my jacket had about a foot-long rip across it which could have been made only by a knife — and I hadn't even realized one of the guys had a knife. I knew, then, my mother was right. But it made no difference.

Bill Johnson was faster than me by about three steps. He dove at the guy just as I had dived at Bill in the ring back at the club, only he dove at the guy's legs, and the guy hit the pavement so fast he didn't have time to put his hands out to cushion the fall and fell right on his chin. He gave out a grunt and swiftly turned. I saw him swing at Bill Johnson's back as Johnson was crawling up toward the man's chest and at the same time Bill Johnson hit the man with an overhand right that brought the guy's head back against the pavement. Then Bill Johnson continued crawling up on him till he was straddling him, hitting him with rights and lefts so fast it was almost like an automatic weapon. Then he got up, grabbed the guy, who was now semi-conscious, by the hair and started dragging him downtown Stone-Age-style.

"You okay?" I asked, walking alongside.

"Yeah," he said, continuing to drag the guy like a sack of flour. "He caught me one on the back but I'm okay."

We headed for a crowd on Tenth Street and Sixth and when we got there, they made way for us to get through and there was a woman lying on the pavement and blood flowing from her stomach.

"Bastard stabbed'er," a man said and just then, the siren of an approaching ambulance in tandem with a flashing police car.

"Got this damn itch in m'back," Bill Johnson said, reaching for his back with his left hand.

"Why's the back of m'coat wet?" he asked.

I looked and touched the back of his jacket. It was soaking and beginning to stick to his body.

"You're bleeding, Bill," I said.

"Son of a bitch stabbed me too, then," Bill Johnson said. "Boy, that nurse gonna be surprised."

# CHAPTER THIRTEEN

**B**ill had to stay in the hospital for two weeks. The guy had just missed his appendix. Bill and the nurse got real close. She was on at night so I think the second week they were doing it right in the room while the patient who shared Bill's room slept. Or maybe he didn't. There was this scene in *The Unbearable Lightness of Being* where this couple is doing it in the compartment of a moving train with a guy sitting there, sleeping, and when the lovers start doing it, the sleeping guy reaches over for his glasses. The nurse's name was Aisha and she really liked him. So now Bill had a girlfriend.

Me, I wasn't even thinking of a girlfriend. I was so busy, running around, taking speech classes, acting classes, body movement classes, doing parts in college plays, I had no time for anything. Except you really do. People will say, "Oh, I'm so busy, I don't have the time," but if you were to do an analysis of what they do, you'd see there always is time. There's a saying, you know, "If you want something done, give it to a busy person." Busy people always have time to do things. It's like love: the more you give, the more you got. So I would've had time for a girl, all right. High time, too, considering I was beginning to have wet dreams.

The important thing was I had a plan and taken the first step toward its execution. Out of the fold of hundreds of thousands of would-be actors looking for a job, I'd put myself on a shortcut route toward achieving my goal.

There is a tendency for people to act like sheep. What's "being done" is what they'll do. All the progress made in this world has been made by individuals who have taken themselves out of the fold of this general "sheep" syndrome and marched out to carve a new reality—and then the sheep would move into *that* reality. It's never been majorities or groups or committees that discovered new things or made advances that benefited humanity. It's always been individuals. But to do that, you have to re-orient yourself into a viewpoint that's truly and uniquely yours and then come up with a bright idea that will conform both to your viewpoint and to what will ultimately make the reality of the world conform to *it*.

All individuals who've achieved fame in one area or another have a ready-made springboard to parlay it into show business. In 1977 Ali starred in a major movie about his life. It was a bomb. Francis Ford Coppola's daughter Sofia got put in a starring part by her daddy in *Godfather III*. She bombed. There are countless instances of famous individuals who, because of their fame in another area, or connections, got an opportunity in show business. Most of them bomb. Why? Because they don't prepare for it. They just go ahead and do it, expecting their greatness or comfort zone in one field of activity to automatically transfer itself to another.

That was where I would not make the same mistake. I had studied Stanislavsky, taken drama classes, written, directed, acted in a lot of scenes—I had prepared. When my opportunity came—I would be ready.

I felt good. Like Don Quixote when he'd decided to go out on his quest. A purity and joy in what I was doing was with me all the time. Because I had a purpose.

But my joy could not be pure nor my purity completely joyful. In the center of it there was this mystery. No question now the guy with the knife, intending to stab me, was going to show up every time I got into the ring. I had been able to pull off three miracles in my efforts to avoid getting the knife plunged into me and, though I could look back and say, "Obviously, these were illusions," they felt real while they were happening.

So I was left with the fact I neither knew what it was, why it was happening, or what the consequences might be if I didn't manage to avoid that knife. Yet I was going into the very activity that would bring about this manifestation.

Like a black panther in your attic. You know the door to that attic's loose and can be opened. Sooner or later, the beast is going to appear. You can huddle in the corner and ignore it and know, like *Candid Camera*, when you least expect it, it's gonna come down and get you. Or you can go get the fucker. I was going after the fucker. Of course, my primary goal was show-biz but the thing was—I was going after the fucker.

Meanwhile, one of my mother's friends arranged for my mother to meet an Italian hair dresser in his forties who had lived in Venezuela for five years and had just come to America to live. His name was Alex and he'd had his own hair dressing shop in a little town called Molfetta near Bari, Italy. He was the youngest of eleven kids and his oldest sister was more like a mother to him than his mother.

He had made a decent living from his hair dressing salon in this little town of Molfetta, staying single till he was in his thirties at which point he got married to the woman who worked for him in his salon. He was very thin and wiry and had one of those natures that constantly has to be doing something. It's really a wonder he was able to live in that tiny town for so many years with just him and his wife working in the shop and then, later, a young man, Emilio, who swept up.

Eventually, though, Fate comes and taps individuals like Alex on the shoulder and summons them to adventures in far away places. Someone came to Molfetta with the news that, if you were a good hairdresser, a lot of money was to be made in Venezuela, South America.

Now, what makes a man living in a tiny town in Italy think he's good enough to travel half across the world to fill the need in a country that must surely have a goodly supply of its own hair dressers is a mystery. But that's part of the mystery of the world and all its doings. It's what makes individuals discover and conquer continents, come up with the idea the world is round and proclaim in a world of barbarism that you should do unto others as you would have them do unto you.

Do you know, by the way, how the word "barbarism" came about? In Ancient Greece, foreigners sounded to the Greeks as if they were saying "bar-bar-bar-ba" and that's how the word was formed.

I think much of it has to do with Destiny and some of it has to do with the fact that Alex had what the Sephardic Jews call in Ladino (a bastardized form of Spanish) "*culu pintudu*," which means "painted ass." The analogy is that when you have paint on your ass, you can't sit anywhere because you'll get paint on it and you'll also probably get stuck to whatever you're sitting on as the paint dries. So you just have to keep moving. There have always been people in the world who've had painted asses and there always will be. Alex was one of those.

He told his wife he would go to Venezuela and work there for a month. If there were money to be made, he would write her and she would sell the store and move there and, with the money from the sale of the Molfetta store, they would buy a store in Venezuela and make a new start.

"I can't sell your store," she told him. "It wouldn't be legal."

So he went to a lawyer and arranged for the store to be signed over to his wife and he went to Venezuela and got a job there as a hair dresser and two months later he saw you could make a good living there and wrote his wife, telling her to sell the store and join him in Venezuela.

But he didn't hear anything back. So he wrote another letter. And again didn't hear. He wrote his oldest sister. She wrote back, saying he'd better come home. He took the next plane back.

He arrived during the day and went straight to his salon. His wife was there and Emilio, the boy who swept up.

"Why didn't you answer my letter?" he asked her. If this were a movie, it would all be in Italian with titles, you understand, and you can imagine the hand motions.

"I didn't want to go to Venezuela," she told him.

"Why didn't you write and say so? We can stay here."

"I don't want to be with you anymore," she said.

"What do you mean?"

He could really not understand what she was saying. It reminded me, when I heard this story from my mother, of my mother after the man she'd been engaged to had told her he didn't want to marry her. People who are truthful and keep their word are not able to conceive of someone who is not that way. They hear stories about people who don't keep their word. But they can't imagine such a person being part of *their* world. And when it happens—the fact has a very hard time penetrating.

"I don't want to be with you," she repeated. "I don't want to be with you, I don't want to live with you."

Emilio sat there and watched them.

Alex turned to him and said, "This is a private discussion between me and my wife. Go take a walk."

"It's too cold to walk," the young man said.

Alex reached into his pocket and took out some money. "Here. Get yourself an espresso and some cake. Come back in half an hour."

"I don't need your money," Emilio said.

"Fine," Alex said, putting the money back in his pocket. "Just go, I want to talk to my wife privately."

"I think I'm going to stay and listen," Emilio said. "It sounds interesting."

"You're playing games with your job," Alex told him. "If you don't leave this moment, you're going to lose it."

"Do I look as if I'm afraid?" the young man asked him. "You might try throwing me out. Would you like to try that?"

"You were always such a nice, quiet boy; what's happened to you? Have you been drinking?"

"Maybe a glass of wine at lunch—in pleasant company—not much more. On the other hand, maybe I'm not a boy anymore, have you considered that? Maybe I'm not someone you can boss around anymore the way you've been doing for years."

"Get out of my store."

"I already told you I'm not leaving. I invited you to throw me out. Or you can call the police."

"All right."

Alex went to the phone and called the local carabiniere. Ten minutes later, the policeman arrived.

"Sandrino," the carabiniere said, hugging Alex, who did not like to be touched but what could he do, everybody in this country loved touching. "You came back to us."

"Emilio here," Alex said to the policeman, "has decided he doesn't want to get out of my store even though I ordered him to."

The carabiniere looked at Emilio. "What's this?"

"If the boss tells me to get out," Emilio said, "I'll get out. This man is not my boss."

"Sandrino's been the boss of this store for fifteen years," the carabiniere said.

"Why don't you find out who the current boss is before you talk?" Emilio said.

"Get fresh with me and I'll hit you with this stick, you delinquent."

"All I'm saying is you should find out who the owner of this store is before you threaten honest citizens who have done nothing illegal."

"You don't tell me who the owner is," the carabiniere said. "I know who the owner is as well as I know this stick that I'm going to hit you with if you don't watch out."

"Maybe you don't know," Emilio said.

"Are you telling me what I know and what I don't know?" the carabiniere asked, approaching Emilio and raising his stick.

"If you don't know this, then I'm telling you what you don't know."

"You open your fresh mouth again and I hit you with this stick *and* put you in jail."

"Are you going to tell him?" Emilio said to Alex's wife.

She had already reached into her purse and come out with a piece of paper, which she unfolded and handed to the carabiniere. The carabiniere perused it and perused it, then turned to Alex.

"This paper says," he said to Alex, "that the store belongs to her."

"I see," Alex said. "I see it all now."

"*Did* you sign the store over to her?" the carabiniere asked Alex.

"Yes."

"Why?"

Only in Italy would a public servant be such a busybody.

"Because I was an idiot," Alex said.

"When it comes to women," the carabiniere said, "we are all idiots."

"I didn't dream of something like this happening."

"Where women are concerned," the carabiniere said, "you have to be prepared for anything."

Alex's wife said, "You men are all so pure and wonderful, aren't you?"

"We are idiot children compared to you," the carabiniere said.

"That's the first sensible thing you said since you walked in here," she said. "You're idiot children—and you have to be treated like idiot children."

It was beneath the carabiniere to dignify her remark. He turned to Alex. "My sympathies, Sandrino. I hope this will not drive you to do anything foolish—I know the temptation is more than great. Although I doubt the judge would be too harsh with you." And he threw the woman and Emilio a withering look—the sort only Italians know how to throw—the kind that if you're watching from the outside strike you as very funny.

In order to avoid doing what he very much felt like doing, Alex took the next plane back to Venezuela, where he worked very hard for five years to save enough money for a new start in the U.S.A.

Eventually, he even got a Chevrolet. See the U.S.A. in your Chevrolet.

I don't know what Alex and my mother felt for one another when they began going together. Older people don't look at love in the same way young ones do. Young people have certain ideals they're looking to fulfill. Older people have been disappointed so many times they feel to have ideals is foolish because, sooner or later, you're going to be disappointed.

What older people are looking for is someone who will help make life easier for them and a little more secure. When Alex and my mother had decided to get married, my mother approached me in the living room and, with tears in her eyes, told me Alex was a good man and, "He'll help me." For some reason she felt she had to explain why she was marrying him and get my approval.

I hugged her and told her I was glad.

Alex was considerate of my grandmother and they often took her along when they went somewhere. One time, when they were in one of those self-service places, having dinner, after they'd gotten their food, my mother said to Alex, "Would you get me a cup of coffee?"

"If you want coffee," he told her, "get it yourself."

My mother got up and got her coffee and came back to the table and the repast was continued.

Later, when Alex had gone to the bathroom, my grandmother said to my mother, "Looks like you're marrying a piece of garbage."

It was an unpromising portent. Alex had come from a country where men prided themselves on their gallantry. If he was acting so rudely now, what would he be like after they were married?

On the other hand, she thought, perhaps her request for coffee and the way she put it reminded Alex of his cheating wife, stirring up feelings he'd tried to put behind. See, there's where wisdom can come in very handy.

She decided to proceed with her plan to marry him and keep a close eye on further signs indicating something was wrong with him that would make her regret the move. She learned to color hair and with her coloring and Alex styling and cutting, they began working in the apartment Wednesday nights and Saturdays, doing the hair of my mother's friends, and Alex's cousins and Italian friends who lived in Hoboken.

Alex had trouble finding a full time job and the conclusion of some of my mother's friends and my grandmother was that it was because he would only look in the fifties and sixties on Fifth and Madison Avenues, where the richest women had their hair done. Even my mother finally offered it might be wise to expand the search and go beyond Fifth and Madison, even beyond the Borough of Manhattan.

Alex was intransigent. He would look nowhere but Fifth and Madison. I thought it fascinating how people from the remotest villages in the world know exactly on what streets the richest Americans lived. Eventually, he was the only one with hope he would find anything on those two avenues.

*On the avenue, tra-la-la-la*

Months passed. Finally, he landed a job in a salon on Madison Avenue in the fifties. It was run by a Frenchman who had faith in Alex's work and Alex did not disappoint him. Women liked Alex's seriousness, his wiry energy, his certainty and definitiveness regarding what they needed in the way of cut and style and soon he began to build a clientele and the money began to pour in. The wiry type of person who is motivated will work without the inclusion of the word "stop" in his vocabulary. It's like with the movie *The Terminator*. You could chop him into little pieces and each little piece is going to keep coming at you.

Alex and my mother got married and he moved in with us. They continued working in the apartment on Wednesday evenings and Saturday all day. When Alex came home every day from work, he would reach into his pockets and pull out fistfuls of bills he'd received each day in tips. At the end of their work at home on Wednesdays and Saturdays they would both pull out bills, Alex from his jacket pockets, my mother from her apron pocket, laying it on the table for counting.

It appeared in time that the incident in which Alex had refused to go get a cup of coffee for my mother at the self-service place was one of those freaky happenings in which he must indeed have experienced some kind of a reminder in regard to the wife he'd left in Italy who he heard was now openly living with Emilio, the young man who had swept up.

Alex turned out to be a good and generous person, begrudging my mother nothing and loving her with all his heart, finally convinced that, just as there were deceitful women in the world, so there were good ones.

For me it seemed perfectly natural things should turn out well and that from tragedy there could come ultimate happiness. It was what I expected of life.

# Chapter Fourteen

I had a date. My first since going out with Maria. It was with the friend of a woman in my English class who thought her girl friend and I would hit it off.

Esther, the girl I was going to go out with was a big girl. Not fat. Just tall and—big. Maybe a little fat. Well proportioned, though. She had a pretty face, nice gentle features, brown, dreamy eyes and straight brown hair. I was not stricken with her but the forces of nature had been beckoning and I was getting curiouser and curiouser about what it would feel like to have sex with an actual woman, and I was getting—eager. Is that the word?

Not so eager it was all I was thinking about. I was doing a lot of stuff all over the place, not to mention my studies, so I had very little time to think about something that wasn't part of reaching my goals. I'm not much into thinking about what isn't happening anyway. I'm into deciding what I'm going to do and then going ahead and doing it.

When this came along, though, I thought, *Maybe IT is going to finally happen and I'll experience—how shall I put this—FUCKING?*

And the idea of this big girl—ever since I'd read the item about African men prizing big asses on women, I'd begun developing an appreciation of big women. Not to the exclusion of appreciating other sizes and shapes but, since I loved women so much anyway, the idea of there being more there to appreciate, to caress, to kiss, to hold, to suck, to penetrate—appealed to me. And having a big girl as my first one—what could be juicier?

Well, this is not the most promising foundation to start a relationship on. Not because a lot of people aren't doing it and making it work for a while but because when you go into an experience with an attitude that goes against your essential nature, something is bound to fuck it up—so to speak.

We went out a few times and she seemed to like me but her feelings may not have had a great foundation either. Many women have strong considerations about the necessity of having a relationship so they will form one even when it may not conform to their ideal scene regarding a mate. As with almost all of us, men and women, we're fairly convinced the ideal scene is unattainable anyway so we settle for what reality offers.

She invited me to her home one evening on a Friday night when her parents were out of town. When a woman who's sharing living quarters invites you at a time when those she's sharing them with are not there, it can safely be considered a done deal.

We were stretched on the couch, watching a Brad Pitt movie and eating a pizza we had had delivered in. Before the last segment of the movie, during the commercial, I leaned over and kissed her and she responded eagerly, slipping her tongue into my mouth and exploring lustily. Of course I got mostly pizza taste, but that was all right. Commercials these days go about five minutes so there's loads of time to do stuff. The way I was feeling, about three minutes would've been enough.

I wonder if broadcasters realize, in their desire to make more and more money and slip more and more commercials into programs, that people who watch can safely leave the area or surf other channels for four or five minutes without fear of missing any of the program. If there were fewer commercials, they might sit through them because they'd know it wouldn't be for *too* long, with the result they might actually *see* the commercials. I understand from the older folks in the olden days there *were* fewer commercials. There was a limit of one minute for commercials then. That was before the Reagan people deregulated the limitations. Will there come a time when there will be more commercials than show? It's approaching that point very quickly.

Well, never mind. We kissed and caressed and I began touching her leg and she was responding and finally the movie resumed and we turned back to the screen, both of us knowing that, when it ended, we would continue kissing and caressing and I felt like shouting hallelujah because, at last, I was going to DO IT! To myself I sang from *Damn Yankees*, "There's nothin' to it but to do it, you gotta have HARD—I mean, HEART."

But, as the Jack Hawkins character in *The Bridge on the River Qwai* said, "There's always the unexpected."

When the movie was over, Esther began offering her own hallelujah's—to Brad Pitt. Now, don't get me wrong, I like Brad Pitt. I think he's a terrific actor and seems like a good guy. But what Esther was ooo-ing and aaaah-ing about was his handsomeness and sexiness. He undoubtedly has those qualities as well. But here we were about to kiss and caress and what have you—and she was going on and on about how handsome and sexy this guy was, *sighing*, mind you, and I'm sure it would be okay with a lot of guys and they would just make use of it as a turn-on—who cares where the turn-on comes from?—and proceed to do what they had come to do.

I found out that evening I'm not one of those guys. I lost my desire to kiss and fondle and even to do the THING with her.

I could see she was ready and waiting to resume and there I was, making a few polite conversational remarks and then up I got and said I had to go. You have never seen such a combination of puzzled and hurt in your life.

Please understand. For four years my hormones had been clamoring. In the summer theatre the previous summer, a Country-Western kind of woman in her thirties, maybe even forties, had come to visit a friend and had been given a room next to mine in the barracks where all the staff slept and she'd come home late one night with Eddie, the lighting man, and they were both drunk. The moment they stumbled into the next room, talking and giggling, I knew what they were going to end up doing and I got excited more than you could possibly imagine. Sure enough, pauses, whispering, and then the rhythmic squeaking of bedsprings. I thought my head would explode and my heart tear through my chest like a rocket bursting in air.

Their coitus was over much too quickly and I was left with this pounding against my temples and an organ that had made a tent out of my pajama pants.

Eddie, the lighting man, a handsome, manly motorcycle-riding-Country-Western kind of guy who was successful with Country-Western kinds of women, got up shortly after and went to his own room. I'm not kidding when I tell you I thought I was going to explode.

It occurred to me I had to do something about it.

I had always had a great attraction for the Country Western type of woman. These women are not necessarily limited to the Western part of the United States. That happens to be the physical location from where they originated and where you will find most of them but to me the genre can be found anywhere, even in Jersey. Yes, especially in Jersey—but because of its proximity to New York, it's a polluted version.

Country Western-ness has come to embody a spirit rather than a location. She cannot, however, be found outside the U.S.—less'n she happens to be on one'a dem Eurepeen' vacations. Though some may think of the type as somewhat contiguous to white trash—which many of them may be—that is not the quality in them that stands out for me. The dominant quality of these women is their fun-loving spirit. They are loud, boisterous, and love to drink and swear but, above all, they love life and fun—and are sexy and love sex. Because sex is part of life and part of fun. And what makes the world go round.

And here in the next room was one of these women and she was drunk and had just made love to my friend Eddie and—what if I were to sneak into her room and slip into bed with her? How could she possibly know who it was? In her state, she would neither know nor care. I was thrilled at the thought I might actually end up fucking a Country Western woman.

This idea simply illustrates how delusional sex hunger can make you. A person in his right mind would not entertain such thoughts. Can you imagine a woman, no matter how drunk, not being able to tell the difference between a hirsute thirty-seven-year old, hundred-ninety pound man she'd just fucked and a hundred-fifty-five-pound eighteen-year-old with a hairless chest and skin that was still the textural cousin to a baby's butt?

I actually got up, left my room, tiptoed to the next room—cursing silently the little floor screeches at each step—opened the door quietly, tiptoed to the bed, kneeled on the floor by the pillow upon which her head lay and leaned over, probing with my lips till I found hers. I kissed her tentatively, catching the corner of her lips. She reeked of alcohol. I found that sexy too. And she was kind of asleep. At the kiss, she roused herself a little and kissed me back. I guess it was an instinctive response, like some dogs that will lick anything you put in front of them.

"Come back later," she mumbled.

I kissed her again and again she mumbled, "Later. Gotta get some sleep."

Suddenly, I felt something in me shooting out and my pajama pant's front was soaked.

"Later," she mumbled again.

And then I experienced some sort of magic that has puzzled me ever since: Not only did I no longer feel like kissing her, I felt like slinking away as quickly as possible.

That struck me as amazing. I had been excited enough to explode, do anything she asked me to, lick her bellybutton from the inside for the privilege of entering her, give maybe ten years of my life—hell, I was eighteen, I could afford it—and now I had absolutely no desire to be anywhere near her.

God, suppose somebody caught me here, wasn't what I was doing some kind of a criminal act? There had to be something in the statutes about this sort of thing. There was an item in the Washington statutes about not copulating with birds so what were the chances of there not being something about this? Birds. Copulating with birds. On the other hand—it *was* Washington.

Had I really done something this stupid? I couldn't get back to my room fast enough.

Next morning when I saw the woman downstairs, she smiled and gave me the kind of look made me feel she might've known it had been me and it amused her. Ah, we are amused.

This was to give you an example of just how horny I could get, especially when the opportunity presented itself. So the fact I was about to leave the prepped Esther, with opportunity practically spreading its legs in my face was an amazing discovery. To walk away from the chance to do IT for the first time in my life with a girl who was sexy and attractive and had something to grab? What did it say? It said I was an idiot.

It did not occur to me to discuss the matter with her, though that would have been the sensible thing to do. It did not seem a discussion would lead to anything productive. There was a certain kind of woman I envisioned falling in love with and it would not be a woman who, while with me, drooled over another guy so, no matter what we said, it couldn't change the fact she was that kind of a woman.

I did not call her and she, being one of those who felt the guy should make the call, did not call me either. The girl in my English class who had introduced us was, I could see, furious and would not talk to me anymore, wouldn't even look at me. Actually, she did talk to me once. A week after this happened, she stopped me in the hall after class, looked me in the eye and said, "You're a bastard," then walked away never to speak to me again.

I admired her for standing up for her friend.

It didn't matter. I was like a shark. I kept moving. From the moment I got up in the morning to the moment I fell asleep at night I kept doing things. Moving, moving, moving. They say productivity is the booster of morale. My morale was in the stratosphere.

# CHAPTER FIFTEEN

**D**an?"

"Bill? How're you doing?"

"Completely recouped. Yourself?"

"Keeping myself occupied. How's your tight-fitting girl friend?"

"Oh, man—there are no words."

Now I felt horny again. The idea of a black woman seemed even sexier than a white one. The way they moved, taking satisfaction in their bodies and the body motions themselves. The way they looked at you for the briefest of moments, then looked away as if they hadn't looked at you at all, not giving away an iota of what they were feeling. And when they danced—dear God, did they know how to have a good time.

"Still feel like boxing?" Bill asked.

Like being awakened from a beautiful, druggy dream.

"Just waiting for you to give the word."

I'd had no idea boxing involved so many other things in the way of training. Bill said it was a comparatively recent development and had hit all sports. Athletes, like almost everybody else, had taken the scientific route. Before, it had been mainly jogging, punching the bag, jumping rope, maybe reps with a few light weights. Now there were so many exercises that worked on specific parts of your body and the various aspects having to do with speed, endurance, being able to take a punch, avoid a punch, tactics, being able to leap, move left, right, back up, clinch when in trouble, cutting the ring, keeping your left foot always slightly to the left of a southpaw's right when you were facing him in the ring, it was a whole regimen of stuff that Bill said wouldn't put me in a ring with an opponent for months. Fine by me. I still couldn't see myself in the ring or hitting anyone or getting hit. Obviously, I had hit Shamaz and Bill but I was not aware of having done it so I had neither experienced getting hit nor hitting someone and I felt an abhorrence for both.

But—I had my plan. I had to keep reminding myself, for me fighting was no more than a springboard. Once I had a name, producers and casting agents would see me, and I would not have to compete with hundreds of thousands of unemployed actors who, from the producers' and directors' points of view, didn't have much to distinguish them one from the other. 98 percent of the agents and casting people looked for someone who already had a career or someone who looked like someone who already had a career. Very few would know a potential star if they tripped over one. I'm not saying I'm a star—but I knew I was *something*. And I knew I had to separate myself from the multitude to stand a chance.

Actually, I liked the training. I had realized even before all this that exercise made me feel good. Later, I learned it stimulated a secretion in your body called epinephrine, which is another name for adrenaline, which speeds up your heart, increases your resistance to fatigue, ups your strength and speed, sharpens your thinking, and causes you to experience a sense of well being. Well—no wonder so many people become so obsessive about so many different physical activities.

I abandoned all my other extracurricular activities and devoted every evening after school, Saturdays, and parts of Sundays to training. Early in the morning before school, I would run five miles. And it felt great. Not only did I keep getting all that adrenaline into my system, which kept me in a state of near-euphoria, but my body, which since adolescence had a tendency toward overweight, causing me to practically starve myself to keep it slim, now started bulging with muscles and strength, giving me still another reason to feel euphoric. I started to wear tight things to show the body off and to take off my shirt whenever opportunity presented itself. I was becoming one of *those* guys. To hell with it. I felt I owed it to myself for all those years I'd been ashamed of my body and hid it every chance I got.

There *was* one tiny concern in the back of my mind regarding the training. If I felt this good because of the exercise, what would happen when I stopped exercising or exercised less than I was doing now? After all, I couldn't go at this pace forever. I had seen a number of athletes being interviewed and the comparison between the way they had been when they were involved in their sport and the way they were now, after retirement, was great enough so you would think they were two different individuals.

I know the response to this is that people age so they change and it happens to practically everyone but with athletes it's not only the joy that comes from being in the fray, the same as with others who have challenging careers, but the physical exercise itself; there's a special euphoria comes just from *that*. There's a deadness ex-athletes exhibit that's peculiar solely to ex-athletes. Sure, there's physical deterioration, an obvious factor that can be readily seen, but I'm talking about the emotional and spiritual side. I read a story about Joe Louis which said, after his retirement, he used to lie around his apartment and the phone would ring—this was before answering machines—and he would just continue lying around, ignoring it. When asked why, he said, "What could happen?"

In other words, he had reached the point where he didn't believe anything he might look forward to and be excited about could happen to him any more. Here was a man who had moved and inspired millions with what he had done in his life and here he was, living out the remainder of his life in a state of apathy. Other ex-athletes may not be quite so badly off or at least not quite as honest about it but there was that same look in their eyes as Joe Louis had had. Not only can't they do what they had done insofar as work is concerned, but they're no longer getting the epinephrine.

As I did not intend to make boxing my life, what concerned me was, in allotting the amount of time I did to training now and getting this much epinephrine into my system, what would happen when I lessened the amount of time I put into exercise and got less epinephrine. Wouldn't I be like the addict whose dosage is being reduced and who starts exhibiting withdrawal symptoms?

I talked to Bill about it.

"Be damned if that ever occurred to me," he said.

"Don't you see it in the behavior of all these athletes who've stopped doing what they've been doing? Don't you see how many try to make pathetic comebacks?"

"They wanna be in the center of things," he said, "that's all. Everybody wanna be in the center of things, doin' what they do. It's nature."

"It's epinephrine," I said. "They miss the epinephrine's effects."

"Then all they gotta do is exercise, right?"

"They don't realize that. Also, if you've been exercising all your life for the purpose of winning a fight, you're not suddenly going to exercise for no reason at all, just to get the epinephrine. Even if they believed it was going to help, it wouldn't strike them as seemly."

"There you go. How in God's name you expect me to make a fighter of you if you keep usin' words like 'seemly'? Hey, look. What I know is what it takes to become a fighter and how you gotta train. So if you wanna be a fighter an' if you want me to train you, this is how you gotta do it. Full speed, full intensity, you gotta give it all you got and to hell with holding back and to hell with epinephrine and to hell with tomorrow. Now you wanna do this or not?"

There're certain things you cannot argue about. Considerations people have about various aspects of life that are impregnable to any kind of argument. If they're convinced the world is flat, for instance, they will sooner torture and kill anyone who might suggest otherwise than entertain the possibility of it being true.

"And, for God's sake, stop usin' words like 'seemly,' " he said, then added,"'tain't seemly." He grinned.

There's a bunch of things in the computers of our organisms we've put there at various points of our early lives that have become sacred cows and, if you know what's good for you, you'll not try to disabuse us of them. I knew I had come upon one of those things with Bill Johnson. He knew what you had to go through when you trained. The prevailing thought in regard to athletes was you gave everything you had in you to prepare for and get the championship, no matter what the cost to your body, mind, or spirit. You stayed in the game and strove for as long as you could and let the future take care of itself.

Until a few decades ago, athletes and artists had the same view in regard to money. You spent it as fast as you got it. Then they started getting smart, putting it away and making it work for them so they could live comfortably after they retired. But they still didn't give thought to something even more important: their emotional, spiritual, and physical life after retirement. Instead, they think, *I'll have money, I can just loll around, sleep when I want, get up when I want, do what I please*. Then they realize how quickly that gets old. And how quickly do they. Some ex-athletes will become commentators and being a celebrity becomes a substitute for what they used to do. But it never takes the place of what they used to do.

I knew Bill wasn't even going to *look* at the implications of what I was saying because it didn't coincide with his ideas on how boxers should train. So I just let it go and agreed I would do what he said. Feeling great as I was feeling, I could be easily persuaded. Part of the phenomenon of feeling euphoric is that you feel the good times will go on forever. Reminded me of the joke about the guy in the hospital, lying in traction, practically every bone in his body broken when his best friend comes to visit.

"What happened to me?" the guy in traction asks his friend.

"Well," the friend says, "we went to this party and had a lot to drink and you went to the window and said, 'Look at me, everybody, I can fly.' And then you jumped from the third floor."

"You're supposed to be my best friend," the traction guy says. "Why didn't you stop me?"

"Tell you the truth," the friend says, "I had a few drinks myself— thought you could do it."

I was beginning to feel like that. Invulnerable. Invulnerable to everything—including time.

When you're feeling good, everything seems to go well. Studying became much easier. Girls were looking at me with admiring glances. But I made no moves toward them.

Why?

It felt as if the purity of the euphoria I was experiencing would somehow become polluted if I started dating. In the olden days, they forbade athletes to engage in copulation while training. I don't think it's so much that ejaculation will weaken you. It has to do more with the age-old concept of females being used to tame troublesome males. It's done with bulls, it happens with gangs. You walk down some New York street and see a bunch of guys, you tend to be a lot more anxious than if you see women with them. When males are getting IT, they tend to be less wild than when they're not. Consequently, when you train them for games or war, you want to keep them hungry and edgy. Best way to do that is to keep them away from women. I could see that.

Also, I was totally engaged in what I was doing. And I loved it. I realized it was one of the qualities children had that I wanted to keep as long as I could. To be totally engaged in what I was doing and to keep going. A child keeps going from the moment he opens his eyes to the moment he's so tired he can't keep them open any more. And, as the saying goes—'s all good.

At some point in our lives we start thinking of how nice it would be if we could just hang out and not have to do anything. And then we become the opposite of what we were when we were children.

# CHAPTER SIXTEEN

Time for sparring," Bill said six months later. "This time, unlike what happened with Shamaz—or even with me—we gonna take it real easy. Real slow so you can learn everything from the ground up. When you spar with this guy, I don't want knockouts. I want you to stick to your basic defense, covering your face and head, bending, weaving, ducking just like we practiced, and throwing a punch when you see the opportunity. When your opponent attacks, I want you to turn that left shoulder in toward your chest while you bend your head down, blocking your face with your left. Then, swing your right leg over and hook'm with your right, letting that right leg support you. I want you to be patient. None of that diving and lunging stuff you pulled on Shamaz and me. We're sticking to basics here. We gonna box, we gonna be patient, we're *not* goin' for the knockout. Stick it out and get out of the way, stick it out and get out of the way—jab, jab, move. Jab, jab, move. Patience. You hear what I'm tellin' you? No cowboy stuff. Boxing is like chopping down a big tree. You work the body, you jab the face and you are very, very patient—till the time he's ready to come down. Then you give'm the one-two and down he goes. Box—box—box. Duck and weave—got it?"

"Got it."

He set me up with this picture book handsome, light-haired guy who looked no more to be destined for boxing than I was. I don't know that there *are* any white guys who can hold a candle to the black and Hispanic fighters. I know there're things that are politically incorrect even to think, let alone say, and I understand the reason why African-Americans resent even the hint of an implication there is a difference between races but, hell, consider the fact slavers used to go over to Africa, probably the toughest continent in the world, pick out the best physical specimens to bring over and, even among those, it was the fittest who survived and the descendants of those specimens are right here, walking and working among us and, even though they excel in every sport they get into, you're not supposed to even hint there's a difference between them and the whites. Well, I'll grant you there are no significant *genetic* differences, but when you take into account life was always a hundred times tougher in Africa than anywhere else and still is, and when you think in terms of the best physical specimens having been selected from *that* tough a continent, how're you going to escape the conclusion the descendants of those people *have* to be superior physical specimens?

I understood why Bill got me this comparative sissy to work against; he didn't want me to panic to the point where I would want to take him out as quickly as possible. I could picture box against this guy without worrying he was going to hurt me.

Except Bill didn't have one salient factor in this equation: The goddamn Roman with the knife was a wild card. He might show up—or he might not.


*At the bell, this white glamour boy turned into my nightmare man in sheets with the knife, heading right for me.*

*I went into my diving act, roaring, "You ugly one!" before hitting him. It had become almost an automatic thing. A neuron path had been cut and that was the way this thing played now. It knew no other tunes.*


When I opened my eyes from my horizontal position on the canvas, there was the glamour boy, lying under the bottom ring rope, bleeding from the nose like a babbling brook, his left leg twitching like a dog having a nightmare. Oh, Jesus.

And they couldn't revive him. They called an ambulance and carried the boy out on a stretcher.

Bill and I went to St. Vincent's and waited in the ER waiting room.

Because of Aisha, Bill's girlfriend, they took care of the guy quickly and the doctor came out to talk to Bill.

Afterwards, Bill came back and said, "The kid's come to but they're keeping him for observation. And his nose is broken, of course. I'm gonna go talk to'm, then I'm gonna call his folks—or whoever he's living with. How come you always go for the nose?"

"Didn't break yours."

"That's 'cause they took out the bone in *mah* nose a long time ago, you *can't* break mine."

"Maybe it's like those animals that have an instinct for the most vulnerable part."

" 'Vulnerable.' There he goes. Vulnerable. Shit."

"Don't like that word either?"

"Not a word a fighter uses. A psychiatrist might use it—a faggot might use it. Not a fighter."

"Hey, Bill—fuck you."

"See, now that's more like it. On another note, I decided I'm not gonna train you any more."

"Because I used 'vulnerable'?"

"Don't be a wiseass. I'm not gonna train somebody who doesn't do what I tell'm. If this had been a real fight and I gave you the instructions I gave you and you went and knocked the guy out, I'd say, 'Congratulations, you did great.' But this was a sparring session. A specific lesson in something I wanted to teach you how to do. And you go cowboy on me again. You did exactly the same thing you did before you started trainin'. If you're gonna go in there and do this one thing every time, what's the point? No need for trainin', no need for sparrin', we just book you fights and you go in there and crack the guy's nose open and they take'm to the hospital and we go on to the next fight. But I'll tell you one thing. It won't be long before the guys in the other corner are gonna be on to what you're doin' an' they gonna be ready fer ya and *you* gonna be the one on the canvas with the broken nose."

"You saw what I did to Shamaz twice. You weren't able to defend against it—and you told me yourself you were still world class."

"I underestimated you. I thought of it as a Mickey Mouse move. I still do. I didn't give it enough importance. Others are going to give it enough importance. They gonna study the tapes and they gonna have a move waitin' fer ya."

"If you underestimated me, why don't you get in the ring with me again and prove me wrong?"

"That's it. You and I are done. You wanna fight? Find yourself somebody who's just gonna book you some fights and then go out and do what you do, you don't need trainin'. You didn't do one thing we worked on. You just sprint across to the guy who's hardly left his corner and you dive at'm, growl whatever it is you growl—somethin' about 'ugly,' and you whack'm on the nose, split it open, and they take'm to the hospital. That's not boxin'. Might as well take a baseball bat and hit the guy across the nose and say, 'There! I won the fight.' Better yet—bring an M-9. She-et!"

"You said the reason the whole world was excited about Tyson for so many years was because he was vicious and knocked his opponents out."

"The man trained, sparred, boxed when he got into the ring. He's a trained boxer. He didn't just dive at his opponents like Batman, throw one punch, and the fight was over."

"You think the public cares about anything aside from the knockout?"

"*I* care."

"Talking about the public now, Bill."

"The public cares too. They wanna see some boxin' before a guy's knocked out."

"They used to say that about tennis too, that the public wanted to see the players smack that ball back and forth a few times before one of them wins the point, yet the player who's considered the greatest in the history of tennis has earned that reputation purely on his serve and his matches rarely consisted of rallies but depended almost totally on his capacity to win the point on one serve and all he needed to do to win was hold his serve—which he did without exception for the six years he was number one—big serve, that's all. All his opponents had to do was make a mistake on *their* service game and he won. As far as boxing is concerned, I think you were right the first time you talked to me about it. What they want is the knockout. They don't care how it comes, from where it comes, or when it comes. Just that it comes."

"They wanna see *some* boxin'."

"How about you and me conducting a little experiment? Book me a fight in one of the little clubs. Just like you did for Shamaz. If I win, book me another one. Keep booking me until one of us is proved wrong."

"Ridiculous."

"What've you got to lose?"

"Just my rep, that's all. Just have everybody in the boxin' world think I've become a total jackass, that's all."

"I haven't done badly so far."

"That's what *you* think. You've done terribly. A clown in a circus. Like that fat guy they call the king of the four-rounders. Just add a couple'a hundred pounds and you can be Butterbean. A circus freak. A geek. One thing to knock Shamaz out with your high school crowd watching. Bad enough to knock me out in front of my fans with a punch and a style nobody's ever imagined in their wildest dreams. But I can override that because you haven't been trained and accidents will happen even to the best—and I'm fifty years old, I haven't been training, and I'm years away from having been in the ring. But now I've trained you for six months, trained you intensively every day, and I put you in the ring with the understanding on everybody's part this is just a sparring session so I and they and everybody can see what you've learned so far from all the work we been doin' and what areas we have to concentrate on between now and the next sparring session and that's what the poor guy who's your opponent thinks too and you go ahead and pull the same exact stunt. You know how it feels to realize you haven't made an iota of difference and to have your peers look at this and ask, 'What the fuck's he been doin' with the kid all this time?' You have any idea how that feels?"

"I must admit I haven't really thought about *that* aspect of it."

"Bet your ass you haven't. And now you askin' me to book fights for you out there in the world where people remember me as a very good professional? All I got left, my friend, in the entire world is what people remember me as. An' you wanna go out and pull this freaky stunt and have people say, 'Bill Johnson trained this guy?' You may not have been punched yet, my friend, but your thinking is fuzzier than any punch-drunk fighter I've ever seen."

"Bill—out in Hollywood in the thirties there used to be a brilliant young producer who was directly responsible for many wonderful films made in that era."

"What's fuckin' Hollywood got to do with it?"

"Could I finish my thesis, Bill?"

"Thesis! Shit! You got a cocky, pompous attitude and it's really startin' to tick me off, you know that?"

"That's because I'm a teenager and we think we know everything. When I get to be your age, I'll be much humbler, I promise. And you're also ticked because you've decided to dump me and your hopes are going down the drain and you're trying to make yourself hate me for it."

"Cocky know-it-all to the end. All right, go ahead, tell me about your brilliant Hollywood producer, Irving Thalberg."

"You know about Thalberg?"

"I know a few things. Go ahead."

"Thalberg was apparently a man who was wise way beyond his years. One of the things he said was, 'All is forgiven if the footage is good.'"

"Except the footage in this case isn't good. You keep bringing Tyson up. Tyson left his corner at the bell with his guard up, his fists up around his head, he jabbed, he probed, he ducked, he felt his opponent out, people could look at him and see he was a fighter. *Sprinting at your opponent the moment the bell rings, diving at him and managing somehow to whack him on the nose or the chin or the forehead is not boxing; none of that in the remotest way resembles boxing.* I am not going to be connected with something that reduces a sport I respect and love into a catch-as-catch-can farce."

"All I'm asking is that you get me booked for one fight in one of the clubs around the city. One fight. And that you keep your mind open long enough to see what the public reaction's gonna be."

"I know what the public reaction's gonna be. It's gonna be what it's been. Shock. But I can also tell you another thing. You're gonna be up against professionals who aren't gonna fall for the sprinting and diving shit. Professionals who're gonna eat you for breakfast. Who're gonna be waitin' fer ya with a cocked fist when you're diving at them and—hey, you know that commercial where the kid tells his buddies he'd fight Holyfield for a million bucks and you see'm in the ring and Holyfield punches'm an' the kid's head gets separated from the body an' goes flyin' to the canvas? That's gonna be you. Listen, the idea was for me to train you. I *been* trainin' you and for all the good it's done, I might as well not have lived. It's obvious you're not lookin' for anybody to train you because you haven't taken one thing I've given you. You goin' through the motions. You're exercising. But you might as well join a fitness club. What you're looking for is somebody to book fights for you. Sign up for the Golden Gloves. Compete. You make a splash there, guys'll be walking all over themselves to sign you up."

"I want to work with you."

"Why?"

"Because you got me into this and you got principles and principles mean a lot to me and I want to be loyal to you."

"Well, it's those principles that won't allow me to take a position where I'm of no use except as a booking agent. I'm not gonna train you, that's that. Just sign up for the Golden Gloves. Win there, you won't have any trouble getting booked."

# CHAPTER SEVENTEEN

The concept of entering the Golden Gloves seemed like the equivalent of going to California by way of Australia. Not much more practical than competing with thousands of unemployed actors for a part, the very thing I was trying to avoid. Also, I didn't know how long my genie with the knife was going to stick around or, if he did stick around, how long it would take before I got used to the idea enough so it wouldn't give me the spurt of super strength, speed, and co-ordination it had been giving me.

There had to be a shorter way.

I thought of Alex. He always found a shorter way. One of his dreams from way back in Italy had been to have an American car. He went to buy a Chevrolet in the Bronx. But he didn't have a driver's license. And, because of his limited English and very limited education—writing and reading were his mortal enemies—he figured his chances of passing the written part of the test were nil. So he told the dealer the only way he would buy a car was if they got him a driver's license.

Don't you know the dealer got him one?

Picking up his license and car from the dealer in the Bronx, Alex, with only a few driving lessons under his belt, took the wheel and he and my mother headed home. At some point, they found themselves on Amsterdam Avenue, a one-way street heading uptown. After a while, my mother realized they were heading uptown, north, when they ought to be heading downtown, south. So what does Alex do? Makes a U-turn on Amsterdam, heading south, the other cars all heading north. It's rush hour. Stops traffic for miles. Finally, a cop came. Asked Alex where he thought he was going. Though the perfect reply might've been, "Wherever it is, I must be late 'cause everybody's coming back," Alex, of course, did not say that. He began to cry instead. The cop happened to be of Italian-American heritage and let him go, even cleared a path for him.

At some point in his life Alex had become convinced one could accomplish anything with hard work, money — and in this case, tears. In America, his dreams were coming true. I think this is why America has remained great. New blood from other lands kept re-injecting new vitality into our national veins and inspiring us to keep on our toes. Either that or turning us into hate-mongers.

I remembered Maria had spoken of a cousin who was connected and was into all those things mobsters are into — loan sharking, drugs, protection, prostitution, boxing, you know the deal. And he wasn't just a soldier either, he was pretty high up on the ladder, his domain being just north of Chinatown.

When I called her, Maria was cheerful, thinking perhaps our dates were going to start up again. I asked her to put me in touch with her connected cousin.

"Why?" she asked.

"I have something I want to propose to him," I said.

"Haven't you seen and read enough to know you should stay far away from people like that?"

"You talk that way about your own cousin?"

"I'm telling you what you should know without me telling you."

"You don't want to do it, say so."

"It's not I don't want to do it."

"Then what?"

"Why haven't you called?"

"Involved in something that's kept me very busy."

"Another girl?"

"No."

"Truth?"

"God's truth."

I could feel her relief. Then she went on the offensive again.

"So busy you can't pick up the phone?"

"What's a phone without a face?"

"Better than no phone without a face. Gonna be too busy from now on?"

"Not as busy, no." Which was a lie; if she put me in touch with her cousin, I would be busier.

She took a little pause.

"What do you wanna get in touch with my cousin for?"

"I have something I want to propose to him."

"What?"

"When did you get to be such a busybody?"

"I was always a busybody. I'm a curious person."

"First I need to talk to him about it."

"Then you'll tell me?"

"It's nothing crooked, if that's what you're worried about."

"Then why would you need my cousin?"

"I'll talk to you about it after."

"You sing?"

"Do I sing?"

"Yeah, can you sing?"

"How did that come into the conversation?"

"Can't you even answer a simple question?"

"What would make you ask such a question?"

"You have a nice speaking voice. I wanted to know if you had a nice singing voice too."

"I can sing."

"You want my cousin to make you another Frankie Sinatra?"

"What put *that* into your head?"

"Only thing I could think of people like my cousin did that could be said not to be crooked. Although I have my doubts about that too. You know the story Al Pacino told in *The Godfather* about the band leader giving up the singer he had under contract after a gun was put to his head? True story. About Sinatra."

"I know. I don't want to be another Sinatra—one was plenty, thanks."

I would have to see her, though. Funny that I, who dreamed and thought about women as much as I did, would be in a position where I was going to go out with one because she was doing me a favor. That was like a pimp. Me being pimp-like. Wow!

The other consequence of the move was that her cousin would now be part of the equation and if Maria wasn't happy with how things were going with us, I would have to worry about her cousin not being happy either. Madonna! And not the Material Girl either.

As Scarlett had said, "I'll think about it tomorrow."


Maria's cousin, Joey Mangiacavallo, had an office in the back of a dessert place on Mott Street in Little Italy. Cake, soups, sandwiches, espresso, liqueurs. There were three or four goombahs sitting at a corner table when I got there and a lot of regular customers. When I said to the guy at the cash register I wanted to see Mister Mangiacavallo, he said, "Yeah? An' who're you?"

I told him my name.

"Wait here," he said. He left the register and walked to the back where he disappeared behind a door. The kind of confidence these people have about their property, even a cash register, they can just leave it and not worry somebody's gonna steal from them.

I looked around. Well, here was this busy, happy place, people eating tasty desserts and gelati, enjoying life, the pulse of New York and here were these other people, the mobsters, who had their own enclaves in all the populated places of the nation, making money off the public, maiming and killing those who stood in their way.

I remembered a friend of Alex's had come from Italy to visit, had dinner at the apartment and said, "I see you have more Mafia here than we have in Italy. Makes sense. This is a much richer country."

"A lot of them are in jail," I said, coming to the defense of my country.

"Less than one percent."

Not knowing what the statistics on it were, I couldn't argue. Or could I? Suppose I'd said, *Actually, it's seventeen-and-a-half percent.* He couldn't say a damn thing. He was probably guessing at the less than one percent, just like I would be on the seventeen-and-a-half.

"They do that," the man continued, "so the populace can say, 'Oh, yes, they're putting them in jail, they're chasing them, they're fighting them.' But that is no more than a token. Do you think a mighty government like of the United States would allow something to exist they did not want to exist?"

"How could the Mafia possibly benefit the government?" I asked.

"It doesn't benefit the government, if by 'government' you mean the representative embodiment of the nation," he said and I marveled at how well he spoke our language. But that was the difference between the way the foreigners learned our language and the way we learned theirs. They really learned ours. And that was the thing about us. We didn't have to learn anything about anybody. We were Americans, for Christ's sake.

"But if you mean the politicians who are elected to their official posts by the people," he went on, "then you're talking about something else. Today, in order to be elected to any post, you need money. Not just a little bit of money. You need a great deal of money. When a source appears that will give you a great deal of money if, upon election, you close your eyes to certain things that source does and vote on certain bills favorable to that source and if it can be worked out that this money is in the form of cash that can be slipped under the table through seemingly bona fide fronts, do you think you're going to say no to this source? And so you have these people operating all over and some of them, less than one percent, are selected to go to jail so it can appear the government is fighting them. But to believe they could not be eradicated, were the government disposed to doing it, is to be very, very naïve."

I had bristled at his theory. But in the coming days and weeks I gave it thought. For World War I and II this government had turned night into day and performed a miracle in getting the nation war-ready, which had to be unique in the history of humankind. It had eradicated all diseases except cancer and AIDS and from certain viewpoints, considering the billions involved in *those* diseases, it would be economically counter-productive to eradicate them in the near future. There was nothing this government could not do—if it wanted to.

I came to the conclusion Alex's friend had been right. The Mob was tolerated because it provided the politicians with an almost infinite source of money. In exchange, the public had to pay an additional tax in the form of increased prices for construction, services, and food ten to twenty percent above what it would be if the Mob weren't involved. It's a ten-to-twenty percent tax paid by the public in addition to what the IRS gets. The money from the Mob, then, becomes a source into which the politicians dip when they need to get elected and officials partake of when they want their kids to have an expensive college education and a Mercedes or three. It's the state-of-the-art version of the "little tin box"—that a little tin key unlocks.

There's a myriad of things going on the government knows about but does not feel inclined to stop because it would be deemed counter-productive. The phenomenon of illegal immigration. There're hundreds of thousands of illegal immigrants in the country. Being illegal, immigrants are willing to work at jobs Americans don't care to perform and at wages way below what Americans would get. They are tolerated because they fulfill an important need and are not going to cause trouble or complain about low pay and bad working conditions because they fear deportation.

Bill Johnson refusing to train and manage me worked out for the best. Though he would've been fine for the local clubs, he had nowhere near the altitude to get a big time fight arranged. Guys like Mangiacavallo did.

And if Mangiacavallo wasn't high up enough on the ladder or if this wasn't his area of responsibility, I was sure these people had agreements like doctors in regard to referrals and fee splitting. Okay—if the government tolerated them and if the public made *The Sopranos* the most popular show in America, then why should I not make use of them? In a way, it was like what happened in nature. All manner of beast and foliage co-existed and they were all inter-dependent. Symbiosis—the balance of nature. I was part of it—so I would make use of it.

The goombah returned. "Goombah," by the way, is a perversion of the Italian word, "compadre," which means "godfather."

"Go tru det door over dere," he said.

I walked "tru de" crowd and "tru det door over dere" and found myself in a studio apartment with a couch, a bookcase, a dresser, a curtained divider behind the couch  and a walk-in kitchen to the right. The couch was soft tan leather and on it sat a man of very large and husky proportions who in the olden days of charging the enemy on horses you would loved to have had on your side. Diagonal to the couch was a leather armchair that looked very comfortable.

"You my cousin's friend?" he said.

"Yes sir," I said.

"You don't gotta call me 'sir,' you gonna make me feel old."

"You don't look old."

"Da prime'a life. Siddown, you wan'a espresso, a nice piece'a home-made cannoli?"

"If you'll have some with me."

"Atta boy. Ei, Ciccolino," he shouted to someone, "go get us some."

A tall, skinny young man came out of the kitchen and went "tru de door," closing it gently behind him.

"Siddown," Joey said, "Din' I say siddown?"

I quickly sat down.

"Dat chair comfy or what?" he asked.

"The most comfortable chair I ever sat in," I said.

"Dat's what I say. See dat lever on your lef' below de a'mrest? Yeh, dat's it. Pull it."

I pulled it. Suddenly, there was a whirr and the whole chair started vibrating. On the back of the chair lumps started forming, pressing into my back, moving up and down and sideways. Taken by surprise, I moved forward.

"No, no, no, you gotta press *against* it, right up against it—like when you gettin' fucked in de ass, you know?"

I pressed my back against the back of the chair, trying to delete from my mind the image of getting fucked in the ass, the lumps from the chair's back probing, massaging, it was—whoa—immoral, it was so good.

"Ain't dat somp'n?" he said, watching me with a child's glee. "Tree tousand smackaroonies dat ting cost me. Wort every penny. G'ahead, lean back, let it give it to ya, it's de best fuck you gonna get, g'ahead."

I suppose if you've been in prison, the concept of getting fucked in the ass doesn't leave that easily.

I leaned back and enjoyed the lumps probing my back and he watched, proud and happy there were such toys in the world and he could get them.

Ciccolino came in with a tray on which were two demitasses of black coffee, two small plates with cannoli on them, and two glasses of water. He set the tray on the dresser, pulled out two folding tables from behind the curtained divider, unfolding and setting one by Joey and one by me, laying out the dessert, coffee, and water on each table, then returning to the kitchen.

Joey Mangiacavallo dug into his cannolo. This was serious business for him. I got a glimpse of how everything he did turned into serious business. He wasn't using the fork so I didn't use mine. After he'd gobbled his cake, cream extending from the corners of his lips, he settled back on the couch with the espresso between his fingers and said, "So, what, you been goin' out wit my cousin, is dat it?"

I put the part of the cannolo I hadn't finished on the folding table while he slurped his espresso.

"We went out a few times some months back," I said, taking a sip of my espresso. Man, that was some bitter stuff, that coffee.

"So, what, you din' like her, or what?"

"Well, I didn't think she was the love of my life and then I got involved in this thing I'm going to tell you about."

"Love'a your life, huh? You fuck'r?"

"No," I said very quickly and very definitively.

"Well, that's one for your side, ain't it? 'Cause if you fucked'r and den dumped'r, I would not take dat very kindly, I wouldn't take it kindly ad all."

"Oh, no, I wouldn't do that, I would never do that."

"'Cause you fuck a decent girl, you take'r heart. You take somebody's heart—a decent girl's heart—an' break it—dat's very bad. Very, very bad. It's a mortal sin is what it is."

"I agree with you, sir. I would never do that."

"Joey. You call me Joey."

"Thank you—Joey."

"You kiss'r?"

"We had one kiss. A very short one."

"See, now awready dat's somp'n. You know dat song—? 'A kiss is just a kiss, a sigh is just a sigh'?"

"'The fundamental truths apply.'"

"What?"

"That's the rest of the words to the song." I sang the next two lines of the song.

"Dat's it, dat's it," he said. "Hey, you know what? You got a nice voice."

"Thanks."

"You could do, you know, a gig, right here in the store some night. People sittin' aroun', drinkin' likyoor, coffee, havin' cake, listenin' to you singin'. Be like *Casablanca*, huh? Do it again, do dat song again, Dan, g'ahead. You get dat? Sing it again—play it again? You get dat?"

"Yeah—play it again—it's good—Joey."

"G'ahead, sing."

These guys, when they tell you to do something— no question of saying no. Doesn't even occur to you. I'm not really a "no" guy anyway.

Fortunately, I happened to know the song. Part of the speech exercises I did every day, I would record poems from a book and then listen back and after that I would open up a book I bought called *The World's Greatest Fake Book*, which has hundreds of songs in it, and I would pick out songs I knew some words and the melodies to and record that on my tape recorder and listen to it and remember the things I did in it that could stand improvement and it's a funny thing. You start correcting things you weren't even aware of doing wrong. And also, without being aware, you start improving and you sound better and better and then you sing for someone—like this guy—and it doesn't sound bad.

I'd read that Sinatra, when he started out, used to do something like that. He would listen to great instrumentalists and practice for hours, trying to make his voice manifest the seamlessness, the fluidity and purity of a wind instrument. They say he kept it up too, did voice exercises every day well into his sixties. Funny how you can be ultra great in one area and a total schmuck in others.

So I sang a couple of phrases of "As Time Goes By" for the guy and put my soul into it.

"Yeh," he said when I was done. "You could sing here at night, we got a piano, we get you a good pianist, it'd be like, like, you know, de old days. I been tinkin' of doin' somp'n' like dat around here, I like dat idea. When can you start, you wanna start tomorra?"

"I need time to get a bunch of songs ready."

"Next week den."

I was about to say I needed more time but he said, "Listen, when I make up my mind sompn's gonna get done, I don' like to wait, know what I mean? It's settled. Next Monday you show up here eight P.M.

an' sing your fuckin' heart out. Meanwhile, you leave me your number, I get you a pianist, you two get togedder'n rehearse an' you come here Monday night an' bang my box, know what I mean? Who knows but this could be de start of somp'n big. I love dat Steve'n Edie. Awright, so write me your number dere on de pad on de dresser, write it down, g'ahead."

I went over to the dresser and wrote down my name and number on a pad that lay there.

"Now what'd you come here to see me about?" he asked. "G'ahead, siddown."

I sat down and got the lumps in the chair moving up and down my back. How had I managed to live so long without having experienced this?

"How come it was a short one?" he asked.

"What?"

"De kiss. When you kissed Maria. How come it was a short one?"

"Well, I realized—I realized—" Let's see, how to put this?

"She wasn't de love'a your life, huh?"

I opened my palms, facing them upward and moving them slightly to the sides. As if to say, *such is life*.

"You feel'r up?"

"No, sir—Joey." Sir Joey, that was good.

"'Cause if I was to talk to her an' she was to tell me odderwise—"

"No, sir—Joey." Sir Joey. The concept tickled me.

"Well, you know what? I ain't *gonna* talk to'r about it. Not only would it embarrass de girl but I judge you to be a stand-up guy—an', when it comes to people, I trust my judgment."

"Thank you, Joey. And I hope you know I would never do anything to dishonor or disrespect you or your family—or your friends." Did I know my *Godfather* or what? I'd only seen it nine times.

"See, I like dat. Dat's a stand-up ting to say. I like stand-up stuff. An' I like you—you got a good face. Sei simpatico." (You are likeable)

"Grazie tanto, signor Joey." (Thank you very much, Mister Joey)

"Ma parli italiano?" (But you speak Italian?)

"Mi piacieva la gente italiana e la lingua tanto che l'ho studiato." (I liked the Italian people and the language so much that I studied it.) Didn't want to tell him I'd learned it because of Maria's friend Stella.

"Bravo. Allora sei proprio un paisano." (Good for you. Then you're like a countryman.)

"Quasi." (Almost.)

"Bene. Bene." (Good.) "So what'd you come to see me about?"

"Would you be able to book fights for a fighter?"

"Like who?"

"Me."

"You? You, a fighter? What're you, a comedian? You don't look like no fighter to me. You a lover boy, dat's what you are. Dat's why I'm gonna have you sing here, I tink de ladies gonna love it. Forget about it."

I had been waiting years—ever since the Al Pacino movie where he explained what the various definitions of the phrase are—to hear a real mobster say, "Forget about it." But, of course, mobsters are not above copying things from the movies.

I told him about my knockout experiences but not about the man with the knife.

"You KO-ed Bill Johnson?"

"And his guard was up."

"What is he, about fifty now?"

"About that."

"I seen Bill Johnson fight. He was good. Fifty ain't like he's dodderin', you know. Foreman regained de championship when he was in his forties an' he tried to make another comeback at 55. Johnson in good shape?"

"Saw'm chase down a man who'd just stabbed a woman and I couldn't keep up with'm. Caught the guy and beat him almost to death."

"Stabbed a *woman*? I like to catch up wid *dat* guy."

Boy, what a difference when a mobster says *I like to catch up with that guy.*

"So I thought, since this has happened four different times with guys who knew how to box, it might be worth the effort to run it up the flagpole and see who salutes."

"Run it up the flagpole, huh? Haven't heard *dat* one in a while. How *you* know dat sayin', dat's like from de fifties."

"I read a lot. Watch old movies—old TV shows."

"Like history, huh?"

"Truman said all news is is history you don't know."

"Truman was like a President, right?"

I was tempted to say he wasn't *like* a President but said, "After Roosevelt."

"See? I know history too. You still workin' out wid Johnson?"

"No. He says it's too freaky, no boxing involved, just knockouts, feels like it doesn't make any difference whether he trains me or not, I keep doing the same thing."

"Hey—de whole boxin' world dyin' for a KO artist an' he's bitchin'?"

"Feels there should be some boxing before the knockout."

"Who gives a shit? De KO is de cum, everythin' else is foreplay."

"I hear women can't do without foreplay."

"You *hear*? What're you, still got your cherry?"

I felt my face turning red—like a dog whose wagging tail betrays him.

"I'm, uh, uh, I'm—"

"Um-uh-nuh, um-uh-nuh, you sound like Ralphie Cramden dere. What's'a matter, li'l-a bambino embarrassed he still got his cherry? Oh—poor li'l-a bambino, still got his cherry."

"Talking about women in general," I said.

"Uh, uh, yeh, yeh, you still got your cherry. At'sa nice-a, bambino still got his cherry. Dat's somethin' in dis day'n'age. You a good boy. Hey, Ciccolino," he shouted. "Anodder couple'a cannoli here."

I did not feel like another cannolo because I'm always watching my weight but you have no idea how hard it is to say no about anything to a guy like Mangiacavallo. And saying no to a cannolo I find hard to begin with.

"So, anyway," he went on, "dat KO stuff sounds interestin'. What I could do is I could arrange a lil' private showin'. I know a couple'a fighters who're pretty good. Get a couple'a people togedder, get you two in de ring, we take a look."

I began to feel nauseous. It had felt so good when he asked me to sing. Why had I not jumped at the chance?

Ciccolino brought in the two cannoli as if he'd had them ready and waiting. It did not help my nausea. Mangiacavallo took a big, sloppy bite out of his, the white cream spreading to the sides of his lips and the tip of his nose so he looked like a clown. That did not help my nausea either.

I had this thing where I rehearsed acting out a song so it was just like a scene you were doing in a drama or comedy. I would do motions, movements, facial expressions, the works. Like, when I was working on "Mack the Knife." At the end of the song, I took out this retractable knife and plunged it into my stomach—that was Mack the Knife stabbing this guy—and then I'd fall to my knees, then on my face. It was like a little play, a little tragedy about this pimp and his life. I had a knack for creating physical movements and I'd put them in and rehearse them and then it would be like watching a whole play with all the movements so it wasn't just somebody standing there, singing a song, it was something you could be interested in visually as well as through sound.

I could do that at this man's place and I would be performing. People would start to get to know me and if the Mob liked me, they could push me like they'd pushed Sinatra. It had felt so good, this guy was giving me a job, performing, what did I need boxing for, he was giving me the opportunity to do what I was going into boxing for in the first place. Maria had mentioned that very thing before I came to see this guy, it was an act of prescience on her part. Why hadn't I listened to her?

And now he was going to arrange a fight with a pro who I knew was going to be tough. Everybody was going to consider it a big joke, me fighting this guy. Me fighting anybody. I remembered watching guys fight on TV and thinking, *My God, how could they be taking these punches?* I'd always felt if one of those punches connected with my face, my face would break, just literally break and fall in pieces like porcelain to the floor and my brain would shatter inside and be oozing through all my openings. And now I was putting myself in a position where the best possible scenario was, after I got my ass kicked, Mangiacavallo was going to look at me as a blowhard, a loser, and lose interest in me as a performer—when you look at someone as a loser, you look at him as a loser in everything. Damn! I could sing songs like "As Time Goes By," and act them out, this could be a place where people would flock to see me and Mangiacavallo might say, "Hey, let's push this guy, make'm anodder Frankie." This guy might do that, he already liked me. Maria had been on the money. Women's intuition. Damn, and I had put my foot in it.

Not only that but I was going to be facing the guy in sheets, carrying the big knife and wanting to plunge it into me. Sometimes you make a plan, like I did about becoming famous through boxing so I could parlay it into show business, and something else comes up, stares you in the face but you're so fixated on your original plan, you ignore the opportunity that could be even better. Certainly easier.

Maybe it wasn't too late. Why couldn't I just say to Joey Mangiacavallo, "Hey, let's forget about the boxing thing, I'll just come and perform in your club"?

Because it was too late. If I had accepted when he'd made the offer, it might've worked out great. Now I had put this delectable item on the table before him and he'd agreed to go along because it had titillated his fantasies and if I withdrew it, the King would not be pleased.

I had entered a world where it was not good to displease the king.

# CHAPTER EIGHTEEN

The event took place at the very club I had trained in with Bill Johnson. When I got there, the members of the club and the guy who ran it were just clearing out. One of the guys on his way out was Bill Johnson. He looked at me, looked at Mangiacavallo, and imperceptibly shook his head like—*My God, what have you done?*

No one at the club was evidently pleased at not being able to train that evening. But that was how things worked. When guys like Mangiacavallo said they needed something—you gave it to them and were happy you got the opportunity to do a "piacere" (favor) for them.

"Hi, Bill," I said.

"Hey," Bill said, shaking my hand. "What's this?" he asked, nodding toward Mangiacavallo and his cohort.

"Hey," Mangiacavallo said, coming over, "you're Bill Johnson." He extended his right hand. "Joey Mangiacavallo."

Bill shook his hand and nodded.

"You heard'a me, right?"

"Oh, yeah."

"I used to watch you in de old days. You was good, you was a stand-up guy, like Arturo Gatti. I used to love to watch you fight. Ting is when you a stand-up kind'a fighter, you gonna get hit. If you can give more'n you take, you can prevail. It's a beaoodeeful ting to watch. Unfortunately, a lot'a times you got more'n you were able to give. Win or lose, people love a stand-up fighter. Dat's why you kept on gettin' fights even dough you had so many losses. Dat's why people never liked to watch dat Whitaker, champion or not. He was a weasel, twistin' aroun' like a snake, dat's not fightin', dat's bein' a geek. An' dat John Ruiz—anodder weasel—Roy Jones—fightin' pussies. Arrogant bastard. Pound-fer-pound my ass. Worms. You take somebody like Trinidad, Hopkins—stand-up fighters. Tyson—even dough he's cuckoo, a wild animal in semi-human form—stand-up fighter—and de on'y way anybody could beat'm was to fight like a weasel—what dey call fightin' 'smart.' Shit. I call dat fightin' like scum, people don' wanna see dat kind'a fightin', dat ain' fightin'. Trinidad, Hopkins, Gatti, you—dat's fightin', dat's what bein' a real man is all about. Chavez in his prime—dere was anodder stand-up guy. Dem Mexicans, dey got chins made out'a rock altogedder, dey ain' goin' down noway, nohow. Hey, we got a lil' exhibition goin' tonight, Tommy gonna get in de ring wid your kid here, pop'm aroun' some, you wanna stick aroun' an' watch?"

"Tommy's gonna fight'm?" Bill asked.

"Ain't dat what I jes' said?"

"Tommy's one fight away from bein' a contender, why would he fight someone who hasn't had one amateur fight, let alone a professional one? And, by the way, I don't know if Dan told you but he's not my kid."

"I could see dat, you be black, he be white, how could'e be your kid? Heh-heh, preddy good, huh? Nah, I know, he tole me you don' wanna train'm no more, I'm sayin' your kid 'cause you used to train'm, am I right?"

"I tried to," Bill said.

"An' he did knock you out in de ring while you had your gloves on an' your guard up, am I right about dat too?"

"Yeah," Bill said. "He did that too."

"Now, to answer your question why Tommy's fightin'm. See, I find people are nice. You ask'em to do you a favor an' dey do it. So, even dough Tommy's up to a half a mill a fight an' HBO coverage an' all, I ask'm to do dis in a crummy lil' club on de Lower East Side in fron' of five or six people an' he's glad to do it. People are nice, don't you find dat?"

"Oh, yeah," Bill said. "I find that all the time, gotta fight'em off to keep'em from doin' me favors."

"So you wanna stick aroun', have some fun?"

"Thanks, Mister Mangiacavallo," Bill said. "I'd love to."

It was a win-win proposition for Bill. If, as he was certain it would happen, I got knocked on my ass, he could have a reality affirmation that he had been right in not training me any more and disassociating himself from me. If, on the other hand, the freaky thing happened and I took the guy out, he could enjoy the fact Mangiacavallo knew I was Bill Johnson's "kid" in that he had discovered and trained me.

As for me, I felt I still had my genie. Which may not be too different from anybody else who possesses a special talent in a certain area. Somebody who can hit home runs, for instance.

There have been hundreds of baseball players stronger and better built than the Bambino. But why couldn't they hit home runs? There have doubtlessly been tennis players who had been and were stronger and faster than Pete Sampras. So why couldn't they hit the kinds of serves he hit? And if you compared Ali's build with so many of his brutish, finely chiseled opponents, you might ask, "How come, if they got so many more muscles and are obviously stronger, they can't beat him?"

The answer is that special talents are—special. The difference between what I had and what all those individuals with special talents had was they considered their talent as part of them, their inalienable right. I considered mine a freaky thing I could tell no one about, that always caught me by surprise and sent me into a great shock which, then, produced a strange surge.

When I saw Tommy the Terror walk into the ring, all these ruminations went down the toilet. This guy had had 21 fights, 21 victories and 19 knockouts. He was to have one more warm-up fight before fighting the champion. What was I doing, getting into the ring with this man?

That Mangiacavallo, though. What happened next convinced me these guys were the bona fide descendants of and the closest thing we have in modern times to Roman emperors.

The hottest announcer in the world was in the ring, holding a microphone—the cable station's top flight announcer and boxing analysts, all wearing tuxes, all sitting at ringside. The top referee was in the center of the ring, ready to work.

Yes, the President of the United States could have arranged something like this if he really wished to. But you could bet there'd be no end of derisive publicity about it—like the time Clinton had held up commercial air traffic at JFK for an hour-and-a-half while a barber was brought into the plane to cut his hair?

Bill Johnson had disassociated himself from me because he didn't want his reputation sullied and Mangiacavallo was showing he had so much power, he could be completely reckless with it. Even in the thirties' movies the characters didn't do anything as foolhardy as this. Suddenly, for me, this had become the nightmare of nightmares.

Tommy the Terror was one of those finely chiseled boxers. All the sports commentators thought it was inevitable he would win the title. Months ago he had knocked one of his opponents into a coma and the guy was still in it. How could Mangiacavallo put me in with somebody like that? When you groomed a boxer for the title you picked his opponents very carefully. You nurtured him like a delicate rose, making very sure you didn't overmatch him. It took at least two years to bring a fighter up to the level where he could fight the champ. Sometimes it took a lot longer than that to get the opportunity to fight the champ.

Mangiacavallo had to know the guy would make mincemeat of me. I had stepped into the dark, violent side of life. Boxers, gangsters. Why did I think I could step into that world and expect it to dance to my music? I had gone to Mangiacavallo and said, "I can do this." And he had gone ahead and made a spectacle of it and probably told Tommy the Terror, "G'ahead, give it to'm, give it all ya got."

It was not Marlon Brando with wads of cotton inside his cheeks; it was a man who killed for a living, a man who went all the way in terms of putting his life on the line. We see stuff in the movies and get the idea life can be like that. Underneath the performance an actor puts on in playing anybody—even a gangster and a killer—we can feel what he really is. He's an actor, for Christ's sake. He goes around pretending he's this or that but how can he be like a real killer—or a real anything? There's gold and there's fool's gold and if you mistake the one for the other, you're in a lot of trouble.

I had a bunch of people in my corner, people Mangiacavallo had hired for me; they were all pros, a trainer, a cut-man, an assistant trainer. The man who had done the honors for Holyfield and other fighters of that ilk was in Tommy's corner. I realized the only way this spectacle could be justified was if Tommy the Terror did make mincemeat out of me—or outright killed me—or put me in a coma. That I would have my nose broken in the process I didn't doubt for a moment.

What was it made people do such stupid things? We were obviously following an atavistic ritual millions were paying good money to see. It explained why it had become a big business. But why were so many so fascinated with it?

The referee was signaling us over so my time for ruminations had run out. Most people believed ruminations were useless anyway. Most people didn't even know what ruminations were.

"Let's have a fair fight," the referee said, "obey my commands at all times, no low blows and you stop when I tell you to stop. I'm firm but fair. Any questions?"

Tommy the Terror was looking at me the way you look at someone you just can't take seriously so you just kind of go through the motions. Like in the seventies, when George Plimpton, society's and media's darling, used to suit up and play with some professional team, like baseball, basketball or football for one game, making like he was one of the team members and the media would cover it and it was supposed to be, I don't know—chic? Or, as Nixon's vice president, who was disgraced just before Nixon, said—effete?

Personally, I have contempt for such things. I neither like doing things I'm not very good at nor do I like to watch others do things they're not good at. I have nothing against their doing it, just don't put me in a spot where I have to watch it.

Generally, Tommy the Terror glares at his opponents, working up the adrenaline, but with me, it was as if I were there to amuse him. And he was probably right. The whole thing was an amusement for the benefit of Joey Mangiacavallo. Emperors and kings can do such things. As Mel Brooks says, "It's good to be king."

We went back to our corners. The old man who was my trainer said, "Jab and move, jab and duck, don't let'm get anything going, jab and move, keep movin'." He was talking mechanically, from memory. I thought of how many true things there are in the world whose value has become nil because they've become a cliché.

I nodded as if I were listening. I could understand all those fighters who go to their corners between rounds and their trainers talking at them a mile a minute and they look as if they're in another world, not hearing a word. But then, nowadays, the trainers, well aware the camera's on them, are giving a performance. Everybody's performing. It's become a PR world, baby. People listen to each other for two reasons—there's something practical to be gained from it or as a courtesy, the understanding being that if they listen to you, you'll, in turn, listen to them. A fighter sitting in a corner after being steadily battered for three minutes doesn't give that kind of courtesy.

*The instant the bell rang, where Tommy the Terror had stood, the guy in sheets with the knife showed up, moving toward me with upraised knife.*

*Running away was not an option.*

*As in dreams, you seem to do the opposite of what you'd thought you'd do.*

*I sprinted toward him as if I were doing the fifty-yard. I could see he was thrown by my running toward him. For a moment, he stopped.*

*That was the moment I dove at him.*

*Sailed toward him—toward the knife.*

*Sailing through the air, I felt everything turn slow. Leisurely—as in a pleasant dream. Flying through the air—like superman.*

*Approaching my target, I could see the moment of hesitation and question on his part: plunge the knife into my back from above as I approached his midsection, or bring the knife down and stab me in the chest from below?*

*That moment of hesitation on his part was critical.*

*The synchronization, co-ordination, and timing of my body, arms, and legs remain a mystery to me. Had I practiced doing it as I've seen me do it on tape, I could try it a thousand years and I wouldn't get close to bringing it off.*

*Because it was simultaneously reality and nightmare for me—it worked exactly right.*

*He brought his knife-wielding hand down just as I was upon him. I blocked it with my left forearm, screaming, "You ugly one!"—while my right executed an uppercut that caught him on the bottom part of his chin.*

As before, I found myself on the floor—or the mat—opening my eyes to the prostrate figure of a body lying quasi-parallel to mine.

This time it was the finely chiseled one of Tommy the Terror. The place was in a state of pandemonium. My corner guys ran over to me, picked me up, and carried me on their shoulders just as if there were ten thousand people watching. Tommy's corner men were trying to revive him and the referee was reaching for my hand to raise it in triumph and I thought, *My God, this is the most exciting moment of my life. Will there ever be anything to equal it?* And I immediately thought, *Yes, when I have sex.*

And then I remembered a story an old time television director had told me about Milton Berle, the vaudeville comedian with the reputed biggest dick in show business, who had been the first to popularize TV to the extent of causing most of the populace to stay home or be glued to wherever his weekly show was being telecast. The streets and restaurants were near empty on Tuesday evenings. It appeared some years later, after canned laughter had been incorporated into TV entertainment, Milton Berle was watching and listening to a playback of a show he'd taped and, as is usual in most of the shows, canned laughter was being substituted for a live audience. Milton Berle, on this occasion, so engrossed in his work, actually succeeded in making himself forget it was canned laughter and, after a line in the playback he thought he'd done particularly well, rose from his seat shouting, "Listen to them, they love it, they love it."

And that was what this was like. Everybody making a big to-do over something that wasn't real. It was okay for everybody because they didn't know what had caused me to pull off this weird miracle but I knew so why was *I* getting excited?

Because I was the center of attention? Was that what it was about? In the final analysis, was that what everybody really loved best of all? To be admired, to be the center of attention? People could act like sons of bitches all their lives but put them in the limelight and they acted like saints—or rock stars, according to what age and position they had in life and what their surrounding environment was like.

A space was cleared and the fight analyst was approaching with the microphone. How many times had I listened to him commentate and then interview the winner and sometimes the loser after a fight. In no fantasy had I come close to imagining I would ever be in that position.

"Dan," he said, putting his arm around my shoulder, "Dan—that's your name, right?"

"That's it," I said.

"Now, tell me, Dan—where—what—where've you come from? Have you fought before? *I've* never heard of you. Have you fought before?"

"Not professionally."

"You fought as an amateur, then. Where?"

"Right here."

"Here? You mean in this club?"

"Yes."

"Who've you fought?" He sported that slight smirk of perennial amusement with more than a touch of cynicism mixed in it.

"Bill Johnson—and another guy who trained here."

"You mean like a club fight?"

"Yeah."

"And what happened in those fights?"

"I knocked them out."

"You knocked Bill Johnson out? Nobody ever knocked him out while he had an active career. What?" He was listening to his earpiece now. "Okay, right." He turned toward the camera and spoke to it. "It appears they cannot revive Tommy the Terror and the paramedics, even as we speak, are getting into the ring to take him away to a waiting ambulance."

The shot on the monitor changed to the paramedics putting Tommy on a stretcher and carrying him out.

The shot returned to the analyst and me with him facing the camera and speaking to it.

"Of course, we all wish Tommy the best and hope things'll turn out well." He turned to me again. "So what—how do you—how do you feel, watching a man who was one fight away from challenging the champion for the title being carried away on a stretcher and knowing you knocked him out, probably changing his life forever?"

"Wasn't an official fight, just a little private exhibition."

"I don't know how private it's going to be. Were you aware of the fact everyone has signed documents to the effect that, if warranted, this fight will be telecast?"

"I wasn't aware of that."

"Didn't you sign documents to that effect?"

"I signed documents but I didn't read everything they said. They told me it was just absolving them of responsibility in case I get hurt."

"Well—okay—to get back to uh—what's the next step in your life?"

"I guess I'm gonna have some professional fights."

"And I guess we're gonna be right there to telecast them." He turned to the camera again. "I'm with Dan, uh, uh—"

"Kahn," I said.

"Kahn," he repeated. "Dan Kahn. A young man who has had no training to speak of, no professional and no amateur fights, according to his account, nothing but a couple of club fights which he says he won by a knockout, including the KO of the great Bill Johnson whom you may recall watching in some previous decades and who, though very likely a far cry from what he was as an active fighter, I can't imagine to be a slouch at any age. Be that as it may, this young man has tonight, in the most unorthodox manner I have yet seen, with movements that far more resemble those of a  Bulgarian gymnast than a professional boxer, knocked out the hottest prospect for the middleweight crown with one flying trapeze punch, causing Tommy the Terror to be carried away on a stretcher in a state of unconsciousness. Dan says he's going to fight professionally at which time we'll see if this was one of those crazy, freaky accidents or if this young man actually has something. At any rate, we'll certainly be there to record it. Back to you, Jim."

People were bustling all around me, I could see the man with the cartoon hair making his way toward me but Joey Mangiacavallo got to me first, putting his arm around me with the cartoon hairdo man coming over, putting his arm around me from the other side so their arms intertwined on my shoulders. When the cartoon hairdo saw, however, there would be no cameras on us and no more pictures being taken, he took his arm away and moved on. In his eagerness, he had probably momentarily forgotten there would be no pictures taken with Joey in them. There *was* a photographer later who took pictures but he was one of Mangicavallo's men.

"Looks like we got a future, kid," Mangiacavallo said.

Was I re-dramatizing the *Faust* legend? As someone of a journalist's ilk might say, "Only time will tell."

In the locker room, while I was changing, Bill Johnson came in and sat on the bench nearby.

"That's somethin'," he said after a while, "knocking out Tommy like you did me and the other guys—just as easily."

"Thanks."

"But, you know, once other fighters see the tape, they'll know what you're gonna do and they'll be ready fer ya."

"Maybe."

"What do you mean, 'maybe'? They'll see the tape."

"So?"

"They'll be ready fer ya. They'll knock you on your ass."

"Maybe."

"Again with the 'maybe.' They'll knock you on your ass."

"You saw me knock Shamaz out twice. You didn't knock me on my ass."

"Yeah, but they'll knock you on your ass."

"Okay. You want the last word? They'll knock me on my ass."

"I was thinkin'—I could maybe give you some stuff that could help you."

"Yeah?"

"Yeah."

"What's changed between the time we had this conversation and you said you didn't want to have anything to do with me, and now?"

"I just—watchin' you—I just thought of some ways I could help you."

"You trained me for six months and said it made no difference. I did the same thing tonight I did with Shamaz, with you, and with that glamour boy. What makes you think it'll make a difference now?"

He stared at the floor.

"Come on, Bill, you didn't hesitate when you told me you didn't want to sully your reputation with me, why're you hesitating now?"

"Because it occurred to me I could help you."

"It still doesn't tell me why, after training me for six months, you tell me you can't help me and now suddenly you can. Where's the difference?"

"You don't need to break *cajones*, my friend. All I'm telllin' you is I could help you. You don't want it, all you have to do is say so."

"You told *me* some things the last time on the basis of your principles and now I'm gonna tell *you* some. *You're* the one who arranged for me to put gloves on the first time and you're the one saw me knock Shamaz out and then you arranged for me to fight him the second time and you saw me knock him out again. Then you wanted to really test me and said you were gonna knock me out yourself just to show me I needed training. *You* got knocked out instead and taken to a hospital. You, then—"

"Why're you tellin' me things I know?"

"Did I interrupt you when you were talking?"

"All right. Talk."

"After training me, you put me in with a sparring partner. I knocked *him* out and *he* got taken to a hospital. Everybody I've been in the ring with got taken to the hospital. After—"

"Your point—get to it."

"After experiencing all of this, you decided you didn't want to have anything to do with me because it would ruin your reputation."

"All right, so I was wrong, so what? Is that what you want to hear? That I was wrong? Fine. I was wrong. You wanna get Mangiacavallo to have me shot for it? I'm comin' to ya with m'hat in m'hand. I was wrong. Now I say I could help you. Yes or no? That's all you gotta say—yes or no?"

"We're not in a court of law. You wanna let me answer my way?"

"Fine—your way."

"Mangiacavallo never saw me knock anybody out. He just talked to me. On the basis of that talk, he arranged this whole circus."

"Mangiacavallo don't have to worry about his rep. The only rep he's got is as a killer of the first order. The only reason he pro'bly arranged all this is to have Tommy either kill you or make a vegetable of you, that's the only genuine amusement these guys have with the lives they lead—to watch somebody or somethin' get destroyed or maimed or tortured, that's all it is. It's amusement for him and his friends. Like any despot, that's what they do. And this is who you chose to go with."

"I chose to go with you, Bill. You threw me out."

"Believe me, you would've been far better off stayin' out than goin' with this guy. You don't know what you're in for. This guy gonna use you and then flick you away like a cigarette butt. For the rest of the years you can be useful to'm, he's gonna tell you what to do an' if you cross'm, he's gonna kill your mother an' if that doesn't work, he's gonna maim you or kill you. And your life's gonna turn rotten. That's your future, my friend, that's who you signed up with."

Just then, we heard footsteps and who should come from around the corner locker but Joey Mangiacavallo and two of his cohort.

I could imagine what Bill Johnson was experiencing at that moment. I myself quickly reviewed if I had said anything that might be offensive to Mangiacavallo. Fortunately, though, I had had a small part in a play called *Born Yesterday* at the Cape Playhouse the summer before and there was a line in the play, spoken by the heroine in which she says, "My father always said, 'Don't say or do anything you wouldn't want printed on the front page of the New York Times.' " It struck me as very good advice.

"What do you know," Bill Johnson said. "We were just talkin' about you."

"Yeah?" Mangiacavallo said. "What'd you say?"

"Dan was tellin' me how you gonna get him some fights."

"What, you gonna lie to my face? You don't tink I heard what you said?"

If there is such a thing as a black person going pale, then Bill Johnson went pale.

"G'ahead," Mangiacavallo said, "lemme see you try'n weasel out of it."

"I can't," Bill Johnson said. "All I can say is—I'm very, very sorry—an' it'll never happen again."

Mangiacavallo gave a little smile. You would not want to see a smile like that directed at you.

"'Course it won't," he said. "Know why?"

"'Cause you're gonna have me removed from the land of the living."

"You get an A plus. Now tell me why'm I gonna do dat?"

"'Cause I spoke out against you."

"But if what you said was de troot—and troot is beauty—and will set you free—why would I do it?"

Bill Johnson shrugged and looked down. What was the point?

"See, the worst ting," Mangiacavallo said, "about talkin' agains' somebody behind deir backs is—it's like cancer. Don't show up right away. It grows in dere—it grows'n grows—till it's ready to kill ya an' you can't do nothin' about it. When you talk agains' somebody behind deir backs, you can bet your life someday in de future it's gonna bear fruit. See, whether you're tellin' de troot or not, you're bein' an enemy. An' if you're gonna be *my* enemy—you can bet your bottom dollar I'm gonna be yours. Dat's how it works, pal."

"If you go around, getting rid of everybody who says what I've said, you're gonna have a lot of killing to do."

"But I'm hearin' *you* sayin' it to somebody I have a relationship wid. Somebody I'm gonna be workin' wid. See de difference, pal?"

"Excuse me, Mister Mangiacavallo," I said.

"Joey. You call me Joey. He calls me 'Mister Mangiacavallo,' you call me 'Joey.' "

"Thanks. Joey. This is a good man. What he said, he said because he wanted to help me. If what he said had no effect on me, then nothing was really done against you. I would really appreciate it—as a matter of fact, it would take the heart out of me if you did anything bad to him. I would feel so bad I wouldn't have the heart to do— anything—any more."

Mangiacavallo glared at me. Was I telling *him* what to do and what not to do? No, I had been very careful about that. I'd told him only how I would feel.

"You want dis guy to continue trainin' ya?" Mangiacavallo asked me.

"No," I said. "He's already chosen not to do that. If he didn't have faith in me before, I don't need him now."

"Atta boy," Mangiacavallo said. Then, to Bill, "You owe de kid your life, you know dat?"

Bill Johnson looked at me. "Thanks." He turned to leave.

"I don't want you in dis town no more," Mangiacavallo said. "Go over to de odder coast. De Pacific one."

Bill Johnson stopped and said. "My whole life's been New York."

"Hey, I'm on'y wastin' all dis time talkin' to ya 'cause'a de kid. But kid or no kid, you show your face in dis town again, you a dead nigger. Now get de fuck out'a m'face."

Bill Johnson left without a word. It was Nixon who had said, "Get them by the balls and their hearts and minds will follow."

# CHAPTER NINETEEN

**P**rior to my Moses-like experience in connection to boxing, there was a brief period before my last high school semester when I hung with a bunch of guys on the corner who one night took it into their heads to steal a car. They broke into it on Riverside Drive and one of the guys knew how to hot-wire it and we all piled in and were off.

Riding around the city in that car, I felt there could not be another place in the entire universe where I would rather not have been than in that car. Here was a bunch of guys, one of whom had the idea of stealing a car. The others might not have come up with such an idea but they were willing to go along. Now here was me who definitively did not want to steal a car, did not want to ride in it. Yet—such is the pressure of people you hang out with that you don't say, "No." You go along. Say "no" to drugs indeed.

After about half an hour, when I thought I'd proved the point of not being chicken, I said I had to go and had them drop me off. They, on the other hand, continued driving around until, as I heard on the news later, they were inevitably signaled by the police to stop, at which point they did what a lot of kids do because it seems so exciting when they see it in the movies. We have so much to thank the movies for. They gave it the gas and the chase was on. They ended up in Brooklyn, crashing into a Mack truck. The driver of the car got decapitated, the guy in the passenger seat went through the windshield and the guys in the back—well, one had his spine broken, the other had his neck snapped when his head hit the back of the front seat, and the third one had both legs and one arm broken. He was the only one left alive and facing car theft charges.

The experience of teaming up with Mangiacavallo felt like being in that stolen car. I had stepped over to the other side. Doesn't matter how much or how little you step over. Once you step over—even to the extent of buying goods you know are stolen—you've stepped over.

What the hell, though. You justify it the same way you justify putting something over on somebody you're doing business with or lying on your tax return or cheating on your wife. It's like the story of the guy who goes to the bar, meets a beautiful woman and they get to talking and he says to her, "Would you go to bed with me for a million dollars?"

She says, "Sure."

"Would you go to bed with me for half a million?"

She hesitates a moment, then says, "Well—yeah."

"What about five bucks?" he says. "Would you go to bed with me for five bucks?"

She says, "What do you think I am?"

"We've established what you are," he tells her, "we're just quibbling over price now."

We justify the multitude of occasions when we lie and cheat by saying to ourselves, "It's just a little thing, everybody does it, it's normal," so we keep doing that, distinguishing it from the "big" things the big boys cheat on.

And I was now on that side. I had prided myself on all the stuff I'd read about in books: chivalry, grace, romance, integrity, honor, courage, principles, decency, benevolence, nobility, dignity—things that no longer had any value but things I loved dearly, things people rationalize as being childish and come under the umbrella of "When I was a child, I saw as a child, spake as a child. But now I am grown, I put away childish things."

Well, now all those ideals were gone. I was with Mangiacavallo and could no longer lay claim to those qualities that seemed so valueless to most people of today anyway.

But I missed them. I missed them dearly.

One bit of rationalization I could still take umbrage in: Even though I was working with Mangiacavallo, I was not actually doing anything wrong nor, at this point, was he—in matters that had to do with me—as far as I knew, for now.

I would do my stint, I thought. I would make my millions, then I would get those qualities back again, with the power of fame and money behind me—qualities that society understands, respects and values. Then I could go on and inspire the world toward those characteristics I loved so dearly. Amen.

One thing about guys like Mangiacavallo; they get things done and fast. They pick up the phone and say, "Do this," and people fall all over themselves to do it. There's no, "I couldn't do it because—" There's doing what people say and not doing it. And not doing it when you're dealing with guys like Mangiacavallo is not good.

I remembered a story about a man named Tito, the late dictator of the former Yugoslavia who, unbeknownst to even the most knowledgeable historians, played a vital role in preventing Hitler from winning World War II by causing so much havoc for the Germans in Yugoslavia at a crucial time that Hitler, instead of using 20 German divisions, which would have made the difference between winning and losing Stalingrad, sent those divisions to Yugoslavia to quell Tito and his Partisans, where these German divisions got bogged down and were unable to get to the Russian front in time and Hitler failed to take Stalingrad, which was the turning point of World War II—and he failed to quell Tito's Partisans to boot.

Tito was not the man's real name. His name was Josip Broz. But to the world he was known as Tito. Tito in the Croatian-Bosnian-Serbian language means, "You, this." He got the name when early in his leadership he assigned tasks to various individuals. He would say, "You do this, you, this, you, this." "Ti" means "you," while "to" means "this." So he got to be known as Tito: "You, this."

After the war Tito was the only one of the Iron Curtain countries' leaders successful in breaking away from Russia and succeeding. Under him, for the next thirty years, Yugoslavia prospered. When he died in 1980, various factions began bickering, which then, in 1991, became one of the bloodiest wars ever fought. Ti-to—you this. Mangiacavallo—"Do dis." Mangiacavallo—eats horse.

Mangiacavallo took over the whole thing. Got me a trainer, a cut man, a handler. And he arranged fights. HBO had wanted to telecast my fight with Tommy the Terror but Mangiacavallo wouldn't let them. He had a plan. Number one, he didn't want other fighters to see what my "method" was and, two, he wanted better odds for himself in the betting. With fighters it's like with horses. You look at their track record and bet accordingly. As I had no professional track record, there would be rumors but rumors would not affect the odds much.

It's well known, when you're bringing up a fighter, you set him up with pretty easy fights till he's gained enough experience and confidence to take on the big boys and go for prime time. In the meantime, you're gilding his resume so it can say so many victories, no defeats, and so many knockouts. The more knockouts on your record, the more impressive. But no one is very impressed till you come up against a name fighter. Tommy the Terror was such a one but if it got out I had put him out, how much money could Mangiacavallo make betting on me?

Everyone who had been at that fight had been sworn to secrecy. Then why had Mangiacavallo arranged for all these people to come in the first place? Why hadn't he just asked Tommy to fight me privately with no witnesses except his own cohort so he wouldn't have to worry about secrecy?

Well, because Bill Johnson had been right. Mangiacavallo had expected Tommy the Terror to brutalize me, put me out. It's the kind of thing Roman emperors had done in their day. Get one gladiator to cut up another for the public's amusement.

Tommy the Terror was in a coma for three days and stayed in the hospital for another four after that. The story they put out was that he'd injured his hand sparring and then had an intestinal virus. When the doctors declared him completely well, he got back to training for the fight that was to stepladder him into the championship match. This was another reason Mangiacavallo didn't want it known Tommy had been knocked out and put in a coma by someone no one had heard of and who had not fought anybody under any recognized organization's auspices. Their not knowing this meant the heavy money would be on Tommy and Mangiacavallo could bet against him and win a bundle.

"He was my guy," Mangiacavallo said to me. "He was gonna be champ. I was gonna have my own champ, make lots of moola on'm. Now I'm gonna make one last bundle on him losin' an' dat'll be dat. But dat's okay. Now I got you. Life always woiks dat way fer me. One door closes, anodder one opens."

"The doctors say he's okay," I said. "All the sportswriters say he looks to be in great shape, nobody thinks he's gonna lose. This guy he's fighting's considered a warm-up."

"Know what happens to somebody who's been winnin' an' winnin' an' suddenly he loses?"

"What?"

"He's a different guy. And he'll never be the same guy again."

"There've been instances of guys losing after winning and winning and then coming back to win again and becoming champions."

"Like who?"

"Muhammad Ali, Lennox Lewis. Roy Patterson, Joe Louis."

"Roy Patterson. Fuck, you do know your history, don't ya. Look who Patterson was fightin'. A Swedish glamour boy pussy. Swedes can't fight, dat whole 'Toonder'n lightnin' shit was a farce. A circus. Muhammad Ali's Muhammad Ali. Lennox Lewis was lucky enough to link up with Emmanuel Stewart and even den he fucked up. All Tommy's got is me. I don't inspire an' I don't give fighters de kind'a tactics dat're gonna make'm win. I can make fights happen an' I can get away wit fixin' certain ones. But on'y certain ones—odderwise de whole ting gets, what do you call it—counter-productive. Hey, you like dat woid? It's your kind'a woid, ain't it? Counter-productive?"

"Not bad, Sir Joey."

"Dis fight wit Tommy—before you come along—I was gonna bet on'm even though de odds are way in his favor—somethin' like eleven-to-five an' it'll be even higher as de fight gets closer. But I was gonna bet on'm 'cause I was dat sure he'd win. Just as I'm now dat sure he'll lose."

"Just because of something that could've been a freak accident?"

"Did you come to me to set you up wid fights 'cause you tought you were havin' freak accidents when you knocked out de guys before Tommy?"

The truthful answer was, of course, I had thought just that. They were freak accidents. "Well—yeah."

"Yeah? Dese were all freak accidents?"

"Yeah."

"Yeah?"

He stared at me in such a way I thought any moment I could be dead. You're talking more or less normal and friendly-like, you forget who you're dealing with and then suddenly you're looking into the eyes of death. It's like with wild animals. When they're not pouncing, they seem so peaceful.

"Except," I said, "they do seem to happen invariably."

"What's 'invariably'?"

"Means 'constant,' 'always the same.' "

"So why can't you say dat?"

"What?"

" 'Always de same.' Why can't you say dat? Why do you have to say 'invariably'?"

"Because it fits better than 'always the same.' There're certain words that fit better to describe what you want to describe than other words. Not only that but it's one word as opposed to three. Don't you want to learn new words?"

"I don't need no new woids, de ones I got I'm happy wid."

"So you're telling me I can't use words I like because you don't know them?"

"I ain't sayin' dat."

"What're you saying?"

"I don't know what the fuck I'm sayin', you're fuckin' confusin' me. You wanna say 'invariably'? Fine, say fuckin' 'invariably,' I hope you two will be very happy togedder, okay?"

"Okay—gangsta Wop."

For a moment, his eyes flashed with anger but then he caught on.

"Fuckin' kike," he said.

"Greasy meatball."

"Money-grubbin' circumcised prick."

I thought of another one but then I thought this could end badly.

"So why do you think Tommy'll lose?" I asked.

" 'Cause, where before, he had the idea he cou'n be beaten, now he knows he can be beaten by a nobody nobody ever heard of. He don't got de feelin' of a winner no more, you know what I'm sayin' here? If you don't got de feelin' of a winner—you ain't gonna win, dat's jus' how it is. Now you want I should advance you ten thou on your future earnin's an' bet it for you on de odder guy? You could end up wid eighty, ninety thou, you wan' I should do dat?"

"That'd be fine."

If there had been any question in my mind before about having stepped over the line—there sure as hell wasn't now. Of course, I could always say to myself it wasn't really my money yet and it wasn't me who was betting it and the fight wasn't actually being fixed, it was only a matter of some inside information. Should I pass it on to Martha Stewart? Oh, what a web we weave when first we—

We had ringside seats at Tommy's fight in Madison Square. It was telecast on HBO. Lampton and Merchant both stopped by to say hello, this amused smile on their faces like here was this weirdo who just might someday become one of those freaks like Prince Naseem that lights up the world and they get to have a lot of stuff to talk about on the air 'cause everybody wants to hear them talk about this freak.

There was a number of celebrities in the audience because Tommy was a comer who was thought to be a shoo-in for the championship. They kept on showing them one after the other on the big monitor. But they were all disappointed. Tommy, who had been a stand-up, risk-taking fighter, making fans tingle with excitement, played it very safe in this fight, jab-jabbing, then pulling away, jab-jab, clinch, he was playing the game of *try-not-to-get-hit-at-all-if-you-can-help-it*, it was like Oscar De La Hoya against Trinidad in the last five rounds of their fight and it was like Lennox Lewis against Tua, or Sugar Shane in the rematch after his loss, the most boring and gutless things you could watch and then the winner prides himself afterwards on having been smart and they always say how they gave the other boxer a boxing lesson. But the irony is guys who do that usually lose because the judges, unless the fix is in, hate that kind of stuff almost as much as the fans. Fans hate boxing lessons. They want to see a fight, they want to see courage and heroism, they want to see fighters batter each other with only one of them left standing. When Galota refused to come out at the bell to continue fighting Tyson, fans threw soda and popcorn at him as he walked back to his dressing room. They couldn't give a shit that his jaw was broken. Ali had continued fighting after Norton had broken his jaw. Other fighters had fought with broken hands, broken noses, broken ribs, deep cuts where the blood kept running into their eyes, you name it. That was what lifted audiences. Not gutless exhibitions. They could have that stuff at home and in the street.

The ring is the only place where men and women can contact the memory and feeling of the primeval that lives in their cells. The age when it was this strength, this heroism, this persistence, this physical cunning that made the difference between life and death. It lives in all of us and the ring is the only place where this atavism becomes incarnate.

But the audience did not see it that night. Tommy the Terror played the game of warding off the vicious beast and running from it. Rather than fighting to win, he was fighting not to lose. It was cringing and succumbing to your worst nightmares. Jab-jab, move away and when the opponent lunged to get to you, avoid the blow and tie him up. All night long. The kind of thing Ruiz did with Holyfield—wormy stuff.

The audience booed. Tommy didn't care. Public figures like George Foreman, who still lived with the nightmare of what Ali had done to him, propagated playing it "smart," not taking chances and doing whatever was legal to win—and if you could do things that were illegal and get away with them why, God bless you—as long as you won. And from this kind of talk there was this philosophy born and prevalent across the board, exemplified by "Sweet Pea" Whitaker throughout his entire career, that it doesn't matter how weasely you get or how debased what you express feels—as long as you win. Not only that—some get the idea it's the only way to win—being a weasel.

Arturo Gatti, a throwback to the years of Graziano, Zale, and Basilio, lost a hell of a lot of fights and they flocked to watch him because he gave them the primeval heroism that lives in all of us. And there're still guys who're stand-up and heroic and who win—like Trinidad, Hearns, and the former Julio Chavez—and who finally lose—but while their star shines—boy, does it shine.

But not Tommy. Not that night. Jab-jab, move away. Jab-jab, duck. Jab-jab, tie him up. All night long, baby.

Finally, it was over—and Tommy lost. And I made a hundred thou. I wasn't nineteen yet, I had a hundred thousand dollars and hadn't done a goddamn thing but be the effect of some sort of weird illusion. God bless America, God bless the world.

I had a thought. Get out right now, invest the hundred thousand in an off-Broadway show you can act in and direct and you're on your way.

Ah, but you're not on your way. A hundred thousand means nothing in show business. A few warped individuals who are critics because they get relief by hurting and destroying and who hate anything that's about honor, principles, integrity, chivalry, heroism—unless you're making fun of these characteristics—do a blitzkrieg on you that'll leave you for dust and you're history. It's like a subway token, it can disappear in a trice. You have memories. Memories are made of this. But memories—and a subway token—will get you into the subway.

Even having done a show and having it on your resume means nothing. Absolutely nothing. I still keep looking at different shows—movies, TV, off-Broadway, Broadway—to see if I can recognize any actors from previous shows—any previous shows. I don't find many.

People in show business, like products, have become disposable. You use them once and throw them away. Unless they become stars. Then they'll last maybe three or four years. If they become super stars, in the case of women, they'll last ten, maybe fifteen. Men can go as many as thirty, thirty-five. But those are rare. Rare stars.

No. A hundred thou meant nothing. The only way of reaching my goal was through this weird gift that had come to me from God-knew-where. I could exploit this gift, and then move over into show business. The idea was as weird as the chimera that appeared every time I got into the ring. But, hell, you played the cards you were dealt.

Mangiacavallo arranged a national tour. I had a time convincing my mother and managed to get her blessing only by solemnly promising I would return to complete college. As in every case with a fighter who's being brought up with care, my opponents were hand-picked.

But it would not have mattered. I could've taken on the champion even then and the same thing would've happened. I was in possession of something that transcended reality as most of us think of it. The transformation that took place as soon as I got into the ring was—magic.

That's looking at it from the outside.

What I felt when the apparition appeared was fear for my life. The strength that came with it is the fight-or-flight syndrome during which your power, speed, thinking processes, and co-ordination can become super-human, as in the case of the mother who was able to lift the back end of a car to save her child.

Picture a nightmare that keeps happening to you while you're awake. Unlike with ordinary nightmares, I was able to remember this one in full-blown horror and remember living through this horror each time I anticipated getting into the ring. Because I knew there would be the man with the dagger and his goal would be to kill me. What I didn't know was whether, during any given encounter, I would succeed in evading the dagger. Useless to say it was not a man with a dagger, it was a guy with boxing gloves and the worst he could do was break my nose or knock me out. The guy and the dagger became more real than any reality there was. And there was no talking myself out of it.

A part of me felt I needed to keep doing this not only for the sake of my projected career in show business but for the sake of finding out what this was. After all, it was like having a monster in your attic and going on about your life, ignoring it and wondering if, at any given point, it was going to break through the door and come down and devour you and your loved ones and then go out on a rampage.

It was somewhat like—yes, it was like—*The Strange Case of Doctor Jekyll and Mister Hyde.*

That was what I'd meant about being in a canoe, heading for a waterfall. There was this thing I had absolutely no control over. I was utilizing it for my benefit temporarily but it was like having a deadly wild animal for a pet that you did not raise or train. You merely confronted it on a regular basis, managing somehow to avoid getting mangled and eaten, wondering each time whether *this* time was going to be the time it lashed out and got you. Like the guy who'd kept a tiger in a Harlem project—till the tiger finally did what tigers do: mauled him.

Inevitably, they began videotaping my fights, showing them on news telecasts and writing about me in the papers. I finally saw myself on one of these segments—although why I'd not had someone tape me in the ring beforehand so I could take a look at it, I don't know. Maybe it was like with some of those movie stars from the past, like George Raft and Katharine Hepburn, who would not look at themselves on the screen. It was not easy to glimpse yourself as others saw you.

On the videotape, the bell would ring and I would run out like a man possessed straight for my opponent and he would put up his gloved fists in an effort to protect himself, having in mind the idea of picking me off as I rushed toward him and then, when I was about five feet from him, I would turn into—SUPERMAN. That is, I would leap into the air and—well—fly. It wasn't for a long period, I'll admit, but fly I did. Of course, they would always run these in slo-mo so it seemed like a long time and there I would be, flying through the air with the greatest of ease.

The length of my body sailing through the air was at a 20-, 25-degree angle to the mat and my left arm was outstretched—just like SUPERMAN on take-off—except for the left fist heading toward the right side of the opponent's face. He would instinctively shift over his guard so it protected his right side, slightly uncovering the left side. Meanwhile, from my flying position, I would send a right hook around to the left side of his face, catching him on the left temple or the nose.

"Now we got tape," Mangiacavallo said when it came out and media people came buzzing around. "Now we got to train—really train. Dey gonna see dat, dey gonna study it in slo-mo an' dey gonna be ready fuh ya. Now we gotta get off'uv our asses an' be ready fer *dem*!"

So what did the trainers do but go back to the orthodox training methods of keep your guard up, jab-jab, move away, jab-jab, duck, jab-jab, clinch, the keep-cutting-down-the-tree mentality most fighters use.

I would guess since life began there's been an orthodoxy about every subject, including the long-held belief the earth was flat, until somebody came along and proved 'tain't so.

Any subject you can name. Sports, for instance. Say, tennis. There had been a time when two players banged the ball over the net as artful and self-satisfied as you please. It went on for years and years like that. At some point, along came somebody who served the ball, ran to the net for the return, whacking the ball to a part of the court the returner could not get to.

Oh, what an outcry there must've been at the first player who did that. How dare he? Outrageous!

But what a shock to find he was breaking no rules. He had just found a better way. When Ali came up with the rope-a-dope tactic against Foreman, everybody thought he was a goner. He had revolted against the orthodoxy. But he won. Once you win—you're in. "Everything's forgiven," Irving Thalberg had said, "if the footage is good."

I had the feeling that, no matter what happened, I had to stick with the cards that had been dealt me. As with all such feelings, if they were true, they held true across many endeavors. The stars you see on the screen. They brought their unique qualities to the table and that was what the public was thrilled by. Robert Redford would not speak with an English accent in *Out of Africa*, even though that was what the part had called for, because he sensed an English accent would remove him from the uniqueness that was his quintessence. When Clark Gable sang and danced in an early movie, *Idiot's Delight*, thousands of letters were sent to the studio by fans, protesting they did not want to see him sing and dance; he was CLARK GABLE. Certain kinds of individuals do *not* sing or dance. King Vidor, the director of *The Gunfighter* was convinced the movie did not do well commercially because the fans did not want to see Gregory Peck with a mustache.

It comes down to a very simple formula. What you do is who you are. If you're not sure of who you are, watch what you do and you'll know. That's not easy; the mind, like a spiritual and emotional prism, has a tendency to pervert what is unfavorable to the mind's owner. That's why there're so few stars—and heroes. That's why one's own farts never smell.

# CHAPTER TWENTY

**M**y next opponent and his trainers had obviously not only seen the tape of me "fighting" but had studied it.

I had been obedient regarding my training. I listened, executed the moves in the drills as they taught them to me but, as far as I was concerned, I was simply getting some very good workouts. Once they put anybody in front of me—even if he was a sparring partner—he turned into the guy with the knife, I turned desperate, momentarily super-human, and took him out. It happened so frequently I began settling into the idea it was just going to keep happening.

Not that I was being stubborn about the matter. It was just I knew there were guys out there so strong, tough, and fast all you had to do was look at them and know they were born for fighting. Fighting on their terms, I would not stand a chance.

I was not constructed for fighting. I don't have a bad body; matter of fact, if somebody said, "Would you like to change your body for another one, if you could choose any body in the world?" I would most likely say, "No thanks, I'll just keep working on this one;" but no, it is not a boxer's body and, speaking both for my spirit and flesh, I still could not imagine anybody punching any part of me. I can't really imagine anybody punching anyone, there's just something doesn't compute for me in this respect. I can't imagine people hurting each other in any way, physically or otherwise. But I know they do and have always done it. On the news I heard about two seventeen-year old kids standing on an overpass in Long Island and throwing boulders of ice at moving cars on the highway below. Going through the windshield, one of those could easily kill somebody or at least cause an accident. There is a teen-age game called "spunkball." A bunch of teen-agers in a car pull up alongside a car stopped for a light. If the window of the car is down, they suddenly yell, "Spunkball!" and throw an oval shaped piece of aluminum foil wrapped around a firecracker through the car's open window. The foil's been dipped in gasoline and after it lands inside the other car, the firecracker explodes and the silver foil ignites, igniting, in turn, whatever is near that is susceptible to fire.

And there isn't even any emotion involved, nobody is angry at anyone and these are supposedly not even psychotics or criminals; it's just something these kids who are old enough to go into the army, drive cars, and make babies have decided to do as a way of having fun.

As far as I'm concerned, anyone who wants to hurt anyone who is not an actual danger to people or animals has to suffer from some kind of insanity. But, as so many are hurting so many, you would have to conclude there is a preponderant amount of insanity in the world.

I can understand how many, many years ago one's life depended on physical prowess. And how this continues to live in our cells. And how, when communication fails us, we call upon our physical side.

It seems to me, however, that someone who gets kicks out of doing something creative like acting, writing, painting, playing music—is someone who will not, as a rule, like fighting. And who will not have it in him/her to understand why anybody *wants* to fight. Are the two activities—fighting and creating—the opposites of one another?

Well, if that's the case, then that's where I was—on the creative side. And here I was in the ring, *hitting* people. Why was I doing something my essence cried out against?

In the eyes of the law or anybody else, I was doing nothing wrong. I was not hitting anyone who was not there willingly, offering himself to be hit and looking to hit me—all under the auspices of legality, publicity, hoopla, politics, and dick-sucking.

So the point cannot be dependent on what is legal or illegal, acceptable or unacceptable. The point would have to be what is right for *you*. You and your essential reason for living.

They gave me all kinds of things to prepare me for the fact that my opponent, having seen the tapes of the way I "box," would be ready for me. To prepare me in the way of counter-acting what he would do. But you know what? All these things are very good as part of the way boxers train. The bottom line, however, was I was not going to go in there and face a guy carrying a knife with my guard up and jab-jab and move away and jab-jab and duck. When you're facing a guy holding a knife, either you finish it immediately or *you* are finished. And I was the only guy in the world who knew what I was facing each time I got into the ring. Everybody else saw something completely different.

*This time in the ring, having the sense that the sheeted man was expecting me to run to him, I walked—deliberately and with assurance. As if I knew exactly what I was doing.*

*When I reached him, he did what I'd expected: he thrust the knife toward me. I put my left hand in the knife's path.*

*I would take the knife through my palm—like the son of god.*

*I had heard of a man being mugged in New York and taking the knife of the mugger through his palm—hitting the mugger with his other hand and making his getaway.*

*Made sense. Even animals do it. Caught in a trap, an animal will bite off its trapped limb to free itself.*

*As the knife was going through my palm, I hit his left temple with a right overhand, howling, "You ugly one!"*

I found myself standing. My opponent lay on the mat after bouncing off the ropes. He was not moving. In the audience there was the roar that comes when something very thrilling takes place. There had been a prediction by my opponent that, knowing what was coming, he would be ready for me.

I looked at my left hand. My glove was on it and there were no holes in it. I had felt the knife plunge into my palm and yet I felt no pain in it and my glove was on and there wasn't a scratch on it. Wow! This was like *Groundhog Day*. It always ended the same way. If I took the knife in my face or chest, would I still be just fine?

What had happened with the knife had felt as real as this was.

What was it, then? Twilight Zone? Were there other dimensions one could tap into? Was I experiencing science fiction? I had no interest in science fiction. Once I saw the costumes, my interest flew right out the window. Yet, here I had faced a man who wore sheets and carried a knife and it had been real and then the man would disappear and my life would continue and I would reap the real benefits of this fantasy experience.

But had I not felt that knife plunge into my hand and was my hand not perfectly all right anyway? Yes, but I might have only *thought* the knife had pierced the hand when it really hadn't. I might have hit the man a moment before the knife had actually made contact and that might have been enough to halt the knife's journey. And then the transformation had immediately taken place and the knife and the man in sheets went back to wherever they had come from.

The lid was now really off. The tape of what had happened this time as well as tapes of what had happened previous times were telecast everywhere and there was more written and said about it than there were pages on the Web about Anna Kournikova, which numbered in themselves twice what Michael Jordan, the most popular athlete in history, had managed to accumulate.

For me, what had been more or less settled with that match was what I'd suspected all along—which is, when you're fighting for your life, you either give up and collapse, or you really and truly become superman. The twist here was that the other guy—neither the apparition *nor* the real opponent—were fighting for *their* lives. They were fighting to put me out—not nearly as potent a motivation. In fact, the real one was merely fighting to win a boxing match so, in terms of the kind of speed, strength, and timing he was able to conjure up based on *that* motivation was peanuts compared to what *I* was able to pluck from mine.

I had also been right in not adopting what they were giving me in the way of training and they, of course, couldn't care less; they didn't even remark on the fact I had done exactly what I had done previously except for not going into a flying dive but just marching toward my opponent and putting up my left hand to take the shot. I saw in the tape of it afterwards that what it amounted to was a parry on my part with my left and a right hook that had more bad intentions than Tyson had ever envisioned.

And that opponent was taken to the hospital and spent a week there.

Now, of course, there was nothing but talk about putting me up against the champion.

I was the "real thing," everybody said. The real thing. Holyfield had been "The Real Deal," I was the "Real Thing." I was Coca Cola.

The flavor of the month, just like everybody else.

In fact, I was a greater fake than anybody else. Whatever talent anybody else had in whatever area, it was something they had that was a part of them like anything else about them that was part of them. Me, I had this aberration that had somehow been doled out to me as some kind of afterthought on the part of whoever took a hand in the creation of the entity that was me, it was something that neither belonged to me nor something I wanted. Who wants a nightmare, after all? It was like something patched on to a house that had already been designed and built and then you add a monstrous eyesore to it.

So I was a greater faker than anybody around. The public's excitement about me, faker or not, would last only so long as I won. This was the difference between sports and show business. In show business, you could have two or three failures and people would still come see you, hoping to experience the thrill you once gave them. In sports, they know once you lose it, it's not comin' back and you're a pariah. Except for Kournikova, of course, who'd been able to parlay her losses into fame for a number of years before she went the way Andy Warhol's philosophy would have it.

All the more reason for me to move over into show business as soon as possible. There, you could have a number of failures and they'd still keep coming back in the hopes you'd come up with another winner.

"If we match you up with de guy who beat Tommy," Mangiacavallo asked, "tink you could take'm?"

"Why not?"

"'Why not?' he says. 'Cause you beat Tommy by surprisin'm an' dis guy beat'm honest."

"In boxing, if you exclude illegality, is there such a thing as honesty and dishonesty?"

"Why does everythin' wid you have to get philosophical? I don't even unnersan' what you jes' said. Who gives a fuck? All I'm askin' ya is are you ready fer'm or not?"

"I'm ready not only for him. I'm ready for the champ right now."

"You know, bein' cocky never leads to no good. Look at your Bible—'Pride falleth before...' No, wait. 'Pride—pride—' How de fuck does dat go?"

" 'Pride goeth before a fall.' "

"Might'a known you'd know it."

"People like it when you're cocky. Look at Ali."

"Yeh, look how he ended up."

"There's always a trade-off."

"No need to rush tings. I want you should have a lil'l more experience, a lil'l more seasonin' before you take on de champ. Remember, when you're on your way up in dis business, you get one chance. Blow it an' it's a long way down."

People are amazing that way. They get into the rut of thinking a certain way, doing things a certain way and it doesn't matter what comes along that makes their way of thinking obsolete, they won't change their mind set. Take tennis again. They have judges who determine whether a ball falls inside the court or out and they have a referee who can overrule the judges' call. Often, they're wrong. This makes the players and the fans unhappy. Now this system was the only way to do business when we didn't have the technology we have today. But now they have cameras that can pin-point exactly where the ball landed and it takes no more than a second for the image to be seen on television and on monitors all over the court. And that's what the TV telecasters do. They replay it within a second or two for the audience at the game and the world. Except they don't make the decision on the basis of what the camera shows. No, they make it according to what the judges and the referee say happened—even though it is often the opposite of what actually happened. It's the same way in baseball and most other sports. People would rather die than be proved wrong.

"I always do the same thing," I said, "haven't you noticed?"

"Less do de guy who did Tommy. Woik up some interest before we tink about de champ."

"You don't think there's enough interest?"

"Hey, you can make more, you make more. It's like foreplay—you gotta know when to bet and when to fold."

"Can you arrange the fight so it's during holiday break?"

"What holiday break, what're you talkin' about?"

"I wanna take some college classes while I'm training."

"College? What de fuck you want college for?"

"I promised my mother."

"Dat's different."

Though I'm not a morning person, I'd get up early in the morning and go running around Central Park. I must admit, even though I am a night person by nature, it feels great to get up in the morning and run through the streets of New York and in Central Park. Must be the *Rocky* syndrome.

There're people who tell you, "I wouldn't live in New York for anything." I understand them. New Yorkers keep their distance and can appear unfriendly—unlike in smaller places where people are all too ready to say hello and exchange a few friendly words. They might be banalities for the most part but they're friendly. And that's nice. It's nice to exchange friendly words with people. But for those who live outside of New York, it's important to remember that New Yorkers are almost daily exposed to all kinds of crazy individuals and occurrences. In smaller places the moment someone starts acting weird, about ten different people will go find a cop or call one on the telephone and the cop will be there in a flash.

In New York, if you went to look for a cop or called one every time you saw something weird happening, you wouldn't come near filling your quota of appointments or work or leisure—not to mention your knowing there isn't much a cop would do about weird behavior anyway, there's too much of it. That's if you could find a cop, which is not very likely. So you continue on your way and keep your distance. And keeping your distance becomes a way of life in the same way that your attitude in life will be a reflection of your job and your attitude on the job.

But—I love N.Y. I really do. I love, first of all, the multitudes. Every time you go out in the street in New York, you see multitudes of people and they're all different and you can go on doing that for years every day and you'll never run into the same person twice, and if you do, you won't know it. There's an infinity about it that parallels the infinity of life and creation. It just goes on and on without beginning, without end. But you have to have an interest in life and in people for that. And I guess I must have that.

I love the idea that New York is the center of the world. Wall Street is here, Broadway is here. As a matter of fact—there is nothing you could not find in New York. America is a dream the whole world dreams—even when they pervert the dream into hate and a desire to destroy us. And New York is the first place they will mention regarding which city they would like to visit.

And even in this day and age, when store chains predominate and you see the same stores and the same malls every place you go, there are things in New York you cannot find anywhere else but there are no things anywhere else that you cannot find in New York.

I admit I love the natural friendliness of small town America. I love everything about the small towns of America, I love driving through them, stopping and eating in their diners, above all, I love talking to the people, but you know what? I have taken up the challenge of breaking down the barrier of any New Yorker I deal with and inspiring them to *get* friendly. If I go into some store and they're particularly sour, I'll say, as the transaction is being completed, "Do you think I can get a smile?" And, of course, they'll smile, people love to smile. Rarely, they'll sourly say, "Nope," and *then* they'll smile. People do love to smile, they just need sometimes to be provided with the opportunity. So I get New Yorkers to be friendly when I'm in the mood and when I'm not, I go on about my business as distant as they are.

*Listen, you New Yorkers, I hear some gossip goin' round*
*That some of you good folks wanna blow this town*

So I'd run around Central Park, rain or shine, get all that epinephrine into my system and feel euphoric for the rest of the day. Going to college now was even more fun. Much more fun, I think, than if college were the only thing I'd been doing. It's a secret I discovered during those years. The more you do, the more you can do. As a matter of fact, there is a saying about it. "If you want something done, give it to a busy person." Actually, the saying is, "Give it to a busy man," but you wouldn't want to say that today.

It's like with love. The more you practice it, the more you've got. It was terrific, going to school and having something on the side, earning you lots of money so you didn't really need to go to school, which meant you were going to school not because you needed to but because you wanted to. A different matter. Then, of course, when word got around that I was the guy who was knocking people out with one punch, why, I was a full blown celebrity.

Being a celebrity is fun. But you get the feeling people are no longer liking you for who you are. It's like being a very rich man, all these people who are bowing and scraping and flowing out to you all that liking and respect, you know damn well it's not simply because you're you and they would not act that way if you didn't have the money or the fame.

Sure, you can say "Fame and money are a part of me just like anything else," and you would have a point but you keep thinking fame and money are really appendages and who wants to be liked for his appendages, it's hard enough being liked because you're handsome or beautiful—although people who are handsome or beautiful don't seem to have nearly as difficult a time with that one.

There were plenty of free periods during the day so I could do most of my homework during those but wherever I went, people were always aware of who I was. It seems fame is the most valuable product in our society, for the young it has even more value than money. Male instructors and professors made jokes, naturally, about how they'd better pass me or I might knock them out and everybody always laughed disproportionately because they were so pleased to have a celebrity in their midst, it made them kind of famous by association and I could be sure they would not neglect to mention it in pretty much every conversation they had with anyone they thought didn't know about it.

People remembered I'd done some acting so they offered me parts in school projects and I would have loved to take them but, what with homework and training, I had to draw the line somewhere. You can be wired and go on euphoria night and day but there's a hefty bill waiting down the line somewhere.

# Chapter Twenty-One

The fight with the guy who beat Tommy was arranged for the week after Thanksgiving. It was held at a Connecticut Indian reservation casino and telecast by HBO.

Richard Steele was the referee and got booed like he always does, ever since he stopped the fight between Caesar Chavez and Meldrick Taylor after Taylor had been beating Chavez up for almost 12 rounds and got knocked down with five seconds left in the fight. Taylor got up immediately and, with three seconds left, he could have easily lasted it out and won the fight hands down but Steele stopped the fight and Chavez was declared the winner. People said it was because Chavez was a Don King fighter and the fix was in. It broke Meldrick Taylor. He was never right after that. Fans have long memories and they kept on booing Steele year after year. Then everybody started beating Chavez but he continued fighting for another few years and it was a sad thing to see, like that photograph of Joe Louis being knocked out of the ring by Rocky Marciano, only with Chavez it just kept dragging on and on. But the crowd kept right on booing Richard Steele.

We were the main event and there was a lot of hoopla. The guy I was fighting was coming out in one of those carriages like in Roman times and he was going to ride it like a centurion and they had four of those miniature horses that were the size of dogs pulling it. I love those horses, they're so cute. I watched them on the monitor from my dressing room. Mangiacavallo had had the idea I should come in dressed in one of those Greek costumes, like the God Zeus, carrying a bolt of lightning.

"No way," I said.

"Why not?"

" 'Cause it looks ridiculous. Ever since Naseem started putting on a show before his entrance, every fighter feels obligated to do it. I'll watch Naseem when he does it because he really seems to enjoy making a jackass of himself but the others don't. They just look uncomfortable and silly. The whole thing's ridiculous. It's not the circus, it's not wrestling. And I'll tell you something else. When I come out without putting on an idiotic costume, it's gonna be so unique, everybody's gonna be talking about it."

"Awright, awright, you got a life story for everythin'; you don't wanna put on a costume—don't put on a costume."

You could see he agreed with me even though he wouldn't admit it. Sometimes people fall into doing something because it happens to be in, never looking at how silly it might be. Then, when you make them look at it, they often see it. Of course, sometimes they don't. When people say or do something, it usually becomes more important for them to be perceived right than for what they're doing to actually *be* right.

One thing I did think would be very striking was if I walked to the ring all by myself instead of with a whole bunch of hangers-on like all the fighters. But I didn't mention that because I knew how much everybody loves being on camera and for the hangers-on, this was their one moment in the sun. So I came out like everybody else with all of them semi-encircling me, holding, pushing. I had the sound people play "When the Saints Come Marching In." It's the kind of thing people can clap and dance to, which was what they did. People love anything that'll make *them* be the performers.

Then there was the period in the ring when everybody tried to get camera time, milling around, doing things for their fighters, talking to them but what it was in reality, was they were performing. Everybody thought of himself as a star.

You watch old documentaries, old photographs, read about stuff from long ago and it didn't use to be that way. For the most part, people used to be modest and humble. If someone was cocky or a braggart, it was considered unusual and not in a nice way either. Nowadays, everybody, people who are namby-pamby, non-entities, all feel obligated to act as if they were stars. It's a rarity to run into a humble, modest person—refreshing.

Then Michael Buffer makes the announcement, Steele talks to us, and we go back to our corners.

*As soon as the bell rings, there's the guy in sheets with the knife.*

*I run at him. I can see him as I run, pulling his knife-wielding hand back so he could plunge the knife into me when I got close enough.*

*Five feet from him I do my dive, flying for his stomach, you might say below radar range.*

*Too late for him to change his position so he could stick me from under into the belly, he keeps the knife high, probably having in mind plunging it into the back of my neck when I reached the right position*

*I put my left hand out, extending it just a little above my head, palm out.*

*He flicks my left with his left to get it out of the way so he can bring the knife into my neck or back without interference.*

*That's when my right does the parabola. It's as if an outside force were choreographing and determining the synchronization and timing of the movements. "You ugly one!"*

I was on the canvas on my stomach and the guy who beat Tommy was lying unconscious parallel to the ropes at a right angle to me. The guy with the knife was nowhere to be seen. My trainers and Mangiacavallo were yelling for me to get up because the referee could not start counting my opponent out before I was up and in a neutral corner. So I got up and went to a neutral corner and, amid flashing cameras and a lot of screeching, waited for Steele to count the guy out. I needn't have hurried; he gave no sign of moving.

And then the doctor came in and they tried to revive him but couldn't and ended up carrying him away on a stretcher.

Well, this is what they must mean when they talk about being on top of the world. My trainers picked me up and carried me on their shoulders, people were yelling, the fight analyst was trying to get to me to interview me and, once my trainers realized it, they put me down and the analyst made his way to me, holding the mike in his right and putting his other arm around my shoulders as he talked to me. My trainers huddled close to me so they could get on camera.

"Now—now—now—Dan—you—you've knocked out every

opponent you've faced in the ring with one punch. Now that has—that has—never happened in the history of boxing. Can you tell us—can you tell us—how and why this comes about?"

I toyed with the idea of uttering some Hebrew prayer the way most fighters thank Jesus Christ or Allah for granting them the victory but I remembered how impatient interviewers get with these and I didn't think they'd realize it was a joke so I decided to skip it. Also, I had never been religious so I wasn't really familiar with prayers enough to recite them the way they ought to have been recited.

"The truth," I said, "is I can't conceive of myself getting hit so I've come up with this way of making it real short so I don't get hit."

"You've never been hit?"

"Never."

"Not in sparring or training or a street fight or anywhere anytime?"

"Never."

"Can you tell us what in the world possessed you to go into boxing?"

"I found out by accident I could knock people out before they were able to hit me so I decided to go with it."

"You realize that, after this fight, you're very likely to be fighting Victor Trujillo, the champion, and that his level is way above what you've encountered so far and that you are definitely going to get hit."

"Well, we'll see."

"Are you saying there's a possibility you may *not* get hit when you fight Trujillo?"

"I said, 'We'll see.' "

"Are you saying you may be in possession of some information we don't have regarding your probable fight with Trujillo?"

"All I said was 'We'll see.' All this other stuff is what *you're* saying."

"Yes, but what does that mean? The reason I'm pressing you on this is because we're talking about boxing. The very idea of not getting hit in a championship match negates the entire concept of boxing. I mean, without getting hit, there is no such thing as boxing."

"Nobody's saying nobody's going to get hit."

"So we're back to the contention you're going to knock Trujillo out with one punch before he ever has a chance to hit you."

"We never left that contention."

"I see. All right. Well, thank you very much, Dan Kahn." He had no trouble remembering my name this time.

He turned to the camera. "Well, there you are, Jim. A young man who has publicly predicted something that no fighter in the history of boxing has even thought of, let alone achieved. A first-punch knockout of a champion who has never even been knocked down, let alone knocked out. A champion who has disposed of his opponents with the ease of a Pete Sampras going through his early Grand Slam rounds during his peak years. Can he do it? He's done it with previous opponents, but can he do it with a champion of Victor Trujillo's caliber? For all of you out there watching—we'd like to hear what you think. Our web site should be on the bottom of your screen, so let us know what you think. Back to you, Jim."

It's difficult—if not impossible—to describe how the world changes when you reach super-stardom. Everybody—I mean everybody, I mean your own mother—looks at you differently.

I find that hard to understand. Let me correct that. I don't find it hard to understand. I find it hard to accept. Let me go a little further; I don't accept it. Even before I was famous, I had never looked upon anyone as having more worth than me. Put the most famous person in the world next to a nobody and I will feel and accord them equal consideration and respect. I don't mean this as a PR statement. It's how I feel.

I've never considered anyone above or below me—until they did something that placed them either above or below me. I mean, think about it. Ronald Reagan was as famous as it's possible for a man to be. But then he lived out his last years not remembering he had been a famous Hollywood actor, the Governor of California, President of the United States, or even remembering who he was married to.

But, of course, I don't take that out on the people who gawk and goo. I'm as warm and friendly to them as if I didn't have that particular consideration about fame. I once saw Paul Newman interviewed in his later years and he seemed rather bitter and antagonistic in regard to fans. That was kind of a surprise. If someone had told me he was like that, I wouldn't have believed it; his character seemed so different projected on the screen. And there were all his salad dressings from which the money was supposed to be going to charities. Then there was the popcorn. But I saw the interview myself. He was livid about some fans approaching him in a restaurant and interrupting his meal to tell him how much they adored him.

I became a media darling and everyone wanted to interview me. It was always about, "How can this be that you dive at someone, avoid getting hit, and always get through their defenses in such a way as to knock them out with one punch?"

It was one thing you could rely on about the media. They seem programmed about certain aspects of any given situation and they'll keep talking about it way past the point when you feel like vomiting.

I could've told them I got into a state where, even if I got hit, it wouldn't deter me and I'd still end up doing what I did. But what would be the point? It wasn't something they were interested in. It's like their stories are pre-written and they ask the kinds of questions that'll give them the answers conforming to what they'd pre-written.

And the thing is I'm not a guy who's by nature secretive. I like to tell people how I feel and what I think and I like to hear their views and build something climbing the ladder of our combined thoughts. Holding back something as important as this was hard for me.

I always danced around the questions. I kept playing with the idea of telling them the truth and just sitting back and enjoying their reaction but then the potential consequences would always kick in. So I'd continue to dance. Norman Mailer wrote a book called *Tough Guys Don't Dance*. Well, I danced, all right; more like *My Fair Lady*, I could've danced all night.

Maria had called a few times since the time she'd referred me to her cousin and we talked on the phone and got together for dinner occasionally. Finally, she asked whether we would amount to anything besides being friends and I said, "I don't think so, Maria."

"You called me that time after all the time you didn't call me so you could meet my cousin?"

"Yes."

"And he was useful to you?"

"Very."

"And I can be used and then tossed away, right?"

"Not right."

"What, then?"

"We're friends."

"Those times we went out before, we didn't go out as friends. You kissed me."

"It was when we kissed I knew we wouldn't be any more than friends."

"Was there something wrong with the way I kissed?"

"No."

"Do I have bad breath?"

"No."

"What was it about the kiss, then, that made you not want to go on?"

"Sometimes—something physical makes you aware of something emotional and spiritual."

"Kissing me made you realize I wasn't the girl for you?"

"Yes."

"What about sex? Isn't that the way you really tell?"

"Sometimes."

"What about you and me having sex?"

"What about it?"

"Wouldn't that be the best way to find out?"

"Ever hear the story about the guy and girl having sex and, while they're having it, the guy's trying to kiss her but she keeps avoiding his lips, turning her head this way and that to avoid his lips, all the while they're having sex. Finally, the guy says to her, 'Why won't you let me kiss you?' and she says, 'Are you crazy? We shouldn't even be doing this.' "

"You're saying you don't want to have sex with me?"

She was not taking my detours.

"It's not I wouldn't want to have sex with you. You're pretty, you're attractive, you're desirable. It's just it wouldn't be happening under the conditions we would both want."

"How do you know what conditions I want?"

"I assume you would want to be in love with the guy and the guy to be in love with you and both of you being together for a long time."

"You remember the episode in *The Odd Couple* about how when you assume you make an ASS out of U and ME?"

"You don't care about the guy being in love and wanting to be with you for a long time?"

"Maybe I'm willing to take a chance on his feeling that way after we make love."

"Maria, that's not you talking."

"I'd be willing to swear on the Bible it's me."

What guys' fantasies were made of. A girl offering herself to you on any terms you chose and demanding nothing in return. Not counting the ethical considerations, I could picture Mangiacavallo if I deflowered, then abandoned, his cousin. He might postpone whatever he would do to me until I was no longer making money for him but sooner or later he would pay me for it. He was Sicilian, after all.

But, strange as it might seem, it wasn't fear of Mangiacavallo that was my main concern. It's got to do with when you agree to enter into a state where something is implicit and then you renege on it simply because the "i's" weren't dotted or the "t's" crossed, you're doing what Mangiacavallo said: you're committing a sin. And while, with today's morals and ethical standards, that seems laughable and I was already committing a sin just by joining Mangiacavallo, I wanted to cling to what vestiges of decency I could. Decency still struck me as the most valuable commodity in life and I longed to get back to the totality of it.

"'Maria," I said, "enjoyable as it might be—I wouldn't feel good about doing such a thing. What I suggest is we continue being friends, see each other occasionally and make love if both of us reach the point where we really want to commit ourselves to the relationship."

"I don't require commitment. This is a modern age, after all, and a modern country."

"Could we do what I suggest for *my* sake then?"

"Do I have a choice?"

Ethics aside—eager as I was to have sex, my anxiety also lay in the consequences that would result from it. For some reason, this loomed large in my universe. I felt, once indulged in, it would rock my world in ways that would collide with my current goals.

We've all heard how fighters and athletes in training are not supposed to participate in coitus because it saps their strength. In the old days this was a sacred, unbreakable rule. Today, it's pretty breakable. Still, there're a hell of a lot of athletes out there who are sticking to the rule. Not because of old traditions but because they feel there's something about sexual intercourse that does completely change your universe.

There is a certain purity of purpose you can envelop yourself with when you're not indulging in carnal intimacies even if there were no physical proof there is a difference between being and not being celibate. Athletes are the most superstitious beings in the world and if they have it in their heads that not having sexual intercourse can help them win—by God, when they're in training, they're not going to be having sexual intercourse.

With me, this idea went way beyond these normal earthly concepts. In my case, there was a genie that appeared every time I got into the ring who caused me to perform miracles. I sure as hell didn't want to do anything to muck this phenomenon up. I kept thinking of that scene in *The Cincinatti Kid*. Steve McQueen playing poker with the great Edward G. Robinson. Winning and winning and winning. He's on his way to being the world champ, "gutting" Edward G. Then, at some point in the game, he takes a break, has sex with Ann-Margret, the femme fatale prototype, comes back to the table and— loses. He's been "gutted." And he's a loser—forever and ever. At the end, he even loses to the little black kid whom he's been beating at coin tossing throughout the film.

# CHAPTER TWENTY-TWO

The training was intense. The trainers thought they were doing what they were supposed to do, that is, get me into the best shape of my life. I, on the other hand, was training because I loved the exercise. It was pouring epinephrine into my system and I was in an almost constant state of euphoria. The difference between me and every other fighter was they all thought victory and championships were going to make them happy. I was convinced it was the joy that came from the doing of it and the epinephrine.

I remained convinced that acting, writing, and directing would give me both the short and the long range thrills I was looking for.

So I kept training and getting all that epinephrine and my body was looking good but above all, my genie would appear in the ring and, when I became champion, I could get bit parts in movies and TV shows and eventually work my way into becoming a real actor and put boxing and the genie behind me forever.

People generally live from event to event. Waiting for something tangible to happen at a certain time. The in-between periods don't really count. Everybody around me was looking forward to the day when he would be part of the championship team.

What does it say about how we feel toward ourselves that it's so important to be on the championship team? Or for your home team to be champions? Everywhere you go, people are rooting for their home team. What is that? Being able to say to the world, but more than that, to yourself—I'm better than everybody? What kind of a game is that?

I'm better than you, I'm better than everybody. Why is that so important to people? Is it something that springs from way back when being better than others meant you survived and they didn't? Did there exist a time when men roamed the earth and fought with anyone they met and the winner lived and the loser died? And later, when they formed groups, wasn't there one who was better than everybody and didn't that one get the best women, the best food, the best everything and didn't everyone else have to obey the one who was the best?

Is that where all that comes from, the game of my country, my town, my group—me—having to be the best?

I don't root for a team because it's my home team. I take a look at two teams, two players in any sport and I pick the one my guts like better—and root for that one. It has to do with what I glean from a team or a person in the way of the kinds of characteristics they possess. Out there when you see them move and when you see the close-ups of their faces and eyes, you see what they're made of. How do you explain that in the game of tennis, which essentially has to do with hitting a ball and keeping it in court, some players are adored and by others you are bored? Why did Agassi cause excitement and adoration throughout the world while Sampras, as good as he was, was always considered boring? Why, when the Williams sisters play anybody, does the audience inevitably root for their opponents? Yet, they love to watch them play. Why did Kournikova, who has never won anything of importance, create so much interest? Arthur Miller said it in *Death of a Salesman*; it wasn't important to be liked, it was important to be *well* liked.

As the time of the bout approached, the hoopla grew. It's true the way the public feels about a knockout puncher. It makes everybody terribly excited. And I can't help feeling that that, too, must come from way back when to put an opponent out in the field of battle was considered the be-all-and end-all of life.

There are so many things that stay with us through the centuries even though we have no need for them any more. They seem to be on no less than a cellular level. I had a collie used to walk circles on the living room rug before lying down. I wondered why she kept doing that. Eventually someone told me that, thousands of years ago, when dogs were in the wild, they had to make a space in the tall grass before they could lie down and sleep and it obviously became something that was now a part of their cellular make-up.

I've even thought such things as the fashion of earrings, piercing the various body parts of men and women throughout the world had to come from the times when we were savages and pirates and it strikes a chord within us.

As for me, I was interested in this phase of my life being over so I could get to the phase I loved and looked forward to where I could spend my time creating and taking joy in it.

I kind of sleepwalked through the TV cameras in my dressing room where I was instructed to warm up so they could telecast it to the watching audience. Everything is being done by the numbers. The announcers talk in phrases they've used hundreds of times, the referee automatically tells the fighters he's read them the rules in the dressing room (so he won't have to bore the audience), the playbacks are predictable and repeated an-nauseam and people have become mechanical and automatic in what they say and do. There are very few surprises left. When the country was being built, there was too little of everything—except work and battle. Now, there is too much of everything and work is something we try to do as little of as we can; as much as we need to accumulate the property we desire.

That was the game they could play if they wanted to; but not me.

After this fight, my real life would begin.

I told them again I did not want any music or rap or any kind of a circus while I walked to the ring. I did remember, though, I used to admire the way Tyson, at the beginning of his career, would walk like a gladiator from his dressing room into the ring without a robe, just trunks. Probably took me and everybody else to thoughts of Tarzan and the primordial times, which is, after all, what it ultimately is all about.

"Why *don't* you wanna do it?" Mangiacavallo wanted to know, again nagging about staging some kind of a show for my entrance. "Everybody's doin' it. The crowd loves it, they expect it."

"They expect it or accept it because that's what they're being given. Would you buy a ticket to watch Naseem wiggle his ass now he's lost the championship? Like when a judge tells jokes in his courtroom. Think anybody would laugh if the joker weren't the judge?"

I made my entrance like Tyson used to, wearing nothing but trunks, only mine were designed in the pattern of Johnny Weissmuller's in the Tarzan movies. It was crass but I couldn't resist it. It was one of my dreams. As a kid, I used to climb trees and tie ropes from branches and swing on them and run around in the woods, thinking of myself as Tarzan.

Besides, the gym shorts they wear these days that come down to the knees I find ludicrously unattractive. It's like the more of their flesh women expose, the more of ours we cover up.

It's funny, you got all this women's lib stuff about women not wanting to be regarded as pieces of meat yet they keep showing us more and more of it.

It felt good walking down the aisle with screaming fans all around. I was Tarzan, roaming tall through the forest, going after some wild animal.

Approaching the ropes, there *was* one temptation I almost gave in to. I thought about the way Naseem somersaulted into the ring. I wondered if I could do it. I remembered I had learned how to do a somersault when I dove into the water. What were the percentages, though? If I succeeded, everybody would say I was a copycat. If I failed, I would be the laughing stock. Hey—that might not be a bad idea. I loved Laurel and Hardy and Charlie Chaplin. What if—?

When I got to the ropes, I jumped up, grabbing hold of the rope and deliberately missing so I slipped and fell. The camera was on me and it showed on the big screens situated about the hall and everybody laughed. I did it again—deliberately. That got an even bigger laugh. One of the trainer's assistants held the ropes apart for me to get through and I put my foot between the lower rung ropes and got my foot entangled and pretended I couldn't get it out. The audience roared.

I remembered how in high school I had been in a play where I portrayed a chef who got nauseous when food was mentioned. Everybody had been in stitches and I couldn't figure out why I, who am essentially a serious person, could cause so much laughter. But it was precisely *because* I was so serious and committed to what I was doing at the moment. I was making myself experience the emotions of being sick and it was expressed in my features and body movements.

And then, during the curtain call, I somehow got stuck in front of the curtain after it had closed and, in trying to get back to the other side, I couldn't find the spot where the curtains parted and frantically spent about five minutes looking for it and the audience had a great time. That, I was beginning to understand, was really the key to comedy. You had to be deadly serious about it. That was why I'd never found those campy things funny. It was like, when they were doing it, they were telling me, *Look, this is very funny, you're supposed to laugh here.* Good comedy, I thought, happened when the person doing it conveyed that he did not realize it was funny and was making sincere efforts to do something that, in spite of all his efforts, wasn't turning out right. I say *his*, here deliberately because, for some reason, I can't visualize a woman indulging in physical slapstick being funny. Maybe because I feel that kind of stuff is beneath them. Lucy made it work, though—but not quite in the same way the male comics did. There *are* some things that still belong to us guys. Like being experts at making idiots of ourselves.

Now, in the ring, like after my high school curtain call, I kept getting tangled in the ropes and slipping as long as I kept hearing fresh laughter. Then, just before sensing it was going to begin receding, I squeezed seemingly with hardship between the ropes and fell onto the canvas inside the ring. I immediately stood up and took a boxing stance against the ropes as if the ropes were my enemy and I were going to fight them. Laughter. Somebody tapped me on the shoulder and I quickly swung around, my fists up, again as if I were going to fight whomever was there, this time it being my trainer. Someone else tapped me on the shoulder and I turned, my fists poised and this time it was the ring announcer who wanted to check something about my background. All this was accompanied by bursts and waves of laughter from the audience.

People love to have something to laugh at, especially at events that are serious to the tune of millions of dollars. Take a match at Wimbledon. One pigeon flying around the court during play will cause the audience to bust its gut with laughter. A pigeon. All he's doing is flying around the court, he's not doing one goddamned thing that's a bit funny. It's the unexpectedness and contrast that make it funny.

181

I milked it for all it was worth and my trainer, assistant, and cut-man all fell in with it and pretended to jump me and grab my arms and forcefully guide me to my corner so I wouldn't hit anybody and the audience really didn't know if I was being funny or if I had gone Tyson. I decided I would continue along that line and kept on struggling, thinking it was a good way to warm up and it changed things around from the usual cliché claptrap that takes place in the ring before the bout.

Trujillo, apparently deciding I was getting too much camera and audience attention, rather than make me wait, as champions often do, having the privilege of coming to the ring after the challenger, began his march from the dressing room much sooner than he might have without my shenanigans. And I, the moment I heard his theme music and saw him march down the aisle, broke free, jumped over the ropes, and ran down the aisle toward him as if to fight him. My trainers and security ran after me and I slowed down a little so they could catch up and when they finally caught me, I strained and struggled to get out of their grips the way Ali used to do before his Liston fight.

They were dragging me back into the ring and I struggled for all I was worth.

"All right," my trainer was saying, "that's enough now, settle down, enough."

They literally lifted and carried me into the ring. The audience was beside itself with excitement. Out of the corners of my eyes, I glanced at the announcer and fight analysts and they all seemed to think I wasn't kidding. I could see the announcer talking into the microphone, probably telling the viewers the challenger had gone ballistic. Well, this announcer loved describing what happened in the ring just as if it were a radio broadcast. After a while, nobody thought I was kidding.

The referee, a former fighter and marine, came over and said to my corner people, "Now, look, if you can't control your fighter—"

I tugged at the guys who were holding me, almost breaking away so I could get to the referee and he instinctively backed away, bringing up his fists in a defensive stance. In the process, I winked at him, trying to do it away from the camera.

He got it and decided not to pursue the matter. He figured the corner men could hold me throughout the proceedings until the bell rang, after which they could let me go. The referee was a bit of a showman himself and he evidently decided to go along with my gag, probably enjoying the idea that he and I were the only ones who knew I was kidding.

And that was the way it went. They kept holding me and I kept struggling, sometimes almost managing to break away. For me it was an acting exercise and, because I feel real when I act, it looked real to everyone else as well.

The referee was even nice enough to let my corner men come with me and hold on to me during his instructions to both of us before the fight and then they dragged me back to the corner where we waited for the bell, at which point:

*Victor Trujillo turned into the man wearing sheets and holding a knife.*

*When they released me, I ran as if a racing gun had gone off and I was doing a fifty-meter sprint.*

*The man with the knife—as much as he thought he'd be ready—just couldn't be. It felt as if he had just pulled out the knife and as if I'd known he was going to so I was ready for him and he wasn't quite prepared for me having known he was going to pull out the knife.*

*"You ugly one!"*

*Down he went.*

Afterwards, with the commentator honing in on me like a vulture on a corpse, holding the microphone and standing before me in the ring, I watched it on the replay where they always ask the winner to describe the action.

The move is like a football tackle. Only you don't grab the guy and bring him down. You hit him instead, and then *you* go down, and if you hit him in the right spot, he, too, goes down—and out. With Trujillo, he hit my upraised left hand that was flying ahead of me— and I hit him with a right hook—and then I hit the canvas. And when I opened my eyes, down he was. I rose, scurried to a neutral corner, and waited for the ref to count him out.

The audience was screaming at full volume. You would think they'd feel cheated to see it end so quickly after they'd invested all that effort, time, and money but they didn't. I had put on a show for them and then I'd backed it up by giving them what they longed for more than anything—except perhaps having sex and, as far as fight fans are concerned, don't be too sure.

They had stretchers nearby—they'd been doing that for my last few fights. Mangiacavallo's idea. He thought it was a good gimmick. And it was.

And just like that, I was Middleweight Champion.

And Shakespeare—as usual—had been right when he talked about there being more things in this universe than our philosophy could encompass—Horatio.

I wondered if other people who became champions of this or that felt surprised. There are probably thousands upon thousands of people who go into some athletic or show business endeavor with the thought they want to become champions and stars. Only one out of hundreds of thousands becomes a champion or a star. Is that person surprised? Or are all those who *don't* become champions and stars surprised and the ones who do simply think, *Well, I said I was going to do it and I did it and am it?*

On my way to the dressing room people yelled at me, saying praiseful things and reaching out to shake my hand, to touch me. I touched their hands as I walked and then decided, *Why am I rushing this joyful occasion, why shouldn't I enjoy it to the fullest?* So I stopped along the way and shook hands and talked to people and then further on toward the dressing room I saw Ashley Judd and she was coming toward me and I stopped because she looked like she wanted to talk to me. And then, when she was right in front of me, I saw it was not Ashley Judd but a woman who looked just like her.

"Mister Kahn," she said, "my name is Sandra Williams, I'm a writer. Would you mind if I walked with you, I'd like to talk to you?"

"Nobody can come wid us, honey," Mangiacavallo said. "Security. Give'm your card wid de number, sweetheart, he'll call ya."

"I'd really like to talk to you now," she said to me.

"Hey," Mangiacavallo said, moving toward her, "somp'n wrong wich your hearin'?"

"She can come," I said to Mangiacavallo.

He turned to me and gave me that angry flash and I looked back at him with full awareness of what kind of power I wielded now.

"Okay, honey," he said to her. "He's de champ. Whatever Lola wants—Lola gets. On'y we gonna have to frisk ya first, honey."

"Who's gonna do it?" she asked. "You?"

"Much as I'd love ta oblige ya, honey, we got female security to do dat." He snapped his fingers toward one of the women security guards.

"Joey," I said, "that's not necessary."

"On *dis* subject you don't tell me what's necessary."

A heavy, square-bodied, short-haired African-American woman security guard came over, checked the woman's purse, then checked her body. I looked at Sandra Williams's body and thought how nice it would be to be checking that body and wondered if the guard were gay.

When the woman was declared weaponless, we continued our parade to the dressing room and she walked right alongside me.

When we reached the dressing room door, she said, "Can I come in with you?

Mangiacavallo began to say, "Uh—" but when I looked at him he said, "Sure, honey, sure. Glad to have ya company."

She stood on the side while they unwrapped my hands and out of the corner of my eye I kept glancing at her. Her presence made me very excited. I don't know exactly why. Maybe it was the "thunderbolt."

In the book *The Godfather*, the author talks about the thunderbolt. People see somebody and they get struck. For reasons you can't name and don't know, you see a person and that person makes you very excited. That's the thunderbolt. It had happened to me once when I was twelve years old and it had happened with Stella. And now it was happening again. Déjà vu all over again, as Yogi said.

I knew from the eventual dissipation of my crush when I was twelve that the thunderbolt doesn't mean this is the person you'll live with for the rest of your life. It just means it's somebody who gets you very, very excited. And not necessarily—or only—in a sexual way either. Just somebody who makes you feel wonderful about life, about yourself—and about themselves. And then there is one other thing. I read it in another book, *The Accidental Tourist*. They made the book into a movie with Geena Davis and William Hurt. Toward the end of the book, the protagonist says to his ex-wife in response to the question of what he sees in the woman he's met and thinks he's in love with. Know what he tells her? He tells his wife he likes who he is when he's with that woman.

I think that's what the thunderbolt means. You like who you are when you're with this person and you like what life feels like with this person around.

"Do they call you Sandy?"

"Yeah, they do."

I used to love Sandy Dennis. I'd see all her movies. She had those slightly protruding teeth and those full lips. Ashley Judd had those too. Judd looks a little like Sandy Dennis. I guess there's something about that look that gets me.

Sandy Dennis won the Oscar for *Who's Afraid of Virginia Woolf*, which gave her the muscle to choose what movies she'd star in. Unfortunately, she also had a tendency to choose weird movies with weird stories, weird characters—so her career slowly careened, till she got cancer and died. Later, I read she'd been gay. Well—bi-sexual.

Ashley Judd has made some weird choices in movies. But I like the look and the personality of those women. And Sandra Williams was like a combination of Dennis and Judd. And she was in my dressing room. And you're going to tell me there is no God?

"Would you like to have a drink somewhere and talk?" she asked.

"You must have ESP," I said.

I suddenly had one of those great life cognitions—an epiphany, if you will: The moment Bill Johnson paired me off against Shamaz in that gym class some secret door of the universe opened up and I'd entered some kind of dimension where exciting, magic happenings were *de rigueur*.

"Don't forget," Mangiacavallo said, "I'm trowin' a party to celebrate. You can bring a date." He winked at Sandy.

"You didn't tell me anything about a party," I said.

"Suppose to be a surprise. You suppose to walk in an' everybody sings, 'Hooray for Captain Spaldin'.' But now you steppin' out, I don't got no choice, do I? Can't be no surprise no more."

"We'll have a drink," I said, "and see you afterwards."

"I'm trowin' de party fer *you*," he said, "so don't get waylaid. Now you de champ, every skirt gonna wanna fuck ya."

There it was again. The idea somebody was coming after me

because of what I'd become rather than for—my soul? Ah, sweet mystery of life.

I looked at her and thought, *She could have anybody she wanted, anybody in the whole world. She could have Brad Pitt, she could have George Clooney—she could have anybody.* There was that look about her. The Ashley Judd look. God, she was like a clone. The Ashley Judd of a few years ago, not the one who's so skinny now and whose fame is fading.

She didn't seem to let Mangiacavallo's remark get to her at all. They can be so impervious, women like that. And haughty too. Because they know they have the upper hand. They are like magnets. Speak softly and carry big tits.

I went into another room that adjoined the large dressing room and showered and changed. Meanwhile, I could hear knocks on the door and people wanting to interview me. They tried to get into the adjoining room from the hallway. Somebody even tried to pick the lock. People are weird about fame and celebrities. You think some kind of connection with a celebrity makes them feel better about themselves?

"Don't forget," Mangiacavallo said as we were leaving, "my place—where you came to ask me to manage you? Where it all started?"

He nodded for a couple of his goons to run interference for us so we wouldn't be badgered on the way to the street.

Reporters waited outside the dressing room and I answered their questions as we walked.

Outside, there were a lot of people milling around and they extended their autograph books as soon as they saw me. I signed them all, just like those tennis stars at Wimbledon.

Sandy pulled me to the right where there was a silver SL600 Mercedes waiting. The goons came with us so nobody would bother us and they stood around while we got into the car and Sandy started it and we drove off.

Suddenly, there was just the highway and the lights ahead of us and we were alone. I looked sideways at her. Here was a woman who could be anybody. She could be somebody fronting for someone who wanted to kidnap me. The World Trade Center disaster had made us all crazy. But you look at her and you say ridiculous. If you can't look at a face and know what's going on behind it, well—Tant pis pour vous, as the French might say.

*The Picture of Dorian Gray.* What you've done, what's done to you, how you react, and what you are are written on your features, in your eyes, your movements, your voice. If you look at somebody and can't pick any of that up—well, it's like choosing not to look at an obstacle that's right under foot and allowing yourself to be tripped up and sprawl into the gutter and then you get up and rant against the thing that tripped you.

This woman—hell, this woman was top of the line, what dreams were made of. "Memories are Made of This." I was in the zone. Everything was coming up roses.

*Startin' here, startin' now—*

The road whizzed by ahead of us, zooming under us, lights on the other side whooshing in the opposite direction—and I was excited more than ever. And life seemed more wonderful than ever. I wondered if this was what people who took drugs felt and if that was why they kept taking them, why there were billions of dollars' worth of drugs being bought and sold everywhere at great risk.

Or was it that drugs took away the emotional and spiritual pain the way aspirin does physically when you have a headache or aches and pains, enabling us to experience the joy of life by removing the constant pressure of pain and anxiety that resides to a greater or lesser degree in everyone?

She reached up and turned the interior light on. Then she pulled a cell phone out of a holder under the dashboard.

"Take the wheel," she said.

I took the wheel and she pressed a button on the phone, then replaced the phone in the holder. She took back the wheel.

"What you've been doing in the ring has never been seen before. The leaping is a little like what they do in wrestling, only with a lethal punch. I'd like to write the story behind it. How you thought of it, how you developed it, how you manage to do it time and again even though they've seen tapes of what you do and should theoretically be ready for what's coming—I think somebody who can come up in this day and age with something no one's ever seen before is worth writing about. Only, instead of asking superficial questions about it, like the reporters do, I'd like to do an in-depth book."

"I'll give it some thought."

It was disappointing she'd had an ulterior motive in reaching out to me. I have this idea of how you see someone and a bell rings. You don't know anything about the person except the look and sound of him/her. And just from that, you have a feeling amounting to a certainty.

On the other hand, if she hadn't said anything, I would have been burdened with the thought she'd reached out to me because of what I'd accomplished and it would have kept nagging at me. This way, she'd been up front about it.

Considering it further, I was always happier when there was a purpose to any activity. Writing a book was goal-oriented. I liked that a lot better than a short-range goal like, *Let's have dinner and fuck.*

On still another hand—how could I write about my life that culminated in my becoming champion without mentioning the knife-wielder who appeared in the ring every time I entered it? And if I mentioned it—well, you get two psychiatrists to sign a paper and you're in a confined space as long as they want to keep you. Hell, they'd climb all over themselves to grab some publicity. They'll do anything for a fee anyway.

On yet another hand, if I turned this woman down, she might lose interest.

"I'm going to give it some thought," I said.

"You said that."

"The repetition was to stress it was going to be serious thought."

"Well, that's good to know."

"Can we see each other while I'm thinking?" Testing, one, two, three, four, testing.

"We're seeing each other right now."

There was silence for a while as if to emphasize the idea that she wanted to do this book.

"Do you have a goal other than boxing?" she asked after a couple of minutes.

I told her about wanting to be in show business.

"Well, then this would work hand in hand. Plus it would provide you with a hell of a lot of cash. But there's a small window to these things. Like Andy Warhol said, you get fifteen minutes of fame—then you're yesterday's news."

# Chapter Twenty-Three

When we got to JFK and she parked in long-term parking, I said, "Where're we going?

She said, "Trust me."

There's a New York Jewish saying that "Trust me" means "Fuck you."

But I was willing to put my money on this woman. First of all, I felt invulnerable; second, she had class written all over her. I was not willing to mistrust my judgment.

I followed her and a presidential bodyguard type through a special door marked "Security," then through a couple of more doors onto the field and toward a big airplane that stood there in the dark fog like an updated version of *Casablanca*. Except this was not the ending of the picture. It was the beginning.

"I thought the Concorde wasn't flying any more," I said.

Sandy looked back over her shoulder as she and the bodyguard type walked ahead. "There're exceptions to every rule. And you're about to meet people for whom rules were made to be broken."

In the Concorde, excluding the crew, there was a party of about fifteen people. Several movie stars I recognized right off the bat. The rest, Sandy said, were producers, writers, and directors.

For fear of getting the billing wrong, I'm not going to list them.

Joseph Schildkraut, who had played Captain Dreyfus in the movie *The Life of Emile Zola*, told a story on a talk show about his father, who had been a famous international star in Europe. It seems there had been a question regarding in which position on the marquee his

190

billing should be for a certain play he was starring in, and the wily old actor had said, "It doesn't matter where you put my name or how large or small the letters. They'll know who it is."

It's not quite like that today. There is a lot more ego that grew in the last two-thirds of the 20th century. John Barrymore had once said the only thing he regretted about acting on the stage was that he couldn't be in the audience, watching himself perform. And Oscar Wilde had said that, whenever he took a long journey, he carried a number of his own manuscripts with him in order to be sure he had something interesting to read.

The seats inside the plane were not lined up in rows the way they are on a commercial flight. They were scattered about as they might be in a lounge; armchairs, sofas, tables. There were several large screens scattered about as well and one had a choice of watching any of the first-run movies and, of course, the older ones.

Turned out all the celebrities there had been at the fight and decided on the spur of the moment they would all go somewhere afterwards for a kind of a party. And it turned out I was to be the guest of honor. Sandy had been given the task of fetching me. For these people who could have anything they wanted, anytime they wanted it, I was to be the toy-mascot for the evening.

It was weird to have all these people I'd seen in movies and the ones who had produced, directed, and written them talk to me and make a fuss over me as if I were the famous one. They all loved the routine I'd done getting into the ring and asked me if I did any stand-up.

"No," I said, "but I do some acting."

"Where did you act?" a man who'd been introduced as a producer asked.

"Cape Playhouse, Broadway."

"Good for you." He pulled out his card and gave it to me. "Have your agent get in touch."

Of course, they all wanted to know how I had developed the idea of running at my opponent, diving at him, and being able to knock him out before I hit the floor.

"If I figure out what the answer is to that one," I said, "Sandy and I are going to write a book about it."

"You don't know how you developed it?"

"Not really."

"Well, that's certainly mysterious, isn't it?"

I shrugged modestly.

"You're not telling 'cause you wanna save it for the book, don't you?" one of the male stars said.

"You got it."

I felt a tiny bit of triumph. I had something that this big super-star, who Esther, the woman I'd walked out on because she'd drooled over him, did not have.

When the plane began to taxi for take-off, it was like sitting in a large building and the building suddenly begins to move. Here I was, flying with a bunch of movie stars and people who made movies happen. These were the individuals who influenced billions of people, making changes all over the world.

I had always wondered, watching movies, plays, and television shows, how people who were part of making it happen got to the spot where they — well, the spot they were in. I knew how other people got to where they were—engineers, lawyers, doctors, dentists, teachers, scientists, accountants—they went to school, they got good grades, and there you are. But with the hundreds of thousands of people competing for all the jobs that are part of show business, how does it work that you constantly see new people doing different shows and there're really no formal qualifications for any of the jobs? How do all these new people in show business keep getting in?

Well, here was part of the answer. Someone introduces you to someone else and he says, "Get in touch with my office," and if you're halfway qualified, you've got the job. But being qualified is not the criterion here. There're plenty of places where you can learn to be qualified. The all-important thing—in this country more than in any other—is, as Arthur Miller had Willy Loman say, "To be well liked."

And being well liked in the entertainment field is more important than any other quality. These people could give me a job. But if I was not well liked by the public, not even Irving Thalberg rising from the grave could help me. I was seeing Arthur Miller's theme in action.

I looked out the window and thought about all the space and planets and worlds that existed out there. How had they all come into being? And the intricate, interrelated systems that made all living

192

things function? Was it an ineffable intelligence separate from us all or were we all individually in on the creation of it, choosing to forget it and disassociate ourselves from it, making our way in this universe, struggling along like the meanest of animals and feeling like puppets pulled by strings?

How would that work—if we were all in on it? Would it be something like the creation of a nation—in which the people were all part of creating it but, at some point, they chose a king to whom they gave all the power and then everything about them and their lives belonged to the king? Good to be king.

"A penny," Sandy said, holding the arms of the chair I was sitting on and leaning over me.

"Where're we going?" I asked her.

"Don't you want to be surprised?"

I smiled. "Yeah, I do. You have a phone?"

"Be right back." She went to where she'd left her purse and came back with a cell phone, handing it to me. "You want to let your girlfriend know where you are?"

"Don't you want to be surprised?" I asked, dialing.

The phone rang on the other end.

"Hello?"

I wasn't quite sure of the voice. She must have dozed off.

"Mom?"

"Where are you?"

"Flying."

"You got drunk?"

"I'm on the Concorde."

"The Catskills?"

"Flying in an airplane."

"I can hear the noise. What're you doing in an airplane?"

"I think we're going to another continent."

"Which one—and how come?"

"I don't know which one. They're holding it as a surprise."

"Oh my God! You've been hijacked!"

"No, no, no, it's a bunch of people from Hollywood. Pleasure trip."

"Just like that? You take off and you go to another continent? You don't tell me anything?"

"I'm calling you now. Did I wake you?"

There was a short pause as she explained to Alex what was happening.

"You know I can't sleep till I know where you are," she said to me, "and that you're all right. Maybe I dozed off a little. So you're all right?"

"I'm fine. It's like a party. Only it's on an airplane."

"We went to your friend's party that we thought was going to be in your honor downtown. Only you weren't there."

"What friend?"

"Mister Mangiacavallo. He threw a party for you in his coffee shop down in Little Italy. He invited us to come as a surprise."

"Oh, boy."

"He was getting very worried about you. I heard him tell somebody if anybody hurt you there was gonna be hell to pay."

"Oh, boy."

"Does he know you're on your way to another continent?"

"He's going to soon as I finish talking to you."

"He seemed pretty upset."

"I'll talk to him. You going to get some sleep?"

"As long as I know you're all right."

"I'm fine."

"Then I'll get some sleep. Call me when you get to wherever you're going. "

"Call you tomorrow."

"Don't forget."

"I won't. Goodnight."

"Goodnight."

I clicked off and looked at Sandy.

"That's so sweet you have such a nice relationship with your mother," she said.

"Don't you?"

"Not so much. Obligatory stuff. 'Course, I'm a little older than you."

"I'm gonna have to make another call."

"Mangiacavallo was throwing a party for you, wasn't he?"

"My mom tells me he's pretty upset."

"I guess it was pretty rude not to go when he ordered you to."

"He threw a party for me and invited me and invited my parents and my friends. That's a little different from ordering me."

"Right."

"He made it possible for me to get to where I am. Very few other individuals in the world could've done it and I didn't know those others. Mangiacavallo did it."

"You feel you owe him?"

"Yeah."

"You don't feel it was as beneficial for him as it was for you? Maybe even more?"

"I don't know about more."

"All right—the same. So who owes whom what?"

"Your point?"

"If your becoming what you became benefits you both the same, nobody owes anybody anything and you can go where you feel like going whenever you feel like going. Unless—he has something to do with you winning all those fights?"

"Like what?"

"Like your opponents are maybe supposed to lose."

"That's what you think of me?"

"It's hard to know what to think of you. You fly through the air with the greatest of ease, as the old song goes, and send your opponents to the E.R. and you're obviously hesitant to have a book written about it and you don't want to talk about it. So either you're even-Steven with Mangiacavallo—if you're on the up and up—or you do owe him."

"Well—you've got a point."

"I thought I did."

"I'm gonna call'm."

"I'd like to stick around and listen. Okay?"

She was a spitfire. I liked a spitfire. I dialed. After a few rings, a man answered. There was a lot of noise in the background.

"Yeah?" a man said.

"Ciccolino?"

"Who's dis?"

"Dan."

"Oh, yeah. Congrats, dat was great de way you took'm out. Hey, where're *you*? Joey's shittin' garlic."

"He around?"

"Just a sec."

I listened to the sounds of the party as Ciccolino put the phone down. I heard him say, "It's Dan."

"Finalmente," Mangiacavallo said. Then, the phone close to his mouth, "Where are ya?"

"I'm far away, Joey."

"How far?"

"I'm on the way to another continent."

"You got waylaid by the bitch like I tole'ya ya would?"

"I don't go in much for name-calling."

"My party don't count fer nothin'? I had your folks here'n everythin' 'n you do dis? What're you, in a plane?"

"Yeah."

"Tell'em to turn aroun' 'n fly back. Lemme talk to whoever's in charge, I'll get'em to turn the fuckin' plane aroun'."

"No, Joey, we're not going to do that."

"*We* ain't gonna do it. *I'm* gonna do it. Lemme talk to'm."

"No, Joey."

"Hey! So far, I ain't interfered with nothin' you wanted to do. I trow a lill' party, tell people dey gonna get to meet de champ an' you do dis?"

"You didn't tell me anything until after the fight about any party. You can't expect to spring a party on me out of the blue and expect me to drop everything."

"Drop what? Some fuckin' bimbo who picked you up on your way to your dressin' room? You wanna fuck de bimbo, a real man tells'r, 'You're comin' wid me, bitch.' You could take'r upstairs right in de middle'a de party an' fuck'r, I got a beudeeful bedroom upstairs for dat very purpose, clean sheets, towels, everythin—hey—I travel foist class, remembuh?"

"Not the point."

"Not de point, huh? Not de point? You don't show up after I tell people you gonna be here, make me look like a fuckin' *stronzolo* an' dat's not de point?"

"The point is you sprang the party on me at the last minute, after I'd committed myself to something else."

"So what? You fuckin' uncommit yourself. Dis is *me*! You don't forget dat."

"Yeah, but I *don't* uncommit myself. When I give my word, it's my word—whether it's you or anybody else. My word is my bond."

"Dat's very admirable, I have to say, but we're talkin' about between me an' a fuckin' bimbo."

"I told you I don't go in for name-calling, Joey. If you keep doing it, we're not going to be having this conversation. Secondly, it doesn't matter, who it is. My word has to do with me, not who I give it to."

"It was a surprise, de party was a surprise, how could I tell you about somethin' dat was a surprise? When you was leavin' wit her I *had* ta tell ya."

"You plan surprises, you take chances."

"We wasn't gonna have no party if you lost, what would be da point?"

"Just tell everybody I had to make an emergency trip to another continent and there'll be another time. After all, aren't you the king? A king can turn something on and off without batting an eyelash. You're the king, Joey, you're a Roman emperor, nobody holds you to account, nobody questions you. You clap your hands and tell your subjects, 'You're all dismissed, I'll have you summoned when I want you. Out!' "

There was a pause on the other side and silence. The party had quieted down. When Joey talks, people listen.

"You got a pair'a balls on you, kid, you know dat?"

"That's why we got the championship, Joey. You're the Roman emperor and I'm the gladiator. You point your thumb downward and I kill them. What do you say, *stronzolo*?"

"Don' call me dat, dat ain' a nice woid."

"I do it with affection, Joey, it's all affection."

"Dat ain' a nice woid, I don' like to be called dat."

"All right, Joey. In my book you're not a *stronzolo*. How's that?"

"You one lucky bastid, you got more luck den brains, you know dat?"

"I know, Joey, I know. But I can't marry your sister. No matter how much you beg me, I can't marry your sister."

"You gonna push it too far."

"All right, what about your mother, then, Joey, can I have your mother?"

"One'a dese days—"

"One of these days," I sang in a fair imitation of Sophie Tucker, "you gonna miss me, honey."

"How you know dat song?" he asked, just when the people on the plane had turned to listen. "My grandmother used to listen to Sophie Tucker sing dat song when I was a lill' boy."

"My grandmother did too, that's how I know those old songs. All right, Joey, I gotta get back to my bimbo now."

"You fuck."

"*Va fa'n culo*," I sang, "*a rivederci, Joey*," to the tune of "A Rivederci Roma," then said, "can I still sing in your coffee shop, Joey?"

I hung up without waiting for an answer.

"Whoa!" Sandy said. "I didn't think anybody could talk to Mangiacavallo that way."

"Clean heart," I said.

We landed at a large airport. The celebrities started getting recognized as soon as we deplaned. You could hear the buzz as people turned to watch our passing. Announcements in French were being made everywhere. Charles De Gaulle Airport. Man, we were in Paris. The city of Hemingway and all those great artists. The City of Light.

As far as I knew, we could've been going anywhere. I was glad it was Paris and not London. There was something in me that was not drawn to London. Maybe it was the calculation that if I was to travel long distances it ought to be to a place where they spoke a different language. On the other hand, wasn't it George Bernard Shaw who'd said that America and England were two countries separated by the same language?

It may have been more than that. I think it has to do with the English nature in terms of what they feel and communicate. I admire their civilization and the great individuals they've produced but I like feelings to be articulated rather than bottled up till you get to a soccer game.

The French, on the other hand, are haughty. Unless you're French, you don't belong to their club.

I thought of the way such things had been portrayed in our old Hollywood movies. There seemed to be a different feeling about foreign countries and foreigners in those days. There used to be lots of foreign actors in Hollywood pictures and the public loved them. And their accents were interchangeable, serviceable for any foreign character they portrayed.

Now there are no foreign actors to speak of in Hollywood pictures. Gerard Depardieu made a valiant effort in the eighties but it didn't work and he went back to France, getting fatter and fatter, making, among other things, a picture called *Uranus* in which he was supposed to be portraying a striking, starving coal miner who hadn't had anything to eat in weeks and weeks. The audience had a wonderful laugh over this Oliver Hardy hulk who stood there, wearing loose, black raiments to mitigate his weight, announcing he hadn't eaten in weeks and was at the point of death from starvation. There's Antonio Banderas, also making a valiant effort, but never reaching the A-level of stardom.

So we've gotten more provincial than even the French. I remembered that inspiring scene in *Casablanca* in which Paul Henreid conducts the denizens of Rick's café in a rousing version of "The Marseillaise."

I got this urge. A little crazy. But it came over me—and I decided to give into it.

As suddenly as it had come, so quickly did I separate myself from Sandy and the crowd we were walking with and marched to one of the counters where airline staff were making announcements. I took the microphone from a svelte, chic French woman in her forties—for, bear in mind, a French woman is almost by definition svelte and chic and flirty and inviting, ready to work you over the moment you take the bait. I switched the microphone on. Having seen me with the crowd of celebrities, she didn't resist but just stood there, her very stance bespeaking seduction.

Ah, French women. There is nothing like them anywhere. For centuries, around the reigns of the Louis', in the courts, they had developed their skills to the point where, in their sixties and seventies, they were still able to charm, seduce, and pleasure men young enough to be their grandsons.

I jumped up on the counter, mike to mouth, and sang:

*Allons enfants de la patrie*
*Le jour de gloire est arrive*

It was something to behold. I was, after all, singing their national anthem. Sandy had stopped when I separated myself from her and, when they heard the singing, everyone in our crowd stopped.

But, then, so did everyone in sight. They stared—frozen. One of the actors in our group joined in first. Then another and another—everybody, in fact, was singing along. Everybody in sight was singing along. Some of the older men and women in the crowd were crying. It was fantastic. Everywhere you looked, people were standing and singing "The Marseillaise," it was like the scene in *Casablanca*. And when you thought about it, it wasn't surprising. The scene in the movie was a time when evil was making a real bid to take over the world so emotions had run high. Now we were living in a time when evil had struck again and was rampant in the very way corruption, cheating, and lying had become something taken for granted. And here, for the duration of the song, bunches and bunches of people stood and declared, *I believe in and love the forces of good.*

Standing on that counter and leading them in song, I thought how the world is really waiting for someone to get up and lead them toward what they knew was best in all of us and is being suppressed more and more. I thought of the song Gene Lockhart, the actor who'd played the drunken doctor in *The Sea Wolf*, had written for his daughter, who played Lassie's mistress in the TV series, and put her through college with the song about the world waiting for the sunrise, the song which for decades had been played by the Radio City Music Hall organist.

Yes, that was what the world waited for and I'd never felt so good in my life as I had at that moment, watching the faces of all those at the airport who sang with one voice, expressing what was best in them.

And when it was over, they applauded and yelled and shook each other's hands and hugged, it was a little like the celebration when World War II ended, and some of them went and had drinks and others got into conversations and I returned to my crowd and we continued marching and the actor who'd joined me in the anthem first put his arm around me and said, "Awesome, man, awesome," and one of the women stars looked back over her shoulder and winked at me and Sandy walked on the other side of me and slipped her arm about my waist.

Limos took us to a Champs Elysees outdoor café, where they put a bunch of tables together for us, all facing the most famous avenue in the world.

A pantomimist appeared almost immediately, entertaining us with an imitation of the various individuals, couples, and groups walking by the café. The thing was these people whose walk was being imitated weren't aware of it. They'd walk by and hear the laughter of the café patrons and look puzzled because there was a faint suspicion they might be the object of this laughter so they'd look around and see the pantomimist walking behind them but the pantomimist was uncanny in the way he was able to stop imitating them when they turned to look and walk just as if he were another one of the walkers and then, when they turned forward and continued walking, he would go back to imitating them again. Then he would shift to another individual or couple walking in the opposite direction and the routine of their looking to see if they were being laughed at was repeated. He kept us in stitches for about twenty minutes like that, imitating everyone's walk, yet exaggerating it just enough to make it funny.

When it was over, the café patrons applauded and he went around to all the tables, hat in hand, for money. He would look at the money patrons dropped into the hat and react with an appropriate pantomime. If the tip was generous, he would hold his chest at the heart with one hand, step back and put his other hand over his mouth, opening his eyes wide in astonishment and, if he thought they were stingy, he would press his nostrils together with thumb and forefinger to indicate a bad smell in the air.

When he hit our tables, one of the producers gave him three hundred-dollar bills and pantomimed that it was for all of us. The mime prostrated himself on the pavement and pantomimed the kissing of the man's imagined garb.

Meanwhile, our food had arrived and we all began to dig in. The mime, bowing and waving his hat, retreated, pantomiming bumping into things on the way. He even stepped off the curb and pantomimed getting hit by a car, being knocked into the air and landing on the pavement. The man was an artist.

It was a beautiful sunny morning in Paris and I reflected on the fact that I was sitting smack in the middle of the City of Light with the most famous Hollywood stars in the world and I had just become middleweight champion and was with the most beautiful woman I could have wished for. How long would this feeling of wonder last? I looked at the stars I was sitting with. They were not in a state of wonder as I was. It was a natural thing for them to be in all kinds of places perceived to be exciting and interesting and where they were gaped at and adored the way they were at this very moment by the other patrons and passers-by.

I supposed it was like having a new car—or a new anything, for that matter. When it was new, you kept looking at it, appreciating it, wiping the dust and the little spots off it and, inside, it had that new smell and you felt like your whole life had a newness and a magic to it like the car.

Alex had been like that with his new car. When he first got it, he fussed over it as one might a baby. Supposedly, he had gotten it as a surprise for my mother after she'd gone to visit her brother for three weeks and Alex fully realized how much he needed and loved her. When he met her at the airport and told her he had a surprise for her, after he'd shown her the new car, she made a face and said, "This is a surprise for you, not for me. If you want to surprise me, buy me a house." My mother, as you might have gathered, was not a reticent woman. On the other hand, she had a clean heart and could say things like that.

Sure enough, next day, Alex plunked down thirty-thousand dollars as a deposit on a piece of waterfront property in Island Park, Long Island, and they were at this very moment building a house on it.

After a couple of months, though, he didn't fuss with the car so much. And after six months, he didn't fuss with it at all. It got washed once a week, got its maintenance, and that was that.

Things and beings were wonderful when new, like a little puppy. After a while, they were just something you took for granted.

I remembered the game I used to play by myself as a child, pretending I was different characters. I used to look forward to doing it and did it for hours at a time. I would rather do this play-pretending than anything. It never got old for me, I never took it for granted, always looked forward to it. These people I was sitting with, did they feel that way about the parts they played in the movies? There was all the business surrounding it. The amount of money you got, the billing, the dressing rooms, the respect you perceived you were being given, how much money the movie made, what the critics said about you, did you have a chance of being nominated for the Oscar, was your career on the upswing or were you slowly slipping? And then you had to worry about what kinds of movies you were in. If you had enough muscle, you could pick your projects. If you picked good ones, your career flourished. Bad ones and you went downhill.

Paul Newman was an actor who had picked good projects. Somebody like John Travolta sometimes picked good ones, sometimes not so good. If you were not in a power position, you had to be lucky enough to have people in charge of good projects pick you and then your career flourished to the point where you could pick the projects. Even when you picked a good project, like Kevin Kostner, who was also a producer for *Thirteen Days*, it could get tainted in that the microphone picking up the actors' dialogue showed up on the screen about fifteen different times throughout the picture, which is something even the most amateurish productions don't do. So there're all these questions you had to ask when you were in show business and if the answers weren't right, you were in trouble and it could send you plummeting.

Playing by myself in a corner as a child, I never had to ask those questions. I just looked forward to the joy of playing. These people lived with those questions all their lives and the answers to those questions became much more important than the playing itself.

Was it possible to love something more and more the more you lived? Could you go against the general agreement that it's normal to appreciate and enjoy things less and less with the passage of time?

The whirring sound of a helicopter underneath the consciousness level suddenly made its presence known and grew. Grew louder and louder. And then really loud. People all around looked up. The machine painted black and blue hovered over the Arch of Triumph. Somebody was being lowered onto the top of the Arch. He swung a little back and forth till he hit it, then, on his knees, disconnected himself from the line that had lowered him. Everyone watched. Some kind of a stunt? Like the fellow years ago who walked on a high wire between the towers of the World Trade Center? Or the one who parachuted off it? Or the one who climbed up the side of it? Or the Arabs who had blown it up?

The man on the Arch of Triumph stood facing the Champs Elysees, put his hands to the sides of his mouth and started shouting. He had a portable speaker system strapped to his body which magnified the sounds so we could all hear him. Like those muezzins who shout from the mosque minarets to the four corners of the world, he howled to the four corners of Paris.

Suddenly, there were shots coming from different directions. The man's body shook, went limp, then, with what looked like a great effort, straightened up again. He took a step to the edge, stretched his arms out to the sides, and did a beautiful swan dive to the pavement below.

The entire area—as far as you could see—was like a photograph. Nobody—nobody was moving. No, sorry, there were some pigeons flying around—which made it even more eerie—this still photograph of people and cars and things with pigeons flying around in it.

We keep forgetting what extremes life is capable of. We move in this narrow area of our own little, well-delineated worlds where what is important is a job, shelter, food, fornication, and entertainment. Ergo, everything we strive for and experience belongs to one of those categories. The wonderful, but more often the outlandishly horrible things we hear about, read, or view on TV are things that happen to other people and belong to the realm of entertainment. We are removed from them by the mechanisms that deliver them to us and by our own desire to individuate ourselves from anything unpleasant. The World Trade Center disaster changed all that—for a short while. Then people went back pretty much to where they'd been before it, as you heard the once-venerable Red Cross had pulled a fast one with the contributions that had flowed in after the WTC disaster and groups and individuals took to squabbling over the amounts of money being or not being doled out by the government for the families of the victims and the businesses suffering from the disaster and there was squabbling over the kind of memorial that was to go up and then the news came that eleven of the firefighter heroes had left their wives and taken up residence with the wives of their fallen comrades. Will people ever stop surprising you?

I looked at Sandy, then at the celebrities on either side of me. They were still staring and in a state of shock. This must be even more shocking to them than to the rest of us. Although, I was kind of one of them for the moment. But still so new to it, I didn't consider myself as anything but what I had been since birth. They, on the other hand, lived a fantasy life. In many ways, they were like King Midas. Everything they touched, everything they wished turned to gold. They told somebody they wanted something to happen and it happened. They saw or heard of a person they wanted and they could have that person. They wanted a certain project to come about and it came about. Everywhere they went people adored them. It was a life in which everything worked exactly as you wanted it to and you literally had to create things over which you could work up some emotion other than, "Yup, everything is satisfactory."

The movie, *Sphere*? Where the guy, after entering that extra-terrestrial globe, suddenly began making things happen just by thinking about them? Haven't you had that feeling sometimes? That your thoughts could make things happen? Even thoughts you weren't aware of? Ever swim in deep water and think of a shark and suddenly get scared that your thought might materialize some shark right under you—or attract it to you from some distance? Happened to me after I'd seen *Jaws*. I'd be swimming and, suddenly, I'd think of a shark. And then I'd think, *At this instant, a shark is getting my telepathic message, making the turn in my direction and starting to head for me.* And I'd swim furiously toward shore.

What if, instead of sitting back and believing everything that happened to us was caused by some unknown, unpronounceable, mysterious force—we began to suspect it was really us that caused things to happen?

The thing about it is, no matter what kind of tragedy befalls you, you either let yourself fall and give up—or you continue living. Inevitably, people choose life.

The limos took us to a hotel called George V. Sandy and I had a suite on the top floor with a terrace overlooking the avenue and much of Paris. We had a B&B on the terrace and another in the Jacuzzi. Sandy's personality was so strong and so unselfconscious that her nakedness didn't call attention to itself nor cause me to have an erection. I wondered how that could be, seeing from high school on, whether in a classroom or on the subway, I would visualize or see some woman and the erection would come *toute de suite*. Sometimes it would happen just when I was approaching my stop on the bus or subway, sometimes at the end of a class when I would have to pretend I was in the middle of doing something and couldn't possibly stop. On the subway or bus, of course, many's the time I would overshoot my stop and ride a couple more, forcing myself to think of my mother in order for the erection to go down.

Sandy had a beautifully constructed, juicy body. It was as if she'd stepped out of the Playboy centerfold—only without the artificial breasts most of the women in that profession seem to have. She walked sinuously, with natural fluidity, perfectly aware of the effect her body created, yet, unlike most beautiful individuals, did not seem to invest the majority of her life forces into the achievement of her goals via those physical assets. None of it called attention to itself as the senior item on the agenda.

That was the thing. Most people didn't pay attention to their voices, speech, or body movements and the very few who did tried to improve these characteristics for a tangible, practical purpose. They were generally actors, dancers, lawyers, or politicians. Sandy was a writer. I have heard and seen writers on television and they are personality-wise nowhere near what you might imagine them to be from what you read in their books. It was like it used to be with radio actors and, in reverse fashion, the silent screen stars. With radio actors, people used to imagine them to be as they sounded. When they saw them, it was always terribly disappointing. And, of course, with the silent screen stars, when the talkies came in, it was a blood bath.

What it said to me was you could develop every part of yourself to the $n$th degree—that is—to a level of greatness; and the more things you were great in, the happier you were and the more happiness you brought to the world.

People, for the most part, though, chose to stop developing in body, mind, and spirit at some point shortly after they completed high school. There was a popular book on the subject a few decades ago: *Is There Life After High School?*

People might hone some skill to serve them in a practical way, but their minds and spirits remained more or less the same for the rest of their lives—except for the agreed-upon deterioration that took place as they got older.

Sandy had obviously thought about that. She moved with grace, the tone of her voice was mellifluous and melodic, yet it had the energy in it that comes with a strong joy of life. The large brown eyes had that glow, reflecting panache—in short, she must have put some thought into bringing to the table all she could. And that was probably why she was moving in the circles she moved, these people could choose anyone they wanted as friends in the same way they could choose anything else they wanted. Because they, too, were bringing a hell of a lot to the table.

What it really came down to was the kind of thing we saw in the movie *Cast Away*. When all the appendages—conveniences and entertainments—of civilization are removed, it is then you realize that what you have *in* you is the only thing. So in any relationship. Take away the money, the house, the car, entertainment—the APPENDAGES—and what do you have? You have what each person has inside him/her. That is the sum total of your riches.

But take it still further. Think about when you had a break-up in your life. How much pleasure did all those APPENDAGES give you then? How much pleasure did anything give you then? What was there in all of it that you weren't willing gladly to trade for your love to return?

Ergo—every appendage, every machine, every relationship, every entertainment, every activity, is informed, dominated—no, dependent upon—what exists inside the person partaking of it. Our entire *world* is dependent upon what exists inside each of us. It is the irony of our millennium that our society enters it placing less importance on those qualities than whatever tidbits they can acquire at the flea market.

We luxuriated in the Jacuzzi, sipping our drinks, chatting and staring at each other.

"Isn't life a thing of wonder?" she said.

"It is."

"Yet you see so many people walking around, bathing in misery and constantly creating more."

"Why do you think that is?"

She smiled. Her eyes smiled. It was a smile that accentuated her joy of life. Spontaneous and real, unlike so many used as a means of impressing.

"Why do people make themselves and others miserable?" she said. "Let's see. Stupidity?"

"I guess some kind of stupidity plays a part in anything that turns out badly."

"How do things turn out for you?"

"Pretty good."

"Seems that way so far, doesn't it?"

I wasn't thrilled by the modifier. Yet, she was right. All you could be sure about was what's happened—so far.

# CHAPTER TWENTY-FOUR

I remember watching a documentary about boa constrictors in which there was a section of the film where a rat was placed in a cage with a python. The point of the documentary was that animals won't eat unless they're hungry. So this rat and this python co-existed in this cage for several hours, each peacefully going about his business. There did not seem to be an innate feeling in the rodent that the python was going to harm him for he was perambulating about the cage with what appeared to be a sense of freedom and security, nibbling, sniffing, doing all those things rats do in their daily existence.

But you knew, watching, that even though the rat appeared to be unaware of it, the situation was as a wit had described it when he talked about the lion and the lamb lying down together but the lamb not getting a good night's sleep. You knew, sure as shootin', the rat's minutes were numbered.

You look at the faces of these animals and at their eyes. That's where we look when we want to see what state someone is in. But animals don't have expressions. The lips of those species that growl and hiss may move and you're getting the communication of a certain mode but there is no change in their eyes and features. Even when their limbs and testicles are in the process of being chewed upon by a feline while they are still alive, their expressions and the expressions of those doing the chewing remain as they had been when they were lolling in the sun. To me the expressions of those being chewed upon in their gentleness always seemed to say, "That's how it's been, that's how it'll be and I have no questions about it."

At some point, without any kind of telegraphing, the serpent struck and if you blinked you would've missed it. Half of the rat was in its mouth, half out, you could see its little hind paws wiggling. You watched in horror and fascination at the interminable amount of time it took for the rat to get transported from the outside in. During this time they showed you in slow motion how the python's jaw unlocked enough to accommodate a newborn baby, never mind the rat, while telling you on the sound track how the snake's secretions and enzymes were already at work priming the rat for dissolution, beginning the process of digestion. They, then, showed you how the rat's body in very slow, wave-like movements made its way down the serpent's innards.

I have always felt a kind of horror of snakes. I know many people do. Could it be the PR regarding what a snake did to Adam and Eve? Could it be more than that? Like a genetic remembrance? Doesn't matter, really. The point is I had a number of nightmares following this viewing. After that, whenever I would come across something about snakes, I would look for a few moments, riveted, then quickly move on before the images could imprint themselves on my dream-making mechanisms.

I took away from the experience something unexpected. The concept of timing being everything. Now I know there's an old saying about timing being everything. But a saying is worth nothing unless you can somehow transform it so it belongs to you so you can experience it down to your toenails.

On this particular occasion with Sandy it was this concept I had in mind — the timing. I gave no thought to sex but concentrated wholly on creating as wonderful and magical an occasion of this as I could. I wanted the magic and the romance to be as it was for Don Quixote or Don Juan or Romeo or Byron, I wanted all of life to be like that. Not an illusion but *like* that. I wanted it to be real. I wanted all these things to shine and be noble and large spirited and great as I sensed they could be. I wanted to seek out those in the world who *were* large spirited and noble and benevolent and gracious and kind and loving and honorable and courageous and honest and truthful and I wanted those who were that way to together inspire the whole world to be that way.

I tried willing everyone I came in contact with to be that way. If they weren't, well, either they would become it or I would have less contact with them. Ultimately, if I worked on myself more and more and more, I would have more and more wherewithal to inspire them toward those qualities. I envisioned Sandy to be this way. So far, she seemed more large spirited than anyone I'd met. Bill Johnson had seemed large spirited and had many of the characteristics I idealized. But in the end he had flunked. So we had gotten disconnected. Mangiacavallo was a crook so he didn't count and would disappear from my life as quickly as he'd entered it.

But now there was this and the whole thing was like being in heaven and there was nothing about it I was going to rush. It was like the old Heinz commercial—*Anticipation is making me wait.*

When we came out of the Jacuzzi, she dried me off with a towel and I dried her. Now I was beginning to feel the blood rushing to that place with which we men think. Then we were in bed, gazing at the sky through the open French windows and the parts of Paris we could see from our vantage point. From somewhere I heard Edith Piaf's voice singing, "*Je ne regrette rien.*"

I decided to just lie and wait and have Sandy make what moves she felt like making. I sensed something very important about life: when you wanted and reached for things too much, they went away from you. If you wanted them, but also put in a clause in your desires that if you got the things you wanted you would be fine and if you didn't get them you would be fine, then it became much more probable you would get those things. But the proviso was you could not put that clause in for the purpose of getting those things; you would have to be sincere in your belief that if you got them you would be fine and if you didn't, you would be fine.

I also thought about the choices this woman had at her disposal in regard to the men she went with. Her choices were practically infinite. Her choosing me might be a whim or she might have sensed something in me she wanted to be part of her life. The things I did during our time together would determine how much and how long she wanted to be with me and the things she did would determine the same for me.

She was the first woman I'd been in this situation with so this had a special meaning and magic that would overlook many things. Later,

I would learn the beginning of most relationships caused people to overlook so much it almost always turned out to be too much. And then the memory of the beginning kept them going through the roughest of times, sometimes for decades, until they finally realized what existed in the beginning would never come again.

A snake had my penis in its mouth.

"Ah!" I shouted and sat up, horrified at the realization it had felt good.

I was sitting up in bed. I remember thinking I'd always made fun of all those scenes in movies where, for decades, in every single scene where a character in a movie wakes up from a nightmare and always sits up. Never just opens his eyes and thinks, *My God, I was having a nightmare*, staying in a prone position. No, in the movies they always have to sit up. And here, goddamn it, I was sitting up myself. To paraphrase Job, what I have derided has come upon me.

Then I saw the outside and it was late afternoon and my penis was still in the snake's mouth. Car horns were blaring and distant voices of people talking, laughing, and shouting. Had I overslept, was I late for school?

Oh. I wasn't in school any more. Middleweight champion. Oh, no, that was silly. That had been the dream; I was late for school, that was the reality.

But my penis was still—Oh, my God! There was the lump under the light-weight midnight blue blanket at my groin, sucking so deftly and with such heat I thought I was going to faint.

No, I had to stay awake. The lump under the blanket. It wasn't a snake. And then there was the feeling of something inside me coming from way below and I realized, if I didn't take drastic action, I would have my first ejaculation in Sandy's mouth.

Since the age of thirteen I had dreamed about the vagina and the fluffy bush around it. The goal of my existence had become to enter it with my penis. I did not want my first ejaculation to be in somebody's mouth. And now I could feel the rush of the nascent sperm like a red truck to a five-alarm and I did not want it to happen that way, not my first time.

Calling forth upon thoughts of my mother in emergency situations when I would have an erection in class or on the subway was bad enough. But to do it in a situation when I was with a real, live woman—'tweren't decent.

But to hell with it. I did it anyhow. I thought of how my mother had cried about the lump on her breast. Then I remembered her heart-wrenching sobs when the man she'd been engaged to told her, after the removal of her breast, he would not marry her.

It worked—the thoughts, like the little Dutch boy at the dam, stopped the onrushing flood and the spermatozoa, like the lions and tigers before the crackling whip of an audacious trainer, slowly, under protest, moved back—and back! Stay! Stay! Stay! Sit!

She seemed to want to suck it out right then and there. I've since encountered that characteristic in other women. They don't necessarily like to swallow but a lot of them love to get into the game of causing you to come while they're sucking you. It's like a challenge for them.

Is it because they care for you so much and think you like coming in the mouth so they want to make it happen for you? Or is there some part of them that wants to put you under obligation so it's, *Oh, well, I've satisfied you, you came in my mouth and now you can't satisfy me and now we have to wait at least forty-five minutes to an hour and you'll probably fall asleep and here I am all hot and bothered and unsatisfied.*

The more she kept sucking and licking, the more I summoned thoughts of things that would work against it. I had read in Havelock Ellis how Turkish men had trained themselves to stay in a woman for hours, placing near the bed various desserts and delicacies so, when they felt they were about to ejaculate, they would reach over for a "locum" (a Turkish jellied candy with powdered sugar on it) and place it in their mouths and chew on it and that would counter the need to ejaculate and, when the storm passed, they would get going again, repeating the process over and over.

I had no locums and did not consider the chewing of food or desserts as candidates for what I thought to be my style but, in preparation for the great act, I did utilize thoughts that would postpone ejaculation so I could stay in there for a long, long time and get as much pleasure from being in the vagina as possible.

I utilized these thoughts now but she did, yes, she did, take it as a personal challenge and used every skill she had garnered from her vast experience to cause my ejaculation. But I'm here to tell you I discovered during this watershed event of my life that my will and strength of purpose were weapons of considerable magnitude.

I was more shocked than surprised at the fact that one's will and considerations could overpower something as mightily physical as the urge I was experiencing and the forces pent up for a jet-like release. It was probably this more than anything that prepared me to reflect on what else one's consideration and will were able to accomplish.

There came a time, as attorneys are wont to say in a courtroom, when she gave up. At which point she furiously crawled upon my body like the snake of my dreams till she was sitting on my lips, straddling my face. Ah, yes—"Sit on my face," as Henny Youngman might've said—"please," memories of that little girl with black panties sitting on me when I was six passed through and meandered as memories do.

From the way thousands of people look and behave, how many could you envision naked and doing all kinds of erotic things? I could never envision any of them. Yet, the homeliest and the dullest have done them. In olden days, sex was well hidden and never talked about except under the most secretive conditions. Nowadays, it's talked about and inserted (so to speak) into as many communications as possible as often as possible and people who talk about it make every effort to treat the subject as if they were talking about grocery shopping. They've become experts at desexualizing sex. For centuries, its secretive aura caused us to long for it with every fiber of our beings. Now it's being thrown at us from every direction, it's like McDonald's, you can have as much as you want very cheaply and everybody's getting very fat and the pleasure of eating, now there is plenty, is nothing, I imagine, like it used to be when there was never quite enough and when it was a mystery.

She raised herself slightly so my tongue could have some play. I'd read enough to know, ever since I'd heard the saying, "Show me a guy who doesn't go down on his girl and I'll take her away from him," what needed to be done. Knowing, however, what needed to be done and having the dexterity to do it are two different things.

As the song says—there's nothin' to it but to do it. You gotta have hard (forgive me).

214

There are odors—and tastes—involved in this. There are things on the market that remove the odors and the taste but you cannot remove all of it. The thing to do, I discovered quickly, was increase your saliva secretion and, if you don't have a taste for it, neutralize it. On the other hand, there was Napoleon who had written to Josephine, when he was on his way back home from the battlefield, "I am coming home. Don't wash."

The delight is that in this as yet unexplored territory you have an infallible guide in the person of your lover who, through sounds and movements, communicates to you with absolute certainty what specific spots are sensitive and how much pressure and what kinds of rhythms are required at each progressive stage.

And what a turn-on it is. To feel your tongue gradually finding its way and causing what grows into a tidal wave and you say to yourself, *I did this, I did it.*

It was a chain reaction that kept going and going and seemed as if it would never stop, yet it was so monumental, you couldn't see how it could possibly last long. And when it began to recede, it would start up again and grow, it was as if it met something on the way, like a bouncing ball, that made it go up again.

It slowly ended, like D.H. Lawrence's world, with a whimper and her head lay limply on top of the headboard. Not for long, though. Slowly, in a very, very relaxed fashion—just when you thought all was at peace—she began to crawl south upon me.

I was very erect. When her bottom end touched my penis, it was like radar, causing her to raise her lower part and again, as if powered by a homing device, her vagina found my penis and, without any help from her hands or mine, impaled itself.

Mercifully, she lay still, my penis in her. Had she moved the tiniest fraction of an inch, not even thoughts of the Spanish Inquisition could have stayed my ejaculation.

So this was what heaven was like.

But my desire to ejaculate was still so strong I had to summon the worst thoughts I could possibly think of to keep from jetting her up to the ceiling with what I had in me, just raring to surge.

Finally, it was thoughts of those Turkish men eating their locums in the middle of lovemaking that made it distracting enough for me to compose myself. It was a funny image.

She must have sensed the lessening of the crisis for that was when she made a move—slight enough so it gave me gobs of pleasure, but not so much it would cause the sperm to come shooting forth. She waited. Then she made another move up and down on me. Oh dear God, what have I done that You should be so good to me? I remembered the Godfather in the book saying at the end of his life, just before expiring that life was wonderful. Oh, yes, yes, Godfather, yes.

She'd move up and down on me once—then stop—and wait. Again—and again—and again. It was the reverse of Chinese torture. Oh, dear God, I knew this was going to be wonderful but there was no way for me to know how wonderful. I remembered those experimental monkeys pulling the lever connected to the prongs inserted in their brains and causing themselves to experience orgasm after orgasm and never stopping until they killed themselves.

Why would anyone want to have it any other way?

You just lie around with someone you love making love to and you do it and wait around a short while and talk and sleep and eat in between but mainly you just keep doing it. Why would you want to do anything else? Ever?

And then she started going up and down on me a little more frequently—and a little more and more and more till she was riding me like a bucking roan and I knew there was no way I was going to stop the flood that would momentarily ensue from my—"loins."

But then she suddenly stopped—and it was as if my semen, surprised by this unexpected maneuver, balked.

The stop was only for a moment. There was something she had encountered in my pubic bone that had gotten her attention—because her clitoris began rubbing against it the way a cat rubs itself against your leg. And then the pressure of the rubbing grew heavier—and heavier—and faster and faster. And still heavier. It began to hurt. But there was some magic at work there. The hurt seemed to become pleasure even as you were actively aware it was pain. Was that what happened to masochists? They were able to put themselves in a mode where they could turn the concept of pain into pleasure? An alchemy of sorts, what?

There she was, writhing on my pubic bone, her features contorted with intentness and ecstasy and I thought how did we manage to get into a million other petty complaints regarding life when there was this? All you had to do was think of this and the fact you could and would be doing this at some point or other and how could you be sad or angry or depressed or even annoyed or anything but ecstatic?

Was that why Bill Clinton always had that little smirk? *Fuck you all, I got this thing?*

JFK too. Only his was classier, a little more intellectual— endearing, actually.

She was in some kind of a trance and looked as if something other than she were guiding her movements and there was no force in the world that was going to stop her from reaching her destination.

The pressure against the pubic bone worked at neutralizing the pent up desire to spurt forth. Instead, it felt as if I would last as long as my pubic bone could hold out.

Harder and harder she pressed and now I knew I would feel pain in that bone for days to come, if not weeks, but I knew, too, instead of annoying, it would excite me. And what did that say about the strength and durability of what she was pressing my pubic bone with? But I already knew about women's capacity to bear pain from the time I learned childbearing to be considered medically the most painful natural experience there is.

And then she went into it. I don't doubt for a moment the witnessing of a woman going into her orgasm to be the most riveting phenomenon in existence. And right then and there was when I decided Mrs. Engels, my high school English teacher, must have been right. "I could not love thee, dear, so much loved I not honor more," indeed.

How could honor or anything else compare with this ecstasy? All the books I'd read, all the movies, plays, operas I'd seen, most about the travails of love, now instantly fell into place. I could now understand why millions of men and women throughout the ages did such far-fetched and unreasonable things for love.

Watching Sandy's twisted features as guttural sounds ensued from her mouth, body undulating every which way to music unheard, her eyes reflecting the stamp of trance, her hair gently swaying with the movements, I knew my goal hereafter would be to re-experience this as often as possible and every other goal would be subsidiary. Is it any wonder a male of any species, once having experienced coitus, will risk, sacrifice anything for the sake of—getting another piece?

Don Juan and Casanova had had it right.

And this led to a realization about goals. People could tell you this or that was their goal and that was what motivated them but this self-analysis of what motivated them was probably further from what really motivated them than anything else. Alexander—Napoleon—Hitler—who knew what truly motivated them?

Take Clinton. What had motivated him to seek the Presidency? The obvious answer would be the power that came with the position, the excitement, the attention, blah, blah, blah. But, looking at his actions, I understood it clearly. He was a man who was driven by a great hunger for organic sensation. And what greater sensation than sex? Ergo, what greater fulfillment? What else could explain the stupid risks he took for its sake?

That would be me from now on. And I wouldn't have to worry about being discovered at it. I was heading for show business where anything goes, as opposed to the olden days when a glimpse of stocking was looked on as something shocking.

I could have ejaculated while she was in her throes but I didn't want to. I wanted every fiber of my being to be watching and bathing in it. I didn't want to be *doing*. I didn't want to make sounds while making love. I didn't want to do anything that would subtract from taking in everything the woman was doing, including making sounds, which might be selfish on my part because she might want to hear my sounds as well but, often, people want to hear sounds so they will feel convinced the other person is into it, like they want somebody to say, "I love you," so they can say to themselves, *Yes, he/she loves me because he/she said so.*

So sounds sometimes serve to convince someone the other person is enjoying it. It wasn't why I loved the sounds a woman made. I loved them because they were part of the miraculous phenomenon and because they seemed to come naturally to them—and they didn't for me. I appreciated it all in another way. The way you might appreciate something sacred or a great work of art that fills your being so completely there is no room for anything but the taking in of what is happening.

The orgasm seemed to go on and on. And when it was over, it would serve to bind the woman to the man and cause her to care for him in a way she could not have cared for him before. It also worked for some men. On the other hand, it caused a lot of men to care less. Men had this joke about the definition of eternity being the period between the time he comes and she leaves.

I loved the feeling between a man and a woman when, knowing you were civilized beings who tended to all the daily actions of thinking, working, and creating but then, there was the time when you both stepped into this other dimension, this world that seemingly had no connection to the everyday world of mundane affairs and you became pure animals. You looked the way animals looked, you acted the way animals acted and the more civilized, culturalized, and intellectualized you were, the more incongruous it became. There was never, never any way you could logically make the connection between the way you acted, felt, and communicated throughout your daily life and the moments when you went at each other, doing things you never gave a hint of being capable of during your routine existence.

To me it made sense keeping it up for as long as you could. There seemed to be some kind of direct correlation between the pay-off and the amount of time and effort you put into the journey toward the pay-off. We were living in an age when things happened instantly. Actors reading their lines off prompters is the rule rather than the exception. Yet, actors working on a part in a theatrical play, if they know how to do it, can create the kind of magic aeons away from whatever can be gotten off prompters.

So my instinct even that first time was to make it last as long as possible. It made every sense in the world. Not only was it pleasurable to be on the edge of coming while experiencing the even more pleasurable feeling of having your penis rubbed by the velvety, warm, juicy vagina but there was the contact of the bodies, the caressing, the kissing, the exchange of unspoken feelings through eyes, all this added to an experience so monumental and unique, it was as ineffable as Jehovah and the longer you made it last, the bigger the experience imprinted on your memory and the greater the pay-off when you finally came.

To hold on while you are being the stallion and your rider is the one who is wild and out of control is the biggest challenge I'd faced or could think of facing—and the most wonderful. Because my pubic bone was still being assaulted, I was able to keep from coming, staying and swaying with her through the entirety of her orgasm. It was like one of those space rides in Disney World where you held on in fear of flying off from your little cart into space even though theoretically you knew you were supposed to be safe.

Her capacity was amazing. I had nothing to compare it to but it was amazing. There is a saying that a man falls in love with a woman because he is sexually attracted to her while a woman is sexually attracted to a man because she has fallen in love with him. Sandy and I had just met, how much in love could she have fallen? Was it the idea for her of a younger man? A flying boxer who knocked people out with one punch? She did not strike me as being that shallow or possessing those kinds of aberrations but you didn't really know. Was it what they've talked about through the ages along the lines of love at first sight? The way Puzo had put it in *The Godfather*, the "thunderbolt"? Meeting someone and knowing right off you were going to love him/her? It is said women know within three minutes of meeting a man whether they want to sleep with him or not. I personally think it may be less than that.

Eventually she was spent. Her head once again leaned against the top of the headboard. I had wondered, thinking about sex as I'd often done, whether the woman, once she'd had her orgasm, lost her desire to keep having sex in the same way the man did. In the Shire book *Women in Love*, a number of women interviewed said there was a definite sensual thrill and pleasure in having the penis moving inside them after the orgasm. That had certainly seemed the case with Sandy.

And a whole bunch of other things regarding the differences between men and women made sense as well. Were our desires not dictated by the physical, we men would not lose those desires once the sperm left its nest. The women, on the other hand, not having their orgasms dictated by the mechanical aspects of having to get rid of pent up secretions were able to have orgasms that were dictated purely by feelings. Ergo, they could have them much more frequently, chains and multiples galore, depending upon their feelings toward their partner—or whatever it was that carried them away.

*Ah, sweet mystery of life at last I found you —*

And then she was at it again. But this time there was something different about it. Her purpose this time was evidently not to have an orgasm herself but to see to it I had one. She moved up and down on me—

*First you move your tootsies round'n'round*
*You sway'em left and right, then you make that sound*
*Tuck it nice and tight lest the bedbugs bite*
*Then you push it in, push it in with all of your might*
*Let your arms enfold her and hold her right*
*Then you do the nasty right on through the night*
*Arch your butt just so and bring it forth*
*That's how you do "the gentleman's sport"!*

There is the story of the Frenchman telling the American, in answer to his question regarding how many positions there were, "*Mon dieu*, in France we have one hondred posissions," and the American saying, "My goodness, a hundred; I know only one, the one with the woman lying on her back and the man on top," and the Frenchman saying, "*Sacre bleu*, zet makes hondred and one," and all that time Sandy kept staring at me so intently it was as if she were hypnotizing me, my entire attention on those eyes, they would not let me go and I could no longer think of anything except staying riveted on them which, in turn, eliminated further ideas of prolonging my ejaculation.

That was okay, though. I had prolonged it enough. No, there was no such thing as enough of sex in the same way they say there is no such thing as too rich, too good looking, too intelligent, too sweet, or too thin.

But there is. There is an end to everything and there is a time to move on. One thing I learned from Hemingway was you should stop things just before you feel you've had enough. That gave you the impetus to come back to it. If you went beyond the point where you've had enough, you would start finding reasons not to go back to it. He used that in his writing but it works for everything. It was hard to see how you could have enough of this, though.

The best and the worst things in life seem to come in waves. And they grow. Bigger and bigger. And what gushed out of me felt like quarts and quarts. Once again I thought of the line in *Hamlet* about there being more things in this universe than our philosophies could ever dream up. The ecstasy of it, the manner of it, whoever thought it up *has* to be ineffable.

You know there's a bird, a tiny bird that weighs less than a pen and you know what this bird does? The male builds a nest. The female inspects it. If she finds it not to her liking, she tears the nest down and the male builds another one. They go through this process again and again and he keeps building that nest over and over till she indicates she is satisfied with its workmanship. I mean, for God's sake. But you can bet she doesn't let him alight on her till he's built that nest just so.

So, Doctor Pangloss? "Everything happens for the best in this the best of all possible worlds?" We may negate it. But how do you argue with Whomever or Whatever created all of this? The crocodile that lays its eggs in an obscure spot and then covers them with sand so they wouldn't be seen? Who thought this up?

And this thing, copulation. That it would be so pleasurable we would want to be doing it more than anything even when we are not procreating and that we would want to continue procreating even though we no longer have to procreate in order to have sex? What of that? Childbirth being the most painful experience there is and bringing up a child perhaps the most difficult and you *don't* have to do it to have sex—and you still do it? What is that?

Two mystics sit in isolation a few yards from each other in the mountains of Tibet. Months pass. One of them finally says, "Life—life is like a well."

The other one glances out of the corner of his eye at the one who spoke and says nothing. Months pass. Finally, the second one says, "Why? Why is life like a well?"

The first one glances at the speaker out of the corner of *his* eye but says nothing.

After more than six months, the first one says, "All right, have it your own way. So life *isn't* like a well."

And that's the measure of our philosophies, Horatio.

There are ecstasies we can experience and there are horrors beyond imagination.

Why is some poor schmuck at this very moment being tortured by the death throes of cancer while this beautiful woman is riding me and I am experiencing heaven, pouring my semen into her?

Is there anything the poor schmuck did that led him to his destination and is there anything I did that led me to mine? And am I someday going to be in his place and was he at one time in mine?

As I was coming, she kept staring at me with just a hint of a smile, as if proud of her handiwork and knowing of the fact that, as a woman, she possessed this the greatest of weapons and that, when, excuse the expression, push came to shove, we needed them more than they needed us.

And then I was empty and went so limp everywhere, it was beyond dead. It felt like, if someone had yelled fire, I would've said, "Forget about it, I'll burn."

I wouldn't've but it *felt* like it.

On her knees, her upper body and head lay on me, my arms around her, caressing her lightly. Every once in a while I would touch a spot that would make her shiver and then I would go back to those spots and she would tremble again and again.

We were like that for a while, the sounds of Paris—our song. I thought of Seward Park High and Bill Johnson and Mrs. Hopper and Mrs. Engels and Stella and Maria and college and summer stock and Broadway and this weird thing that happened when I got into the ring. All these stars and celebrities had had their own Seward Park High and the rest of it, they had all gotten to where they were through something that was equivalent to a genie. It was all, when you read their biographies, a string of coincidences catapulting them to fame, power, and riches. Each of them could probably say, if such and such hadn't happened—.

Sandy unimpaled herself to lie beside me, my arm around her and still saying nothing. There were times when saying nothing was much more than anything you could possibly say. It was then you realized how inferior words were to some ways of communicating.

There was a knock at the door. Sandy got up, saying, "Just a minute," put on one of the thick, terry cloth robes that hung in the bathroom, and went to the door. When she opened it, two bellmen rolled two clothing racks full of dresses, suits, shirts, ties, and what not. Two other bellmen brought three full suitcases, which they laid on the floor. Still another bellman rolled a table with plates, glasses, silver, napkins, serving dishes, tea, and coffee.

Then three men came in, all with violins. They stood off to the side and began playing "Fascination." They were good. They had probably trained in the conservatory for years to play Mozart, Chopin, Beethoven, etc., and were playing in the suite of two spoiled Americans as gilding to their fucking. Ah, life—is like a well.

Sandy smiled. "*Un petit homage* to *Love in the Afternoon*. Only this time the woman is the older lover."

She got a roll of bills from her purse and distributed wads to the bellmen. They all left, thanking her in French. I remembered one of the sequences in *The Sun Also Rises* where Hemingway talks about how easy it is to make friends in France as opposed to how challenging to do it in Spain. In Spain, he'd said, people had to like you before they'd consider being friendly to you. In France it was far simpler. All you had to do was give them money.

I looked at the racks with all the clothes that hung on them.

"One of the women traveling with us," Sandy said, "does wardrobe in movies. She probably did some shopping for all of us, seeing as how none of us brought anything."

"And the suitcases?"

"Underwear, socks, shoes, condoms."

"How did she know sizes?"

"For her kind of job, you have to be a genius. Let's eat."

# CHAPTER TWENTY-FIVE

**W**e went to see Moliere's *Le Burgeois Gentilhomme* that evening. Then to the Folies Bergeres. I remembered *Moulin Rouge* from the John Houston movie about Toulouse-Lautrec who had two short stubs for legs and the misfortune to be portrayed in the movie about him by Jose Ferrer, the F. Murray Abraham of yesteryear. No less unfortunate than Ali in the two movies that were made about *his* life.

That night Sandy and I made love eleven times. Next day we went to the Louvre. Afterwards, we stopped at an American card shop where she bought me a card that said, "Seven—eleven—" and then a question mark.

We went to an outdoor place for lunch, then all of us were driven back to the plane. The plane took us to Athens. There, Sandy and I stayed in the hotel room for a couple of hours, then we were all driven to the Acropolis, where several picnic tables were set with food and we all sat around in those plastic armchairs you blow up and ate lamb and rice and vegetables and drank wine and watched *Oedipus Rex* in Greek but, as in Paris, they had set up a special marquee on which a running English translation moved in co-ordination with the speeches so we'd know what was going on. They had also constructed a temporary picket fence around us so we would be separated from the general public.

Sandy was sitting on my lap and I was caressing her body with little caresses so it wouldn't be too obvious and every once in a while she would lean over and kiss me, rubbing her clitoris against my knee, and here it was, the Acropolis, the Parthenon, all this nature and people, this Ashley Judd look-alike sitting on my lap, the thick, homemade dark Greek wine, all the endorphins from the lovemaking and all the rest filling my head, not having slept much causing even more exhilaration rather than tiredness, I'd had no idea life could get so wonderful.

Except I had this feeling that I really *had* had an idea. I don't think it could be so wonderful unless I first had an idea it could be. I don't think anything happens unless you first have an idea it *could* happen. I remembered reading how an ancient Chinese philosopher had once said a vision was like a picture puzzle. If you had it, all the little pieces would come together.

I looked at Sandy, at all the celebrities I was traveling with, other people who were stealing glances at them. Everywhere we went people were stealing glances at them. This was, after all, something these celebrities were used to, they could have this or they could have anything they wanted anytime they wanted it so it must be kind of old hat for them so how did they sustain that joy of life and the electricity they exhibited in the movies? I guessed, when you did something supremely well, something you'd begun doing in your youth and got to be masterly at, so good that you were pretty close to God-level in the area, as the years went by and other things in your life started going to shit, in this one thing you did so well, your life remained charmed and you remained close to God, the magic in this one endeavor remained.

I remembered watching Ali after the illness had advanced and his right hand kept shaking and how surprised I was when he did some pretend-boxing with Roy Jones Jr., at how nimble he still was and how he was able to jump around and show us the shadow flashes of the old Ali. I remembered seeing a fencer once jump around, lunge and fence his heart out and when it was over and I saw him later on the street, limping like an old, crippled man, I said, "What happened to your leg?" and he said, "Oh, I've had this arthritis for years," and I said, "But I saw you lunging and jumping and moving back and forth like a son of a bitch out there on the strip, I didn't see you favoring that leg at all," and he said, "Oh, yeah, when I fence I'm okay but the moment I stop fencing it all comes back."

And I learned later most athletes are like that. So something similar must hold for these celebrities, only in the spiritual and emotional realm. When they're doing what they do, they've got the electricity, the communicativeness, the capacity to experience the strongest and the subtlest of feelings, the intelligence, the power, the benevolence, the affection, the sanity, in short, the most wonderful and ideal characteristics you can imagine but the moment they're not doing what they do, they become somebody you wouldn't necessarily, if they weren't famous, care to have any connection with. They become petty, boring, shallow, totally self-involved, narcissistic. Well, we've all seen them on talk shows and it's boredom incarnate; whenever I run across one of those, I switch channels immediately, I want to hold them in my heart the way they are when they're doing what they do, rather than the way they are when they're working without a script or a good director.

Who can forget Sally Field accepting the Oscar and saying before millions, "You like me, you really, really like me," and Jonathan Demme, a great director, accepting *his* award for *Silence of the Lambs* and blathering and blathering and blathering, the entire audience laughing at the fact he couldn't stop, continuing to babble even as they dragged him from the microphone.

And suddenly, during intermission, two dark haired men with white suits and burning dark eyes stepped over the picket fence and stood in our midst. One of them held a greenish, egg-shaped object in the air and shouted in Arabic.

The other shouted in English, apparently acting as a quasi-simultaneous translator:

"We are de Islam Order of Houri!"

"Dis is bomb I hold in mine hend!"

"Somebody rrrong move—I ixplode everrbody!"

*I no longer saw two Arabs. I saw two men wearing those Roman looking sheets, holding knives. One I recognized as the one who appeared each time I'd been about to fight. The other one, skinny, with a long hook nose, looked familiar, though he had not made an appearance before.*

*I raced toward the one I recognized in the same way I'd raced toward him each time he'd appeared in the ring.*

*As during each occasion we did this, he froze for a moment, surprised by my running at him full speed.*

*I leaped from my usual distance of four or five feet, howling, "You ugly one!" catching him with my right on the bridge of his nose, then plopping to the earth.*

From my prostrate position, I saw one Arab on the ground and several policemen and men in civilian clothes piled on top of both Arabs, beating the hell out of them. I got up and went back to Sandy. Everyone in our group stared at me just as the kids had done the first time I'd knocked Shamaz out back in Seward Park. As if I were the Elephant Man.

# CHAPTER TWENTY-SIX

Sandy and I remained on the scene at the Acropolis because the police wanted to talk to me, while the rest of our group disappeared. The police gave us a lift back to the hotel in Athens. There, we discovered the group had checked out and left. We were informed that any additional stay on our part would cost one thousand two hundred American dollars a night for which we would be personally responsible.

"Hasn't tonight been taken care of?" Sandy asked.

"Oh, yes," the manager said. "Tonight has been paid. I speak of from tomorrow."

"Fine," Sandy said. "We'll let you know in the morning."

"Verry good, Madame."

When we got to our room, I said, "What's going on?"

Sandy poured us each a glass of vodka and orange juice and we sat on the terrace. We touched glasses and looked at Athens.

"My friend," she said, holding up her glass and trying to peer through the drink that was in it, "whatever notion you might have of trying to parlay your fame into a show business career, I'm here to tell you, wipe it clean off your itinerary."

"Why?"

"The word is going to go out from one end of Hollywood to the other end of New York that you're a maniac and very dangerous to have around. You won't be able to get a job as an extra in a second rate touring company."

"What happened to the concept of 'My hero'?"

"What're you, Israeli? He could have pulled that pin, those guys thrive on blowing themselves up, that's how they get into heaven. Islam even has beautiful women waiting for them in paradise. They're called *houris* and their sole objective is to pleasure the men who sacrifice their lives for Allah. And you wonder why these men are killing themselves off like flies? Do you realize billions of dollars' worth of stardom and movies could've gone up in a poof?"

"But they didn't."

"I hate people who keep telling you what you damn well know. The point is not that they didn't. The point is you had no way of knowing they wouldn't. You took a chance that was foolhardy by even Israeli standards. You had no way of seeing in that semi-darkness whether the pin on that grenade was in or not. He could've taken the pin out and pressed the safety with his finger, in which case, when you hit him and he dropped the grenade, all of us, including you and a lot of people who were around, would've been blown to bits. The fact the grenade did not explode might be improvidence or bad luck on his part but it does not absolve you of irresponsibility to the *n*th degree."

To the *n*th degree.

*I could not love thee, dear, so much loved I not honor more.*

Had that concept ever really existed?

We sipped our drinks for a while. From somewhere, a recording of the *Zorba* theme drifted through the city.

"What about you?" I asked.

"What about me?"

"Are you through with me too?"

"Bet your sweet dick. You're certifiable."

"All right."

It's strange what happens when you experience a loss. I'd been perfectly happy without her just three days ago and now it felt as if the whole world had fallen on me. I was middleweight champion, I had oodles of money, there were very likely loads of women who would be happy to go out with me, yet none of it mattered. It didn't even matter that what I'd done was supposed to have screwed up my show business aspirations. This loss—this loss of someone I'd suddenly gotten to care for made everything seem dark and hopeless. Why was that?

"Doesn't mean we can't have a good time tonight," she said. "Like maybe ten or eleven goodbye fucks."

I looked at her. "No thanks."

"Really?"

"Really."

"Pity." She shrugged.

We sat there for another while and, eventually, she got up and went to bed. I sat out on the terrace for a long time until, finally, the lack of sleep during the past couple of days slowly overcame me and I just went and flopped on the other king-sized bed. For a few moments I was roused by the idea of Sandy in the other bed and the memories of all the pleasures we had given one another during the past couple of days which had now turned into a heavy sadness and tears came to my eyes and, even as I was silently crying, my eyelids were falling from tiredness but then I heard a movement from Sandy's bed and then faint sounds on the carpet and then a sound and pressure on my mattress and her body next to mine, her hand going directly to the source, starting gently to work on it.

"Don't do that," I said.

"Make a deal with you," she whispered. "You don't have to participate or do anything at all. All you do is lie there and do nothing—unless at some point you feel like doing something—at which time feel free. In exchange, you let me do what I do—and we see what happens. What do you say?"

And all the while she kept on massaging and caressing.

I got up and flicked the light. She blinked, turning her eyes away.

"When a certifiable tells you he doesn't want to do something, are you sure you don't want to take him at his word?"

"I didn't really mean that—about your being certifiable."

"But you meant it about not seeing me any more."

"Publicly anyway."

"Get off my bed."

"You *may* be certifiable after all—you know?"

She got up and went to her own bed.

# CHAPTER TWENTY-SEVEN

**I** was awakened by the phone's electronic sound. It caused a pleasant feeling. The phone was one of life's great messengers. It brought you new things. Things you could play with. We took all this stuff so seriously—life. We were spiritual beggars, whiners. "Common people," George Bernard Shaw had said, "do not pray; they beg." Oh, let me make a little more money, let me have some more fame, let me have some more power, let me get laid, let me have five more years of life, let me have two more years, let me have an extra day. We groveled like ants carrying crumbs to their domiciles and, when you got old, it was, "Put a couple more prunes in my bowl—please?"

Georges Clemenceau, French statesman and prime minister back in the early part of the 20th century, had the kind of spirit that would today be far out of the realm of reality. Throughout his life he fought duels. On one occasion, when he was dueling with his arch political rival, he kept lunging and the man kept retreating till, finally, Clemenceau tucked his sword under his arm and said, "Monsieur is leaving us." On another occasion, when Clemenceau went with his second to the railroad station, he bought a one-way ticket to the site where his duel was to take place. His second, noting it, said, "Isn't buying a one-way ticket rather pessimistic?"

"Not at all," said Clemenceau. "I always buy a one-way ticket to my duels, then use my opponent's for the return trip."

In 1918, during World War I, when he was prime minister for the second time and in his seventies, he insisted on going to the front lines and was escorted by Winston Churchill to an area where a fierce battle was taking place. At one point during their drive, a shell fell upon a group of horses nearby and one of the wounded animals began running in panic. Clemenceau, to the consternation of all those who were escorting him, jumped out of the car, ran to the horse, caught it and quieted it down until others arrived to take over. When the attending officers pleaded with him to move from the danger area, Clemenceau reluctantly returned to the car and said to Churchill, "*Quel moment delicieux!*" (What a delicious moment.)

How do we reconcile that with the spirit of the yuppie that prevails today?

The spirit of Cyrano, Clemenceau, Don Quixote. The fun you feel when you have a worthy goal, when you play a large spirited game. *Largesse d'esprit,* the French call it.

Maybe that was why Sandy broke up with me. So I could have this epiphany. And maybe that's why the guy dressed in sheets and threatening me with the knife keeps appearing. So I would have the kinds of Cyrano-Clemenceau-Don Quixote kinds of adventures my soul yearns for.

The last person who had that kind of panache was Muhammad Ali. And how he ended up. Almost as if God were saying, "Hey, look how dangerous it is to be like that."

Unless, unless it goes beyond that—to the flaw—the fatal flaw of Greek tragedy. The concept being that, when you were in a high place, it was a flaw within you that caused your fall—a fall that was always steep and devastating. Think of the other person in modern times who had that kind of panache. John F. Kennedy. Both Ali and Kennedy had a bad ending. Suppose—suppose—there was a flaw in each of them.

Suppose—cheating and lying a la Clinton was Kennedy's flaw. "Happy birthday, Mister President." And suppose, as documented accounts have it, Sonny Liston was visited by two Moslems during his training period for his second fight against Ali and suppose he was told, "Lose or die." Ali was not necessarily part of that but he was part of it in being part of the group that did it. And he was part of the group that assassinated Malcolm X. So, though Ali subsequently proved himself heroic and great, there was that little corner that was dirty.

Could there be panache—without a flaw? Clemenceau lived to be 89, not bad.

It's been said, when certain situations in the world arise, the individual that's needed appears.

Does the world want that kind of spirit now—after WTC?

I had been used to Sandy answering the phone but it wasn't being picked up so I picked it up and looked toward the other bed at the same time. It was empty. The bathroom door was open and there was no one in it. I had the sense there was no one in the other room either. The bird has flown. If you love something let it go. To which the NRA might add, "If it doesn't come back, go after it and kill it."

"Hello?"

"Misterr Kahn? Dis ist Mister Populopolis, de managerr of de hotel."

"Yes?"

"Dere are peeple from de telebishion and newspaperrs who vould like spik vid you."

"About what?"

"Last night. De terrorist, de bomb. I didn't know you vas herroi."

"I was what?"

"Herroi, herroi. Doing brave tings."

"Most people would say stupid things."

"Oh, no, brave, verry brave. Verry herroi. Dese people—dey vant spik vid you. Dey say you also kampion box. Dey vant spik."

"I'll meet them at the hotel restaurant in twenty minutes. Have them order me a big breakfast, I'll talk to them while I'm eating. And then have someone book me a flight to New York this afternoon."

"Miss Williams ist alrready make reservation forr you. Four P.M."

"What a woman."

Wasn't I supposed to wake up all depressed, devastated by this beautiful woman leaving me? What was it about rejection that made you feel so terrible? The way I had felt the evening Stella had dumped me. The kind of thing that drove so many to acts of horror?

Did it hark back to something primeval? Of being left alone in desolation? And what happened that brought you from the state of desolation into a state of euphoria, which was what I felt now and what I had felt after I'd gotten over being upset with Stella having rejected me? Some, throughout the ages, reacted to this kind of thing by killing the person who'd rejected them or by committing suicide or both and, nowadays, picking up an automatic weapon and killing a whole bunch of people for good measure. That was likely why all those terrorists kept on committing suicides. They were so miserable in their spirit the only solution they could think of was to kill themselves and then all they had to do was find a seemingly logical reason for doing it and that's always easy; a man trying to take your parking space will do.

A few rare individuals, once over the initial upset, had the opposite reaction. The world suddenly became a wonderful place.

There is an Italian song called "Vivere," meaning "to live," in which a man sings about how this beautiful woman whom he has loved and lived with for many years has left him and how wonderful, free, and alive he feels and how she had promised never to return and now, more than ever, he wants to enjoy life to its fullest for as long as he can.

If some of those individuals who committed horrible deeds as a result of rejection and disappointment had waited a certain period of time—might not they, too, have awakened one day, feeling good and free and hopeful?

Of course, in the case of terrorists—and probably other kinds of individuals—there are unknown third parties who see to it these potential suicides continue to be miserable, until no other solution than suicide seems viable. Gild this lily, then, with what kind of heaven they will get into, with all those beautiful *houris* who will attend to them if, in killing themselves, they destroy certain designated targets, and you have yourself a cheap and potent weapon. Over there in Iraq, they're killing themselves over Saddam. Over Saddam, for God's sake.

There must've been over thirty reporters in the hotel restaurant when I got there. It put me in mind of all those animals you saw in the documentaries on TV that had other little animals clinging to them and feeding off them. When during the latter stages of his/her life, a reporter asks him/herself, "What have I done with my life?" what's the answer?

If it turns out to be something like Watergate or revealing there are forces goading the states to write a new Constitution or publicizing the exportation of jobs to foreign countries—it could be a wonderful thing. But if it deals with things like who Jennifer Lopez is currently fucking—well, that's all right but how will you feel about it down the road when you say to yourself, "That's what I did with my life. I told people who was fucking whom, who was cheating on and killing whom and what celebrity's birthday fell on such and such a date?"

Seated at a table that had been set up for me with a microphone, I faced the reporters semi-encircling me. Wow, like those press conferences you see Presidents and generals hold in the middle of a war or athletes and managers after a big game.

"Yes," I said into the microphone, "what would you all like to talk about?"

I pointed to a dark haired, pretty woman in the third row.

"Why don't you be first?" I said to her with what I imagined to be a devastating smile.

She got up. "Tenk you," she said with a harsh accent and she didn't seem as pretty any more. I had an instant understanding of what had happened in Hollywood back in the twenties when the talkies came in.

She introduced herself as Hagit Albahari, a reporter for Israeli television. "You vas herre vit movie starrs ant directors ant producers. *Verre* dey arr?"

"I think in the United States."

"Vy dey liv you herre?"

"I decided to stay an extra day and see a little bit of Athens. And see how lucky it was? We got to meet."

There was a forced ripple of laughter as acknowledgment of the flirting.

I pointed to an elderly man sitting in the last row. Why should it always be the ones who are sitting in the first few rows?

The man rose, seeming very dignified. He was balding with patchy strands of gray in the little hair he had left above the ears and the construction of his head appeared to be rather square, the veins in his temples swelling to a darkish blue. The eyes, grayish, had lost, as with most elderly people, almost all their light and joy, now existing only to watch and make sure harm didn't take them by surprise.

"Did you know the terrorist had not taken the pin out of the grenade when he was holding it up as a threat?" He was a baritone with an English accent who, as with a preponderance of educated British people, made up in pronunciation what he lacked in the expression of emotion.

Whatever I said here was going to be heard, seen, and read throughout the world. It was a story everybody was interested in. The sports fans because here was this weirdo who knocked people out with a dive and a right hook, the star-worshippers because I'd traveled with a bunch of Hollywood people, and the rest because here was an incident involving terrorists, while the young generation, the ones they make all the hi-tech movies for, would love the idea of this dude tackling a terrorist with a bomb. There was even a tape of it, which they played for me on a monitor they'd set up.

I remembered all the interviews I'd watched of celebrities responding to set questions with set answers, each one more or less a replay of all the previous ones. Ali, of all the ones I'd seen, was the only one who responded to questions with sincere, spontaneous answers that had flair.

Everyone else responded according to whatever public relations image they thought they were constructing and it never went with what you felt were their real personalities. It's funny how you can never hide what you really are, it's boldly written on every part of you but no one seems to be aware of it. So what they always try to show is what they want you to think they are.

I didn't want to do that. I didn't want to stand there, telling lies to serve some self-serving public relations image. I knew why everybody else was doing it. When confronted by a circumstance in which one realizes the public is watching, one decides the way one speaks and behaves in private is not good enough for the public to see. So one constructs a personality one thinks is acceptable to the public.

There's also the phenomenon of the reporters taking what you said and putting it out in a way that would make you look ridiculous. That was their business. There were no sales, they perceived—and who's to say they're not right—in portraying events that had peace, harmony, honor, love, and integrity as their subject.

If I weren't going to lie, though, wouldn't I have to tell them about the man wearing sheets, carrying a knife? That was how it worked. You either told the truth—or lied. So most people ended up lying.

Everybody had something to hide. How wonderful if you could just go out there and tell people the truth and didn't have to hide a thing.

Maybe—maybe there was a way of telling them enough of the truth without actually telling them about the guy with the knife.

"The truth of the matter is," I said, "when somebody threatens me—and this is why I've done what I've done in the ring—it feels as if it's a matter of life or death and something happens to me that gives me super-strength, super-speed, super-co-ordination, and super-luck. And I'm successful."

Several news people began to speak but the dignified man, through his British doggedness, prevailed.

"Are you saying, then, that, for all you knew, the terrorist might've had the pin out?"

"That's right."

"So you put yourself and hundreds of people in danger because of something that overcomes you when you're threatened?"

I could see him calmly weaving this spider web that would, with my co-operation, engulf me.

"That's true." It's chilling when you perceive some things being looked at from another point of view.

"So the fact you, a number of movie stars, and a great many men, women, and children are alive is due purely to the fact this particular terrorist freakishly didn't do what it would have been normal and more than likely for him to do?"

Now he was tightening his web and they all knew it, tense with expectation. What a headline this would make.

"True."

"Is there anything you can tell us beyond the fact you were 'overcome' by strange forces that caused you to perform such a dangerous act?"

"I've come to the conclusion that there are parts of us, deep within us, that know and plan things we consciously don't seem to be aware of. They cut a path that goes way underneath the surface, one that is synergistic not only to what we as individuals think we want, but to the direction in which the entire universe is going."

I could feel them all salivating at the prospect of my getting weirder and weirder with my theories.

"Are we talking about fatalism and Destiny now?"

They were not even thinking of interrupting him as the dialogue took on this hue that sent us all into a dimension which they thought might pay big journalistic dividends, depending on how far I was willing to put my foot in my mouth.

"No. We're talking about the combination of visions, wishes, and doings of different individuals and groups all converging at any given time upon a single point and one force prevailing while others are being submerged. Which force it is depends on the powers of those who are sending these forces out."

"I'm not sure I understand what you're saying specifically and I'm willing to wager no one else does either." He pronounced "either" with "I," of course.

"I'm saying, sometimes you can do the unexpected, the wrong, the ill-timed thing and execute it badly and it'll come out right. I'm saying I felt with what is very deep within me it was going to come out okay."

"Just like that?"

"Just like that. And I dare say, if you check your history, you'll find the most significant world-changing events didn't take place because of superior forces, greater planning and organization, or logical thinking but because of freakish, outlandish, seemingly spontaneous and illogical coincidences—much like this one. Take the assassination in Sarajevo that touched off World War I. A fanatic with a pistol who, though not a particularly good shot, somehow managed to hit the Austrian Archduke. Another example is World War II, caused by a crazy house-painter, whom no one would have bet on to rise even to middle class status, let alone become the head of his nation and cause an international Holocaust. To add to the irony, this crazy house painter fails to complete his conquest of the world through the purest of flukes. His failure to keep Einstein in Germany and/or to plow on to Stalingrad. It's all material for a French farce. So, please."

See, now this was a gas. The papers, the other media, were never going to communicate the point I was making. They were going to print something equivalent to HOLLYWOOD STAR-FUCKER-CHAMPION-MYSTIC ALMOST BLOWS UP ACROPOLIS and the sub-headline would read, HUNDREDS INNOCENT NARROWLY ESCAPE MASSACRE!

We went on like that for a while and they asked me questions about my one-punch knockouts and I told them again about the feeling my life was being threatened and what happened to me when I got that feeling and then how did I get to know all these stars and what was my connection to them and I told them the truth about that and how what I really wanted to do was act, direct, and write. Like that t-shirt, you know? WHAT I REALLY WANT TO DO IS DIRECT. How would it play out in media language? They'd find a way to make me look silly. But, hell, in for a penny, in for a pound.

They popped questions at me all through breakfast and I answered them truthfully, thinking, *Let's just see what they do with it, there's no way they can really harm me, there's no job they can cause me to lose, nothing anybody can sue me for, as long as I don't tell them about the sheeted man with the knife, let's just have fun with this.*

After breakfast, I excused myself and went back to my room. The phone rang. It was the manager saying I could stay in my room till time for the flight and I was not going to be charged for the extra day.

"That's very nice of you," I said.

"You arr herroi. Ve arr honorrr you herre."

"Aw, gee-whiz, shucks, but thank you, you're very gracious."

"Excuse me, vat ist 'gee-vizz, shucks'?"

"Well, 'gee' is short for Jesus, 'whiz' means something is very good, 'shucks' means 'it's nothing.' All in all, it means I'm very pleased and it's nice of you to say that."

"It is mine pleasurrre. De carrr vill be in frrront at two o'clock dis afterrnoon. Meanvile, if you vould like to heff a turr off de city—"

There was a knock at the door.

"Let me give you a call about that."

"I am yourrr serrviss."

I could swear I heard heels clicking.

"Thank you," I said. "I'll call you." I hung up and went to the door.

I stood before it and wondered whether I should open it. I had become famous, I had downed a terrorist, and therefore, I was fair game for somebody. We lived in a world where, once you did something, you became a target for somebody. That was part of fame if you wanted fame. Anybody could be behind that door and they could do anything to me. It behooved me to be circumspect. Everything, once you were famous, behooved you to be circumspect.

Of course, nowadays, even people who were not famous got struck down, there no longer needed to be a reason.

It had struck me, watching the film *Wild Man Blues*, a documentary of Woody Allen's jazz concert tour through Europe, how sweet, modest, intelligent, and humble the man was and how, no matter how much he tried, he could no longer have a conversation with anyone as his own persona but was always forced to have it as the persona of a celebrity. I don't think it is possible for anyone not famous to understand how frustrating, wasteful, and mechanical it becomes to be talking to one person after another who is having a conversation not with you but with that famous person whose raiment you happen to inhabit.

By the same token, the intimates around you have the consideration that, having gone beyond your famous persona façade and evaluated you for what you really are, they are, in most respects, worthier than you and, therefore, the entire phenomenon of all these crowds adoring you and gaping like sheep is for them a gigantic farce, which they can see right through but have to play along with because the rules are sometimes just as foolish as those crowds. You can see that attitude plainly in Allen's young lover who talks to him with the affection and patience of a caregiver toward a ward whose physical and mental faculties are failing and with whom she has to deal slowly, gently, speaking just a bit louder and more clearly than she normally would. Of course, she is also performing for the cameras but enough of the attitudes come through so you could see where everybody is.

And the man deals with it pretty well, considering, not whining too much as I imagine he might've done when he was younger, almost as if he were doing it because he was expected to, there's a wisdom there that rises above it all and his sense of humor is always there and he cracks a few during the movie, which those who are around him don't seem to catch and appreciate fully because they're too busy dealing with the fame aspect of it all but he's trying to get what he can out of it with all these handicaps heaped upon him.

Out of it all, though, there's a poignancy that comes from this sweet little man playing this wonderful music, being able to get intense and deep enjoyment out of what is truly valuable while everybody else hovers about, bathing in the illusory significance of rubbed-off fame in the manner of all those tiny living forms that cling to the big fish and feed on whatever comes off it.

I wanted to transcend that. I wanted to deal with people as me and I wanted them to be talking to me, not my fame persona.

I opened the door. And there was Hagit Albahari, standing straight and proud as a marine, staring me in the eyes and saying in her thick Israeli accent, "You vont to fock?"

Why, how nice of you to think of it, my dear. And nicer yet to act upon it.

But Israelis were known for not beating about the bush. There is the joke how in the U.N. a Russian, a Pole, an American, and an Israeli are talking and a man approaches with a pen and a note pad. He says, "I beg your pardon, gentlemen, we're conducting a public opinion poll on the current world meat shortage," and the Russian says, "What is 'public opinion'?"

The Pole says, "What is 'meat'?"

The American says, "What is 'shortage'?"

And the Israeli says, "What is, 'I beg your pardon'?"

And why was it that the question of whether she'd come to my room because I'd become known or whether she simply liked me didn't occur to me at the moment?

# CHAPTER TWENTY-EIGHT

Lovemaking with Hagit turned out to be closer to Greco-Roman wrestling than to the poetry of Shakespeare. It's not the way I would idealize it; on the other hand, not much can go wrong when you're making love, no matter what kind of riders you attach to the bill—unless you go into the S&M stuff, which isn't what I'm talking about.

This was just doing things in a very strong, very rough way, banging away, rolling around and around, even falling to the floor and continuing right on, she was like a pouncing tigress bringing down her prey and then it was like she was mauling it the way a dog might take a rag doll and fling it back and forth. And when she came it was a growling howl that I'm sure was heard throughout the hotel and street.

When it was done, we were sweating profusely. She fell asleep immediately and deeply while I gazed about, thinking not many people wait till they're twenty before they make love; but here it was, two wildly different women within a week and I'm in Athens, the very seat of art and culture. There were billions of people in the world, working at jobs they hated, doing things they had to do after work, none of which they particularly liked and, if they were lucky, sneak an hour or two of television, having sex, stuffing themselves with something tasty, or doing whatever they had a fondness for. If we were to divide it up in percentages, what portion of our lives did we spend doing things we really enjoyed and would do if we didn't have to?

And then there were the movie stars I'd been with for a few days. Technically, everything they're doing is something they enjoy doing. But from the look of them and from everything I've read and heard, it's not so. Woody Allen said something that might speak for many. When he's in Europe, he wants to be back in New York, when he's in New York, he wants to be in Europe; wherever he is, he's dissatisfied and would like to be somewhere else. There's even a medical term for it, which he mentioned but which went unacknowledged as so much of what he said seemed to. His young lover admits she hasn't read his books.

Woody doesn't seem to mind, though. He seems to keep struggling, doing things to survive even though the things he's doing are things most of the world feels if *they* could be doing them, they would be wildly happy. Which is what most of the world feels about the lives of all of these stars. Just look at the kinds of places they stay in. An apartment with a swimming pool right inside it, the kind of stuff dreams are made of. But what happens instead? They're dissatisfied. They're not getting good parts, they're getting good parts but not being nominated for the Oscar, they're being nominated but not winning it; it's being bought; they're getting divorced and publicly accused of all kinds of things, they're getting the Oscar but then their careers go downhill, they haven't had a hit movie in five years, the fans are being unreasonable. There's always something not going right and that thing that's not going right is more important than anything else.

Yet, you look at their work and ask yourself, *How can they not be ecstatic, never mind happy?*

But they're not. We're all the same. You get a new car, new puppy, new relationship super-stardom and you're in heaven, life is magic. A short while later, the newness is gone and you're in a worse place than before because here goes another time you thought something was going to make and keep you happy and once again you were betrayed and it takes you down another notch.

That part is the same for everyone even though different things occur to each of us. Is there some kind of control mechanism about all of this stuff each one of us is operating that we're not aware of or familiar with and are, therefore, operating it much as a blindfolded person might shoot at a target he/she has a one-in-a-million chance of hitting?

Hagit was in a deep sleep, mouth slightly ajar, her breathing rhythmic. Her body was what you might call *zaftig*, breasts large and hanging slightly to the side. It was refreshing seeing large breasts that had not been constructed artificially. All those artificial breasts you see on TV and in movies, it was like inflatable dolls.

Why was I wide-awake, alert and full of joy? Wasn't the man the one supposed to roll over and go to sleep after sex? Life had become so exciting I had the feeling I never wanted to sleep. I remembered having felt this as a child. All children fought going to sleep. So much fun for them being awake and playing they want it to just go on and on. Later, the main business of life turns into work and work is something we're not supposed to enjoy and we get tired and never get enough sleep.

I got up, went to the terrace, and sat there naked, looking out at the city. Why couldn't everything be fun? Why couldn't we be gods about everything rather than just a few chosen ones being gods in one activity and shitty like everybody else in all the others?

Why was the guy in sheets and the knife appearing, causing all these fantastic things to happen? I dream of genie.

Secrets. Secrets out there. Could they be unearthed? Or do you just go on with life, living it like animals do, day to day, doing your daily work and eating your daily bread and not giving a thought to the how and why of it all? Give us this day our daily bread.

In all the centuries before the last three decades of the twentieth, people were innocent, full of awe and wonder at the endless miracles, mysteries, and magic of the universe. Then we became oh so cool and matter-of-fact about everything, we made an effort to act in such a way as to give the impression nothing ever surprised us, let alone made us open our mouths in wonder.

Then came the WTC attack and we realized there were things out there we could not be cool about after all. The biggest mysteries, we began to suspect once again, the biggest magic is still out there. If any of us had the slightest thing to do with why this, as opposed to that, is happening out there, we damn well wanted to know about it.

If it's all an accident and coincidence, why, I could be a messenger, a factory worker, a soldier, or a blind man begging on the corner. Things could fall on me, I could get robbed, tortured by the worst diseases, I could die though I might not want to—anything could happen. Are we at the mercy of accidents and coincidences?

This guy wearing sheets, wielding a knife—okay, so he appears only to me. But he's part of this life in which anything can happen and we just stand around, meekly going about our business as if we had no control over any of these things. And if we think we don't, we don't. But the few rare individuals who have in one activity or another risen to the level of gods show us it is possible to rise to that level.

My personal mystery symbol comes in the guise of a man wearing sheets and wielding a knife. He is my key to it all. When I find the answer to why he's there and what he's doing there, I feel I will have the answer to everything that matters.

It's my quest. My glorious quest. To dream—the impossible dream.

Nice. Nice to have a quest. Like Dostoyevsky prescribed. Then everything else falls into a much more manageable perspective.

I went back to bed. Hagit turned and placed her fingers about my penis. Her eyes were still closed and she seemed asleep but she hadn't searched around, it was as if some kind of radar were guiding the hand that landed right on my organ. And, of course, the penis immediately began swelling.

The question of protection had crossed my mind when Sandy had asked me to go with her after the fight. I had dealt with it briefly and simply. Sex with a condom had, ever since I'd learned about sex at the age of ten, felt antithetical to everything I felt about sex—and life. The thrill of it all was in my flesh being in *her* flesh, rubbing against *her* flesh. Flesh to flesh, dust to dust.

Rubbing against the condom, which, in turn, was rubbing against her flesh didn't give me that thrill. I'm not saying I couldn't do it, just it's not the same.

In regard to catching something, I have a sense that humans, like water, seek their own level. Further, I trust my judgment of people with the same certainty that authorities trust dogs to smell out drugs and detectors to ferret out bombs.

There is something else at work here. You know how kids are especially interested in other kids and animals especially interested in their own species? In a similar way—and this is where that law comes into play—we are drawn, whether through repulsion or attraction, to individuals who are emotionally and spiritually on approximately the same level we are.

A great way to test this out is, you work day in and day out in a certain place, you travel about town, look at people, exchange communications with them and you don't notice anything about them aside from their individual characteristics. Then you go away on vacation. You come back. You look at those same people and, lo and behold, they look—tired. Weary, tense, nervous—as people in cities tend to do-- -permanently on guard, dejected, worried. But— why hadn't you noticed it before? In a few weeks you'll no longer notice it. But then, when you return from your next vacation—you'll notice it again.

When you're in the same state they're in, you don't notice their condition. When your condition has changed during your vacation, you notice their condition because now it's different from yours, you're on a different level. But only for a short time. After a few weeks back, you're working and tired and weary, on guard, nervous, and dejected and you no longer notice those qualities in the people around you. You've gone back to their level.

The moment Sandy talked to me after the fight, I had this vision. There would be women. I could engage my thoughts and spirit in making sure I was protected and always have the condom be a spiritual and emotional symbol as well as physical reality between us, or I could trust myself to pick the kind of individual who is on the level I fancy myself to be. That is, not carrying a disease.

Hagit's hand deftly and with surprising gentleness worked on my organ and then, eyes closed, put a leg over and, with uncanny accuracy, impaled herself upon me. She sat there for a while, still somewhat asleep. She made a movement. Then another. Then another. Suddenly, her eyes opened. And then she began moving in rhythm, faster and faster—till she was throwing herself on me, you could hear the thud of flesh against flesh, she turned into a growling beast, grabbing my hair, my flesh, suddenly swinging me over so I was on top, then rolling again so she was on top again, moving faster and faster, coming out with howls that resounded for all the city to hear. I didn't care, though. I realized, since the time Bill Johnson had put the gloves on me and that sheeted knife carrier appeared, I no longer seemed to have my attention on how I was coming over as far as others were concerned. A lack of self-consciousness had come into being. The kind children and very old men and women exhibit, when they're in the mode of saying and doing what they feel like as opposed to what will make the impression one is bent on making.

No matter how many times I thought the strenuous activity, the howls and the growls on Hagit's part were receding, they would pick up again in waves and come pouring out, it was more like two cats that make you wonder whether they're killing each other when they're copulating.

She was doing too much too forcefully and I was unable to hold back as I'd wanted to, the sperm was more or less forced out of me and, after I'd come, she still kept going and I realized there was nothing quite so unwanted as a continuation of lovemaking after ejaculation.

But she was impervious and just kept moving and moving till I was so limp my penis slipped out of her, at which point she moved down, put it in her mouth and started sucking on it and sucking on it and, though I felt she didn't have a ghost of a chance, by God, I had not been acquainted till that point with Israeli persistence and in ten minutes it was growing and swelling again and she came right back on, mounted and resumed her wildness.

This time, since it was such a short period after my last ejaculation, I was able to last much longer and kept up with her till she'd gotten her last explosion out. Then I let mine go and she collapsed on top of me.

A prim elderly woman sits on a bus and hears a man talking to another behind her.

"First-a come-a Emma, den come-a I, den two asses come-a togedder. Den I come-a again, den two asses come-a togedder anodder-a time-a. And again I come-a. Den de two pee-pee, den I come-a again!"

"This is outrageous," the elderly woman shouts to the driver, "to allow such vile talk for decent people to have to listen to."

"What's-a matter for you, lady," the man who had been talking says, "I just teach-a my friend-a how to spell-a Mississippi."

This time both of us fell asleep. As I was drifting off I thought, *You are in Athens for the day, shouldn't you be seeing the city?*

On the other hand, isn't it the height of luxury when you can say to yourself, I'm doing what I *feel* like doing, not what I *should* be doing?

We did not disconnect when we fell asleep and the way I woke up the next time was by her starting to move up and down on me again.

And that was the moment in my life that I said to myself, *There is nothing more ecstasy-producing than this.* This pleasure that two people can induce in one another. A woman from another part of the world—from any part of the world—and me. Just lying together—for hours and hours—making love again and again.

This time she moved very slowly. She would stop for a while, then move again. Very, very slowly—gently—kissing—caressing. After about twenty minutes we rolled over so I was on top. We changed positions every once in a while, trying different ones—but it was all slow and gentle—and loving. We kept it up for an hour.

This time she did not come but I did and then we disconnected and lay, sweating, next to each other.

"Do you have to go back tonight?" she asked.

"No." I could call my mother and tell her I'd be delayed. There was Mangiacavallo. He's upset anyway.

"I could take another day," she said.

I called the manager and told him I'd be staying an extra day and to book a flight for tomorrow. Suddenly, I had arrived at the point where I could tell people that's what I wanted and that's what would happen. Like those stars. Wow!

"Are you hungry?" she asked.

"Starving."

I thought it would be nice to take a walk around Athens, have a bite in some outdoor restaurant like Robert Jordan had dreamed of doing with his girl Maria after the war, then return and sit on the terrace with a liqueur before we went back to lovemaking.

"Let us order room service," she said. "Let us not go anywhere, just stay here and order room service."

Well—all right. If you have to, you have to.

Did you ever stay with someone for hours and all you did was make love and talk and eat and go to the bathroom? It's a wonderful thing. Nothing on your mind except that. Out there, especially if you're into something exciting, you can get carried away. With your work, your games, plans, with your increasing knowledge, it can absorb you.

People like George Bernard Shaw, for instance, didn't have much use for sex. The exercise of his intellect turned him on to such an extent sex came in way down on the scale. He thought, for instance, the positions two grown people had to assume during sex were ludicrous. Well, of course they are. But isn't that part of the excitement? Isn't anything that's part of sex part of the excitement?

Someone who reaches the kind of mental altitude GBS reached looks at things from a different perspective. You take conquerors like Alexander, Napoleon, Hitler, or great minds—Einstein, Diogenes, Plato—I get the feeling none of them gave the kind of importance to sex the rest of us do.

Right now I keep thinking such a thing could never happen to me. But if I continue to be as voracious about reading, learning new things, accomplishing feats I consider to be important to me and the world, who knows but that for me, too, sex would diminish in importance.

Nah.

Someone said sex is like money; when you don't have it, that's all you think about. When you have it, you think about other things. There's something to that too. But from what I can tell, with the passage of time, there is a tendency on the part of individuals to shift the areas upon which they place a sense of importance. It seems to me the problem arises from their fear of this change and their desire for things to stay the same. They constantly strive to prove everything is as it used to be. Or else they go into apathy of succumb and deteriorate like nobody's business. And then they tell you, "You know how it is—gettin' old." "You'll see how it is when you get old." "Let me give you one piece of advice—don't get old."

People think your strength begins to wane as you grow older and that's why you shift your attention from the physical to the intellectual. I think one's attention moves toward the intellectual and ethereal because those provide the truly satisfying things of life. My feeling is the physical recedes because it's less and less important to you while the intangible stuff grows more important. The consideration that this means you're deteriorating came about when your survival depended on your physical prowess. Even when you were young in those days, if your proclivity didn't happen to be physical prowess, you were held in contempt, of no use to anyone. So the loss of physical prowess, whether due to a change of interest or whatever, equaled deterioration and eventual deletion from society. That, of course, equaled death. The Eskimos used to put their old people on a floe and send them out to sea to die.

When you're no longer of any practical use, you're condemned to death. We're not as obvious about it as we used to be, we put the old in old age homes these days where they can live as wilted vegetables for a few years and then die. But they know no one has any use for them any more, they're being tolerated because it would be bad PR these days to put them on a floe. Besides which, most places in the world don't have floes, but the old know they're considered burdens and sense what the wishes of their loved ones underneath the conscious level really are.

There was a French movie years ago, *A Month in the Country*, about this thirty-year-old teacher who is undergoing an emotional crisis in her life and who goes to the country to visit her parents. She feels a great love and respect for her father who has always tried to improve himself and add to his knowledge, but he's suffered a stroke and had great limitations imposed upon his thinking powers, physical movement, and speech. His daughter sits at his feet, hugging his knees. Tears come streaming down the old man's face and he manages the words, "I—I—know—so—so—much."

Think how it would be if, as you grew older, you also grew wiser. Think what wisdom you could reach as the years passed.

But we don't. There was a book once, *Is there Life After High School?* Making the point that, after high school or college, we stop learning, stop dreaming. Or at least stop dreaming about ideals or forming ideas about wonderful things that really matter. After school we start dreaming about possessions and tangible benefits, things you can see, feel, touch, get a sensory kick from.

Not much stock in wisdom placed by society in this day and age. With cable, video games, and the internet around, what in the world would you want with wisdom? Even in the Far East it isn't what it used to be. As America goes, so goes the world.

Yet—sooner or later we all find out it is the most valuable thing there is. The most valuable thing in relationships, business, health, longevity, and happiness or the lack thereof.

But, we think at some point in our lives, when we realize this, of all the things we have sought and possessed, this—wisdom—is what is most valuable, what is most wanted and needed—the alleviation of the emotional ulcer that constantly keeps tugging at our innards— but where is it, this wisdom that brings alleviation? How come we don't have any? Oh, well, it's normal, nobody has any. Where do you get it? Ely Lilly has the answer: take a pill.

So you take a pill. And whatever it was that's been burdening you, handicapping you, goes away—temporarily—coming back with a vengeance bearing a far higher interest rate than credit card payments and you take more pills and it goes away and comes back again till you end up calling for Doctor Kavorkian.

What if you could call upon Mom or Dad or Grandma or Granddad and they'd accumulated so much wisdom in their lifetimes they actually had something that was useful to you—and you were able to regain your emotional and spiritual homeostasis?

I called room service. Ordered all the things Greeks are famous for—and two bottles of wine. And two hard boiled eggs. In memory of the Marx Brothers and the state room scene in *A Night at the Opera*.

While waiting for them to bring up the food, we made love again. I remembered a documentary about male and female monkeys in a cage. Every minute or two they were copulating. From their expressions you couldn't tell it meant anything to them, it was no different from their picking something up off the floor and examining it or putting it in their mouths or picking their noses or ferreting out lice on one another's bodies.

We humans recognize we're supposed to get into a loving mode when we make love. At one time, a long time ago, making love meant total commitment. It had always been the fantasy of man that this be not so. Sure enough, during the sixties, when women thought they were making advances in regard to equality, this fantasy came true for the men. That you could make love to someone you met at a bar or a club or on the street and that you never saw the person again, or see her when you felt like making love again. This fantasy and the fantasy of being able to live with a woman and not have to marry her had been more far fetched than the concept of extra-terrestrials, yet men have pulled them both off during those same sixties when drugs began to run rampant.

We had the waiter set the food out on the terrace. As we ate and drank, we could hear the strains of *Zorba* coming from somewhere in the area. Funny, I thought, that a movie about a Greek played by a Mexican in Greece, distributed and popularized by America, provided the song that became the favorite in Greece and throughout the entire world when there are arrays of folk songs in every nation that are every bit as catchy and inspiring as the *Zorba* theme. I once hummed "Politics and Poker" from *Fiorello* to someone who was with me in a restaurant and a woman sitting at the next table joined me, singing the same exact notes but in Slav words I couldn't understand. Turned out she was Croatian and hardly spoke English. She gave us to understand, though, that it was an old Dalmatian tune dating back at least a couple of hundred years. Through some kind of coincidence or strange sub-conscious processes, *Fiorello's* composer had scored as one of his songs the same notes that had already existed in a foreign nation's folklore half a world away. Later, several music lovers told me the main theme from *Evita*, "Don't Cry for Me, Argentina," was a note-for-note duplicate of a classic melody. Had Harry Truman been right when he said, "The only news is the history you don't know?"

Hagit dug into the food with the same lustiness she had manifested digging into my body. I joined her, not managing to be quite that lusty. I remembered *Tom Jones* and the sexy food-eating scene that has since been replicated in a number of movies. For me, the concept had never worked to begin with. In my universe, food was food and sex was sex and the twain would never meet.

"So what's going to happen with the Middle East?" I asked Hagit. "Is it ever going to be resolved?"

"Not until we and the Arabs all know and understand who lit the original fire that's continued burning all these years."

"Who lit it?"

"The English. Unwilling to give up their holdings, they fixed it so trouble in the area they used to occupy would continue through the decades and people could say, 'It was so peaceful when the British occupied it,' and possibly someone might get the idea they should come back. Of course, the British never learned the lesson that people would rather be miserable, fighting and starving but independent than being forcefully occupied by another power. The only reason the British let go of any of their holdings is because they were forced to by their inability to control such things from a great distance. Ireland has not been so lucky. And you in America are not going to experience true happiness and morality until you settle your debts with the African-Americans and the Native Americans."

"You have any ideas on how that could be done?"

"Details on how something could be done are never a problem. Agreement on whether it *should* be done is always the problem. And this problem has a double foundation. First, you have to admit a wrong has been done—that's very difficult for people to do, to admit it as opposed to giving it lip service—second, it's inevitable that people who have something are going to have to give up something. That may be even more difficult. It may, in fact, be impossible. Our conflict in Israel has always been out there in the open. Yours is constantly brewing, like an ulcer—corroding things inside—until it comes out in the open. The terrorist attacks may be a manifestation of that. Of course, America has been lucky. During every crisis in its history, the right individual has appeared to save it and guide the nation to a higher level, with the rest of the world following. Maybe your luck will continue."

"I'll drink to that," I said, raising my glass.

"Of course," she said, raising hers, "this thing with the Arabs may all come down to the simplest of equations. For, when you consider how Arabs treat their women and how they treat one another, it may simply come down to a question of the civilized against the primitive; good against evil. So, regardless of how it got to that point and all the things that need to be done to set things right, the first thing that needs to be done is that those who have shown themselves to be a danger to the world must be neutralized."

"I'll drink to that too," I said.

We clinked glasses and drank.

# Chapter Twenty-Nine

We separated without allusions to a reunion. When she got to the States, if she felt like it, she would look me up and if I felt like seeing her, I would take a plane to Israel and see her. Might be interesting to see Israel. It *was* supposed to be the homeland. Though, like all things that were *supposed* to be, you had to really check with yourself to see if it was something you felt or something you were *supposed* to feel, or something you had decided a long time ago you were supposed to feel and were now just pulling it out of the file. Neither my mother nor I were very religious. Strangely enough, my grandmother wasn't either, although she was probably more religious than my mother and I, I being the least religious of the three. Each generation got less religious.

I wondered why. Religion was supposed to be the link to our souls. Was the falling off of religion a way we were cutting our links to our souls—or was there a new religion needed to do the job that had to be done in these modern times?

Whichever, it was a cinch we would all be cast further and further adrift without it—like those old Eskimos on their floes.

I loved the freedom and fun of being able to go where I wanted whenever I wanted and with whom I wanted. It wasn't full freedom, though, as long as everything I had was due not to Jeannie with the light brown hair but to the genie with the knife. At any time, that genie could disappear and everything I had would disappear right along with it. There is nothing as insignificant or as pathetic as an ex-champion or an ex-star.

What I was experiencing now could make me a very sad person in years to come. To have had a taste of being independent and famous and then sink into anonymity and no money—. The person who'd said, " 'Tis better to have loved and lost than never to have loved at all," may not have had it right.

Life, unlike our universities, did not offer you tenure in anything. One was always rolling the dice—and then living out the consequences of the roll.

It was F. Scott Fitzgerald who had said the only difference between poor people and the rich was that the rich had money. And money makes so many things so much easier.

There are people who take the bus to the airport and others who take the train. If you're in a strange country and don't speak the language, you wonder whether you're getting on the right bus or train, then you wonder if, once on the train, you're in the right car. Then you wonder at which stop you're getting off. Is it the right one or is it going to be that, somehow, there had been a miscommunication and you should've gotten off at the stop before or after? True in New Jersey as well—even if you speak the language. You ride on a bus there and it seems the driver will be caught dead before he'll announce what stop he's making and what the next stop is going to be. Communication, dear Lord.

When you have money, all this is eliminated. Somebody carries your bag, puts it in the car that has come to pick you up, the car deposits you exactly where you have to go, somebody takes the bag out of the car and puts it where somebody else takes it and so on.

And then you travel first class. First class on a plane epitomizes what being rich means. It means you board first and settle into wide, comfortable chairs with plenty of room all about. The primary idea is to have you not wait, the bonus being that, as the coach passengers are boarding, you are already sitting in your comfortable chair from where you can watch them marching past and say to yourself, "Those poor schmucks."

You have your oversized overhead bin where you put your bag and whatever else you've got without having to squeeze it in with a bunch of other people's stuff. The flight attendant takes your jacket and hangs it up for you. They ask you if you'd like a drink or a snack—

whatever. Not only do they ask, they encourage—they make you feel it would please them if you had some champagne, or whatever. If they're young and attractive, they make you feel, if you asked them for a date, they'd jump at the chance. It is, I understand, the way it used to be many years ago for coach travelers. Those were the days when flight attendants, a.k.a. stewardesses, wrote such best sellers as *Coffee, Tea or Me?*

One of the ways the world fundamentally changed after the attack on the World Trade Center was we all realized, without anyone voicing it—it didn't really matter whether you traveled first class or coach.

The attendant who took care of me was a young woman named Rachel. She was red-haired, slim, medium height and, if you saw a photograph of her, you'd not think her beautiful, yet there was something about the eyes that was beautiful because gentle, benevolent, delicate and—vulnerable. She had that melodic, resonant, Mid-West-American-prototype voice that could be heard distinctly but was not loud. I watched her as she went about her work and I was overcome with the realization that there was an infinity of people, things, happenings and they were all different from one another and there were so many people who were so appealing in such a variety of ways I thought what a pity when a person gets stuck on one experience or one person and feels there will be nothing to equal it and the threatened loss of it results in tragedy. If all those people changed their consideration and projected themselves a little in time, they would see how true it is that each ending begets a beginning and within weeks spiritual spring begins to blossom and new, equally wonderful, sometimes even more wonderful experiences come around to take the place of those past.

A popular forties' character film actor, Walter Slezak, told the story of his father, Leo Slezak, who had been a famous European opera singer. The story was about a scene in an opera where Slezak the elder was to sing an aria front center stage, after which he was to hop onto a boat moored behind him, in the rear part of the stage, and sail away into the sunset.

The boat was constructed in the shape of a swan and the scene in which Slezak sings the aria, after which the swan-boat is pulled away by concealed stage hands off stage as Slezak, having sung his song, stands proudly on the prow, was the highlight of the opera, greatly appreciated and anticipated by audiences everywhere.

During one particular performance the stagehands jumped the gun and pulled the swan-boat off the stage while Slezak, facing the audience, was still singing the aria and could not see the boat had sailed without him. Completing his song, Slezak turned and, marched to where the boat had always been, but now wasn't.

Without missing a beat, he turned to one of the extras standing on the "dock" and said, "Excuse me, what time does the next swan leave?"

Rachel brought me champagne and I thanked her with a smile that told her how much I liked her—not for the purpose of getting her into the sack but for her unique endearing characteristics.

I wonder, really, how sincere we are when we tell ourselves we are being charming to a woman for reasons other than getting her into the sack and wasn't the success of the world's Casanovas due partly to the fact they were in there pitching all the time?

She kept bringing me stuff throughout the trip and asking me was there anything else I wanted. She asked the other passengers as well but I felt there was something special in the way she looked at and spoke to me. For all I knew, the other passengers might've felt the same. The entire atmosphere in which people were being treated as if they were important and worthy created a kind of holiday feeling, somewhat like the Christmas season during which everyone is in the thrall of that special magic where life is being lived as if it were a wonderful and wondrous experience and encounters between people reflected that magic glow.

An old Japanese woman came in from coach and was trying to communicate with Rachel but her English did not seem to be up to it and Rachel began talking to her in Japanese. They exchanged several sentences and Rachel appeared quite fluent in the language. At the end of the conversation, Rachel bowed to the woman and the woman bowed back and returned to coach.

"What did she want?" I asked Rachel.

"She said her back hurt and could she lie on the floor in the aisle here."

"What'd you say?"

"I told her she couldn't."

"Where did you learn Japanese?"

"I live in Japan."

"How long have you lived there?"

"Three years. As a rule, my route is Tokyo to Newark and back. This was an exception."

"So I could get to meet you," I said.

She stared right into my eyes. "That's right."

"What appealed to you about Japan?"

"They were the only people I'd met anywhere who didn't exhibit an attitude. The only thing they exhibit is helping the person with whom they're dealing. It's almost as if they were able to erase their egos in the process. I find them civilized."

"Interesting. My only contact with them is the few I've seen from a distance in New York, taking photographs, and the depiction of them in World War II movies."

"People who live away from their homeland are fish out of water—flipping around but really dying. As to their depiction in World War II movies—what is there to say?"

"Still—there *is* World War II itself."

"That part is difficult to explain. I'm not sure myself of the reason—except, perhaps, convinced they were superior, they felt the need to make it a tangible reality. Not that war or conquest can ever be justified. I just think they chose the wrong way to spread their influence."

"Like the Germans?"

"They're nothing like the Germans. Go around the world and ask natives of various countries which people they dislike the most and it's invariably the French first and the Germans second. No one ever has a bad word about the Japanese."

"Still—trying to conquer the world is not exactly a slip of the tongue."

"This is several generations later. Don't you believe people can change?"

"You think the Germans have changed?"

"I don't think Germans *can* change."

" 'The fundamental things apply—as time goes—'?"

I gave her one of my cards and she moved on to service other flyers who had begun to glance at her with the kind of resentment people feel when someone is being given preferential treatment and, as far as the other male flyers, there was the age-old tradition of resentment springing from the *Coffee, Tea or Me* syndrome.

I leaned back and closed my eyes. No—life was not like a well—it was a thing of ecstasy. Sandy and all those stars had left and there was Hagit and then Hagit left and here was Rachel—life was a thing of ecstasy—every moment. If I had dwelled on the person and the adventure that had been—would I have been open to the adventure that was coming?

Was there anything more delicious, delightful, and wondrous in life than to love and to have those who can be your partners in love appear one after another to provide you with an infinite number of joys and pleasure?

"This is the captain speaking," came over the system, "we have a slight technical problem which needs looking into. Nothing to cause any alarm but we *are* turning back to Athens where we'll have this little matter attended to and then we'll be on our way. No, we are not being hijacked so rest easy."

There was a lot of looking by the passengers from one to the other. Rachel and I exchanged glances and she smiled at me. I smiled back and wondered if we were thinking the same thing.

I remembered a Joan Rivers routine in which she'd talked about standing in line to get on a plane when she heard the booming voice of a man say, "If God meant us to fly, he would've given us wings," and when she'd looked at who'd said it, it turned out to be the pilot.

# CHAPTER THIRTY

**A** glorious adventure on the town with Rachel that ended up in a hotel room. She was just as sweet to be with over a sustained period as she was over the short. She had a family in New York and a fiancé in Osaka, Japan.

"I don't know why I did this," she said after we'd made love the first time and were lying in bed side by side. "I'm not the unfaithful type. Never thought I'd cheat. I guess it shows what can happen when the right circumstances and opportunity all come together."

On the plane ride back, Rachel was even more attentive and this time we shared our little secret and re-lived in our glances all the wonderful moments we'd spent together in Athens. If she wanted to, she could call me when she hit New York. My own special secret was it wasn't something I would give thought to. If it happened, great. If it didn't, there was an infinity of wonderful beings and adventures out there.

"Where'd you go, you bastid?" Mangiacavallo wanted to know when I called him from my apartment. I had rented a one-bedroom at 365 West End, four blocks from Schwab House, where my mother and Alex lived. They had found a one-bedroom for my grandmother in an apartment building half a block north on West End Avenue, where a lot of old people lived.

"You missed my fuckin' shindig," he went on without waiting for my answer. "I had everybody come down to see ya. Was it wit de bimbo came to your dressin' room?"

261

"Yeah."

"So you're in wid de glamour crowd, I guess Maria's outta de pitcher."

"Maria was never really more than a friend."

"Dat's not what she tought."

"I can't help that."

"You kissed'r, din'ya?"

"Once."

"Once, twice, ten times, what's de difference?"

"You kiss somebody and you get the real feeling of what it is."

"You don't know what you feel before you kiss?"

"Kind of, but when you kiss you know for sure."

"You can't play wid a girl's heart like dat, you know. Women put deir hearts on de block dere, you know, an' de man, he's holdin' de axe. You not supposed to chop dat heart in two. It's a sin, you know? 'Specially a girl comes from de old country, dey're serious about stuff like dat dere."

"You're right. I didn't really know that much about it, I was kind of innocent too."

"Not any more, dough, huh?"

"Not any more."

"Well—what can I say. Pro'bly just as well for you not to settle down yet, we'll find somebody for Maria—somebody ain't gonna chase after glamour pussies. We gotta start makin' plans about who we gonna fight next. How about we have lunch tomorra, you'll come down to my coffee shop."

"I was thinking of taking some time off."

"You just took some time off. Listen, nobody's hotter'n you right now, we gotta make hay here. You got what dey call a li'l wind'a opportunity here. It closes like dat. Make de money while it's open, it closes like dat."

"Guys take six months to a year between fights."

"For tax purposes and to work up a big gate. Different for you. We have ways of gettin' around de tax and you gonna be a sell-out no matter how often you fight, a guy dives, knocks de udder guy out wid one punch—people eat dat up—forget about it. You come down to lunch tomorra at one, we discuss it."

I went to visit my mother, stayed for dinner. My mother was upset over Alex leaving a remunerative, secure job at an established salon on Madison Avenue and striking out on his own by leasing a place on 57th Street between Madison and Fifth. They had been doing so well on his job and on the Saturdays and Wednesday evenings when they worked out of a little room on 55th Street and now Alex was about to ruin it all by investing all their money in a posh salon of his own where whatever money they made would be eaten up by the rent. And then you had to hire stylists and manicurists and a receptionist, my mother got sick just thinking about it. Then the stylist would take his clients and go to another place or open up his own shop, it happened all the time. Heartaches. One heartache after another.

*Heartaches, heartaches,*
*Why does it happen that your heart aches?*

But there was no holding Alex back. He possessed the kind of energy that just had to keep exercising itself. Not only did he strike out on his own but, at my mother's insistence, he had bought a plot of land by the water in Island Park, a suburb of Long Beach, Long Island, where he was building a house into which they were planning to move. But even that wasn't enough. Already he was looking for a place he could rent in Long Beach where they could open a beauty salon to operate Saturdays and Wednesday evenings when they weren't working in New York.

He would wake up at five A.M. every day and start preparing for work. On Sundays he would drive to Hoboken for fresh Italian bread just as it was being taken out of the oven. On the way back, he would stop at Manganaro's on Ninth Avenue and stock up on all kinds of Italian delicacies. Then he would spend the next several hours cleaning the apartment. If it was summer, they would go to Sherwood Park and spend the afternoon at the beach, roasting and eating the goodies he'd brought from Manganaro's and the bread from Hoboken he'd begun to eat chunks of much earlier.

Alex was born in Molfetta, the southern part of Italy, the youngest of eleven children. Because there is a strong class distinction in Italy between those who are from the north and those who are from the south, the dividing line being roughly Rome, for a long while, Alex told people he was from Milan, which is about as far north as you can get without stepping over into Switzerland.

He was the only sibling who'd left the village in which they were all born and raised, another example of individuality triumphing over environment and circumstances. Here were eleven children all raised in the same way, living in the same place, yet one strikes out and moves to another part of the world, one goes to another part of the country while all the others stay right where they are.

Generally, it turns out to be like that. In every family there's one whose vision goes beyond what's around. And it's like that all over the world. We happen to be lucky in the U.S. but in most places, people live in misery and you wonder why they stay there. Some go, of course, but most are content to stay where they are. Probably, if things were bad in the States and good somewhere else, most of us would also be content to stay where we were.

And then there're people like Alex. People who are always looking for a new lane. People who keep scrambling, hustling, not going around cheating or stepping over others but working very, very hard. They're the ones who keep the economy going. In their own countries they manage to keep their heads above water but in this country they get rich with a fraction of the work they did in their homeland.

They eat and work and get bits of pleasure here and there and take care of themselves and their families. They're the woof and warp of every society and always have been.

Theoretically, we are aware there is more to life. Prophets throughout history have reminded us of it time and again. They have told us exactly how we should act toward one another to reach the state of grace. Abe Lincoln had gone so far as to say, "A man is as happy as he chooses to be." Of course, it holds for woman as well—especially seeing as how, according to statistics, six times as many women get seriously depressed as men.

How much has that knowledge affected us? Not very much. We are willing to be moved by great feelings and deeds we witness but unwilling to consider they have anything to do with us. Unwilling to move above the level of animals—except technologically.

Gary Larson of *The Far Side* has a cartoon in which two explorers get a flat tire on a jungle road and stand around, looking in helplessness at their vehicle and you get the idea they've never changed a tire in their lives. Suddenly, an ape swings down from the trees on a vine, grabs a jack and changes their tire, then swings away up into the trees again and one of the explorers says, "What a great ape!"

Technology—mechanics. When you are at close quarters with someone you love and who loves you—what you know or don't know about technology and mechanics makes not the slightest difference. It is only for a very short period that a person will be struck by your expertise or fame or stardom or wealth—after which he/she will look at, judge, and deal with what's inside you. If we were to get a private glimpse of how the famous people we idolize are being treated by their intimates and vice-versa, we would be shocked to our core. In no way does it resemble the feelings and actions they manifest publicly.

Alex, like so many billions, was looking out for himself first and his family second, third, fourth, fifth, etc. And, like so many other millions, he longed for his homeland. Going to another land when you are past the age of seven or eight, you are as Rachel had said, a fish out of water. You never get quite integrated with your new land and the older you are when you arrive, the less integrated you are. Alex would say to my mother, "If one of us dies, I'm packing my bags and going back to Molfetta."

"If one of us dies," my mother would say each time, trying to point out the irony in the way he'd phrased it, but Alex wouldn't get it.

After he got word from his legal connections in Italy that his American divorce would be recognized and he would not be arrested for bigamy when he set foot upon Italian soil, Alex went back to Molfetta for a visit.

When he returned to the U.S., he was not nearly as enthusiastic about Molfetta as he had been before the trip. "Everything's shrunk," he said. "The people too, they're all smaller. One fellow's bent over so far that when he joined us at the table I couldn't see him. I'd keep hearing his cackling and have to remind myself there was someone sitting in that chair."

The talk to my mother about his going back to Molfetta if one of them died ceased.

I went to pick up my grandmother so I could walk her to my mother's for dinner. It wasn't she couldn't've come by herself but she liked to have me visit. First thing she did when I got there was put some meat pies and strudel in the oven so I'd have something to eat.

"We're going back to have dinner," I said.

Didn't matter. In the olden days food was the most precious item and when you wanted to make someone feel good, you offered them food. So the old timers always insist you eat. So I ate.

I could see the chair near the window that looked out on West End Avenue. My grandmother sat there for various periods throughout the day, watching people and traffic. She had grown up in the years when there was no television, when your entertainment and stimulation came from other people so that was what she was used to. She'd look out that window for hours and hours.

For me it's incomprehensible. I don't like a minute to go by without pouring something I consider useful into this brain of mine. Been that way ever since I'd read a book called *The Brain*, written by a well regarded scientist, in which he said the brain was like a muscle with respect to its capacity for development and power proportionate to how much you put into it and exercised it. Simply put, the more you used it, the better it got. Like love. Ooo-la-la. It got to me. Epiphany.

After this, I started buying books on different subjects, reading from each one every day and marking off the spot where I'd left off. The concept of the brain and mind growing mightier by the day appealed to me above all else. Well, not above all else, I still thought sex was the best but I could also see, as time went by, how the pleasure I might experience from a very high level functioning of the mind might, as in the case of George Bernard Shaw and people of that ilk, prove to be greater than the sensation of orgasm and the games surrounding it. After all, if the real name of the game was for humans to achieve their highest potential, then the spirit and the intellect were the areas to be explored rather than the realm of sensations, which any animal could indulge in. Of course, animals didn't tie and whip each other as part of sex play but a lot of them certainly did a lot of scratching and biting.

"I'm thinking of getting a dog," I said to my grandmother.

"Why?" she asked.

"I like them."

"What use is a dog?" she asked. "They can't even bring you a glass of water."

"No, but maybe I could train it to flush the toilet or turn the gas off on the stove in case I forget."

She gave me a look. My grandmother was not into teasing.

"Who's going to take him out when you're away?" she asked. A dog was always a "he."

"That's my only consideration. If I got a Jewish dog, you think you might take him out for me sometimes?"

"What do you mean, a Jewish dog?"

"You know—a collie."

"Why is a collie a Jewish dog?"

She was frowning heavily.

"Has that nose—you know?"

She stared at me. For quite a while. Almost as long as the pauses actors take on the screen before saying a line. "You could get slapped for something like that."

"You haven't heard that in Germany, during Hitler's time, collies had to wear a yellow band around their left front paw, saying, '*Ich bin ein Juden*'?"

"One more remark like that and you're *going* to get slapped."

It's not that my grandmother didn't have a sense of humor. Just you'll find that Jews, when it comes to jokes about them, tend to lose their sense of humor—even if the jokes are being made by other Jews. Probably because every time a group took to persecuting them and ended up by slaughtering them, it always began with jokes.

We walked back to my mother's place. My grandmother was short and somewhat plump with heavy legs that had, for as long as I could remember, been swollen from the knees down. These swollen parts were always full of scratch marks, redness, and pieces of old, flaky skin dropping off. They itched and she scratched them with a comb. It was the same with her arms below the elbow. As a child, I wasn't bothered by the scratching. Growing up, as with so many things, I began to be disgusted by it.

"Hey, champ," a slim man with a thin, light brown mustache said as my grandmother and I were walking toward Schwab House.

My grandmother looked at him, then at me, puzzled.

At first I thought I must know the guy from somewhere but then I remembered I was now in a position where thousands knew me whom I didn't know.

"Hi," I said, trying not to assume the air of a celebrity but that of a friendly guy who's in the same boat as everybody else.

He stopped. I stopped too and held on to my grandmother's arm so she could not continue for I knew she'd just keep on walking. Old people have a tendency to lose their inclination for niceties.

"Hey, I gotta tell you," he said, "with all due respect for the interruption, I don't know if what you do can be classified as boxin'. I don't know what you *could* classify it as but I gotta tell you the troot, it's hard to think of it as boxin'. But, hey, people trooout history come up wid stuff most of the world says, 'Hey, dis ain't dis.' Then, later on, it turns out, hey, it *is*. Know what I'm sayin'?"

"I do. Will you pay sixty bucks to watch the next one on Pay-per-View?"

"Hey, I'm there. Except I gotta tell you, I got an illegal box, I get all the channels for nothin'."

"But if you didn't, would you pay to see it?"

"Hey, I'm there."

"There you go."

"Hey, but, you know, there's lot'a people out there payin' to watch wrestlin' too, you know."

"You got a point."

"You got it."

"See you around," I said.

"Keep takin'em out, champ."

"But will you still love me if I don't?"

My grandmother and I began walking.

"Yeah, an' you know why?" he called out after me.

"Why?"

"'Cause you're a good guy, talkin' to me like this, not like the others with their nose up in the air."

"We're all in the same boat, buddy."

By now, my grandmother and I were under the Schwab House awning and it had become a shouting dialogue. *Shane — oh, Shane — my mother needs you — needs you — needs you. Shane — Shane — Shane — Shane.*

"That's the ticket," the man shouted. "Name's Kenny."

"Glad to meet you, Kenny."

"Glad to meet you, champ."

See how friendly New York can be?

My mother liked us all to have dinner together at least once a week. Of course, she saw my grandmother every day and bought things for her and when she and Alex went somewhere, they took her along. Alex was very good and respectful to my grandmother. As a matter of fact, she even rode in the front seat of the car next to Alex when they went somewhere, while my mother sat in the back. I found out that's how you know the depth of someone's love. How much they like your kids, your relatives, and your pets. If they don't like them—there's gonna be trouble in River City.

When the soup was served, my grandmother and I had a set dialogue.

I would say, "Mmm, this soup is good."

And she would say, "You like soup?"

And I would say, "Yes."

And she would say, "Do you want me to teach you how to make it?"

And I would say, "No."

"Why not?"

"Too much time and effort when I can buy it ready-made at Fairway."

"Store bought is never as good."

"Good enough when you don't feel like making your own."

"Mister Big Shot—throwing away money."

Another thing that would happen was she'd always forget to bring something she needed to the table or else she'd get up to go to the kitchen and get something she'd just thought of and I'd always say to her, "Why do you have to get up, just tell me what you want and I'll get it for you," and she'd say, "I can get my own things."

One evening she started to get up and I was ready for her, jumping up from my chair, reaching out for her shoulders and pressing her down back onto the chair.

"Tell me what you want," I said, "I'll get it for you."

"Leave me alone," she said, trying to get up again.

"Keep your seat," I said, pushing her down, "and tell me what you want."

"Let me go," she said, struggling up.

"No," I said, pushing her down again. "You're not getting up. Tell me what you want."

"I want to go to the bathroom."

I rejoiced each time I entered my apartment. I had not been in it long enough to take it for granted.

Actually, I was very vigilant about not taking anything for granted. I kept seeing this phenomenon all around and was convinced this was the very thing that brought ruin across the board, down to the deterioration of our bodies and spirits. You started out by being very enthusiastic about something, then, when you had it for a while, you got used to it and took it for granted and it was like it didn't exist except for the fact you utilized it. I remembered when Alex bought his new car, how he would keep it clean, even get out on red lights to take little spots off it, he couldn't bear to have even a tiny piece of dirt on it. Later on, though, he would just take it in for a wash and that would be that. It was like that with everyone. You saw married couples throwing little barbs at each other all the time, putting each other down in addition to having knock-down drag-out fights. I was determined this would not happen to me. I didn't know exactly how I was going to prevent it if everybody around me was falling prey to it but I was determined it would not happen to me. Somehow, I would work it so, if I appreciated something greatly at the beginning, my appreciation would grow instead of lessen.

If it was that easy, why didn't more people do it? Maybe no one thought of it as a scourge and an enemy as I did. Or maybe they thought there was just nothing you could do about it.

Much as I loved my mother and got along well with Alex, it was wonderful to have your own space, be able to do anything you wished to do whenever you wanted to and have no one else to consider. There was such a sense of freedom in it. As a child, I remembered finding little spaces where I could be by myself and it always felt so good.

The phone rang. I let the machine take it. It was like having a secretary, only better. With a secretary you'd have to indicate you didn't want to speak to the person and then she/he would have to lie by saying you were unavailable. With a machine you simply listened and if at that time you did not want to speak to that person, it was your business and no one else's.

"Hi," this beautiful voice I recognized immediately said, then paused. People who have distinctive voices rarely identify themselves. They know they'll be recognized.

I picked up. "Hi, Sandy," I said.

"How's my baby?" she said.

"From a mother who left her baby on a Greek doorstep for adoption?"

"That what you feel happened?"

"If you're gonna talk like that, let me go lie on the couch, set the timer for fifty minutes and locate my checkbook."

"What do you mean?"

"Wasn't there a definitive goodbye when you left?"

"Is there such a thing as definitive any more than there is an absolute?"

"You're every bit as cute as ever, my darling; I believe even GBS would enjoy conversing with you."

"Why, thank you, kind sir, a worthy compliment indeed, not that I feel for a moment I don't deserve it."

"What's on your mind, honeybun?"

"A hundred and one pounds of fun," she sang, then stopped and switched to dialogue. "I miss you."

"Something you hadn't expected when you said goodbye?"

"You might say that."

"Could we go again over the reason you dropped me as if I were a hot plate just out of the micro-wave?"

"I see we're serving crow tonight."

"One wants to serve the appropriate thing to the appropriate guest."

"Like to see a little crawling, would you?"

"I like to solve mysteries."

"Such as?"

"Why someone as intelligent and calculating as you would do something as decisive and meaningful as breaking up with a guy, making it very clear it's goodbye, and then call up a few days later and get all lovey-dovey."

"Everybody except the studio and the producer feels there was an overreaction about leaving you the way we did. Matter of fact, no one but the producer and the studio were even aware we were deliberately leaving you behind. The others were told we had to leave for security reasons and that you had other plans and that was why you weren't coming with us. I was talking to Brad just today, as a matter of fact, and he said he would never have gone had he known you were being deliberately left behind. Matter of fact, he admires what you did and said he'd like to do a movie about you. I think he's thinking of either producing or directing—or maybe both, who knows. You know how he likes stories about fighting and the way you do it fascinates him. He also admires the things you did on the trip, you know, singing the Marseillaise at the airport and diving on that guy with the bomb just like you do at your opponents in the ring. And, of course, I reminded him how we plan to write a book about your life."

"The fog begins to clear."

"Of course, it doesn't mean that was my motive for calling you. You know how I feel about you, I think you've had ample proof of that."

"If ample fucking is ample proof, I've certainly had ample proof. But let me backtrack for a moment. You say the studio and the producer were the only ones who were aware I was being left in Athens flat as a Hungarian *palascinta*?"

"Your analogies, darling, for some reason, wax culinary, but that's essentially correct."

"Think hard now—wasn't there one other person who knew?"

"Don't do this, Dan. Think of what's at stake here. There's a window here to something that's a dream. Movies. Brad Pitt wants to do something with you, which guarantees a major production. Not only that, but you and I work together, hang out, do what we love to do between writing, take little trips here and there, combine business with pleasure—this kind of opportunity doesn't open up to ninety-nine-point-nine percent of the people anywhere at any time during their entire lives. To the remainder it happens once. Never twice. Why create a problem where a problem doesn't exist? All right, it was panic time. Everybody was leaving, so I left, so what? Nothing terrible happened. I reserved you a flight later that evening, nothing much was lost, just we didn't travel together, is that such a big deal? Why would you jeopardize something so valuable for something as silly as what happened in Athens? Nothing happened, in fact, except we traveled on different flights."

As so often occurs to me at significant, and even insignificant, moments, I think of a scene in a movie. This time it was *It's a Wonderful Life*, the scene in which James Stewart is sitting at the bank with Lionel Barrymore, the bank owner, who tries to talk him into giving up the lending concern left to him by his father and joining forces with him. The deal Barrymore is offering seems so good. Stewart and his wife Donna Reed could have all the things they'd been dreaming of, their future would be secure. He shakes hands on the deal. While shaking hands, he suddenly has a realization. He looks at his hand that shook the old man's and you could see he feels as if that hand were full of slime. And he changes his mind about the deal.

Mephistopheles is always at work. The difference is that in the olden days people actually stopped to wrestle with their consciences a while before going along. Today, there is no such wrestling, not even the phony kind we watch on TV.

I actually considered it—I said to myself, *I could work with this woman, make the deal, and not let it interfere with my personal feelings about what she'd done.*

"You know what?" I said.

"What?"

"I don't want to."

"If you have any idea you're going to get in touch with Pitt and make the deal directly, get over it. If he feels you're screwing me over and there're bad feelings anywhere around the project, *he'll* drop you like a *palascinta*, you can trust me on that. The man's got hundreds of projects being offered him, you think he'll want to get involved in something that comes with bad vibes?"

"Frankly, my dear—"

"Oh, I don't believe this. Could you be *so* egotistical that you would spit on the biggest opportunity that'll ever come your way?"

"Grace under pressure, my dear. The moment of truth."

"You know what? I'm not gonna let you commit career suicide. I'm

gonna keep after you till you say yes."
    "That could be fun."
    "You have no idea how persistent I can be."
    "Definitely fun."

# CHAPTER THIRTY-ONE

Mangiacavallo's place was buzzing. Not an empty table. You take a walk in Paris, Athens, New York in the middle of the day — or any time of day, morning, afternoon, whenever—and if it's nice weather you'll see the outdoor and indoor coffee shops and restaurants full of people. I'm told you can go from Bosnia all over Europe to the Middle East and it's the same thing. From the tiniest villages to the big cities—throughout the entire working day and late into the night—people sitting around, drinking, eating, chatting.

Store windows are full of expensive stuff—in Bosnia as well as in the big, expensive cities of the world. Plus there are flea markets with cheap goods from China, more of them in Bosnia after the war than ever, and more of them now all over the world than ever before. And cars, planes, trains, buses—continually moving, day and night, 24-7-30-365, on and on and on. Our constant whiff of reality on how many people there are, how much motion and how much money.

After embracing and kissing me (something I could've done without), Mangiacavallo led me into his private garden, which was sealed off and soundproofed from his restaurant garden where the public ate. There were all kinds of flowers, greenery, and even grape vines surrounding us. We might've been in some little bower in Italy's heartland. We sat at a table in the center covered with a white tablecloth and Mangiacavallo's bodyguard poured us each a glass of wine.

"So, *paisan*," Mangiacavallo said, "ya popped your cherry, had a good time?"

"Had a good time."

"So what you talkin' about, time off, what is dat?"

"Like some time off."

"An' do what wid it?"

"Acting, writing, directing."

"What do you mean? Like show business?"

"That's right."

"So why you go into boxin'? Why you come here an' tell me you want me to set up fights fer ya? So you could become champ an' den retire?"

When you want something badly enough, you never look at it from the other person's viewpoint. Now I was going to have to.

"I'm talking about taking the amount of time off that other fighters take," I said, making a strategic retreat. "I know you've told me the reason they take time off has to do with taxes and building up the gate but I don't want to do the Joe Louis kind of thing, fighting the bum of the month. That means I'm constantly in training and doing nothing else."

"So what's wrong wid dat? You do dat a few years, you're a billionaire, you don't have to work de rest'a your life. 'Less you stupid like Tyson'n trow you money away. You could put up de money for your own shows or movies or whatever you wanna do, you could have control of all dat instead of goin' to all dese people witch your hat'n your hand."

"I don't want to bury myself for a few years. I don't wanna do it even for a few days."

"You could get your rocks off now and den — like you did dese few days."

"Weekend pass, huh?"

"Dat's it. Meanwhile, you makin' money hand over fist, ain't dat what you people love?"

"You mean us yids?"

"You yids, us wops, de chinks — we all love it."

"Think people'll pay Pay-per-View to watch me fight every month?"

" HBO's awready offered us a contract."

"In three, four months people would get sick of it. Same thing over and over every month."

"Numbers fall off, we stretch it out."

"Once they're sick of you, they're sick of you forever. Not only that, but if you make a contract for a certain number of appearances, you can't go changing your mind mid-stream."

"So we make it once every tree months."

"Still too often. Six months."

"Four months."

"Five-and-a-half."

"Five."

"On one condition."

"Conditions yet."

"The next one to take place in seven months."

"Why such a long time, why?"

"Let the anticipation build. You know that commercial—'Anticipation is making me wait'?"

"It can build in tree months. We strike while de iron's hot."

"No."

"Yes."

"No."

"I don't know what you're about, I swear to God. Here you got de sweetest gimmick in de woild dat can make you millions an' you wanna wile away time bein' a pussy actor. I don't unnerstand dat."

"A year-and-a-half ago I came into this place and talked you into something, didn't I?"

"Dat's what I'm talkin' about—da follow-tru, *capisch*?"

"Listen to me, *stronzolo*—"

"Don't call me dat, dat's not a nice woid."

"I take it back, listen to me, *stronzolo*."

"I tole you not to call me dat."

"I told you I take it back. Listen to me, *stronzolo*—"

"You know, one'a dese days you gonna get hoit."

"I told you I take it back, who loves you, baby?"

"*Va fa'n culo*, my mudder loves me, dat's who, dat's de on'y one."

"When I came in here a year ago and tried to talk you into backing me as a fighter, you thought I was full of shit."

"I backed ya, di'n I?"

"And how long did it take before I could make you see it?"

"An' your point?"

277

"My point is learn to trust me, listen to me when I talk to you."

"You are so full'a shit I cannot believe my ears. I don't even know what we're talkin' about no more."

"What we're talking about, number one, is there's a good reason fighters take off between fights and it's not taxes."

"When Louis was fightin' de bum-a-de-month dey was interested."

"That was before multi-media and internet. Now their attention span is much shorter, now they want a lot more variety."

"You just comin' up wid stuff 'cause you don't wanna fight?"

"Who came to you 'cause he wanted to fight in the first place?"

"Yeah, but since dat time you apparently discovered show business, pussy."

"Listen to me, *stronzolo*—"

"I tole you not to call me dat, I'm not kiddn' aroun' now."

"Oh, you can call me pussy but I can't call you *stronzolo*?"

"You wanna be in show business, you a pussy."

"And you a gangsta *stronzolo*."

"I tole you not to call me dat."

"You call me pussy, I call you *stronzolo*, that's how it is."

"If I don't call you pussy, you don't call me *stronzolo* no more?"

"All things being equal."

"What does *dat* mean?"

"Means unless you come up with something else that's unworthy."

"I'm not gonna be called a *stronzolo*, I mean dat now."

"And I'm not gonna be called a pussy—or anything else derogatory."

"Dere he goes again. What de fuck is 'derogatory'?"

"Dissing someone."

"So why, why, why, why de fuck can't you say dat?"

"You know why?"

"Why?"

"Because."

"Because?"

"Because."

"*Va fa'n culo.*"

"*Pure tu.*"

"So what we sayin' here?"

"We're saying the public is much more eager to see a fighter if a few months go by after they've seen him and I'm also saying during that time you and I could pool our resources and put on a play that could make us some money."

"Whoa, Whoa, Whoa! What is *dis* now? You just slip dat in like a cock into a wet pussy? Put on a play? What're you, nuts?"

"See, now this is the same reaction you had a year-and-a-half ago when I came to this place to talk you into arranging some fights for me. Remember? 'You a lover, not a fighter.' Remember?"

"Okay, now dis is a whole new ting now, a whole new ting an' you just tink you can jes' slip it in, dat what you tink? An' stop bringin' up how you de brains'a dis outfit an' how you talked me into somethin'. I don't do *nothin'* I don't tink's gonna turn into *somethin'*, so stop fuckin' wit me."

"I bring it up to point out how you should keep your mind open."

"I keep it as open as I like it to be, don't want too much of a draft in dere, so you don't have to bring up nothin', you hear me?"

"I can bring up whatever I feel like bringing up."

"Not in *my* restaurant you can't."

"Fine. Then I'll leave your restaurant." I got up.

"Sit de fuck down."

"Am I going to be allowed to bring up what I want to bring up when I want to?"

"*Va fa'n culo.*"

"*Pure tu.*"

"Sit de fuck down."

I sat.

"You're a weirdo," he said, "you know dat?"

"I wouldn't talk if I were you."

"What de fuck's *dat* suppose to mean?

"You're a fucking gangster, you rob and kill people, what's weirder than that?"

"I can't win for losin' wit you, can I? So what is dis play you talkin' about?"

"An off-Broadway play—with songs."

"A musical?"

"A play. A play with songs."

"So what's de difference between a play wit songs an' a musical?"

"Musical is light fare, a play is serious."

"So what about *Le Miz*, dat's pretty serious, ain't it?"

"That's all singing so it's more like an opera."

"Oh, no," he said, "*Le Miz* ain't no opera."

"Why not?"

"If it ain't Italian, it ain't no opera."

"Who says?"

"I'm tellin' ya how it is."

"Well, you're full of shit."

"Hey—"

"*Les Miz* is an opera. Quit arguing about it. I'm proposing to put on a play—like a regular drama—only it would have songs in it. But it's not like in a musical or opera where a character suddenly bursts into song in the middle of a dialogue. No, these songs would be sung by the main character who is a singer and is doing it as part of her profession."

"So de hero's a bitch?"

"Not a bitch, what're you, from Harlem suddenly? Bitch. You're Italian, for Christ's sake; Italians love women, they don't call them bitches. The heroine is a black woman."

"A play about a black female? See, I was right callin' her a bitch. Where de fuck you come up wid dat? Don't expect *my* friends an' relatives to come see it. Or me, for dat matter."

"What're you, prejudiced?"

"You know any white people who ain't? I don't tink so. An' who wrote dis play?"

"Me. I'm going to write it."

"You're *going* to write it. What do you know about writin' plays?"

"Enough to write one."

"An' what about de songs?"

"I'm going to write those too."

"So now you write songs too?"

"I can whistle it into a tape recorder and have someone write down the notes. I've been making tunes up and recording them on a tape recorder for a couple of years now, I'll make them into a score."

"An' *dat's* for what you wanna take time out from fightin'? Dis sure-fire fiasco?"

"See, now you don't want me to call you *stronzolo* but you can malign something I'm about to create."

"Watch dem words like 'malign,' again. I'm not even gonna *ask* what *dat* means, mainly 'cause I don't give a fuck. Create, my ass. You know dat expression about buyin' a boat? A wooden hole in de middle'a de water into which you pour money? What *you* plannin' is worse. An' what kind'a involvement am I suppose to have in *dat*?"

"I want you to back it."

"You want *me* to back it? What're you, out'a your fuckin' *faggioli*? How much does somethin' like dat run into?"

"Between a hundred-fifty and two hundred thousand."

"Off-Broadway?"

"Off-Broadway."

"Holy shit. So how much would it be on Broadway?"

"You wanna do it on Broadway?"

"I ain't doin' it no place, man, I jus' wanna know how much shit like dat costs."

"On Broadway it'd be three to four million."

"Mudder'a God an' de Holy Ghost. People spend dat kind'a money puttin' on a fuckin' show?"

"Some of these shows run for years and the investors get back five, six, seven thousand percent on their interest. Can you imagine how much the investors of *Cats* have made? *The Fantastics* ran from 1960 to 2002; can you imagine what *its* investors made? I know a guy, a civil servant, was asked to invest in *The Fantastics* and he turned it down. He's an old man now and he's been eating his guts out for over forty years. And *Phantom of the Opera*? Don't get me started."

"Yeah, but de odds must be worse'n Vegas."

"Only if you don't know anything about it."

"Yeah, gamblers in Vegas, *dey* all tink dey know."

"With shows it's not a system. It's knowing what's good and what's not good. It's taste and judgment."

"So why don't *you* back it, you got de moolah."

"A person backs his own play it becomes a vanity production."

"Vanity production? What does *dat* mean?"

"Means you're doing it to please yourself, for your ego, it's like spanking the monkey."

"Ain't it?"

"No, it's something that's going to be a hit and I'm giving you a chance to be part of it and make money on me as an artist just like you made money on me as a boxer."

"I was able to check you out as a boxer. I was able to see how you knocked somebody out. You had credentials. You got no credentials in dis."

"Then let's get some. I'll write a scene. I'll cast the actors, I'll direct them. I'll hire two, three musicians and we'll rent a little theatre for the night and we'll do it and you can watch and, poof, I got credentials."

"An' if I don't tink it's gonna go, you not gonna nag de shit out'a me de way you doin' now?"

"Not a shit, not a piss."

"Dis scene an' stuff is all gonna be at *your* expense, right?"

"Mine. But if we decide to do it and the show makes money, the money I spent on this comes back to me out of gross."

"Jus' like I figured—yid first, artist second."

"See, now that's a lot worse than *stronzolo*."

"It's de troot, ain't it?"

"So's your being a *stronzolo* but you still don't like it."

"Excuse me, you *are* a Jew, ain't ya?"

"And you're a primitive, prejudiced *stronzolo* fuck; fine, how do you do."

"You don't wanna be called a Jew, fine, I won't call you a Jew no more."

"You know—I would explain it to you, but you know what? You just wouldn't get it."

"But I would get backin' your show, I'm smart enough for dat, right?"

"You don't need to be smart for some things, all you have to do is listen and follow directions, I'll draw you very simple pictures."

"You such a superior fuck, somebody gonna bust your balloon real good one'a dese days an' I'm gonna stick aroun' to see it an' have myself de best laugh'a my life. You know what? It could be dis very show. About a black bitch? Who you tink's gonna come see de show? De whites ain't gonna come see it. You tink whites gonna end up spendin' over two hunnert bucks, what wid tickets, baby sitters an' dinner? De blacks ain't gonna come see a play about blacks written by a honky, dey gonna parade wit signs in front'a your teatre, chasin' everybody away. Who you tink's gonna come see it?"

# CHAPTER THIRTY-TWO

DIANA

You wanna do a book about my life? What in hell for? Not enough garbage out there? *My* life? 'Cause people'll shell out when they see a celebrity's name on the cover? Hope to pick up some juicy gossip, the rag sheets and the talk shows aren't enough?

HARRY

Because those who read it will be inspired.

DIANA

What do you know about my life? Could be dull as dishwater.

HARRY

I doubt it.

DIANA

Listen to the man. Because I can turn an audience on when I sing and act? Have you caught actors and singers on talk shows? Have you seen anything as boring in your life?

HARRY

Think of it this way for a minute. A girl from the South Bronx captivates the entire world. Then, in addition to entertaining, goes into competition with Mother Teresa in the field of humanitarianism. You don't think there's food for inspiration there?

DIANA

Where'd you get the idea people wanna be inspired? Shocked, that's what they wanna be. They wanna turn on the TV, go to the movies, and pick up those rags at the newsstand and watch for new ways their fellow human beings can do vicious and perverse things to one another. Even when the World Trade Center got blown up, what'd they keep showing over and over and over? The impact, the impact, the impact. Why? To titillate, my friend, to titillate, titillate, titillate. Inspired, my ass.

HARRY

There're things being made that are inspiring without being vicious or perverse.

DIANA

Like what?

HARRY

It's a Wonderful Life, Miracle on 34*th* Street, Secrets and Lies, Remains of the Day, The Rain Man, Kramer Versus Kramer, The Seven Samurai, Bridge on the River Qwai, Lawrence of Arabia—should I continue?

DIANA

They make any money?

HARRY

Loads. And still making it.

DIANA

Well—you know what they say about exceptions.

HARRY

At what point could an exception *change* the rule?

(DIANA rises, moving left. DESK AREA LIGHTS go DOWN. HARRY moves OFF-STAGE RIGHT. DIANA moves to DOWN CENTER as LIGHTS in that area go UP. SHE kneels, holding a DOLL, making it dance on the floor before her)

DIANA

(Singing)

*Let me entertain you —*

(From another room ensue the SOUNDS of a MAN and a WOMAN arguing. As DIANA sings, the SOUNDS grow progressively LOUDER. The ARGUMENT in the other room turns into a screaming match. Comes a WOMAN'S SCREAM, immediately followed by a SHOT, then the SOUND of a BODY HITTING THE FLOOR. Then there is another SHOT and the SOUND of another BODY HITTING THE FLOOR. Then silence)


DIANA

(Hugging the DOLL to her bosom, singing)

'Bye, 'bye, blackbird


(SHE continues the song. On the SCREEN above the stage we see, as the LIGHTS go DOWN, DOWNSTAGE CENTER, a TEN-YEAR-OLD AFRICAN-AMERICAN GIRL, carrying a SUITCASE, led by a SOCIAL WORKER into a FOSTER HOME. IMAGE ON SCREEN FADES and LIGHTS go UP on DESK AREA where DIANA talks into a PORTABLE TAPE RECORDER)


DIANA

(Into TAPE REC MIKE)

Well, Harry, it appears we have some violence in our story after all. Wouldn't do to have our readers go into deprivation shock, would it?


(LIGHTS DOWN on DESK AREA and UP STAGE LEFT, where HARRY is at PODIUM, talking to AUDIENCE)

HARRY

She was right, of course. Though I was in a state of ecstasy she'd agreed to do the book, I wasn't a bit displeased we were having some drama. I could talk till I was blue in the face about inspiration and what have you but, when push came to shove, I knew as well as your grossest Hollywood producer that conflict and violence never hurt— the gross.


(A SECURITY MAN hands HARRY a NOTE. HARRY reads it. Then to AUDIENCE)

Seems a gate crasher managed to finagle his way into our little shindig here. Six-four, according to reports, African-American— though one can't be certain he's African *or* American. Probably a fan too impatient to wait for the HBO telecast. We know he's not an Arab, so that's something, isn't it? Should you see anyone fitting that description, please let one of the security personnel know and they'll check it out discreetly. Nothing to worry about, I'm sure.

# CHAPTER THIRTY-THREE

First thing you want to do when you're planning a show—after you have a script—is find a place where you're going to hold your auditions, then a place where you're going to rehearse and, finally, a place where you're going to put it on.

*Back Stage* is a weekly newspaper that lists contacts for specific auditions. It is what actors who don't have agents, and even some who do, buy in order to see what auditions are being held for what shows. It is a pretty good rule of thumb that if it is listed in *Back Stage*, it isn't going to do much for your career. The shows that are going to do you any good as an actor are all cast through power agents who wouldn't be caught dead having anything to do with *Back Stage*.

But for the thousands of actors who don't have agents—and for many who do but are not getting work—*Back Stage* is the only game in town. And for producers who are putting on shows that are going to be attended mainly by friends and relatives, *Back Stage* is where you place the ads.

Now it used to be, at one time, the publishers of *Back Stage* were more than happy to list auditions for a nominal sum. Matter of fact, they might've fallen just short of *paying* producers and directors to list auditions in their paper. It was these listings, you see, that made the actors *buy* the paper every week.

But that was a long time ago, in the days when everybody was much more innocent about everything. That is to say, more honest. It was in the days when the public didn't pay for products that advertised the manufacturer and when they didn't have to sit through 10 minutes of commercials that were followed by another ten minutes of previews in high priced movie theaters and when, making a business call, they didn't have to wait for machine announcements to tell them they would have to wait some more and the company knew your time was valuable and your call was very important to them but they made you wait and wait and wait anyway and, after you pressed innumerable buttons on your touch-dial phone, you waited some more.

These days, to place an ad in *Back Stage* that told actors about the audition and whom to contact costs fifty bucks. So the paper gets it both ways: money from the producers to place an ad listing an audition and money from actors who buy the paper to see what auditions are listed.

The paper also listed such things as rehearsal and audition studios, schools and coaches for various phases of performing and they, too, had to pay for those listings and you had to buy the paper if you were looking for any of those things and, of course, all those who bought a listing had to buy the paper to see if their ads had been published. Ah, free enterprise.

I was looking for a studio where I could hold auditions so I bought the paper. There are oodles and oodles of rehearsal studios in New York. There are oodles and oodles of everything in New York. It is when you see listings that you get a reality on how many things and people there are in New York and, by deduction, in the world. Because when you live in New York, it is like that Steinberg cartoon. There is New York, and then there are all these little insignificant places in the rest of the world—such as other states, countries, and continents. But to a New Yorker, not only are they insignificant, they're not really real.

Most of the advertised rehearsal studios did not list their prices. They wanted you to call so they could postpone talking about prices till you had booked a room. I zeroed in on ads that did list prices. I looked for a combination of the lowest plus a certain convenience in terms of accessibility.

I made my first appointment with a studio on 22nd Street between Fifth and Sixth Avenues.

It was one of those old four-story buildings that still exist in New York, with a very slow, rickety elevator and creaky wooden stairs.

Climbing the stairs to the second floor, you found a winding vestibule where you could put a few chairs for actors to wait in and a door that led to the inner hallway. Going through the door, you were faced with a stack of second hand furniture and you knew these were props for shows. They gave you a good feeling. This was a place where people came and carried pieces of this furniture to the stage where they pretended they were certain personages doing certain imagined things and people came to watch.

People who did stuff like pretending to be characters in a story would not physically hurt nor would they steal. That's not to say that later on, when they had "gotten somewhere," they would not do worse than physically hurt and steal. But that's a different subject. At this level of creativity, people tended to be pure, warm, and propitiative. They had dreams, hopes, and ideals.

To your left in the hallway was a door, to the right a small office, and further right another door. A cherubic man with graying hair and a rotund structure was sitting in the office behind a desk, watching a 13-inch color television set positioned on a stand to his left.

I walked in, said, "Hi," and he looked up.

"Hi, yourself," he said with the kind of gleam in his eye that immediately identified him as a breed from the days when there used to be vaudeville and musicals with melodic tunes. The mark of that breed was they lived to entertain you, not because it would advance their careers, but because that was what life was about for them—making people laugh. "What can I do you?"

It occurred to me the man must have a hell of a trust in human nature if he could sit here in this little office in a dark hallway and the door to the outside downstairs open for anyone to walk in. It was New York. Had he never been mugged? No, he could not have been because people who had been mugged remained frightened for the rest of their lives. How had he avoided being mugged with the downstairs door open all day? It once more raised the question in me as to whether each of us acted as a magnet for certain kinds of happenings. Ah, life is like a well.

"I'm looking for a place where I can hold auditions and rehearsals for a scene."

"Come into my parlor, said the spider," he said, getting up and coming around to where I was. "Let me show you our theater and then let me show you our rehearsal room."

He led me to the door on the left of the entrance, which led to the little theater. When I say little, I mean—little. There were about thirty folding chairs lined up on graduated platforms so the audience could look down and get an unobstructed view of the comparatively large stage. I liked it immediately. There are people who go for a big theater. They have dreams of filling it. I personally like little places. I would rather turn people away than take a chance on having empty seats.

The man showing me the space said, "Al Pacino, when asked in a *New York Times* interview what had inspired him to go into acting, said he'd been wandering the Bronx at the age of 14 when he passed a large theater called the Elsmere. He decided to go in. The theater was cavernous. There was a play being performed. It was Anton Chekov's *The Seagull*. There were about 12 people in the audience. Pacino said in the interview he was blown away by what could be done and decided right then and there to go into acting. A friend of mine played Trigorin in that production which, if you're familiar with the play, you'll know is the leading part. When he read the interview in the paper, he decided to write Pacino a letter about how life can be like the movie *It's a Wonderful Life* in that you never know whom you're affecting or how you're affecting them."

"Did Pacino answer?"

"Nope."

"Maybe the letter never reached him."

"Like Hemingway said, 'Isn't it nice to think so?' This is fifteen dollars an hour for rehearsals and auditions, seventy-five dollars for a performance Mondays through Thursdays, hundred-twenty-five per performance on weekends and you get an electrician with that. Now let me show you our rehearsal room."

He led me to the door on the other side of the hallway, which was to the immediate right of the little elevator. This room, though smaller, was a nice size, say that of a large living room, and it, too, had pieces of furniture, chairs, and a piano. One of its two large windows had a fire escape and they both looked out on 22nd Street.

"This one is seven-fifty an hour before five and ten an hour after five."

"I like it," I said. The whole place was clean, acceptably neat, and the prices were quite reasonable.

"Thank you. Pleasing the customer is our motto. I've never been able to actualize that motto in regard to my two wives but with customers I've had no problems."

"What's your name?"

"Milton. Milton Taurus. Like the sign."

"I like you, Milton."

"That's good. When people like me, my sense of security goes up, like when the stock market rises. After a while, again like the stock market, it falls down again. I make jokes so people will like me and my stocks can rise again—and then fall down again. So I make more jokes."

"You look familiar."

"I was in the original Broadway production of *South Pacific*, I was one of the sailors. Perhaps you remember me; I was the third one from the left."

As the original production of *South Pacific* took place decades before I was born, I could only say, "Of course, you were the one with the baritone voice."

"I was a tenor then but why quibble?"

He sang the "There is Nothing Like a Dame," from South Pacific.

I joined him, harmonizing. He looked surprised but continued. We gave it the big finish, then slapped each other a high five.

"I didn't expect you to know anything about *South Pacific*," he said. "I mentioned it, when you said I looked familiar, as a joke. I mean I was in the Broadway version but I wasn't in the movie of it. I didn't expect you to know anything about the movie either, young people today don't have the patience with old time stuff like that, it's too slow for this age."

"I see everything that comes around."

"You might've seen me in some of my current movies. Did you see *One Fine Day* with George Clooney?"

"No, I saw it with my girlfriend."

"Let's get one thing straight; I'm the comic, *you're* the straight man. Milton Taurus is still in the building. One more time; did you see *One Fine Day*—which starred George Clooney—wise guy?"

"Yes."

"I was in that. And the one with Sharon Stone where she adopts the kid and hides from the mob? I was the druggist."

"Oh, yeah, I remember that, where you said you couldn't read the handwriting on the expired prescription when she gave you some money so she gave you a bigger bill and the prescription became legible and you gave her the medicine for the kid?"

"That's right."

"You were terrific."

"Thank you."

"Milton," a man called out. I saw a man stick his head through the door. "I'm here. I'll be in the office."

"Oh, hi, Bob."

The man disappeared and the sounds of footsteps took him to Milton's office.

"Isn't that Bob Dishy?" I said.

"My, my, you do keep up, Bob's not exactly a household name. Yeah, we're friends, when he's not working he comes around once in a while to bug me or calls me and bugs me on the phone. What's your name?"

"Dan Kahn."

"You wouldn't be the Dan Kahn who recently won the middleweight title, would you?"

"Yeah, I would."

"So, what're you, going into show business?"

"I went into show business before I went into boxing."

"Fascinating the way you knock those guys out. What's even more fascinating is that show business and boxing always seemed to me to be on opposite ends of the pole; I can't think of one actor who was a good boxer and I can't think of one boxer who was a good actor. Johnny Weissmuller, who was an Olympic swimming champion, turned out to be our greatest Tarzan but a boxer who turned out to be an actor? Never."

"I'm not really a boxer, I hate boxing. I just have this freaky thing where I get to hit them before they hit me. If anybody ever laid a glove on me, I'd quit on the spot."

"Somebody's bound to hit you, you know that, don't you?"

"Gonna try and quit before that happens."

"Well—in my world nothing is impossible. Welcome to my world and good luck to you."

After booking both the theatre and the rehearsal room for

auditions—Milton wouldn't take a deposit, said he trusted me—I went to the building on Times Square where *Back Stage* had its offices to place an ad for an African-American singer-actress.

The *Back Stage* staff consisted of people who had at one time tried or were still trying to break into show business and who now got satisfaction out of making money from something that was connected to show business and they could thereby feel they were still technically in show business. They tried to act businesslike but couldn't conceal a slight air of superiority stemming from the knowledge they were dealing with people who were coming to *them* for help regarding show business matters.

Though *Back Stage* didn't get to the stands till Thursday, I started getting calls from actresses on Wednesday evening and the calls continued through Thursday, Friday, Saturday, Sunday, and Monday, which was the day of the audition, plus a couple of weeks after that. The phone hardly ever stopped ringing. When I stepped out to the grocery store and returned home, there would be seven, eight messages from actresses sounding propitiative and seductive as all get-out. I scheduled a group of five every fifteen minutes.

The ad in *Back Stage* had said an African-American actress-singer was needed for a scene to raise funds for an off-Broadway show. It wasn't even for the show itself, just to raise funds, there was no guarantee the person who did the scene would be in the show. Yet the number of actors and actresses in New York is so overwhelming and their desire so strong, they will climb all over themselves to get a part, any part in practically anything. Let me amend that. Not *practically* anything. Anything. They'll find a way of justifying the crappiest projects.

I made no provisions for anyone to help me with the auditions. I figured I would have people wait in the rehearsal room, give two women the script to look at before they came into the theatre to audition, then have each come in separately to sing something, then have them come in together and read, one reading HARRY, the other reading DIANA for a page or two, then reverse them while the next two were looking at scripts in the rehearsal room, preparing for their turn.

I came to the rehearsal studio ten minutes before the audition was due to begin. and there were twelve actresses waiting.

There are always actors and actresses who have to be somewhere in a hurry and need to be taken right away. If they look sincere and honest—and they always look sincere and honest—I ask the others if they mind this person going ahead. Because everyone wants to be nice at an audition, they don't ever say they mind.

What happens at these *Back Stage*-begotten auditions is you are getting beginners who know little about either acting or show business, or you get people who, for one reason or another, haven't made it to the level where you get paid for acting so they keep auditioning for things that don't pay anything in the hope something will come of it. As a result, finding talent and professionalism co-existing in one individual is rare.

In this instance there was a number of women who were beautiful but could neither sing nor act, then there were some who could sing but were so unattractive and insipid they were out of the question. No, they were not unattractive to me. I felt about them the way I'd used to feel about the baby sitters who'd sat on me when I was a child. I liked them all, wanted them all to sit on me. But, in this case, I was also able to see how they would appear to others. Some who could act but not sing and so on. And though you might know from the first instant they wouldn't do, you had to go through the whole ritual of letting them read and sing just like you did with everyone else because you wouldn't want to hurt their feelings and because you wouldn't want anyone accusing you of being unfair and making arbitrary decisions without giving them the full benefit of a trial.

Quickly falling behind, I realized it had not been a good idea to go it alone. There were actresses who wanted to ask you questions, others who wanted to tell you things, still others who simply wanted to charm your pants off, then there were telephone calls from some who were running late, some who had gotten lost and wanted to know how to get there, some who had just heard about the auditions and wanted to know if they could be squeezed in, all of these things set you back and, meanwhile, there were more and more actresses coming and I was falling further and further behind.

Then a slim Caucasian woman wearing glasses showed up, saying she'd made an appointment and wanted to audition. I checked her name, Karen Graves, and yes, she'd made the appointment. My first impulse was to ask her if she'd read the ad where it said I was looking for an African-American woman but this would have come off as being sarcastic and, in fact, *would* have been sarcastic so I decided to treat it as if it were a totally fresh experience and neither she nor I knew what the *Back Stage* ad had said.

"This part is for an African-American woman," I said.

"Oh," she said cheerfully, as if this news didn't faze her but was kind of fun to hear. "I'd be willing to do anything."

"Except the part calls for an African-American."

"I mean anything to help out. Keep track of actors who come in, give the next two actors their scripts so they could prepare, help you out when you rehearse—that's what I mean by anything, I just wanna help out in the show."

"It's not a whole show yet. Just a scene."

"Whatever."

"Okay. Grab the list of appointments and get to work."

It went much faster after that.

It was true—build it and they will come.

After three hours there was no one I could genuinely say thrilled me. The process must be something close to love. You have this ideal of what you would like. You may not have articulated it or even brought it to a conscious level in your mind, but somewhere in each of us there is a feeling of what we want. When we fail to come across it, we begin to think in terms of settling for something else. Our area of what is acceptable to us broadens more and more and includes more and more possibilities and we more and more loosen our hold on the idea that there is someone who will ring our bell

As it got closer to the end of the time I'd booked the space for, I began to think I would later review the pictures and my notes of the women who'd auditioned and pick one. After all, if I, as a director, could not charge anyone with the electricity needed to move an audience, what kind of director was I? There were hundreds, maybe thousands, of people in show business who, with a certain director, could be stars but with other directors they were non-entities. It had happened to people who'd worked with Charles Chaplin, Robert Altman, Sam Packinpah, Howard Hawks, John Ford, even with modern-day Tony Scott. These directors made stars out of actors they worked with. Why could I not do the same thing to one of the ones who had auditioned?

As the last two actresses were finishing reading their lines, Milton poked his head in to announce we had two minutes left. As jovial as he was when you talked to him, you could see he was all business when it came down to—business.

And then Karen poked her head in to say there was one more woman who had just come in to audition. I was about to tell her I'd made the last appointment fifteen minutes ago, tell her to forget it. But the euphoria that holds sway when you do a show and the conviction that the most important things in life come in the guise of the unexpected won out and I said, "Tell her to come in quickly."

I heard Karen tell her and then she poked her head in again and said, "She just went to the bathroom."

My eyes rolled up. I tried to roll my eyes only when people couldn't see me. It was one of those sarcastic communications I wanted to avoid. There was another group coming to rehearse and Milton, I could see, did not put up with nonsense in this area. He had probably had too much experience with actors who needed the studio "just a couple more minutes."

"Let's collect our things," I said to Karen, "and get going."

As we were doing that, with thirty seconds to go, the woman burst into the theater.

"Sorry," she said, handing Karen a picture and a resume, "can I still audition?"

Charlene S. White was in her twenties, out of breath, had a pretty, round face, hair done up in curls, Shirley Temple style, a tight leather black skirt with a matching vest and a loose, bright green blouse open at the neck down to her breasts, which were sizeable. She had a disproportionately big butt, at one time considered a societal disadvantage but now fast turning into an advantage. I saw this as ironic or poetic justice, considering the reason many African women have rather generous butts is because generations ago in Africa it was prized greatly by men as an asset, therefore, the women saw to it that it grew and grew and thus became almost a cultural and genetic trait.

"We've got thirty seconds," I said. "Sing something."

"What?"

"Anything. Sing out, Louise."

"Name's Charlene."

"I know. Please sing."

"Who's Louise?"

"A character in the musical *Gypsy*."

"Oh."

She began to sing. "Happy birthday—to-oo-o-o you—"

Oh, dear. Happy birthday, Mister President.

But wait. She was doing something to it. Twisting those tones—making it into a—spiritual? Happy birthday—a *spiritual*? Yes—yes—belting, bellowing, howling out those sounds like old Nell Carter, Ms. Force of Nature herself. Whoa! The door opened and Milton, the people from the next rehearsal group came in. Instead of interrupting and telling me our time was up, as I knew must be his wont, Milton stopped and listened. So did the actors who had booked the studio for this time slot. We were all enraptured—riveted. She went on and on and on, it was the singing equivalent of an orgasm that went on forever. Finally, she howled her way to a wind-up—bring it home, Louise. There was silence. We were all in a trance. Then we woke up. The applause was wild. It was like experiencing a miracle. In the end, I realized this is what I love about life the most. To experience how much people are able to move you by what they feel and create. And that was what it was all about. I glanced at the actresses who had read before Charlene and one would be hard put to see as much devastation on anyone's face, knowing there was now no question as to who would get the part.

# CHAPTER THIRTY-FOUR

**H**ey, babe."

"Hi, Sandy."

"The offer from Pitt's not gonna last forever, you know. If you don't want to be in a relationship with me, why can't we just keep it business? Rent an office where we can work every day, you know, nine-to-five stuff and go our separate ways when day's done."

"Business is relationship."

"I don't know how you can do yourself out of such an opportunity because of a grudge."

"Not a grudge."

"What is it?"

"A resolution not to be connected to people without character."

"Mangiacavallo has character?"

"In his fashion."

"If you're going to start rationalizing—"

"You're right; I'm not going to be connected to him much longer either."

"Nice to know I get prioritized in the evil department over a bona fide gangster."

"All I know about him is what I get from the news and, though you're right he's a gangster, we all know the news is not a place where you get nothing but the truth which, as a result, turns out to be something other than the truth."

"You're still rationalizing—and expounding, I might add."

"You're right again. I'm trying to address the issue of why I disconnected with you first."

"With those standards, you're going to end up with very few friends."

"You know what they say about friends like you."

"Don't believe forgiveness is divine?"

"I forgave you the moment you said you were dumping me; I just don't want to be associated with you."

"Tell you what. I get you and Pitt together, give the project my blessing and you give me ten percent and co-writer credit."

"You get no part of this, Sandy."

"If I get no part of it, you don't get to do it, you lose it all."

"Consider it lost."

"You *are* certifiable, you know that?"

I thought how, when we'd been intimate, I had considered telling Sandy about the man in sheets with the knife. When you're intimate with someone you're tempted to tell them all kinds of things. In *Love Story*, the famous phrase was "Love is never having to say you're sorry." I personally think love is being sorely tempted to give up everything you've got. It was a great lesson on how important it was for some things to be withheld.

A couple of hours later the phone rang and I picked up without screening and the guy said, "This is Brad Pitt."

Your instinct is to think someone's playing a joke on you but, out of consideration for the fact that if this *were* he, it must happen a lot, I decided not to do the "Is this a joke?" routine.

"Listen," he said, "Sandy explained to you about our leaving, didn't she?"

"She did." I still thought it was some actor Sandy had gotten to imitate Pitt so I was playing along.

"She also said she fucked up and you don't want her working on this project." The guy was good. He was really good.

"That's right."

"I admire that. Admire integrity. Don't run into it much."

It really felt weird. Sounded exactly like him. Could anyone be that good? But then, I'd heard Kevin Spacey interviewed on *Actors' Studio* and, if you closed your eyes, you'd swear you were listening to all those actors he was imitating. "It's a luxury I indulge myself in."

"I still wanna do the project. Sandy's fine not being involved. Like that diving at the opponent. Could make it look great on screen—

slow-mo, all the high-tech stuff. Gotta have a hook, though. Somethin' to hang it all on. Make it fly. Can you put somethin' together and get back to me?"

"Sure."

"Got a pencil and paper handy?"

Well, now this was a new twist.

"Yup."

He gave me his number. "My personal line. You can always leave a message an' I'll get back to you. And I mean I'll get back to you."

"Could you do me a favor?"

"Sure."

"Could you tell me what happened the day we got to Paris?"

"Oh, I get it. Sure. When we got to the airport, you sang the French national anthem, then we went to an outdoor restaurant on the Champs Elysee where a pantomimist entertained us for twenty minutes, imitating people's walks, then a terrorist landed from a helicopter on the Arch of Triumph and got shot and did a swan dive to the pavement. Do I pass? You wanna know what we did in Athens?"

"No. Sorry."

"Don't be sorry. Comes with the territory. I could've been in Oshkosh, washin' dishes. Or worse, a male model."

"You happen to have Sandy's number?"

"Hold on a second." There was a pause and he came back. "Here it is." He read it to me.

"Listen," I said after I wrote it down, "at the risk of sounding gushy, I thought what you did in *True Romance* was out of this world. Everything you've done is great but that was the first time I saw you."

"Well, thanks, man, that was, you know, like the springboard, got everything rolling."

"I dumped a girl in college because she was gushing over you too much."

"Don't blame you. Got her number handy?"

I called Sandy. After screening the call, she picked up.

"Did I redeem myself?" she asked.

"Partially. I'll give you fifteen percent of my take, no credit."

"Deal. Any chance we can get together again?"

When I was a kid there was a distant cousin, an older guy looked like Robert Mitchum. Comedian of sorts. Used to do a variation on an old song—"If you were the only girl in the world, maybe—but right now, no."

No big deal; wouldn't mean that much to her. Sandy could get just about anybody she wanted, probably already had. I'd had two others and it was a lot easier for her.

"You know," she said, as if divining my thoughts, "it may seem to you I sleep around and go from one person to another—and I do—but whereas this is a man's fantasy, it's never a woman's. We do it and talk ourselves into liking it in a perverted effort at equality with you guys. But there's a hell of a lot to the saying that men fall in love because they're sexually attracted and women get sexually attracted because they fall in love. It's not easy for us to have sex with a guy and not be quite fond of the fucker."

"If it's a guy's fantasy to have sex with beautiful women, why am I refusing you?"

"Maybe it's not all the guys in the world. Maybe I'm just unlucky. Also you know it's not just a question of sex. You're not trashy enough to have sex and walk away, let alone be capable of saying publicly, 'I did not have sexual relations with that woman.' We did have a great time, didn't we?"

"Yeah. We did."

"We could again, you know." She was being very soft and seductive now.

That was one of the things I marveled at in regard to women: when it came to love—they were just about unstoppable.

We guys, on the other hand, unquestionably think with our dicks. *Why not*, I thought even at this point, *get together with her, have sex, have conversation—she was a great conversationalist—and then, if I met other women I liked, I could have them as well. I could have as many women as— I could have.*

What would happen, then, to all the things I was trying to become, all the characteristics I valued? Integrity—ethics.

Well, I could have them in other areas, in this one area I could be free—function under the principle that my body, my spirit, my emotions belong to me and I could share them with anyone I pleased whenever I pleased without this being the business of anyone else, including the additional person or persons I had an intimate relationship with.

"No," I said. "We couldn't."

"Why not?"

"Do you really want to know or you keeping the conversation going as something to do during the process of looking for a way to persuade me?"

"I want to persuade you, of course. But I'm interested. I really am."

"It's about ideals."

"I've apologized. I sincerely regret it. Are you so perfect you never make a mistake?"

"Far from it."

"Putting all our lives at risk by tackling that man, was that smart? Turned out all right, fortunately, but only because of a freaky accident. The chances were far greater we'd all be blown to bits. I've forgiven you for that and so have the others. You can't do the same?"

"The thing I did may not have been smart but the intention was not bad. What you did afterwards, on the other hand, was smart but—"

"All right, I got that, but was it really that terrible? Is it really so impossible to forgive?"

"Not a matter of forgiveness, I forgave you right after you did it. Just you can't ever have the same feeling toward someone who's betrayed you."

She took a pause. What was there to say?

"Good luck on your project with Pitt."

"Thanks."

There was a pause. She was still on the line. Pulling at my innards. I was tempted. But my sense of ethics—or ideals—or else my stupid pride—it's a toss-up—won—*tant pis pour moi* (so much the worse for me).

"One of us has got to say it, you know," she said.

"What?"

"We'll always have—Paris?"

"And we will too."

"If you need any help, let me know. Think about how it would be." She hung up. Women don't really ever give up—on anything—do they? It's like—eternal hope—about everything.

I began rehearsals with Charlene at the same time I began writing the screenplay for Pitt. Actually, I decided to write the story first as a book. I had read and heard enough about moviemaking to know it's not only an uncertain process in terms of whether it would get done but, even when it got done, most of the time it took years for it to reach the phase where you actually started shooting. You throw yourself into writing something with the idea that, because it feels wonderful to you, it's going to feel that way for everybody. And then you start coming across all kinds of reservations people have about it, all kinds of conditions they have in regard to getting involved with it and negotiations taking place all over the place and time passes and now you begin to look at it as this piece of merchandise you're peddling in a buyer's market and, worse, due to some prehistoric mechanism we all seem to have, you grow obsessively attached to the idea it should be made no matter when, how, or at what cost. You hawk it to anybody and everybody and your own conditions and standards in terms of how it should be done and what changes you will stand for get lower and lower until they become non-existent. You become a whore, willing to do anything for that pay-off. And it's not really the pay-off in money. It's not wanting to fail, the thing that nightmares are made of.

So, knowing this stuff about what a screenplay has to go through before it becomes a bona fide film, I decided, if I wrote it as a book, books being published on the strength of the author's fame in whatever area, I could find a publisher who would undertake to put the book out and the process would go much faster. Not only that, but there would be money and publicity from the book, which would act as an advantage insofar as movie producers were concerned, and then, of course, the publicity from the movie helps the book, hands washing each other all over the place.

Although, if Brad Pitt were behind it, the movie would happen and happen pretty fast. But with the kind of schedule he was bound to have, who knew how many other projects he was obligated to do before this one. The bottom line was that a person peddling a screenplay was always in a no-power position. He/she depended on the kindness of moguls and that always turned into an anxiety-ridden waiting game. The other side of the coin—people in a power position were never in a hurry to do something those in a no-power position wanted them to do. With a published book, on the other hand, you had producers bidding for the right to make it into a movie. You had a product that was already out there, you had nothing to prove any more. *You* were in the power position.

The other, and most important advantage in writing something as a book first, is that when it comes out, it will say pretty much what you set out to say and how you wanted to say it. You'll have conferences with an editor and there will be changes made but they are generally changes that are more or less aligned with your goals and in accord with your theme. In a movie the producers will do anything and everything, including bringing a horde of other writers to put in whatever they feel will titillate an audience and make the movie into what they believe will be a blockbuster.

The all-important question that rises in both movie and book is the very thing Pitt mentioned regarding a peg on which your creation will hang. Every dramatic work has a protagonist who wants to achieve something and who is being prevented from doing it. How he does it or is prevented from doing it and what changes result in him and others from the process is what dramatic creation is about.

I would have to bring out the knife-wielding guy in sheets.

I was pretty certain two psychiatrists could be found to sign papers committing me on the basis of this evidence. On the other hand, if push came to shove, I could always claim this was a story *based* on my life and the guy in sheets with the knife used as a symbolic dramatic fulcrum rather than the literal truth. That is, if push came to shove.

There would be no way of avoiding the subject. There would be the national book tours and talk show appearances where the question would inevitably come up and they would not let me off the hook. They would insist on my answering whether the Roman toga guy with the knife was truth or fiction.

I could tell them this was the story of my life but that particular item — the guy with the knife — was fiction, the dramatic fulcrum I needed to give the story suspense and movement.

Except that would dilute it to hell. Mixing fiction with non-fiction was like saying you were a little bit pregnant. And the question of why and how I was able to execute my knockout would still remain in the air. The public would regard the book as a cheat.

The ending in any piece of creation was another question. I could not end it with me becoming a middleweight champion. At one time, long ago, when we were innocent and entertainment was young and sparse, an ending like that might've been enough. Now we require twists and turns, we want a root canal job on our guts.

It's a maxim in the writing profession that you have to know the ending to your story before you begin it. Because I'd be writing about my life, I wouldn't know the ending of the story any more than any of us know the ending of our lives. The ending of our lives is the thing we would least want to know and if we knew it, we'd do our damnedest to forget it.

However—just as the guy in sheets with the knife is the fulcrum for the plot, Mangiacavallo might be the fulcrum for the ending. I could no more play with his involvement in my career than I had the right to play with Maria's heart. But I did it. I went with Maria even though I knew from the beginning she was not the woman for me. And I enlisted Mangiacavallo to help launch me even though I knew boxing was not what I wanted in life and involvement with a gangster was more dangerous than signing a contract with Satan.

Maria let me get away with dashing what hopes she might've had just as millions of women let guys get away with such things time and again. What can a woman do? She can get hysterical, angry, bitter, vengeful—or gracious and pretend she has no ill feelings and you are still friends. With Mangiacavallo I could expect no such helplessness.

Mangiacavallo was indulging me by giving me a little time. He might even back my play. More indulgence. Eventually, though, I'd have to go back into the ring. Again and again until the magic was gone—and he was a millionaire several times over, a la Don King.

Into the ring—a la Don King.

I had started out thinking about story plot and ended up realizing I was in mortal danger. No way Mangiacavallo was going to let me walk away and cut off his flow of money. And no way I could devote myself to acting, writing, directing, *and* training for fights. Mangiacavallo was fully aware of what happens when a boxer's mind is on things other than training. Witness the debacles of Tyson-Douglas, Lewis-Rahman I. Mangiacavallo would never let me divide my time. This little scene he was letting me put on was a one-time thing. Would he even let me work on the movie with Pitt? He might if there were a generous cut in it for him. I hadn't even thought of that. I'd promised Sandy fifteen percent and now I would have to think in terms of giving Mangiacavallo probably half. I've seen *The Godfather*, *The Sopranos*, I'd read books written by gangsters — with someone else doing their writing, of course — I knew the drill.

# CHAPTER THIRTY-FIVE

**W**henever you are creating—whatever you're creating—miracles happen to you. And this, I now understand, is why so many individuals through history would shut themselves from the world and bury themselves in their creations. Why they could cut off their ears and go deaf and do all kinds of things and continue to be in a state of ecstasy—all because they were creating. It is better than drink, better than cocaine, better—in the long run—than sex. It is better than anything.

Why don't artists, then, live in that blessed state, protected and preserved forever and ever? Why do most of them end up so damnably and often tragically? Hemingway, at 61, put a muzzle of a shotgun into his mouth and pulled the trigger. Rodin, refused a warm place by the French government, which was preserving his works of art in a luxurious setting with perfect temperature, got frostbite out in the street and died in pain and misery.

Why could not art continue to treat them in the manner, as the courts are wont to say about divorced wives, to which they had grown accustomed?

I felt certain there was an answer to that question but I did not yet know what it was, no more than kine know they are being fatted for the hatchet.

I was just as certain that eventually I *would* know.

Meanwhile, I was in the thick of three kinds of creating. I was writing the book that would eventually turn into a screenplay, I was directing Charlene and myself in the scene I had written as part of my projected play and I was acting with her in that scene, playing the part of Harry.

The interesting thing is that each kind of creativity enables you to reach a different form of ecstasy. Writing, for instance, introverts you, placing you in an inner world that has an existence all its own. You walk through and deal with the real world but there is a shield between you and the real world that prevents you from being violated—even in the smallest of ways. It's like the stories you hear about people who take heroin. Or women who are pregnant. There is this self-sufficient, serene air about them, as if they were carrying with them all they needed to make them happy.

Acting, on the other hand, is like taking coke. You're hyped up and the world is a bright place of wonders and games and you could play forever and the attention is always on you.

Directing? Directing is—like being a God—who is on coke.

And I was being all three.

What was knocking people out in the ring compared to that? What was anything compared to that?

I can understand how individuals who get into boxing and become great at it, like Ali, Sugar Ray Robinson and Jack Johnson, can get into a state of ecstasy by creating greatness through their skills. That wasn't the case with me, though. Not in regard to boxing.

All creating is something like being God but, of the three forms of creativity I was indulging in, directing is most like being God—in that you are doing your creating with live people. What I learned about it was that a director created a different world from the one in the script. Insofar as he/she succeeded in creating a separate world, he/she succeeded in creating something that was alive. The mediocre directors, no matter how good the script, always created something that was stillborn because they functioned no more than traffic cops, believing it had already been created in the script and all you had to do was transfer the script to the screen or stage without creating something that was separate, their own, and alive.

The essence in creating something live was creating physical action, a sense of urgency in everyone and specific individual goals. I found in directing Charlene I had a talent for doing that. And it made me feel wonderful. On every line a physical movement would occur to me. Actors love physical movements. They think they love them because it gives them more "business," which brings more attention on them, increasing their sense of self-importance.

But, as in so many things, what we think the reason we like or dislike things is not the reason at all. The reason physical action is important in anything we do is, one, because it engages the person who performs it, removing a sense of self-consciousness, and two, provides the balance required for a fully-dimensional world. Whether we're aware of it or not, there needs to be an equilibrium between what the spirit does and what the body does. Ultimately, that may be the reason why artists don't get full protection from the practice of their art.

You cannot live permanently in an ivory tower. Unless you deal with the world and everything that's a part of it, its battering rams will eventually get you. And it works like the Archimedes Law of Displacement. You weigh an object in air, then place it in liquid and it will lose an amount of weight equal to the water it displaces.

And so with the ivory tower and the world. In the end, the world will bring upon a person the amount of force and punishment equal to the amount in it that the person has failed to confront and handle. That was why these individuals who did wonderful things for the world at large but neglected their families often caused terrible consequences to their families *and* themselves.

The beauty of this ultimate game of life we all play is that we don't know how much we've failed to confront and handle until the bill comes in and we have to pay it. And the bill comes in to everyone— life is more intransigent that way than the IRS.

Another way creativity is similar to drugs is that everything when you're creating seems not only okay but great. Things that might under other circumstances annoy you seem just fine and you love the world and everything in it. You become large spirited, everything you and everyone else would wish you to be. Like the early stages of falling in love.

And so, as I directed Charlene in her part and she began to assume the persona of the character, we imbued her character with the qualities I idealized in great individuals: large spiritedness, nobility, courage, grace, honesty, integrity, honor, passion, sexuality, in addition to great talent. And she assumed those qualities. And that, of course, is yet another benefit of creating. You can put what qualities you choose into a creation. And those qualities can make you and anybody who participates feel great too. This is the beauty and wonder of creation. *That's the story of, that's the glory of—*

She was feeling good about what we were creating, I was feeling good about it and everything else and I began to fall in love with Charlene. Because there was this wonderful individual being created right before my eyes. And I understood why actors kept falling in love with their co-actors and leaving the people they were married to and it kept happening over and over.

As an actor, with the help of your script and director, you had the option of creating the most exciting and interesting character conceivable. The lover who was waiting for you at home had no chance against that kind of competition. And that was why the stars so often fell in love with each other and their directors and why the public fell in love with stars. They saw the characters these stars created and most of the characters were magnificent and they were always involved in adventures that magnified the magnificence. How could anyone help falling in love with them?

The difference is that in a work of art we choose how the character will react to the pressure. Those actions and reactions determine what the character is. They can become heroic, grand, noble, unselfish, inspiring—they can be the most wonderful and exciting actions the world has known.

In life we don't expect a person's actions to be that way. We say, "Hey, this is life, this is reality, real people don't act the way they do in books or movies."

But what about Jesus Christ or Gandhi or Abe Lincoln or Mother Teresa or Joan of Arc? Weren't they real and weren't their actions as grand, noble, inspiring, and significant as anything created in a work of art?

They *can* happen in real life.

But they rarely do. And that's why relationships fall apart. And here's how it works. Charlene and I would rehearse and have a great time creating these characters and actions and there would be all kinds of wonderful interaction and feeling taking place and we would raise ourselves to the level of gods and then rehearsal would be over and, with Charlene, it would be like Dr. Jekyll and Mister

Hyde. The moment rehearsal ended, she would revert to this person who would start worrying about whether she'd gotten a ticket because she'd parked on the street a little earlier than she was supposed to in order to make rehearsal on time or whether traffic would be heavy going home or whether she had enough money to buy what she had to buy or whether she would be able to finish what she had to finish at work tomorrow so she could make it to rehearsal on time—and I would look at her and listen and think, *What made me have a crush on this woman? How could I, whose fundamental ideal is largeness of spirit,* largesse d'esprit *as the French would have it, maintain a relationship with someone who can be so small-minded?*

The answer is we form relationships with people on the basis of their presenting us with a persona in a state when his/her buttons are on hold. As a television comedian said, "You don't meet the real person at the beginning of your courtship. You meet the person's representative." Once the relationship is sealed, they activate those buttons almost as if making up for the time they had to suppress them in order to make a good impression at the beginning.

Once buttons start getting pushed, there are very few bounds.

For Charlene it was perfectly normal she could rise and become a wonderful character in a play but the moment rehearsal or performance was over, she could become as petty as one could possibly be.

Time and again I have seen great stars, musicians, painters, composers, ballet dancers who are in the business of performing and creating great works, yet who in their everyday life are so small spirited it's hard to believe they've ever been exposed to anything great.

And here it was. I was in love with the Charlene I rehearsed with but totally unadmiring of the one I walked out into the street with. And how was I to reconcile it?

That was easy too. I would, while outside of rehearsal, keep in my mind's eye and heart the woman I fell in love with *in* rehearsal—just as zillions of people keep relationships going based not on the person they're currently dealing with but rather on the person they got to know during the early courtship days.

I kept the magic of the idealized Charlene with me. Sometimes it's more fun to have a person you idealize, the way fans idealize stars, and just live with that idealization without ever having direct contact with the real person. It is the way knights used to idealize fair damsels. And the way in some countries in the olden days husbands and wives tried to ward off contempt through familiarity by addressing each other in formal terms.

And then, just when we were ready and I was about to call Mangiacavallo to arrange the date for a performance, he called me.

"You fightin' in tree monts," he said.

"What about this scene I rehearsed for you to look at?" I asked him.

"What scene? Oh, yeah, we can do dat anodder time. Right now we gotta make some moolah."

"You agreed to do this."

"Sure we'll do it. Anodder time. Right now we got dis kid. Puerto Rican. Luis Gonzales. Been knockin' people out right'n lef', he's hot. Big money fight. We gotta strike while de iron's hot."

"You agreed for us to do this play now."

"I agreed to look at de scene and *den* make up my mind. Dis fight has priority. Way lot of priority. So dat's what we gonna do."

I took a pause.

In that one tiny pause I made a decision and a plan and was amazed you could decide such important things, things that have to do with life and death, in such an infinitesimal amount of time. The plan was far-reaching and bold—like that of a chess player thinking ten moves ahead. I pressed the "Record" button on my phone.

"You know what, Joey? I'm not gonna fight any more."

Now *he* took a pause. "You not what?"

"You didn't hear what I said?"

"Yeah, but I can't believe my ears."

"Believe them, it's another fifteen years before they'll start failing you."

"You tellin' me you ain't gonna fight now or you never gonna fight?"

"Never, that's it. I'm quitting fighting."

"So lemme get dis straight. You come to my place, recommended by my cousin who you royally screwed over, you modder-fucker, you ask me to arrange for you to fight, I invest my money, my time, my influence to make you middleweight champ and you now have de balls to tell me you ain't gonna fight no more? Everyting I put in you goes down de drain?"

"Why don't you have your accountant add up the figures of what you spent and put them up against the figures of what you made on my fights and see how it balances out."

"You don't tell me what to do wit my accountant, you superior modder-fucker. I don't need no fuckin' accountant to know what I'd be losin' if you quit."

"Look, Joey, I know who and what you are. I may have had some grand idea that came from thirties' movies and Hemingway about friendship and honor and stuff like that and I may have fantasized that, because of what I thought we were to one another, you might say, 'Hey, good luck, kid, it's been great,' and that we might keep in touch and remain friends but fine, I'm awakened to reality, I realize how ugly you're going to get but let me ask you this. You think you can force somebody to fight if they don't want to any more than you can force somebody to love you?"

"Hey, Nixon said it better'n anybody. 'Get'em by de fuckin' balls an' deir hearts'n minds'll folla.' Yeah, you'll fight, you modder-fucker. Even if you tink you're brave an' ain't scared of what can happen to you, you got a modder, ain't you? You got a grandmodder. Can you protect dem? I can protect *my* family. Can you protect yours? What's'a madder, cat got your tongue? Not so high'n mighty now, are we? You report to fuckin' camp day after tomorra, ready to start trainin'. An' don't bodder tinkin' about no place to go 'cause dere ain't no place we can't find you *an'* your family."

And he hung up. And that was that. I pressed the "Record" button off. And what of my thoughts of honor and romance and dignity and grace and creativity, art, what of all that? Well—I'm sure Nixon and others of that ilk would have something to say about that too. A .38 always beats aces, how's that? Eat shit and die, how's that?

# CHAPTER THIRTY-SIX

That evening I called Charlene. A man answered in a cold, unfriendly tone. I identified myself.

"Yeah," he said in an even colder tone, if that was possible.

When a guy answers like that, you get a picture of how things are. You understand this guy does not trust this woman and they've had a hell of a lot of arguments on the subject of her going out, doing plays. And these have likely spread over into arguments on other subjects.

Charlene had mentioned in passing that her previous boyfriend had beaten her up a few times. Now, if you have any sense at all, you know that getting mixed up with a woman in this day and age who has gotten beaten up by someone she was going with is guaranteed trouble.

And I knew that. But I thought it didn't have to apply to me. I could raise her to another level. Where she was loved, respected, where the conversation she indulged in would be uplifting and stimulating and where whatever came up regarding a difference of opinion could be solved with mutual respect, harmony, understanding, and peace. Shows how wisdom-challenged I was.

There had been another incident with her that one might think would have turned me off. One time, coming to rehearsal, she'd run right to the bathroom. That was in addition to the time she'd done it just before the audition. It took a while for her to come out and, when she did, she told Karen and me how she had trouble with her bladder and, at certain times, she couldn't hold it in and just before rehearsal had been one of those times and she had ended up urinating in her pants.

When she told us this, my reaction was, *How could I have thought I was in love with this woman? How could you go down on someone who urinates in her pants?*

But, you know—that feeling didn't last long. Within three days I was right back in.

"Charlene home?"

"No."

"Any idea when she'll be back?"

"No."

"Could you ask her to call me when she does get back?"

"Yeh."

After hanging up, I was certain Charlene would not get the message. Then I remembered I had her cell number.

When she answered, her tone was melodic and inviting.

"Dan," I said.

"You didn't have to tell me," she said, "I'd know your voice anywhere, anytime."

"Ditto for me for yours. I called your home and left a message with your boyfriend but then I thought I'd better call you directly."

"You did right. Jamal's not very dependable and he doesn't like me being in plays."

"We have to postpone rehearsals for a while."

"What happened?" she asked and I knew the first thing actors think when they hear there's some kind of a problem is that they've been replaced. "You're not happy with my performance. I'm willing to do anything—anything. I really want to do this."

"Oh, no, I'm very happy with your performance. See, I box and I have a fight coming up."

"You box? What do you mean? You actually fight? Like in a ring?"

"Yeah."

"You do this professionally?"

"Yeah."

She wanted all the details, said her boyfriend was an avid fight fan and he'd know me. In the middle of the conversation I heard the little beep on my line and told her someone was ringing me and I had to go.

It was Mangiacavallo. I pressed the "Record" button on the phone again.

"Jus' had anodder tought," he said, plunging right in as if we were in the middle of talking. "Come over to my place for lunch tomorra at one an' I'll tell ya." He hung up. The relationship was obviously going into the mode where he was going to be giving orders and I was going to be obeying them. What a surprise!

That night I looked through bunches of videotapes for one to watch. What I generally did was peruse TV Guide each week and choose movies I wanted to see, tape them, file them and, when I had the time and was so inclined, watch them. I realized at some point in my life, between the movies you could watch on video, the new movies opening up, the best ones from all over the world coming to New York, the plays in the hundreds of theatres, the books, opera, then, on top of that, if you liked to create, if you were an artist of any kind and spent time doing that, what motive could you possibly have for talking to people who were less interesting than all the other stuff you could have access to in New York? Unless, of course, you needed someone to listen to *you* and find *you* interesting. Which very likely was the reason so many boring people sought each other's company. None was interested in *listening*. What they were interested in was talking. We all spent so much time being entertained, what we were starving for in order to balance the books was doing some entertaining ourselves. When you saw John and Jane Doe being interviewed on the street these days or on any kind of a game show, they were no longer modest and humble as in the olden days. No, they put on a show for you, John and Jane were doing a star turn, they all thought they were better than Jerry Seinfeld or Martin Lawrence. They were better than anybody. They were stars. We had become a nation of soi-disant super stars.

What I planned to do with Mangiacavallo was simplicity itself. All I needed was one item. Well, two. Well, three, if you wanted to get technical about it. And they were all things I had on hand. I was ready for him.

The way I looked at it, if I could not outsmart somebody who was stupid enough to be a gangster—I didn't deserve to live, let alone be successful.

I went into the bedroom, turned on the TV, found a French Open tennis match tape, and slipped it into the VCR.

I watched till I was so sleepy I had no interest in watching any more. I imagine it's similar to the way people think when they have decided to die. They must look around and think, *I have no interest in doing anything any more—except close my eyes and keep them closed.* It's that, "keep them closed" clause that makes the difference between going to sleep and going to die.

With that in mind, I went to sleep and woke up feeling refreshed and regenerated, the kind of feeling that everything was going to turn out wonderfully. Wouldn't it be something if dying were like that? Like *Groundhog Day?* Each lifetime a new dawn? I showered, did my speech exercises—which consisted of listening to a tape of Laurence Olivier reading the Bible and then, phrase by phrase, repeating his phrasing and intonation—after which I recorded myself reading from a book of poetry, then listened back for things I needed to do to improve my speech.

"I am an actor," Anne Bancroft is said to have told her husband Mel Brooks, "my body is my instrument," and Mel Brooks is supposed to have replied, "Oh, yeah? Lemme hear it play 'Begin the Beguine.'"

"Your body is your instrument," is what they tell actors. If it worked for actors, why not for ordinary people? Why couldn't your body, your voice, your spirit be your instruments to hone and hone till they performed like the finest of Stradivariuses? Or is it Stradivaria?

After the speech exercises, I did some sit-ups, lifted barbells, and rode the exercise bike. Then I had a concoction consisting of juices, greens, vitamins, minerals, and I was ready for Mangiacavallo, thinking what a nice juxtaposition, filling myself with all this healthy stuff to go see someone whose name is "Eats horse."

I like the idea of stepping out in the street and seeing a lot of people any time of day or night. In fact, I love seeing oodles of people. Each person represents a different world. I like the idea of being in so many worlds. A character in a Chinese movie said how, now that there are movies to go see, it's like living many lifetimes instead of just one.

When I got into a cab there was a brown suitcase on the seat. I remembered the story of the cab driver who'd found a suitcase with thirty-thousand dollars in his cab and had received hundreds of hate letters because he'd turned it in. The writers all thought he should've kept it. We've come a long way, baby.

I reached over and opened it.

"You know you have a suitcase in your cab?" I said to the driver.

"Huh? What you say?" He had an Indian accent enveloped by a tone of belligerence.

Dave Barry had written that one of the qualifications for being a cab driver in New York City was that one must not be able to speak English. To which one might add, "And an attitude of 'I couldn't care less.' "

"Never mind," I said, and looked into the open suitcase.

Inside was a tape recorder-player, a microphone, and a little speaker. A karaoke set. I reached over and pressed play. I recognized the song from the intro, placed the speaker out the window, and let it hang there by its wire. I picked up the microphone, held it close to my lips, and sang "Manhattan."

People were turning to look at the cab. When it comes to stuff like this, New Yorkers are the most receptive people in the world. They go around pretending nothing can shock them to fortify themselves against the bad stuff they expect in New York but stuff like this— they'll eat it up, they're starved for it.

People were smiling and waving at the cab. The cab driver was smiling too. He hummed along. What are the odds you'll find a Hindustani cab driver who knows the melody to "Manhattan"?

When I got to the part about the wondrous toy made for a girl and boy and turning Manhattan into an isle of joy, I thought, *The only thing missing for this boy is a girl.*

Canal Street was a hurly-burly of action. There is your humanity at its most industrious. Nothing you can't buy there and more cheaply than anywhere else. The rest of the world is dwarfed by what you can see and find in New York.

I left the karaoke set in the cab. Hell, maybe the cab driver was honest. If he knew a Rodgers and Hart song from the thirties, it was possible he might be honest.

Mangiacavallo's place was buzzing. I thought of what it might've been like had I accepted his original offer to sing here and never mentioned boxing. Would an agent, a casting director, or a producer have come in and said, "Hey, this guy's got something, let's sign him up"? Would the audience have responded so favorably to me that Mangiacavallo and his cohorts would have pushed me the way they'd pushed Sinatra?

I was conducted into the private garden where Mangiacavallo waited for me. He smiled and extended his hand, seeming glad to see me, without a trace of the harshness and cruelty that had been part of his demeanor when we'd spoken the night before.

That always amazes me about people. How pleasant they can be after they've acted like shits, pretending everything's still just fine, the way it had been before. I keep thinking of John McEnroe when he played. The behavior so ugly, the question of whether he was right or wrong paled into insignificance. And, to a greater or lesser degree, most people are like that. Revealing, under pressure, patches of such slime it's like watching maggots. Yet you look at McEnroe as a commentator and he's interesting, likable, and intelligent, acting as if he had never behaved in an ugly way in his life, tossing it all occasionally aside by saying, "I guess I have a bad temper," and even going so far as to make fun of his famous remark during a match to a referee: "You cannot be serious!"

Mangiacavallo was extra charming and hospitable, as if to make up for the cruelty he'd showed me.

"Siddown, siddown," he said, pointing me to one of the chairs at the table.

I sat down and looked around.

Mangiacavallo sat opposite me, shouting to the waiter in Italian.

"So how *you* doin'?" he asked in the manner of Joey Triviani from *Friends*, in his booming voice, jovial as hell.

"I'm doin' good, Joey, how *you* doin'?" I could do a Triviani as good as any gangsta.

"Been givin' our little talk some extra tought, know what I mean?"

"No, I don't, Joey. What do you mean?"

He paused for a moment, staring at me, not quite sure if I was razzing him.

I looked at him with seriousness and sincerity. I slipped my hand into my pocket below the tabletop where he couldn't see and leaned back in my chair. Oh, I was ready for him.

The waiter brought a bottle of red wine and two glasses. He poured some into Mangiacavallo's glass. Joey tasted it, nodded, and the waiter filled his glass. Then he filled mine and went away. Joey raised his glass and we clinked and drank. I remembered reading about a Persian custom in which gentlemen, when clinking glasses, make sure one gentleman's (it's mandatory they be gentlemen) glass clinks the bottom of the other gentleman's to show the respect of the one whose glass is below for the one whose glass is above. Sometimes, the one whose glass is above will, in turn, bring his own glass below the glass which had been below just a moment before and sometimes they'll keep doing that all the way to the floor like you do the hand-over-hand on a baseball bat to choose sides and then sometimes they'll even get into a fistfight over who respects whom more. Could you just see Americans doing that? Or better yet, New Yorkers?

The wine was smooth, rich, and mellow and, I suspected, homemade.

"Here's what I come up wid," Joey said. "De public loves dis stuff you do, divin' at de opponent, dey jus' eat it up, nothin' like it before, dat's why dey love it. Not only dey love it, dey tink you invincible. I got some pretty big woids myself, ha, paisan. 'Invincible,' how you like dat?"

I just stared at him without saying anything. You think you're ever gonna be my friend again, fucker?

But Mangiacavallo could give a shit. "Now, a few weeks ago," he said, "I hired de top firm in de country to do a survey on who de public tinks is gonna win if you two fight."

"What's the name of the guy you want me to fight?"

"What's'a matter, you don't folla de fight game no more? An' you forgot I tole you de name? Too busy wit show-biz and bimbos? Dis guy's hot stuff. Luis Gonzales. Puerto Rican. He's been vicious. Anodder Trinidad. But de funny ting is—de public and de bettin' people still tink you gonna knock'm out. Dey convinced you got some magic goin' for you. De money's gonna be on you. Very, very heavy odds."

"Let me guess where we're going with this, Joey." Very distinctly, using my best elocution, I said, "You want to put some serious money on Gonzales and you want me to lose the fight."

Even more distinctly, he said, "No. I don't *wanna* put some serious money on Gonzales and I don't *want* you to lose de fight. I'm *gonna* put some serious money on Gonzales and you're *gonna* lose de fight. Now—dere's gonna be a rematch clause. In de rematch, it's gonna be de odder way aroun'. Odds are gonna be against you an' I'm gonna put some serious money on you. Now, needless to say, you can add to dis money out'a your own pocket an' I'll bet it for you, as much as you want, dere's no limit to how much is gonna be dere for de takin'."

For once, I was glad Mangiacavallo had a loud voice and wasn't shy about using it.

I almost laughed right in his face. The scene we were playing was a compilation of all the movies and plays I'd seen about boxing. And the funny thing was it was so true it had become a cliché.

"You want me to lose this fight we're going to fight in three months, Gonzales and I," I said resonantly and distinctly, "and then on the rematch I'm supposed to win?"

"Why you talkin' like dat?"

"Like what?"

"Like you a fuckin' actor—on de stage."

"I *am* an actor. I'm working on practicing my speech, my voice is my instrument."

"When you wit me, you a fighter—so shove dat instrument up your ass. You talkin' to *me*. You unnerstan' dat?"

"Is Gonzales going to be apprised of the fact when it's his turn to lose?"

"What's 'apprised'?"

"Notified."

"So why can't you say dat?"

"We gonna go through that again?"

"Yeah. For de last time. I want you to use woids people can unnerstan'. Get off'a dat fuckin' cloud nine, I don't wanna spend de rest'a my life lookin' up woids *or* lookin' up at you, know what I mean?"

"I know what you mean."

"Good. De answer to your question is, I expect you to woik your magic but, yes, de fucker's gonna be 'apprised' it's his turn to lose— just in case your magic don't woik no more, know what I mean?"

"I think I do," I said with great seriousness.

Again he looked at me, this time with a little more suspicion regarding the possibility I might be razzing him.

"So do you still want me to go to training camp?" I asked.

"What kind'a silly-ass question is dat? You wanna 'apprise' everybody it's a set-up? Yeah, you gonna train an' you gonna train twice as hard as usual. Let de media see an' let de public tink you got serious intentions to keep your crown."

# CHAPTER THIRTY-SEVEN

It's amazing how good you can feel when you're playing a game—say like chess—and you figure out what the opponent is going to do, and the opponent goes ahead and does it.

I had no bad feelings about Mangiacavallo, I didn't even dislike him. Like everyone, he had figured out what the best way was for him to deal with life and this was what he'd come up with. Maybe the main factor in his configuration was some kind of primordial fear, the need to aggrandize himself or keep himself safe through the destruction of everything and everyone around him—it doesn't matter. What matters is I was able to peg it so I could go ahead and figure out what *I* was going to do.

Once I knew what I was dealing with, it was simple.

There're dangers. Look at people who deal with alligators and such. They know what to do but there's always a chance of miscalculation. Statistically, airplane travel is the safest mode of transportation but should something go wrong, the chances of your survival are minimal.

The game between Mangiacavallo and me was on. He was going to do what he was going to do—and I was going to do what I was going to do.

Training can be a pleasure when, as in anything, it's done moderately. Trouble these days was in this, as in anything, they were driving it to the $n$th degree. Trainers worked on muscles and conditioning in a scientific manner and it was as if they were dealing with machines. It had become a pragmatic exercise in which whatever fun had existed was long gone. Athletes kept getting injured and burned out in a few years and hated it—but kept going. The only question was, "What do I have to do to win?"

There is nothing quite so pathetic as an ex-star, whether in sports or entertainment. In sports, your span, dependent as it is on the physical aspects, is shorter but, either way, nobody is ever prepared for how they're going to feel when their stardom is over.

I wanted to develop the kinds of satisfactions that would be with me forever. I wanted to exercise at a rate I would be able to keep up for decades and decades, not the kind of rate that would burn me out. I didn't want to lean in any way on the fame aspect of anything I did. Whatever satisfaction I got had to come from the act of creating, the doing-ness—nothing else.

So I went to training camp and did all the things I was supposed to do—knowing it was the last time I would do them. I got up early in the morning and ran. Then I had breakfast. Then it was on the machines, working different parts of the body. Then lunch. Then bicycling, then chopping wood—the Rocky factor—then hitting the bag, sparring, then dinner, then I went into my room to read, then sleep. Day after day. What a way. All for, "What do I have to do to win?"

They showed me tapes of Luis Gonzales. He was vicious. Even more so than Trinidad. He came at you without regard to what you were throwing—as long as he could get his own punch in. Like Joe Frazier used to be—take three to get one of your own in.

Funny how the public regarded what I did in the ring as some sort of magic. Without knowing it, they sensed some kind of transcendence.

Well, it was all magic anyway—all of life. The difference between the magic of life and the other kind of magic—the kind we all call magic—has to do with the difference between scarcity and plenty. Life has ceased to be magic because there is so much of it all around it's all become ordinary. Somebody walking on water or parting the waters is a scarcity so it's regarded as a miracle—magic. If people were able to do it all over the place, it wouldn't be magic any more.

I had the idea making love might make the man in sheets with the knife stop appearing. I don't know why. Probably because I thought there is a kind of innocence and purity in all of us while we're growing up I think of as not being present when we make love. I realized I'd made love to Sandy, Hagit, and Rachael and the man in sheets still came but I thought I might've gotten away with something there and if I did it again, the genie might stop appearing. Priests were supposed to lead an ascetic life and, for years, so were athletes. There is a strong lore from time immemorial about the man losing his essence when he releases his sperm. In *Doctor Strangelove*, the general who has decided to start an atomic war says he hasn't had sex for years because he doesn't want to lose his "essence." In *The Cincinnati Kid*, the card sharp Steve McQueen portrays loses his winning streak after he has sex with Ann Margaret—the proverbial siren—remaining "gutted" forever more.

It would be funny if the man with the knife *didn't* show up. I remembered reading a comic book when I was little about a baby elephant portrayed as a kid who went to school with all kinds of other animals, all portrayed as human kids. Some of these were tigers, lions, panthers, the array. This little elephant-kid was very cowardly and all the other animal-kids beat up on him regularly. Then, some animal-kid gave the elephant-kid three acorns and told him they were magic acorns and would make him stronger and braver than anybody. And, boy, did that elephant start beating up the bullies.

Then he lost the acorns and became a coward again. But the kid who gave him the acorns explained they hadn't really been magic acorns. It had been the elephant's own thought that had made the elephant strong.

I knew it was really my own mind that had produced a via for my quickness and strength to elevate to the point where I could knock out all these people. But even knowing that, if the man with the knife failed to appear—I thought just about anybody in the world could beat the shit out of me, let alone a vicious guy like Gonzales.

Well, so what? As Bill Johnson had said, thousands of guys had gotten knocked out. Those who had developed brain trouble had had their brains beaten in over a period of years, it did not happen with one punch—often.

I was getting very, very horny. You know—"Me so hawny!" Masturbating I thought to be degrading. I don't really know why. I know why I would not want to go to a prostitute, that answer is very clear to me. But I was never quite sure of masturbating. I had read when younger about the old wives' tales of it making you blind and, when you read something connected to sex, maybe because of the sheer power of sex, there is a tendency to pay attention to this rumor that had been passed on to us by—the Puritans? But then I read somewhere where the writer humorously stated he'd decided as a kid to do it only to the point where he'd need glasses. That little piece of humor blew away some of the considerations I'd had about not doing it. Yet, I still kept on not doing it. I don't know why. Perhaps because I wanted to save myself for the woman I'd fall in love with?

Now there was no one around for me to fall in love with. I supposed I could go into town and find somebody. The joke about the cowpoke in the Old West flashed through my mind. He'd gotten a job on a far-away ranch where there were only guys and, what with their work, they didn't get to go any place where there were women for months at a time. One of the other hands tells the guy, "If you get real horny, there's this Chinee boy, cook's helper, looks like a girl. You could use him."

The new cowpoke is contemptuous of the thought and rejects it out of hand.

Weeks pass, however, and the Chinese boy starts looking better and better. Finally, the new hand asks the old fellow who'd told him about it, "If'n I *was* to use the Chinee boy, be just us three know about it, right?"

"Ackchelly," the old hand tells him, "be five know about it."

"Five," the new guy says. "Where you get five?"

"Well," the old hand tells him, "there's you, me, the Chinee boy and the two guys that hold the boy down."

Or I could call Sandy and have her meet me somewhere and we could do it but I did not just want to "do" it. I wanted the works, all the things I'd had in Paris and Athens, I wanted the magic. After all—we *did* have Paris.

Was that why the man with the knife kept appearing? To provide the magic I liked so much?

On top of it all, it was much harder to abstain now, having had a taste of it.

So I bypassed my considerations and started spanking the monkey. And it turned out there was something exciting and liberating about it. You could imagine the act with anyone at any time in any place and have it just the way you wanted it. And they would behave just the way you wanted them to and no disappointments and no bickering.

I took to doing it three, four, five times an evening. Didn't seem to make any difference in my training. Made me a little more relaxed maybe. I thought of the movie *Spanking the Monkey*, where the boy sits in the bathroom, trying to have a go at it and the dog sits outside the door, sniffing underneath, making sounds till the boy, lest the dog draw attention to them, finally lets him in. But then the dog just sits there, staring at the boy so how can he concentrate with the dog looking on. Probably would not have helped him one bit to remember what "dog" spelled backwards is.

Every few days Mangiacavallo would show up to see how training was going. I was cordial but it was an entirely different kind of cordiality than the one I'd extended to him before. I'm sure he felt it; people always know what you feel toward them, even when they choose not to identify it or give it significance. Mangiacavallo didn't show he noticed a thing—or else he didn't give it any importance. Like all dictators. He wanted to be top dog, spelled backwards, and if you resented it, fuck you. So we were no longer equals, he made sure he let me know he would be the fucker and I would be the fuckee.

I did not let it get to me. When Teddy Roosevelt said, "Speak softly and carry a big stick," this was what he was talking about: make sure you had the wherewithal to handle what needed to be handled. If you did that, you had no need to let your emotions make you miserable. It was so simple you wondered why there was so much trouble in the world. It was all emotions about things that hardly ever had much to do with the matter at hand.

It felt good to be running early in the morning. Something life-giving and nurturing about being in the middle of nature. Like where there was a lot of water around or in the woods or mountains. It kept your mind close to where it felt best. The miracle and mystery of life. Refreshing. More so, I think, when you live in New York than anywhere else. Sometimes I ask myself how it would be if I lived somewhere else. Say in Jamaica or France or Italy or Switzerland—or California—where I could be with nature. And it's fine being in any of those places for a certain amount of time. But when I think of living in any of them—it's like leaving the center of the universe.

Whatever forces are battling for the hearts and minds of the world, New York is the vital spot. That is where the battle will be fought and decided. And that's where I have to be.

So I enjoyed my time in the woods and mountains, breathing the fresh air and thinking of how I had put into effect my plan regarding Mangiacavallo and was in a win-win situation—except if, as with wild animal trainers, there is a miscalculation and the wild animal doesn't do what it's supposed to do.

But that was the thing that made life interesting. If a chess player made the move that was supposed to win him the match in ten or fifteen moves and if it were absolutely certain his opponent *would* make the moves he was supposed to make—a hundred percent certain—the game wouldn't be fun. If all were certain ahead of time—nothing would be fun. Just as nothing would be fun if everything were *un*certain.

The fun was in there being a certain amount of—certainty—and a certain amount of uncertainty. Things you knew, things you didn't know. A question of finding the right balance.

As a rule, I did not meet people during my morning run. One morning, a week before we were to go back to the city, someone was suddenly running alongside of me. I jerked in surprise and almost tripped over myself.

It was Sandy—dressed in jeans, sweat shirt, sneakers, and carrying a backpack, jogging.

"I have something I want to talk to you about," she said. "Can you meet me?"

I was so horny I would've been happy to stop right there and make love to her in the woods. But I didn't want her to see how eager I was.

"I'll meet you here tonight at seven o'clock," I said.

"See you," she said and veered off downhill.

The rest of the training day was extra exciting. I was so eager I could hardly stand it. For years, growing up, I had gone without making love but once that door was opened it appears impossible to go back to where you were before. Male dogs are that way. Once they've tasted it, forget about it, they'll go for miles to track down a female in heat, they'll do anything. It's like that post-World War I song—"How you gonna keep them down on the farm after they've seen Paree?"

I took a shower before dinner and put on a fresh pair of sweats instead of slacks so no one would suspect I was going to a rendezvous. After dinner I told my trainer I was going for a walk and left. Some guys were playing poker, watching pornos and I was into neither of those activities so they were just as glad to see me go.

The night was cool as it tends to get in the country and I was hoping she had driven up in a van where there would be plenty of space in the back. Whatever reasons I'd had for breaking up with her became meaningless. Being afraid sex would make the genie disappear? Meaningless. I remembered the old joke about the family of eleven that was on welfare and the wife was pregnant with the twelfth. In the hospital, waiting for delivery, the father is asked by the social worker if he had he ever given thought to the fact he was unable to support all these children.

"Sure I've thought about it," the father answers. "But at that moment, I feel I can support a million of'em."

I actually ran to the spot, making sure, when I was in view, to slow down to a leisurely walk.

When I approached I acted cool and distant, let her do some more apologizing and begging, let's see how creative she could be, the sex would be that much better.

She kissed me on each cheek, European style, and said, "Let's take a walk."

We walked. I love walking in the country. There's something that surges inside me when I walk in the country. Especially when it's with a woman. Whatever things are bothering you, when you're in the country, they turn insignificant. And nothing really did bother me—except I wanted very badly to get laid. Where had my pride gone? The same place, probably, where all the flowers had gone.

Who cared? I wanted to get laid.

"How's training going?" she asked.

She seemed different. There was a serenity and humility about her that hadn't been there before. Maybe she had had a genuine realization about how wrong she had been to abandon me the way she had and was now genuinely contrite—as opposed to before, when she'd wanted to be involved in the project for Pitt. You see, I was already rationalizing getting together again. I wanted to get laid.

"Fine," I said. I was waiting for her to do what she was going to do to get us to the stage where I would be willing to make love. I was willing right now but it was up to her to come up with the right pitch. When someone did something wrong, the balance of power was awry—and had to be put back in place. And the party that had caused the imbalance was obligated to come up with the appropriate pitch to set it back into balance. It was like what had been played out in the Cuban missile crisis. The Russians had done something to upset the balance so they'd had to eat crow to right it.

"Listen," she said, "you don't have to give me any money for this project you're going into with Pitt, it's your thing and you're right not to want me involved."

What the hell was she up to now? Well, whatever it was, I trusted her to come up with the right stuff that would enable us to have sex.

"I don't have a problem," I said, "giving you the percentage I promised you."

"I don't want it. Credit or money. Getting you two together, that was nothing. Consider it trying in part to make up for the way I deserted you."

"You came all the way here to tell me that?"

"I came to tell you something else but first I wanted to tell you this."

"And the other thing?"

She stopped and stared at me. She kept on staring.

"What?" I asked.

"I'm wondering if you're ready."

"Ready for what?"

"Ready to hear what I have to say."

"You're starting to make me nervous."

"What I have to say might strike you as freaky."

"You in trouble?"

"On the contrary. I'm fine. Most of the rest of the world, including you, is in trouble. I'm fine."

"Now you're starting to freak me out."

"What would you say if I told you I came across something that resolves any problem anybody ever had or ever could have?"

"I'd say you were in the Middle Ages and just discovered alchemy—or you're Ponce De Leon and just found the fountain of youth. Or—"

"Don't do that."

"All right."

"That's really the only difficult part about this whole business. We've been fooled and betrayed so often we can't believe something like this could possibly exist."

"Something like what?"

"That there could be something that could, like magic, solve every problem there is and raise us to a level of unimaginable happiness and capability. All the drugs, sex, all the violence there ever was or could be can't hold a candle to the amount of ecstasy and power we could feel permanently, irreversibly without taking a thing."

She had cracked. How or why she had cracked I didn't know. I didn't want to flatter myself thinking she could've been pushed over the edge because of what had happened between us; it didn't matter why. The fact was she had cracked.

"All right," she said, "now you think I'm crazy, don't you?"

Who was I to think anybody crazy? At least she could talk about her craziness—which she was undoubtedly about to do. I couldn't even mention mine.

"Do you?" she repeated.

"No."

And I meant it. There were millions of people who took drugs, drink, sex, or got into some kind of therapy thinking desperately it would pull them out of the quicksand or at least postpone their sinking. You didn't have to be crazy to do that. No. I was still the prime candidate for that distinction.

I asked, "What is this thing?" (called love)

Of course, all you had to do to one of these people who've discovered some kind of panacea is ask them what is it and they'll go into a monologue that would put the greatest filibusterer to shame. If it was some kind of a therapy, that is. If it was something else—like drink, drugs, sex, or exercise, they won't say a word about it. You'll just see the effects of it. If it's some kind of an improvement thing or psychiatry—they'll talk you to death.

"It's a philosophy slash religion," she said. "It's a technology, actually."

*Here we go,* I thought. "And?" I asked.

"And it does what I told you it does. That's it."

"And you decided to rush here from New York to tell me about it?"

"That's right."

"And the reason would be—?"

"I wanted you to know about it as soon as possible."

"Why?"

"Are you angry with me?"

"No." Which was a lie. I was angry with her for coming at me with a philosophy slash religion when I was expecting sex. How could we get to sex from where she'd put us now?

"Are you annoyed, then?"

I couldn't tell her what I really was so I had to lie again. "No."

"You act annoyed. If you act annoyed but tell me you're not, one of these is a lie."

"I just didn't expect proselytizing on a beautiful country evening."

"You expected hot sex?"

"All right, look. Let's just get to why you had to rush in here and break into my training to talk to me about some miracle elixir."

"If that's how you feel, I'm sorry I bothered you." She turned to go.

"Wait, Sandy."

She stopped and turned.

"I'm sorry for being rude," I said. "I appreciate your coming here to share something you feel is valuable. I have things on my mind that have to do with the fight and I get a little snappy. I apologize. It's really nice to see you. Let's continue our walk; I'd love to hear what you have to say."

I'm not going to lie. I was hoping we'd get around to having sex after all.

We resumed our walk.

"It's a question," she said, "of looking at something for what it really is as opposed to coming at it from a derogatory position without knowing anything about it—except perhaps gossip and innuendo. Where can we go from there except to an argument? Why not wipe the slate clean, be open, and find out rather than taking a closed, antagonistic position?"

"Okay. Let's go back to where you first told me about it."

"Let's go a little further back to just before I told you about it and let's find out what it is you were expecting out of this encounter, shall we?"

"Whatever it was, it wasn't being preached at, converted, or baptized."

"You see how you're playing a game? You won't admit to what you *were* expecting, just what you weren't."

"What difference does it make how I put it? The point is I wasn't expecting this."

"Okay. I'm going about it the wrong way. I've brought this to share with you because I believe, with your professed ideals and ethics, you're evolved enough to look at it. I'm not asking you to go into it, all I'm asking you to do is look at it without having made up your mind beforehand it's something you're not going to like."

"I'm in the middle of training, I've got an important fight coming up, I can't look at anything right now."

"You have time to read in the evening, don't you?"

"Yes."

"If I give you a book, will you read it?"

"Sandy—I'm not only in the middle of training, I'm in the middle of something that's much bigger and more dangerous and has many more consequences than just winning or losing a championship bout."

"Mangiacavallo?"

"Yeah."

"Having somebody like that in your life is one of the indications you've got to pull yourself up to another level."

"If I embraced this philosophy slash religion of yours, I wouldn't have people like Mangiacavallo in my life?"

"That's just one of the things that would happen to you."

"You mean he would just magically disappear from my life? A car would hit him or some opposing gang member would shoot'm down, something like that?"

"How many freaky, unexpected coincidences have changed the course of nations, continents, even the world?"

"If I go into this philosophy slash religion of yours, I could make such things happen?"

"That's right."

"So you're making greater claims for this philosophy than—"

"Applied philosophy."

"*Applied* philosophy. Okay. What does *that* mean?"

"It means it's not something to *believe* in. It's something to *do*. If it works, you believe in it because you've witnessed and experienced it working. If it doesn't work, there's nothing to believe in. The difference between this and every other religion, philosophy, or therapy is that all those others give you precepts you are to believe in and follow on faith without regard to your feelings on the matter or whether they work or not. 'Do unto others,' for instance. George Bernard Shaw said, 'Do not do unto others as you would have them do unto you; they may not have the same taste.' Even beyond that, however, the only reason given for any of these precepts is that it's the 'right way.' Well, we've been through too much to take it for granted that, just because someone in authority tells us something is so, it must be the truth. More often than not, we've discovered the truth lies in the opposite direction. What we demand today is—workability. Prove to us beyond the shadow of a doubt that it works—inexorably. And on top of that, make us *feel* like doing it. *Feel* like it—you know, the way you feel like taking a drink or watching a fight or making love or taking a swim on a scorching day or reading a great book, watching a great play or a movie,or listening to a wonderful song—*feel* like it."

"And this thing of yours does that?"

"Inexorably."

"And you *feel* like doing the right, the beneficial things the way you feel like doing all those delicious things you mentioned?"

"Inexorably."

"And if I went into it, how long would it take me to get rid of Mangiacavallo?"

"If you, for God's sake, look at it in such a petty fashion and think of it as a thing to do your bidding like a magic wand, you *deserve* to have Mangiacavallo in your life."

"Right now, what is sitting right in front of me, staring me in the face, is Mangiacavallo who has me in the kind of a vise that will either lose me my integrity and dreams or my bodily life."

She took a pause, regarding me.

"Okay. Then nothing can be done in the way of your absorbing this technology until that problem is resolved."

"So you came all the way here for nothing?"

"I *can* tell you one thing that will be useful to you until you resolve this and are able to look into this technology more deeply. Problems are not resolved purely on the basis of what is good for one person or one group but on the basis of what is good for the greatest number and what harms the smallest number."

"Greatest and smallest number of what?"

"Beings—things—everything that exists in the world that can benefit the world. I have a book you could read in the meantime. Jump-start you, give you some fresh thoughts, ideas, feelings, a different perspective—a new slant."

She took a hard cover book of, I judged, 300 pages out of her backpack and handed it to me.

"This is going to be an adventure the likes of which you've never dreamed. Read it. If there's anything I can do to help you—in any way—call me. When you're ready, we can get you going and you'll step into a dimension far, far greater than any heaven that's ever been envisioned—compared to which the existence we lead without this technology is like the worst hell anybody's ever imagined."

"And this was developed by—?"

"One man—who goes beyond what we consider genius. Who, with years and years of research and testing all over the world, came up with a technology that's documented in hundreds of published volumes numbering millions and millions of words."

"When did you get into this?"

"Got introduced to it by a friend. I'm absorbing this stuff at a rate of 60 hours a week, I eat, breathe, and live it from the moment I wake up to the moment I go to sleep."

"Something like a Moonie?"

"Nothing like the Moonies. It's nothing like anything. People have ideas about things based not on what they know about the thing itself but on the basis of what they heard, in addition to their innate prejudices. Read this book. Get to know a little about it, then we'll talk some more."

She leaned over, kissed me on the cheek, and was gone.

It was getting dark. I began walking back.

# CHAPTER THIRTY-EIGHT

I tossed the book on the dresser. I didn't have the patience right now to read anything that smelled of self-improvement. At another time I might've given it a look. Right now I was in the process of moving toward a goal. There was something very big in my way that I would have to overcome and if I didn't do it right, it would be the end of everything. I had put my life on the line and it had become the chip on the table. My life—against the best things the world had to offer.

It was like the stock market. If you wanted great gains, you had to take great risks. Most people did not take risks. They went through life, eking out a living and maybe a few luxuries and, if they wanted more, they had to risk something, the risk being proportionate to what there was to gain. The gain was sometimes measured in terms of what was valuable to the individual and sometimes what society thought valuable. Either way you had to take risks proportionate to the perceived value of your goal. Sometimes you did not see the risks until much later, when you became the effect of the consequences.

As fight day approached, more and more media people came to the camp for interviews and video-tapings of my training sessions. One of them was a cute woman, black, very slim, representing a Jamaican publication.

"How come Jamaica is interested in this fight?" I asked her while she was interviewing me.

"Luis Gonzales was raised by a Jamaican family in Brooklyn," she said. "They found him on a park bench when he was a baby and adopted him."

"Did they mistreat him?"

"They're very warm, loving, and kind. Why would you think they mistreated him?"

"When you watch him fight, he seems so vicious."

"When you talk to him he's gentle as a lamb."

"Why does someone gentle as a lamb turn to fighting?"

"An interesting question for a middle-weight champion to ask. Why did *you* turn to it?"

There's a special lilt and melody to Jamaican speech and she had a very sweet voice. I got lost in it and was staring at her. She had a pretty, oval face with large brown eyes, but what captivated me even more was that there was a benevolent look about her with that high clean looking, unlined forehead you see in documentaries about Africans who have been more or less untouched by what we call civilization. It has the purity and good nature of a child ever ready to smile and play with not a thought of anything unclean or evil.

Except, aside from obviously being natively intelligent, she had gotten a modern education and the combination of this raw innocence and purity with the education was beguiling.

"Hello," she said. "Where did you drift off to?"

"I did drift for a moment. What did you say your name was?"

"Morshia Ellis," she said, rolling the "R."

"Morshia with an 'O'?"

"Like Liza with a 'Z.' "

"Interesting."

"Are you going to answer my question?"

"I'll answer any question you put to me. The prime reason being I'd like to keep you around as long as possible."

There're people in this world to whom you feel like telling everything. They're rare; mostly, you run into people who feel like telling *you* everything. I felt like pouring my guts out to her. I told her I hated fighting and how all I wanted to do now was get through this one more fight and how I would then go into what I really wanted to do with my life—act, direct, and write.

Much as I was tempted to, I had not gone ga-ga enough to tell her about the man with the knife.

"If the reason," she said, "for going into fighting in the first place was to make the kind of name for yourself that would open the door to a career in acting, writing, and directing, isn't losing the fight going to go somewhat against your objective?"

As I had not told her of Mangiacavallo's demand I lose the coming fight, this woman was either a psychic or she had access to inside information—or she was taking a shot in the dark. Either way, she was sharper than I'd thought—and I'd thought her very sharp in the first place. If my number one turn-on was goodness, then number two was definitely intelligence.

"What makes you think I'm going to lose?"

"I hear certain kinds of bets are being placed."

"You expect me to comment on this fishing expedition?"

She took the slightest of beats.

"If you were to win, Mister Mangiacavallo would be very upset, wouldn't he?"

This was beginning to feel very weird. There *was* something psychic about her, you could feel it, you could see it. It was something native in her that had persisted through the centuries—right through the modern education she'd gotten and the tasteful velvet blouse and modish short skirt she was wearing to exhibit the shapeliest legs it had been my fortune to gaze upon. Never mind the bets being placed she'd heard about. The knowledge I was sensing in this woman came from a totally different source. I did not want to go there.

"You journalists are quite a breed, aren't you?"

"And when Mister Mangiacavallo gets upset, people have been known never to be heard from again."

"Are you planning to print this theory of yours?"

"A journalist's *raison d'etre* is to put out whatever's newsworthy."

"Even if your theory were true, once you print it, you think it could possibly take place?"

"If there's enough money on the table, the assassination of a president can take place."

"I don't suppose it would bother you you'd be putting me in a very uncomfortable spot."

"How so?"

"If your theory were true, who would Mangiacavallo be likely to think told you about it?"

"Well, *you* didn't—and that's the truth."

"Truth may be beauty but the consequences are often not."

"You have a point. On the other hand, if you're asking me to suppress the story you would seem to be interfering with one of your basic constitutional freedoms."

"I wouldn't think of interfering with such a sacred umbrella based on something as unworthy as my life any more than I would expect a press photographer to help a person in pain when he has a chance to photograph the suffering instead."

"Ouch."

"I would want you to print whatever you feel you ought to print."

"Are you telling me you're depending upon the kindness of journalists?

"I think my tendencies are more in the direction of Doctor Pangloss."

"Everything is for the best in this the best of all possible worlds?"

"Something like that."

"Wow. A literate fighter."

"Almost as rare as a literate journalist?"

"Ouch again. This is turning out to be unexpectedly interesting."

"I was thinking the exact same thing. Except mine was more in the area of 'enjoyable.' "

"Despite the fact that with what I may or may not print I hold your life in my hands?"

"I think you have your hands on something of mine that's even more meaningful."

"Dare I ask what it is?"

"My heart."

She was silent for a while, gazing at me, a tiny smile playing about her lips.

"Considering," she said, "you have a very practical reason to woo me, might that last shot not be considered somewhat below the belt?"

"I don't believe you'd consider it that."

She took a beat. "I don't."

Now I stared at her for a while.

And then I asked the most exciting question there is. "Will I see you again?"

"I live in Kingston."

"Down de way," I sang, "where de nights are gay and de sounds of laughter fill de air—" I went back to speaking. "Kingston, Brooklyn, what matter?"

"You would come all the way to Kingston to take me out?"

"I would go to Australia to take you out."

"On the basis of speaking to me for a few minutes?"

"To know I'd go anywhere to take you out took less than a few seconds. A few minutes is what it took to know I'd want to be with you for a lot longer than a date."

"*Now* you're hitting below the belt."

"Why?"

She looked me in the eyes and said more with the look than either of us could say if we spoke for hours.

But one has to say something. So she said, "Because it's getting difficult to breathe."

"Are you going to come to the fight?"

"My paper will be sending a regular sports writer; a man, of course."

"If I send you a ticket, will you come on your own?"

She took a beat. "Let me give you my card. You can call me when I get back home and we can talk about it."

From that day I stopped being horny. Maybe it was the excitement of the approaching fight and everything that was involved regarding it, but I had a feeling it wasn't. I just stopped thinking of other women. There was something about Morshia that enveloped me, translating itself into a lack of thought about sex. A goodness and brightness that made me feel both happy and certain we were for each other. I thought of a speech I'd heard in a movie where the woman tells the man how she'd waited all her life for what she'd known was the promise of him. It felt like a fait accompli, a matter of destiny that gave no room for equivocation.

Assuming I would be able to handle Mangiacavallo, then make a successful transfer into show business, there was still one underlying problem. The man with the knife. He had caused me to rise and was the key to my future, yet I had no idea how he had gotten there or why. From the time it had begun happening I had disturbing thoughts of it being something that could destroy me—yet I had no idea of what I could do about it.

The one thing we have in this world we are supposed to do when anything dealing with the emotions and the spirit goes awry is go to a psychiatrist or a psychologist. Well, I'd read enough about psychiatry and psychology and met enough of them to be convinced beyond a doubt that not only is it neither a science nor an art, but that it is the biggest bunch of crap perpetrated on humanity since humanity appeared. They ask questions that beg for self-serving answers but what they do most of all is give drugs. Their only significant accomplishment is they've somehow convinced most of the world they are the authority when it comes to emotional problems and, as a consequence, governments, businesses, and private individuals have sunk billions of dollars to enable their thriving. From everything I've read and heard about witch doctors, psychiatrists and psychologists are a lot worse. But it happens to be the only game in town so either you play it or play with yourself.

And just as I've had thoughts the man with the knife was something I shouldn't be ignoring, I've had thoughts of it possibly being something like Faust, a bargain of some sort made with the devil—or the spiritual equivalent of a big lump suddenly appearing somewhere on your body and you're ignoring it. Just as my mother had tried to do with the one that had appeared on her breast.

And just as you're going to one day have to deal with a lump if it appears, you're going to have to deal with whatever goes awry emotionally and spiritually. Ultimately, the bill arrives—and it has to be paid.

I had the sense that, with the direction Mangiacavallo had taken plus the guy with the knife plus Luis Gonzales, it was like a bunch of cars traveling on different roads toward the same intersection, all due to arrive there at the same moment.

# CHAPTER THIRTY-NINE

I received the article Morshia had written for the Kingston paper. It said I was a ruggedly handsome young man who read a lot, was intelligent and thoughtful beyond his years, and what a contrast such an individual was to the game of boxing where the objective was to knock your opponent on his rear end and, if you could do that, you were feted and idolized more than the discoverer of the cure for cancer though you might have the looks and the IQ of an orangutan.

It talked about my modesty and my question of what motivated Luis Gonzales, my coming opponent, to be so vicious in the ring.

"I told him," the article continued, "it was simply a matter of doing something one knew one could do well. Later on, however, I found myself not being able to get off quite that easily. Why *does* one go into boxing in the first place? It is the only endeavor in the universe as far as we know where the sole objective is to hurt the other person. Even in American football and hockey, hurting is merely one of the perks. An important perk, to be sure, but still not the overtly main objective, not according to the stated rules, at any rate.

"What is it, then, that prompts a person to go into an activity where your whole life revolves around hurting someone?

"Dan Kahn's question to me was, 'Did Luis Gonzales' parents mistreat him that he is so vicious?'

"The opposite is the truth. Even though Luis' parents found him on a park bench where he'd been abandoned as a baby, they were not only extremely loving and considerate in his upbringing but they respected his potential sense of heritage so much they kept the name that was scribbled on a piece of paper pinned to his diaper when they found him. Having, in addition, talked to Luis Gonzales a number of times, I found him to be a gentle, benevolent person; nothing like what the public sees when they watch him perform in the ring. What is his real nature? Is it what we get when we talk to him—or what we feel about him when we watch him fight?

"Ultimately, we come back to the original question: what is it in a person that makes him want to devote his life to hurting someone else, make a living off it, and be famous for it?

"The easy answer, one that has become acceptable to the great majority, is that the moment one says, 'make a living off it and become famous for it,' one is begging the question. For, in our day and culture, we deem nothing worthier than making a living and becoming famous. It matters little to us what we make a living off of and are famous for, as long as we make a living and are famous.

"I took the assignment of writing this article about Luis Gonzales and the champion Dan Kahn as a matter of course, like any other assignment. Dan Kahn's question as to what made Luis Gonzales so vicious in the ring caused me to give thought to the entire phenomenon of fighting. The pursuit of that thought brought me eventually to the point where I questioned the very profession I find *myself* in. For, in writing about it, am I not priming the hunger for it? And isn't the public, in hungering for it, mightily fueling the fighters and their sycophants?

"It goes further than that. In examining my profession, I came to the sad conclusion that the stories we journalists write and call 'news' is not 'all the news that's fit to print.' It is, I'm sad to say (I'm on my way, won't be back for many a day), all the *bad* news, most of it not fit to print. When asked why the media so rarely indulge in good news, the journalist inevitably answers, 'People are much hungrier for and willing to spend a lot more money on bad news than on good news.'

"Fair enough. But what happens as a result of it? We journalists and producers of entertainment in general come to rely on the existence and the spreading of anything and everything that's evil, violent, and perverse in order to, first survive, then make more money, then become more famous.

"Artists who are dealing with things they create out of their imaginations have the choice of creating something violent and evil or something beautiful and inspiring. Journalists with or without integrity don't have that choice. We depend on recreating things supposed to be based on fact. Where does that put us? It puts us first in the realm of wishing for, then choosing, then stressing, then re-ordering and exaggerating things so they will come out in a way that will, as it is perceived, get more people to watch, read or listen.

"If we were to give what we journalists do for the most part a name—what would that name be? Well, once again, I'm sad to say—we are the merchants of chaos. It's what we deal with. Our livelihood and our survival depend on chaos. We're not the only ones, to be sure, but ours is definitely one of the professions the survival of which depends on there being chaos.

"I've decided I no longer want to participate in that. I don't want to be part of anything that depends on violence and suffering for its survival.

"And I don't want to be associated with anyone who participates in those kinds of endeavors. It is not enough, I've decided, to abstain from doing things that are bad for all of us; I want to be counted among those who do not associate or support in any way groups and individuals who participate in those things.

"I, therefore, no longer find in my heart the desire nor the capacity to continue in a profession whose aims go against what I find my true goals to be.

"So I bid you goodbye, my dear readers, wish you all well, and may God bless you."

*Wait a minute*, I thought, *what just happened? Could it be that the very person I thought was my destiny has just written me a public Dear John?*

I picked up the phone and dialed. The number she'd given me was disconnected. How could I locate her?

But then, why should I?

She'd made her feelings clear in the article. She did not want to have anything to do with anyone or anything connected to any of the endeavors she defined as those of chaos merchants. Fighting was something she had specifically mentioned as the foundation of the thought process that had led to her decision.

In the future, after this fight, it might be possible for me to agree with her view. Right now it didn't matter. She had gone somewhere.

It might be anywhere. I knew nothing about her or her family or anything except she had worked for a Kingston newspaper. I supposed if I'd gotten some private dick on the case, he might ferret her out but again—why?

*Shall I, wasting in despair,*
*die because a woman's fair?*
*Or my cheeks make pale with care*
*'Cause another's rosy are?*
*Be she fairer than the day*
*or the flowery meads in may—*
*if she be not so to me,*
*what care I how fair she be?*

She might yet call me. She seemed intelligent and fair enough to realize I might agree with her and give me the opportunity to do it.

On the other hand, knowing the corner I'd squeezed myself into regarding Mangiacavallo, she would also know I would have to fight this fight. So there would be no point in her contacting me till the fight was over. And then she might keep her eye on the news to discern whether I had given up fighting, as I'd told her I was going to, or if I was planning other matches in the future. She was smart enough to know that someone like Mangiacavallo did not toss away a goose that laid those proverbial eggs.

I threw myself into the training for the few days that were left and returned to New York three days before the scheduled bout.

I met Luis Gonzales at the weigh-in. We were both surrounded by groups of various hangers-on. The big guy with the cartoon hair was the promoter. He had taken Luis Gonzales under his wing and now stood next to him during the videotaping and the still photography. He loved being on camera. I wondered how a guy who hogged the camera every chance he got, seemed unable to stop talking, kept waving that little American flag whenever his picture was being taken, and who had such funny hair could get to be a multi-millionaire and the biggest name in the business. And, of course he had gotten to Luis Gonzales. He got all the hot prospects—except fighters who had really, really strong principles. I wondered if Luis or

I were in a worse spot. I was hooked up with Mangiacavallo while Gonzales had this cartoon-hair guy who, like Liberace, laughed all the way to the bank while his protégés ended up in Dante's hell. And with all of that, when you looked at the guy and listened to him talk, you had to like him. Or at least be amused by him. You could see some of the commentators hated his guts and weren't above showing it. Didn't bother the man one bit. He just kept on smiling—like Liberace had said—all the way to the bank.

Because of Morshia and her story about Gonzales, I had a warm feeling toward the boy. *Listen to me,* I said to myself, *he's no more than a year younger than me and I'm thinking of myself as the wizened veteran and him as the young gun.* I looked at him, coming barely to the pectorals of his promoter who, with his perpetual smile and the cartoon hair, had his arm around Luis' shoulder. Gonzales was a good-looking boy with a very serious demeanor, giving the impression he was all business. You could look at people, I'd learned, and tell exactly how capable they were. I'd spoken with a man who'd been a table tennis champion and he told me he could talk to a person, not see him play, just talk to him, and tell how many points this person could get on him in a game. And so you could look at someone and tell if he was a winner or a loser. Luis Gonzales was a winner. I had seen him fight a Mexican kid who was pretty tough and they went toe to toe and Luis floored him within a few seconds. *This is a real fighter,* I thought.

Because of his connection to Morshia Ellis, I felt warm toward him and went over to introduce myself.

Everybody froze. I knew even as I was walking that visions of Tyson going over to attack Lennox Lewis before their fight were on everybody's mind. His entourage kind of opened a path so I could get to him—hell, it was great publicity if somebody whacked somebody before the fight—and he looked at me, waiting and, as I approached, I extended my right hand to shake his, thinking that I would first offer this physical gesture of friendship, then we could exchange words.

He must have seen my movement as the beginning of an aggressive action because next thing I knew I was on the floor, gazing up, a lot of people leaning over me, looking concerned, somebody shining a penlight in my eye.

They pulled me up and sat me down and I thought, *Well, now I have been hit, I have been knocked out and the guy in sheets with the knife didn't come to save me.* Had I gotten a "Dear John" from *him*?

I watched everybody milling around me. I don't know how long I'd been out. Time, I guess, means nothing when you're out. Had time existed before we did? Or did we invent it—the way we had invented God? The guy with the penlight put up two fingers and asked me how many and I thought, for some reason, about Bill Johnson and wondered what he was doing. He had started this whole thing and now where was he? Mangiacavallo had banned him from New York so he would have to be somewhere else. Where would somebody like Bill Johnson go?

"How many fingers am I holding up?" the guy asked again. He had a seriousness about him I felt was there not because he was really a serious person but because he felt, being suddenly in the limelight, that was the role to play.

I said, "Anybody can see that's eleven."

I had said it so definitively the guy actually paused, then looked at his two fingers and you could see him reflecting on the possibility the two ones he was holding up, if they were written, would be read as eleven.

"Two," I said, "two. Don't sweat it, buddy, just pulling your leg." Don't you hate it when you make a joke and then have to tell people it was a joke?

My head was pretty clear now and I could see Luis Gonzales being interviewed and videotaped by the media. The rest of the cameras were on me, though, they love showing the loser's reaction. The media love victims. Gonzales looked over in my direction and continued talking and there was an incipient smirk on his face as if, hell, I'm gonna eat you alive, Pops, you couldn't even block my punch.

He had a confident air about him I really admired and, in truth, he had everything to be confident about, not like most who strive to give the impression they're confident. And if my guy with the knife hadn't appeared this time, maybe he was not coming. The Sephardic Jews have a saying: "If your brains haven't arrived by the age of sixteen, they're not coming." In which case the kid *would* eat pops alive. Well, that was all right, I had been knocked out and lived through it and, win or lose, I would be rich enough to finance my own off-Broadway show.

Sure enough, according to the write-ups, Luis Gonzales had said he thought I was moving my right hand to hit him and he was defending himself. With Mike Tyson having made history in those areas, it was the story to go with. But it's amazing how many times you see two fighters at the sound of the first bell, going toward each other in the ring and one of them wants to be a good sport and extends his hand toward the other so they could touch gloves and the other guy, instead of touching gloves, hauls off and whacks him as hard as he can and nobody ever even mentions it and the poor guy who'd extended his glove not only gets whacked for trying to be a good sport but ends up looking like a pathetic fool — *World, thou art base and debauched as can be.*

The time after the weigh-in is fun because you get to eat and drink a lot so you can gain the weight and feel strong. I made a real pig of myself, although, as far as I was concerned, neither losing the weight nor gaining it made a difference. If the guy with the knife showed up, I would knock my opponent out, if he didn't, I'd get the shit beaten out of me and win all the money I'd given Mangiacavallo to bet on me. It was terrific going into a situation where winning was not your goal.

The day of the fight I got a call from Sandy but let the machine pick it up because I knew she'd ask me if I'd read the book she'd given me and I didn't want to tell her I hadn't.

The odds out there on me winning the fight had dropped considerably, a lot of bettors probably figuring if Gonzales could knock me down at the weigh-in, he could probably do it in the ring. Also, as the fight approaches, the odds usually fall anyway.

I worked on the play I was writing, ate, and read all day. It was very relaxing. In the evening the car came to take me to the Garden and I thought of all the great fights that had taken place there. Although not really there geographically but at another place that was the original Madison Square Garden. People talked of the great tradition of a place even when the place had been moved to another location.

I waited and read in my dressing room, getting up to do some warm-ups whenever the media people asked me to at various intervals during the prelims so they could flash them on the large screens in the arena, to the public at home and in the bars.

I didn't feel nervous. It was easier not being nervous when you knew it depended on something other than yourself. Maybe that was why the idea of God had become popular. You could sit back and say, "Well, it's not up to me; it's up to Him." And then, so you wouldn't sit back *too* much, someone had come up with, "God helps those who help themselves." That way you would have to punch the clock and put in your hours but not be running the company.

When it came time for me to march down the aisle, I had them play "La Cucaracha" and then did a little rumba-like dance on the way to the ring. Did you know that "cucaracha" means "cockroach"? Well, all right. I could've waited longer to make my entrance, that's the privilege of the champion, but I felt it a petty thing to do and didn't want to play that game. So, what with coming out early and doing my little dance, as opposed to Luis Gonzales coming out all serious and somber, dressed like a gladiator and doing a little hip movement a la Prince Naseem, the crowd seemed to lean more toward me and shouted all kinds of encouraging things to me, "Kill'm," "Put'm away in the first," "Shove your fist through his brain," stuff like that. And there was another thing that happened. Some people in my last fight, when I'd become champion, had started making the noise of an airplane diving and now a lot of people were doing that. It's a funny thing when you hear a whole stadium do the diving sound with their voices. My favorite is still the one they have in Manchester, England, when their fighter, Ricky Hatton walks to the ring and the whole crowd breaks into "Blue Moon." There's no rhyme or reason why that song should be sung before a fight but maybe just because it's so incongruous it moves me deeply every time I hear it.

All in all, crowds seem to take to fighters who do something unusual and spectacular in the ring and I had been giving them spectacular from the beginning. There is something very touching in the way the public continues to believe in boxing. Wrestling has become a freak show, beloved mostly by what is considered America's multi-racial trash. That, too, however, is a mark of wanting to believe. It is a little easier to believe in boxing because you can see people really getting hit. Even when decisions in boxing are awful and you can see something is terribly wrong, like when George Foreman, after getting beaten up throughout the fight, got the decision over Axel Schulz and in Germany they threw chairs at the screens and American fans called in and wrote by the hundreds in outrage at the decision, the public somehow gets over it and flocks to fights in which a Trinidad or a Gatti gets in the ring and acts the part of the hero, standing up to anything the other guy has to give. Except the public doesn't really get over it. I personally think it stays in the public's soul and, same as the Kennedy assassination lie, grows there like a cancer.

Getting in the ring, Gonzales tried to be flamboyant. Not because he really *was* flamboyant but because, like most fighters, he followed the pattern that had been set by Ali back in the sixties. Ironically, at that time everybody hated Ali for his flamboyance and braggadocio, booing him every time he got into the ring. Until that point, modesty and humility had been the virtues people looked up to as models. Now everybody was trying to act like Ali and it was a painful thing to watch. It's always painful when people are trying to be what they're not. Gonzales tried to incorporate a page from Naseem's book except that, instead of somersaulting into the ring, he held on to the top rope and swung his legs over, which is not too difficult but, as with so many things one tries to do that are not in one's nature, one of his legs got tangled in the rope and he landed awkwardly on his ass. I saw it from my dressing room and it made me laugh but I knew the embarrassment would give him more adrenaline for the fight. Which could be a good thing or a bad one.

That put me in mind of when I clowned around, getting into the ring on my way to the championship. Thing was, you could do that only if you won. If you lost, clowning became pathetic. Everything became pathetic if you lost. I'm not in accord with that, you understand. I love a good loser. When I watched a tape of Henry Ross Perot conceding the presidential election of 1992, even though he had what appeared like a certifiable running mate, I thought him so classy, gracious, cheerful, and dignified in his loss, I was inspired. By God, he even took his wife in his arms and danced with her. But the rest of the country? Comedians made fun of him for years. Almost as if they were mad at him for taking it so well. No—we just despise losers.

So, after I did my rumba to the ring, I grabbed the top rope and was about to swing over—and then didn't. I just hopped as if I were going to—and then didn't. As if I couldn't quite get up the courage. And I kept doing that.

Didn't take the audience long to figure it out and the laughter began. Clowning and laughter are not part of what happens in a fight. There's showboating—but no genuine clowning. It bespoke to the audience flair on my part and they liked it. So they let themselves go and laughed and laughed and even applauded. Luis Gonzales, on the other hand, looked daggers at me. He took it that I was making fun of him. He was wrong. Making fun of him was only a perk. Having fun by putting on a show was what I was after. That, too, I knew would give him extra adrenaline. Too much adrenaline often did an athlete in. Cheerfulness and smiles, on the other hand—well, that was another matter.

Like the American girl who won the diving platform competition in Sidney. Came into the finals in fifth place but smiled every time she got on the platform as if she and the world were in love with one another. And the Chinese who had come into the finals ahead of her and who had been heavily favored to win, and the other competitors who had all been ahead of her, screwed up one by one and she kept smiling and moved into first place and got the Olympic gold.

Finally, I swung over and did a somersault into the ring like Naseem, then raised my hands to the audience in victory and greeting. More applause, cheering. Well, they were in the mood to cheer. If we were to give them a boring fight, they would be in the mood to boo.

And now there was the stuff with prancing around while waiting for the announcer to do his spiel, the referee getting us together and telling us how he had explained the rules to us back in the dressing room, all the stuff I fast-forwarded when I watched the fights on tape. There were so many things that sounded and looked the same each time they were done. All the stuff fighters said about each other and how each claimed he was going to beat the other guy and, if the odds were impossibly high, how the underdog was going to surprise everybody, which has happened maybe three times in a century; Harold Ledderman with his same, impossibly cheerful sing-song rendition of the rules; the march to the ring with whatever unintelligible song the fighter had chosen to be played and sung; the ring announcer with the same exclamatory sound, it had all gotten to be old a long time ago and it was being repeated over and over with the identical mechanical efforts to sound exciting. Very few individuals in the world had managed to figure out that, in order to be exciting, you had to first be excit*ed* and in order to be interesting, you first had to be interest*ed*. The only thing that sometimes turned out to be fresh, and the reason the audience sat through all the other stuff, was what the fighters brought into the ring. What Hemingway had called the moment of truth. That, too, often turned out to be mechanical. Once in a while, however, there was genuine drama, like Bernard Hopkins, this tough, uncelebrated ex-con, outsmarting, outfighting Trinidad, reminding everyone of the levels to which human beings could rise both in the physical and the spiritual realms and that was what the fans hungered for.

It was these other repetitions, I thought, these things that had become mechanical that caused people to grow old and finally die. The same things happening over and over again finally made people say to themselves, "Okay, I've had enough, I'm checking out." But if there could constantly be, I thought, a flowing supply of fresh experiences like the ones great individuals brought to various endeavors that added up to new knowledge and new cognitive insights, new inspirations, then there could be a constant creative process taking place and continued regeneration.

While the referee talked to us, Luis Gonzales stared at me with what he probably thought to be his most intimidating killer stare. I just looked back at him as if I were watching an actor on the stage, performing. I was feeling completely at peace.

And then the bell rang and

*There was the man in sheets with the knife. I ran at him like a sprinter. It surprised him as it had surprised all the others, no matter how many tapes of it they had watched and studied.*

*The reason watching tapes could never prepare them for the real thing was, on tape, they could not see the other-than-human feeling that envelops those who are facing death. The soldiers through history who had been trained for war always realized when they got to the front lines that nothing could prepare you for that.*

*So my opponents, seeing this phenomenon for the first time, either froze or flailed out in an untimely fashion and I got through—because my life depended on it and theirs didn't.*

*I dove at him and caught him as I'd caught the others, "You ugly one,"
and I thought of* **Groundhog** Day, *where the same thing keeps happening
over and over again and you have to face it and treat it as if it were a brand
new thing and—it does become a brand new thing.*

*What suddenly occurred to me as I lay on the mat after I'd hit him was
that, as in Athens with the two terrorists, the guy with the knife might appear
in more and more places on more and more occasions—as Mister Hyde does
with Doctor Jekyll and I looked up and there was the guy still standing,
leaning against the ropes, the knife-holding hand hanging at the side so I
jumped up, roaring, "You ugly one!" and hit him again—and again and
again and again—till I was grabbed and dragged away from there and
encircled and held by a whole bunch of arms while a man was hugging the
bloody man on the ropes and I thought, feeling arms around my chest and
stomach, my god, that's what it'll feel like when they put that straitjacket on
me.*

Medics carrying a stretcher made their way to the other corner and
the crowd cleared and they got Luis Gonzales, whom I couldn't
recognize because his face was covered with blood, and they put him
on a stretcher and secured him with straps and put the stretcher
through the ropes where other people got hold of it and they carried
him away and there was a lot of confusion and suddenly silence in the
arena as I held my blood-soaked gloves before my eyes and
thought—much as Alec Guinness in *Bridge on the River Qwai—What
have I done?*

# CHAPTER FORTY

**W**hen they led me from the ring, there wasn't a sound in the arena. People watched with what felt like greater awe and wonderment than I'd perceived them to feel for Mike Tyson in his halcyon days.

In the dressing room they began taking my gloves off when the door crashed open and Mangiacavallo burst in, screaming, "Out! Everybody out!"

People ran as if someone had announced a bomb was going off. The room was empty in less than five seconds.

Joey Mangiacavallo stood in the middle of the room, glaring at me. And I realized that until now, I had not seen the full extent of what he could turn into.

People can never really hide what they are. Oscar Wilde with his *Picture of Dorian Gray* had it right. Every single thing we think and do is firmly imprinted on our features, in our eyes, our movements, the timbre of our voices, in our very presence. We make great efforts to create a social persona and think we are fooling somebody. What we are is written all over us, all anyone need do is simply read it. A lot of us, of course, don't like to read but we can all feel. Looking into Mangiacavallo's eyes, I could see the cruel killer. Why had I chosen not to see it before but had dealt only with what he put out there for me to see? Simple. Because it had suited my purposes.

"You know you a dead man?" he said.

"You asking me?"

"Yeah. I'm askin' ya. You know you a dead man?

"If I'm a dead man, I can't answer, can I?"

"Wise guy to de end, ain't ya?"

"Isn't that what they call you guys—wise guys?"

Wisecrack upon wisecrack. Same thing I'd done with Shamaz the day he and his cohort surrounded us on the street. Who did I think I was fooling? Sorry—*whom* did I think I was fooling?

"Just for curiosity's sake," Mangiacavallo said, "you *wanted* to commit suicide, is dat what dis is all about? Like dose fuckin' whackos crashed into de Woild Trade? You chose to do dis ta me, ruin me financially, dis me in de eyes of all my friends'n acquaintances 'cause you wanted to commit suicide? You coun't trow yoself da fuck off de Brooklyn Bridge an' leave me da fuck alone? What'd I ever do to you except make you rich'n famous dat you should do dis ta me?"

"If I'm a dead man, I can't tell you anything, can I?"

"I'm askin' ya—for ole times' sake."

I remembered that great line from *The Godfather*—could the guy ask Mikey to spare him—for old time's sake?

"You're gonna have a conversation with me for old times' sake and have me killed for new times' sake?"

"Lemme explain somethin'. You might tink you in de driver's seat 'cause you decided to commit suicide so dere's nuttin' I could do to ya. But, see, dis ain't so. You could go fast'n easy—or you could feel pain for weeks like you can't imagine—an' den you get left at your mudder's doorstep, a paraplegic, how funny you tink *dat* would be? An' den, before your very eyes—your mudder gets raped and tortured an' killed. So who you tink's gonna take care of you for de rest'a your paraplegic life? So now, don't even bother tellin' me what I ast ya, I don't even care no more. 'Cause now awready your wise guy self got me so pissed, I don't even care no more why you did what you did, dat's what I'm gonna do to ya—gonna inflict pain on you for weeks, gonna make you a paraplegic an' I'm gonna have all dose tings done to your mudder *an'* gran'mudder an' den lesse how wise y'are den."

"I—"

"Don't even bother to apologize, mudder-fucker, dat's what's gonna happen to ya an' your family, no matter what you say or do now."

"I wasn't going to apologize, Joey. I just wanted to give you something."

I moved toward my locker. He took out his .38 and aimed it at me.

*And there was the man in sheets with the knife again.*
*I took a running start and, growling, "You ugly one!" dove at the man, catching him with an overhand right and flopping on the cement floor.*

When I looked up, there was Mangiacavallo lying unconscious, the .38 on the floor next to his outstretched hand. Blood was coming out of his nose at a steady rate. Using a towel, I picked up the .38 and put it in the wastebasket under some other stuff, so you couldn't readily see it.

I took the bucket of water they'd brought back from ringside and poured it on Mangiacavallo's head just like I'd seen it in so many scenes in the movies. His head shook a little but his eyes remained closed. I went to my locker and got dressed. There was a knock at the door. I opened it slightly. The trainer and a whole bunch of people, including the reporters and the HBO guys, were standing out there in the hall.

"What?" I asked.

"Is everythin' awright?" the trainer asked.

"We're having a conference," I said.

The trainer, poking his head in a little, looked at Mangiacavallo on the floor, his flowing blood forming a rivulet, and began closing the door so the reporters wouldn't see it.

"Hey, could we ask you some questions?" a reporter asked, trying to push the door open, the trainer at the same time straining to get it closed.

"We're having a conference," I said. "If you want to wait, wait, if not, we can talk another time."

"We'll wait," the reporter said seeing as how the trainer was winning.

Another guy said, "Can you give us a ballpark?"

"Maybe another twenty, thirty minutes," I said.

"We'll wait," the guy said.

The trainer finally got the door closed and I thought about how everything the media people did depended on what someone else had done. And then they took what someone else had done and changed it so it was something else. What a way.

Mangiacavallo's eyes were open and he was looking up at me as if trying to recognize me and then he did. I guess he regained consciousness because I had hit him with my bare fist. If I'd had a glove on, they probably would've had to take him to the hospital. These Mafia people are tough, though, they come from very hardy stock. You're not going into that business unless you're pretty tough.

He wiped the blood from his nose with his sleeve and moaned as he felt his cracked bone. I handed him a towel and he applied it very tenderly to his nose.

"Nothing worse to do to me now than you've already said," I said. "Right?"

"Dere's always worse," he said, lifting the towel for a moment then pressing it back. He looked around for his piece and, not finding it, gave what vaguely resembled a smirk. "So you tink you done somethin' by breakin' my nose? You tink it's gonna change somethin'?" He sounded funny speaking without his nasal passages. A little like a baritone chipmunk.

"Listen, Joey, I could kill you with your own gun and get off scott-free because you're the one who pulled the gun on me and the self defense would stick like glue. But I happen to have something better."

I took a cassette out of my pocket and extended it toward him.

"What's dat?" he asked, looking at it but not taking it.

"It's what I went to my locker to give you," I said. "You could take it, it's not a bomb."

"It's a cassette, I can see," he said, still not taking it. "What's in it?"

"It's dialogues of our conversations having to do with your telling me to throw the fight. The conversation we had in this locker room just now has been recorded on a remote and is now part of the evidence."

"You gonna put me in jail? You tink I can't order a hit from jail?"

"That, too, has been recorded, Joey."

"Fine. You still dead meat, pal."

"I understand that. But now, how about shifting the viewpoint slightly and think about both of us being alive and okay?" I signalled with my hand.

"We still bein' recorded?"

"The recording has just been stopped."

"How come?

"I have a proposition for you."

"Wouldn't wanna record yourself offerin' to withhold evidence, would ya?"

"Exactly."

"So you sayin' here you wouldn't use all this stuff if I laid off you?"

"And my mother and grandmother."

"I was just scarin' ya. We don't do stuff like dat to women. We're Italians, you know?"

"Then Stanislavsky would've been proud of you, Joey, because I believed you completely. So the way it stands now is I have all this evidence in several places where the instructions are that, should anything happen to me, it's all to be sent to the D.A. and the major newspapers and networks—including today's conversation."

"An' if nothin' happens to ya?"

"Then neither of us has anything to worry about."

"Suppose somethin' happens to ya dat has nothin' to do wid me?

"You gotta pray that nothing happens to me, Joey—that I don't get struck by lightning, as Brando said in *The Godfather*, that I don't contract fatal pneumonia or anthrax, that no tree falls on me and that I don't happen to be in the next building the terrorists blow up."

"What about de odder way? How do I know you ain't gonna buy a hit on me?"

"Joey, with all due respect, that's stupid."

"Don't call me stupid; I don't like to be called stupid. Why? Why is it stupid?"

"It's not your fault, Joey, it's your gangster mentality. It's all warped. Why would I buy a hit on you when I've already neutralized you with the tape? I've got copies of this tape all over the place, Joey, don't you see the picture?"

"An' what I got? I got nothin'."

"You have a principal position in the mob, Joey, you're Tony Soprano."

"After tonight I'm shit. You know how many goombahs I told you were gonna lose de fight an' who on my word bet a lot'a money on you to lose? How you tink *dey* gonna react?"

"That's outside my province."

"What're you talkin' about, Province—de place in Cape Cod?

What's dat got to do wid it? Or is it dat place in Rhode Island? See, I know a few tings."

"It's another one of those words, Joey; means it's outside my area of responsibility."

"Oh. So you fuck me over'n walk away, dat's what you sayin'? Not only are all my goombahs screwed by me but dey see you walkin' aroun' wit not a hair harmed on your head, how's dat gonna look?"

"What do you want me to do?"

"Could you at least disappear for a while, go live on some Caribbean island so it looks like I took care'o you for double-crossin' me?"

I immediately thought of finding Morshia in Jamaica. But she probably wasn't in Jamaica any more. No, she wouldn't be staying in Jamaica. She had the kind of spirit that searched for bigger places. People like that, if they're born in a small place, don't stay there. They go to the biggest places.

"No, Joey, I can't do that."

"Why not?"

"Because I require New York."

"What's so special about New York? It's de most dangerous place in de woild? You said you wanted to do some writin', make up plays, stories, stuff like dat. What better place den de Caribbean?"

"Since you think there's nothing special about New York and you like the Caribbean so much, why don't *you* go?"

"I got a business here, I got a family, I got all my goombahs here, what're you talkin'?"

"You said yourself it's all gonna turn to shit. Why don't *you* get out of town, disappear?"

"Dere ain't no place dey ain't gonna find me."

"If they're going to find you, they'll certainly find me."

"Not if dey tink I took care'a'ya."

"That's really sweet, Joey, but we're not bargaining here. A few minutes ago, when you thought you held the winning hand, you were promising to do all kinds of things to me and my family. Now you don't have the advantage, you're talking as if we were buddies. I would've kept you on as a partner in anything I did if you hadn't tried to force me to do things I didn't want to do and that also happen to be illegal. Now you'll have to fend for yourself and get yourself out of the mess as best you're able. I'm going to go ahead and do what I want to do."

"Dat's what I'm tryin' to tell ya. Dey ain't gonna be happy wit you fuckin'em over. Dey gonna get you too."

"Nobody dealt with me except you. You're the one who's taking the hit, Joey. It was your idea, your scheme, you're the one who talked them into putting money into it, as far as anybody's concerned, you're the one who did the double-crossing."

"Awright, awright, nobody's takin' de hit. I was, what do you call it, exaggeratin' to ya before. I didn't tell nobody about de arrangement; I'm de on'y one did de betting, I'm the on'y one lost money here. Tink I'm crazy to tell anybody? Any big money bein' bet on either side changes de odds. Ain't gonna spread somethin' like dat around."

"Why did you tell me that, then?"

"You made me lose a lot'a bucks. I wanted to impress you."

"Joey, you should start learning how to take responsibility not only for the money you make but for the money you lose."

"You could'a tole me you wasn't gonna go trough wid it."

"Yeah, you would've let me get away with it, right?"

"You're gettin' away wid it now."

"I didn't have anything on you then. Now I have you on tape not only threatening me but admitting you made the bets, which'll prove you tried to make money off it."

"Yeah, I didn't figure you to be dat practical. I knew you read a lot'a books but I didn't tink you'd have de smarts to pull somethin' like dis. An' I swore to myself I'd frisk anybody I had a confidential conversation wid. Din' even occur to me wid you. Don't even ask about how much I lost. Lost your money too."

"I don't care."

"If you ain't gonna be fightin' no more—or are you?"

"No. I'm not going to fight any more."

"You could make millions—especially after tonight. Gonzales was good—an' he's out dere in a coma. You could write your own ticket, you could make more money den Tyson ever dreamed of."

"I'm not going to fight any more, Joey."

"Why not?"

"Because I'm going to do what I love doing."

"De show biz shit?"

"That's right."

"Pussy shit. See, I don't understand dat. I don't understand dat ad all."

"That's all right."

There was a short pause.

"I wasn't gonna do nottin' to ya or your mudder'n gra'ma, you know dat."

"No, I don't, Joey. I don't know that at all. That's why those tapes are going to remain in safe places, ready for deployment."

"Deployment? What is that—like not bein' employed? Never mind, I know it don't mean nothin' good. Aw, you can't tink I'd do anything to you an' your family, we're buddies, you'n me, we're partners, I liked you de minute I saw ya, di'n' I ask ya ta sing in my place? Dat offer still stands by de way. "

"Great, then you'll see to it nothing bad happens to me."

"I will, you can count on it. You lost me a hell of a lot'a money, though, I'm hurtin', I'm hurtin' real bad, I might have to go back to bein' a hit man just to feed my family."

"It amazes me to think there're people like you in this world, Joey."

"I'm a rare breed all right."

He was puffed up about being a rare breed. That's what these guys take pride in—stuff like that. It would be comical if it weren't that they cheated and butchered people.

"As long as we're such buddies again," I said, "and in a confessing mood, I have to tell you—I had every intention of going down in that fight."

"So what happened?"

"That's the million-dollar question. Like I told you that first time I came to see you—something happens to me when I feel a threat and I just run into the fray. Like when you had the gun on me—I just rush right into it, no control."

"What's a fray?"

"A noisy quarrel. A fight in public. A brawl. It's a variant of affray. Comes from the old French '*effrei*.' " I pronounced the word with the guttural rolled "R," just like the French do.

"Yeah, you see, dat's a hell of a lot more information den I wanned to own. You know a lot'a words, I'll give ya dat but you such a show-off, you know?"

"I'll have to watch that."

"How about givin' fightin' some more tought? I could get back all de money you lost me, you could save a lot'a people's lives by me not goin' back to bein' a hit man."

"First of all, stop saying I lost you that money, Joey. You know damn well you did it yourself, I don't wanna be blamed for it any more."

"I can't blame myself, for Christ's sake, what de fuck is dat?"

"And I'm certainly not going to take upon myself the mission of stopping you from being a hit man if that's what you have a mind to do."

"You're forcin' me into it—an' it could be so easy, we could make millions."

"Go after the Arab terrorists, government'll give you good money for that."

"Ain't a bad idea, you know? Could just start knockin' off Arabs, some'a dem're bound to be terrorists, know what I mean?

"Joey, call the reporters in and tell them how great we feel about winning the fight and find out how Luis Gonzales is doing and let's get a masseuse in here, I could use one of those sweet, hard massages."

"When exactly did I become your bitch?"

" 'Life's a stage,' old Willie boy said, 'and we are merely players.' "

"Who's Willie boy? Is dat dat Bobby Blake movie from de seventies? *Tell Them Willie Boy Was Here?* Hey, wasn't Bobby Redford in dat movie?"

# CHAPTER FORTY-ONE

**I** went to visit Luis Gonzales at Lennox Hill. It was sobering to see him with all those tubes going into his body, his eyes closed, giving no sign of life. A slightly overweight black woman in her fifties was sitting by his bed, tears slowly trickling down her cheeks as she watched him. There were certain characteristics in the woman, such as coloration, facial expression, bearing, and general vibes that put me in mind of Morshia Ellis.

Though each nation has its own characteristics, those of Jamaicans strike me as standing out in various respects. The combination of playfulness, gentleness, kindness, good cheer, tolerance, humor, patience, and music make them endearing. The three expressions that came from there struck a chord throughout the world: "No problem, mon," and "Don't worry, be happy," —and "One Love." It was those characteristics in the woman sitting by Luis Gonzales that put me in mind of Jamaica—and Morshia Ellis.

She looked up when I came in and I could see she recognized me and, for a moment, I thought she was going to start screaming and lunge at me but then she caught herself and just looked back at the boy and fresh drops slid from her eyes. I remembered *It's a Wonderful Life*; the idea of how many lives one person can affect had inspired me. And here was the other side of that coin. You go along doing what you feel benefits you and think very little of how it affects others. My thoughts had all been on how I would parlay the appearance of the man in sheets into a successful show business career. Here was something I had never given thought to: the destruction. The pain I could cause other people.

I stood by the bed and watched this woman and thought about my mother and how she would feel if something like that had happened to me.

Life was an amazing thing. Anything can happen. Wonderful things—and horrible things. Was there some kind of a pattern to it? Some cause or reason behind certain kinds of happenings as opposed to others?

Suddenly, the woman started to scream. She clutched the boy and screamed and screamed, throwing her body on his, writhing and screaming. Nurses and orderlies streamed into the room. They pulled her off and, while she was still struggling, carried her out. Others checked the tubes going in and out of her unconscious son but, evidently, she had been careful even in her hysteria not to dislodge any of them.

I was alone in the room with him. I thought of how all our lives we strut and prance like peacocks—and here was this boy who had been on top of the world. He could've had the most beautiful women, the finest hotels, the choicest locations to travel to and what? He was lying here like a vegetable. All of us, we walk around, thinking we're cocks of the walk, we watch the old, the sick, the "challenged," and think, "Poor schmucks," and go on, never once realizing it was like that epitaph the man had had put on his stone: "I was once where you are. You will one day be where I am."

I sat there on a chair by the bed, watching him. Weird to watch someone who's asleep or unconscious or dead. I thought about the last scene in A Farewell to Arms. The contrast between a lifeless body and your thoughts and emotions which are so alive is so stark the only way you can experience your emotion is by going back to the past and recreating a time when this body you're looking at was alive and then, like a film editor, super-imposing it on the present.

Luis Gonzales' eyes opened. He stared for a while. The doctor had told me he had been in a coma since the knockout. The doctor was a fight fan and had seen the fight. He had said there was not much hope Luis would come out of his coma. The doctor had asked for my autograph for his son.

"The young people admire stars and fighters much more than they admire people like me," the doctor had said. "We're boring. Everyone, it seems, aside from stars and name athletes, is boring. I don't even know if boring is the right word. I think we're below the level of boring."

And now Luis Gonzales' eyes were not only open but his head was turning. Not much but it was turning. He was looking at me. His lips moved. It looked as if he were trying to speak but no sound came. I leaned over so I was closer to him.

He kept moving his lips and after a while a soft, breeze-like whisper emerged. I leaned further toward him. He kept moving his lips over and over. Something that sounded like what you might hear if a breeze were to start articulating words began to drift through the air. Every little breeze seems to whisper—ah, me.

I got even closer now and then I thought of what it might look like if someone were to walk in and see me that close to his lips. But what came out of him was so soft I knew, if I wanted a chance at hearing it, there would be no other way to do it.

"She, she, she," I kept hearing.

I shook my head to indicate I didn't understand.

He kept repeating it and, seeing I was not understanding, stopped and stared at the ceiling. Tears trickled down his cheeks.

"Take your time," I told him. "However long it takes you. I have all the time there is."

It seemed to inspire him to a new effort.

"She—she—she—" It went on like that for a while until finally "She—eets," came out.

"She eats?" I asked.

He shook his head as vigorously as he could, which was hardly at all; the intention was vigorous.

"She—she—she—" He stopped, and then resumed with what appeared to be a super human effort. "She—she—sheets."

"Sheets?"

He nodded in confirmation as vigorously as he had shaken his head in negation previously.

"You," he whispered and now the sound of the whisper as well as the articulation grew clearer. "You—in—in—in—she—she—sheets. Me—me—wearing—she—she—sheets—and—and—holding—holding—n—n—knife."

And then he closed his eyes and was as immobile as before.

I sat in the chair, as unmoving as he.

The wild card had just been popped into play. I had not told anyone about the man in sheets and the knife. How could Luis Gonzales have known?

At the same time, it occurred to me the staff had to know the boy who had been in a coma for days had just opened his eyes and spoken.

I went to the administrative office and looked for the doctor who'd asked for my autograph. One of the secretaries there said she'd watched the fight with her boyfriend and, though she'd never been a boxing fan, she loved what I did in the ring. She helped me locate the doctor on the floor where he was making rounds. Then she asked me for my autograph for her boyfriend.

I signed the hospital prescription pad she gave me as I spoke to the doctor. "Luis opened his eyes and spoke."

He rushed out to the hallway toward the elevators and I followed. The nurse shouted, "Thank you," after me.

In the room the doctor raised Luis' eyelids, then listened to his chest with the stethoscope. He covered Luis up again and let the instrument hang on his own chest.

"You say you heard him speak?" he said to me.

"Yes."

"No sign of change."

"He opened his eyes and whispered."

"What did he say?"

"Wasn't very intelligible."

He shook his head and shrugged. "His condition is exactly the same. There is absolutely no indication he's any different than he was."

"Are you saying he didn't speak?"

"I'm saying there's no indication anything has changed. But I will make a notation that you said you heard him speak."

He was humoring me. Doctors do that. They give you the feeling that anything you say has no pertinence and they're listening because not to listen would be bad PR.

On the street I just walked and walked. It had always been a relief when something was weighing on me to take a walk, and New York is the perfect place to do that. There is something about all the buildings and the people that helps you put things in perspective. Another great thing was to be out in the woods or at sea. It widened your perspective so much it became impossible to keep the blinders on that made any specific problem loom larger than life.

I had treated the appearance of the man in sheets as a kind of gift horse that I did not want to look in the mouth because he was bringing good things into my life. Had I really made an effort to discover what this phenomenon was about, I might have succeeded — or not. But the inherent risk in poking around was that the man would no longer appear. And if he did not appear, I would no longer have those good things. It's probably like that with anything. Someone approaches you and offers you a tremendous bargain. It's so good it's too good. Well, you want this thing he is offering you, it's a wonderful thing. It could be a low priced Mercedes in mint condition or the box that gets you all the channels without you having to pay Time-Warner Cable a dime, you just pay two-hundred-fifty or three hundred dollars for the box and you have all the cable and pay-per-view stations you want and you pay nothing. That's a saving of thousands of dollars over the years. There's only one catch. It's not legal.

So what do you do? You either say no, I'm not going to be part of that and end up paying over a hundred dollars each month for your cable and fifty, sixty bucks each time you want to watch a boxing event or some such thing on pay-per-view, or you don't ask questions and just pay someone to install that box in your apartment and then enjoy and save.

Which do you do? It's an age-old question.

It was like with all things in life where you're considering a shortcut in the form of a gift horse. You take it and you get to a certain place and you say, okay, now I'm going to switch back to the regular path and what happens? You find yourself soon thereafter — taking another shortcut. And then another and another. It's like *Doctor Jekyll and Mister Hyde*. He takes the formula, becomes transformed, and it feels great but then decides not to take any more and behold — he gets transformed anyway, and horrible things are happening as a result of it.

Well, here we are. A horrible thing had happened because of my apparition and now the guy in the coma was telling me about *my* apparition without my ever having revealed it to him or to anyone else.

What do I do now?

Send the question in to *Jeopardy*.

# Chapter Forty-Two

I've had several periods in my life when there's been an incident and I would just stop and know it was a watershed incident and some life changing experience was taking place—like accidentally meeting someone who turns out to be a fulcrum and it changes your life forever and ever.

While walking on Times Square I ran into Bill Johnson. We stopped, looked at each other, and hugged. You often don't realize how fond you are of someone until the person's not around any more.

"What're you doing in New York?" I asked him.

"I live here, man."

"What about Mangiacavallo?"

"Think I'm gonna let that fucker chase me out'a mah city?"

I shrugged. You can't tell people what to do. "Well, you don't have to be afraid of Mangiacavallo any more." Like, *You won't have Nixon to kick around any more.*

"You think I give a rat's ass about that fuck? How he gonna know I'm here or not? It's like, back in Seward Park, you knew if you could avoid Shamaz till the end of the term, movin' uptown, what are the chances he gonna find you? New York City, man, you can go two, three years without seeing the guy lives on the same floor as you. New York, man."

"Well, good, but now you won't have to worry even if you do run into him. You still seeing Aisha?"

"Seeing her. I'm married to'r, man. Biggest favor anybody ever did me was you knockin' me out."

"So, you're happy."

"Happy! Every mornin' I pinch myself, see if it's real. So, now I'm gonna do *you* a favor. Can we go somewhere and have some coffee, I wanna talk to you about somethin'."

"I'd like to have coffee with you but I gotta tell you—I'm not fighting any more."

"Really? How come?"

"Fighting's not what I want to do, I told you that at the very beginning."

"Tell that to all your fans to whom you are the stuff of legend."

"It's all phony, Bill, it's all a gimmick, a trick."

"The punches, the comas—*they're* not phony; what're you talking about?"

"It's too complicated and crazy to go into right now."

"Now it sounds *real* interesting. But that's not what I wanted to talk to you about."

We went to the Westway Diner on Ninth Avenue and ordered pancakes. Diners have become the big thing for New Yorkers. It's a way for them to feel they're out in the country.

"Actually," Bill said, "I'm not connected with fighting anymore either. I'm still teaching gym but not having the kids box any more."

"What changed?"

"I ran into something that transformed my life as if I'd been transported to another planet."

If he had found, I thought, what Sandy had found, it would be too much.

"Are you going to try to sell me on it?" I asked.

"No. But I will insist that you look at what it is and keep an open mind."

Similar to what Sandy had said: keep an open mind. Was that possible?

"Why do people who think they've found a panacea in the form of a belief in some kind of a therapy insist everybody in the world has to become a part of it while people who find it in drugs or drink are content to just experience it and keep it to themselves? You never hear an alcoholic or a drug addict say, 'Hey, man, you gotta try this, it'll change your life.' "

"Maybe because those who discover something beneficial want to share it so everyone else can be happy, healthy, and able while those who discover drugs or drink know it's harmful and don't want to inflict it on anyone but themselves."

"Always did enjoy our discussions, Bill."

"Then will you listen to me about this?"

"Of course. I'm so happy to see you, I'll listen to you about anything."

"Glad to see you too, baby-cakes. First thing I want you to do, after we finish our repast, is walk five or six blocks with me and watch a short film."

As we approached the awning on 46th Street between 7th and 8th Avenues and I saw the sign on it, I saw it was indeed the same religion slash applied philosophy Sandy had come to the training camp to sell me on.

Last thing I needed right now, with this heavy thing hanging over me, was philosophic feel-good shit.

Then I thought—I'm not really being fair. What do I know about this movement, this philosophy? I recalled reading things about it in the papers—hearing things from the media—but it was nothing about what the movement consisted of—what they did, what they believed in—it was mainly gossip and innuendoes. Yet the effect of these innuendoes was so powerful I had an antipathy toward the movement without knowing the first thing about it. I had seen people on the street, handing out leaflets and I had immediately assigned them the role of zombies, robots— nerds—without knowing them or what they represented. The media had formed my opinion without my realizing they'd done it.

And if it had happened on this, what other opinions, ideas, and feelings had the media formed in me about other things I wasn't aware of?

The receptionist, a pretty, vivacious young woman, seemed neither like a zombie nor a robot. And neither did a fellow named Jerry Indursky, to whom Bill introduced me, saying it was the organization's CEO. Indursky was a tall, dark-haired, dark-eyed, handsome, virile looking man with a deep, strong, slightly raspy voice and a decent, friendly air about him. Where had I gotten the idea they were all zombies and robots? The media, of course.

On many walls were photographs of a large heavyset man in his fifties with red hair, blue eyes, and a good natured, smiling expression.

"He founded the movement," Bill said when he saw me looking at one of the man's photographs.

"When did this movement begin?"

"In the fifties."

"Doesn't it seem strange to you, Bill, that something as beneficial as you claim this to be could exist since the fifties and that the entire world wouldn't be partaking of it so we could be living in this miraculous new world even as we speak?"

"There *are* hundreds of thousands throughout the world who *are* partaking of it and thousands more who are joining every day and benefitting from it but you're right that, compared to six billion existing in the world, it's a drop in the bucket. Does it make sense that six billion people don't know about it and are not using it? You know how people are regarding something new coming on the scene. Look what Galileo had to go through when he came out with the idea the world is round. There are such questions throughout history. They have answers. Your question has an answer too. But we don't need to go into too much at one time, we'll get to the answer another time, I promise you. Right now, I'd like you to watch a tape of this man lecturing; that way you can take a look at him yourself and form your own impression on whether he knows what he's talking about."

To watch the individual responsible I knew would be the best and the quickest way to judge this philosophy. I prided myself on my conviction I could look at someone and know whether the person was true or false. If they were false it didn't matter much what they were false about, false was false. It wasn't important to me whether the economy had been good during Clinton's presidency. The man was a cheat and a liar; that was all I needed to know about him. And all these guys who started movements that promised all kinds of things—Moonies, Hare Krishnas, all that stuff—they were all false and I knew it just by looking at them and what they produced. I'm not saying they were necessarily dishonest. They just struck me as being full of shit, that was all.

The one thing that rang true about what Bill had said related to the beliefs of this movement was in regard to psychiatry. Psychiatrists and their products had always impressed me as the worst of the lot, pretending to help people while succeeding only in filling them full of drugs and making worse idiots out of themselves *and* their patients—all these therapies, they were all counter-productive, all you had to do was look at the people who were part of it and you needed to know no more. Religions, movements, therapies were all terrific at telling you what people should do, how they should be, how they should feel but none—no one—no one ever told you how you went about *feeling* like doing what they told you to do. How do you go about telling a lowlife who'll watch a kiddie porno, then rape and kill a young girl or boy, or how do you tell a priest, for God's sake, not to *feel* like doing what so many have been doing; that there are things that would give them far greater and healthier relief? Misguided souls lost at sea, those who were led and those who were leading. Full of shit. As soon as I saw this fellow who had founded *this* movement, I would see it was the same thing, regardless of how much he had traveled, "researched," and published.

We went to this organization's screening room and I got my opportunity to watch and listen to the man. His voice was deep and resonant, yet rich with laughter and vitality, his eyes were smiling and blue, bright and clean—like the sky on a clear, sunny day. His expression and attitude were benevolent and always with a large proportion of humor and amusement. Though on the heavy side, he appeared entirely comfortable with his body, not in the least bit self-conscious either about his body or his delivery. With all of that, there was no sense of vanity or ego about him.

He spoke in a way that made you feel he was making things up on the spot, yet not a word was wasted and he paused only when it was pertinent to the effect he was creating. What he said was obviously not something he'd come up with in a short period of time but something that had been carefully studied. Now Bill's words as to how many years this man had spent on research began to make sense. And there wasn't anything in his sound, looks, or body movements that made one feel he was in any way eager to have you agree or even accept what he was saying. He was speaking as if everything he said was something that was a matter of fact and it wasn't going to affect him in the least if you rejected it. It was as if he were saying, "Hey, look, the sun is shining," and if you (though it *was* shining) said, "No, it's not," it wouldn't faze him one bit.

Most important, he didn't ask that you accept anything he said on faith. He insisted that everything he spoke of be tested in the real world. If you found it didn't work, then it wasn't valid.

"What is true," he said, "is what is true for you."

This may have been the most amazing thing yet. I had never seen, heard, or read about anyone who did not ask you to take certain things he/she said on faith. Faith was the foundation of every philosophic and religious movement since history began to be recorded.

The centerpiece of it all seemed to be that we all had old hurts that were encrusted in us and when we came upon something that reminded us of them, those old hurts acted up and caused all kinds of disproportionate trouble. Buttons. We were talking about buttons.

It was like when an animal got injured. Everything about the area where it got injured and whatever was connected to the area in the way of smell, sound, location, visual objects, touch, everything that reminded it of anything that had been there at the time of injury is going make that animal afraid for the rest of its life. It doesn't even have to be in the same location; it's sufficient it reminds the animal of whatever was part of the scene when it originally got hurt and the animal will feel fear or pain or anxiety—and not know why.

It made sense. After all, was there anyone in the world who did not have things he/she did not like or was afraid of or disgusted or angered by without knowing why this was so?

Those are the results and the insidiousness of having something in us that affects us without our knowing what it is. The husband and wife who bicker over petty things, our children and other people who appear to be doing things to deliberately spite us, the man who, in arguing with another over a parking space, pulls out a gun and shoots him, that and a myriad other experiences that prompt us to do things for which we don't know the reason and, because we don't want to appear wrong to ourselves and others, we rationalize and come up with some kind of reason we convince ourselves makes sense. Only it doesn't really make sense. There is no rational explanation for shooting someone over a parking space. Millions upon millions of people do things that make no rational sense at all. Yet they do them anyway. They make sure to explain to themselves and others that what they did was right and logical—but it really doesn't make sense. Else the jails, mental institutions, and divorce courts would be empty.

All of that suddenly began clicking into place. This seemed like the kind of information I'd been looking for all my life.

The objective of this technology, then, appeared to be to hunt these encrusted hurts down and erase them so we would not have anything hidden from our awareness that influenced our thoughts, feelings, and actions.

We went out into the hall. A woman was coming down the stairs. She was of middle height, in her late thirties, with smooth black hair, nice skin, she was full-bodied but not fat.

"Dan, this is Lori Jacoby," Bill said. "Lori, this is Dan."

"Hi, Dan," she said, extending her hand, "glad to meet you."

Her voice was mellow and soothing but what was extraordinary were her eyes. They were blue and sparkling, as if they were a couple of Elizabeth Taylor's diamonds. Then I noticed Bill's eyes were like that too, though, of course, not blue but brown. I did not remember them as having that sparkle before. The guy Bill had introduced me to before who ran the place, his eyes had been like that too. And there had been some others we'd passed in the hall that had had eyes like that. I hadn't realized it at the time but now, seeing Lori's eyes brought to mind all the others.

"Are you people wearing some kinds of lenses in your eyes?" I asked.

"No," Lori said. "Why?"

"Your eyes have a sparkle—like jewelry."

She smiled. "Thank you."

"They become like that when you get free of buttons," Bill said.

Yeah, right. And I'm God.

Lori said, "If you have any questions, if you'd like some reading material or if you'd like to take some courses on the subject, we're at your disposal. Glad to have met you, Dan."

We walked out into the hallway, shook hands, said goodbye, and she hurried off while Bill and I walked back to the stairs leisurely. Bill didn't say anything, allowing me to think. Could it be that both Bill and Sandy were right in their enthusiasm and that this movement, this technology *was* what they said it was?

I remembered something an uncle of mine, a very wise man, had said to me once: "Give me a man who reads."

"Is there stuff I could read about this?" I asked Bill when we were outside.

"Enough to see you through a lifetime and then some. There're taped lectures, training courses—the panacea people have been searching for since time began is here. Only it's not in the form of a potion or a pill. It's in the form of hard intensive work but it's doable by every single person and it's unfailing in the infinite treasures it brings. The only belief required is the belief that one could be open to the possibility such a thing *could* be and a willingness to test it without prejudice against reality."

# CHAPTER FORTY-THREE

If there were the slightest chance that what Bill and Sandy believed about this thing was true, then it would be the biggest miracle the world had ever known.

If it *were* true—why *would* people resist it? Why *would* the media malign it? We were no longer living in the age of Galileo or Socrates. If someone came out with something miraculous like a cure for cancer, wouldn't we all embrace it with gratitude?

But would we? We may not live in the age of Galileo but vested interests have always ruled and determined what was to be and what was not to be. It is said that whatever the original reason any organization or committee has been created for, its goal, upon creation, immediately changes to one of—survival. And the thing about survival is the same as what Willy Loman had said in regard to being liked; one doesn't strive to just survive—one strives to survive well. So if a multi-billion dollar organization that seeks to cure cancer comes into being but if such a cure would put this organization out of business, what are this organization's vested interests? And in the case of a woman who goes for a breast cancer test, if a biopsy indicates a tiny piece of a breast need be taken out, but if the surgeon will make fifty times more money by taking the whole breast, what are the vested interests and what kind of literature to support one procedure over another will be sought? Would the medicos, the drug companies, the psychiatrists, or the educators be happy about a technology that promises health and happiness with something other than drugs—or them?

Doctor Linus Pauling, who had won the Nobel Prize, did research on vitamin C, showing how potent a healer it was. Yet none of the medical magazines would publish either his research or his conclusions on the vitamin.

The editor of one of the medical publications told him in confidence, "Drug companies are our advertisers. The AMA and the drug companies are the Siamese twins of American business. They've both made it very clear to us if we publish a paper by a respected physician of renown that shows vitamin C does more to fight colds than the cold remedies and various other drugs these companies put out, we might as well close up shop because they're not putting any more ads in our publications. We survive by those ads."

And, as far as the media are concerned, Morshia had been on the money when she experienced cognition about their goals. How happy would *they* be to have harmony and peace in the world? What in the world would they write about and take pictures of? Happy, peaceful scenes? Good deeds? How often do you see stories of happy scenes and good deeds?

Turned out there was a tremendous amount of material to be read. Not only had the founder of this movement published volumes of books but he'd written out all these processes, he had created drills training people to deliver these processes, he had designed courses with detailed curricula of the theories and reasons why these processes worked.

En route to all this he'd realized that, in order to make it possible for people to learn what he had created, he would have to come up with an educational system far more effective than the current ones being used throughout the world. And in order for the technology to grow and prosper, he had to come up with business methods that were more organized, efficient, and productive than the ones being used for commerce. He came up with all of these, creating both a business and an education technology that were so clear, simple, exciting, and effective that they were revolutionary in how successful they were in accomplishing their goals. Yet, when you practiced them, it felt like you were a kid playing a game.

None of these technologies were destined to please areas of entrenched power.

But they were successful despite the media, the AMA, the drug companies, the psychiatrists, and the IRS. Bill had not exaggerated when he told me thousands of people were joining the movement all over the world, schools were rising up in this country and overseas which were using this man's educational methods, and business institutions using his business technology were spreading internationally faster than any movement or technology had ever spread before and experiencing far greater financial success than businesses not using the technology.

Of course, the Germans who joined this movement in their own country, obsessed with being in the forefront, immediately went to the forefront in their enthusiasm, numbers, and productivity. The Russians, having been oppressed for decades after the abandonment of the Iron Curtain, were catching up fast.

In Germany, however, there was a problem. It seemed too many Germans were joining this new philosophy/religion. The government didn't like it. It responded with a vengeance. They pulled out their favorite page from the history books and began using the same tactics toward the members of this movement that they had used against Jews just prior to World War II, stripping them of their rights as citizens, of their right to vote, of their property and, finally going after their jobs.

*Time* magazine, which had selected both Mussolini and Hitler as "Man of the Year" in their heydays, jumped in once more to give the German government support. They put out a cover story issue in which they blasted this new philosophy/religion with every innuendo and bits of gossip they could dig up. In all fairness to *Time*, its motivation this time was not the same as it had been during Hitler's and Mussolini's time, when Henry Luce, the daddy of *Time*, gave the nod for favorable articles to be written about the two dictators. This time the reason for *Time*'s onslaught was that this particular philosophy/religion had attacked the drug Prozac because of its tendency to cause a large number of its imbibers to become violent and annihilate both themselves and other people, and the stock of Ely Lilly, which produced the drug, was going down fast. It turned out Ely Lilly had a special connection to *Time*, which was subsequently uncovered and documented.

Ironically, despite the *Time* attack and the German persecution, this philosophy/religion grew stronger throughout the world with thousands upon thousands more joining than had joined before. Thousands upon thousands in this country and other countries signed petitions seeking to put a stop to Germany's persecution of a movement which not only did not believe in any kind of violence or any kind of coup against the government but one which had absolutely no interest or involvement in anything political.

The United States and the U.N. both appealed to the German government to pull back and at least give *some* semblance of respect toward a few of the minimal human rights.

So a kind of truce by the German government was instituted where everything that had been taken away from the members of this movement was still taken away but the nail in the coffin of going after their jobs so they could no longer make a living was not instituted.

Which was about the time the French government went to work. They took the direct action of outlawing the movement together with a number of other movements, including that of the gypsies. I think there is a perception that including gypsies magically legitimizes the persecution of any group the government is going after.

Well, the French—what do you say about the French? They've given us some wonderful things—Voltaire and Monet and such— and they also gave us Napoleon. And the Germans, of course, gave us Beethoven and Goethe—and they gave us Hitler. *Ach, du lieber.*

I read on and began taking courses. It turned out the very foundation of this philosophy/religion was ethics. If you were not behaving ethically, the technology would not go in.

What was the standard for ethical behavior and doing the "right thing"?

It was simplicity itself: the greatest good for the greatest number, the least harm to the smallest number.

The significance of this went straight to my guts. Could it be there now existed an actual objective standard people could turn to to resolve their differences? If so, then humankind had discovered the most valuable tool there could be to help itself.

Could this be the army I had envisioned at the age of ten?

The first process I did had to do with rehabilitating sour areas in the past. It took a few weeks for me to complete it, after which I felt so good I didn't feel I had to go back and do anything more, I had arrived. Bill and Sandy both told me this was merely the tip of the iceberg, there was an infinite amount more that could be done and I could feel infinitely better and more able and, yes, even more intelligent but I thought, *Oh, of course, these places are always interested in making more money so they always have more stuff for you to do.* No, I was feeling great and didn't even feel it had much to do with the process I'd undergone; I was just feeling great, it just happened.

I decided I would finish writing the play I'd begun working on, direct it, and put it on somewhere and invite Pitt to come look at it and maybe he'd let me direct the screenplay he'd asked me to write. Unless, like Redford, he wanted to go into directing. Oh, well, we'll cross that when—etc.

If you recall, I'd begun the script about the famous African-American singer-actress who has finally agreed to have a book written about her by the Jewish-American writer, Harry Horner. I'd left it at the point where she's playing with a doll and hears an argument between her parents in the next room, then hears screaming, a shot, then another shot and we realize that her father has killed her mother and then turned the gun on himself.

Parentless and homeless, little Diana has been placed in a foster home. We find her at the point where she is narrating her life story into a tape recorder.

# CHAPTER FORTY-FOUR

DIANA

One of the questions you put to me, Harry, was what is it got me from there to here. The most important thing I realized at the moment my parents removed themselves from the living was—I needed something to save myself—lift me up. I suppose the instinct that worked in our history that caused all those great spirituals to be created during the times of our greatest trials was working in me at that moment. I began to sing. Singing lifted me and saved me. From then on, when anything bad happened I'd break into song—until the bad stuff went away and I felt good. But the purity of song got polluted. Those were the days, my friend, when it was believed psychiatry could help us so the government ordained that a psychiatrist come into our little foster home once a week--to treat us.

(The BAND breaks into a martial tune as DOCTOR FRIEDRICH HIMMLER   marches onto the stage and sits behind the DESK, taking out a FOLDER from his BRIEFCASE, looking at the FILE inside. DIANA approaches and stands before the desk)

DOCTOR HIMMLER

(Looking up)

So—you vould be—Diana Best—tvelf yearss olt, zet ist correct?

DIANA

Yes, sir.

DOCTOR HIMMLER

You are, vat you say, a big girl for your aich, nein?

DIANA

I'm not what you say nine; I'm what you say twelve.

DOCTOR HIMMLER

You are vat you say maybe a vizenheimer, nein?

DIANA

Not nine; twelve, twelve.

DOCTOR HIMMLER

Heff a sit, pliss.

(DIANA sits)

DOCTOR HIMMLER

(Starting to pace)

Tell me mine deer—vat you are sinkink at zis momENT?

DIANA

Sinking?

(Reflexively looking down to make certain the wooden floor hasn't somehow turned into water)

Like when you're drowning?

DOCTOR HIMMLER

No, no! Soughts—soughts—runnink srough your het.

DIANA

My hat? Like—talking through my hat?

DOCTOR HIMMLER

Ach—ach—listen to me, liebschen, listen to me. Sinkink—soughts—you know—runnink srough your het—

(Taps his temple)

You sink off somesink—unt—unt zen—you say it—sinkink.

DIANA

*Th*inking?

DOCTOR HIMMLER

Zet's it, sinkink, ja, goot! Now tell me, mine deer. Vy you sink you here, talkink to me at zis momENT?

DIANA

They just said come here, talk to the doctor.

DOCTOR HIMMLER

I see. Unt do you know vat kind DOKtor I am?

DIANA

What kinds are there?

DOCTOR HIMMLER

Zet ist a goot one. Vat kinds are—two, mine deer. Only two kints. Mind—unt body. Unt do you know vat kind I am?

DIANA

Ain't got a clue, Mister—I mean, DOKtor.

DOCTOR HIMMLER

Bos, mine deer. I am a DOKtor for ze body—unt—ein DOKtor for ze mind. Bos. Unt do you know vat such a DOKtor ist called?

DIANA

This like a test?

DOCTOR HIMMLER

Ha-ha! Your are vat zey vould in zis country call a card, nicht wahr?

DIANA

What's a 'wahr'?

DOCTOR HIMMLER

I don't know; vat's a wahr vis you?

(Laughs)

DIANA

What?

DOCTOR HIMMLER

Vat's a "wahr"? Zet's a goot one. You know, you are a simpatische junge fraulein, effen if you are black. Goot one. Laugh unt ze vorld— ze vorld—ach, tomorrow ze vorld. Nu—ze kind of DOKtor I am ist vat ist called—a pseecheeatrist.

DIANA

A what-a-trist?

DOCTOR HIMMLER

Ah-ha, anozer goot one! Liebschen, you are vat you say keepink me in stitches, ja? Ze trouble ist, you see, ven I laugh zo hart, I heff a tendency to farrrt. So, pliss, careful, ja?

DIANA

Thing is—I feel fine so what I need a doctor for?

DOCTOR HIMMLER

Your parents blow zeir hets off unt you sit zere unt tell me you feel fine, ja?

DIANA

It's been over a year. You can't cry forever.

DOCTOR HIMMLER

You got repression, zet's vat.

DIANA

What I got?

DOCTOR HIMMLER

Repression. It ist a condition in ze mind like cancer in ze body.

DIANA

I got cancer of the mind?

DOCTOR HIMMLER

Exactly! Unt if ve don't take care off it, somesink terrrible vill happen to you—unt maybe somebody else too.

DIANA

Who?

DOCTOR HIMMLER

Whoever happens to be around ven ze explosion occurs.

DIANA

There's gonna be an explosion?

DOCTOR HIMMLER

(Banging his fist on the desk)

Bang! Unless ve begin treatment immediately.

DIANA

You can fix it so the explosion don't happen?

DOCTOR HIMMLER

I am a DOKTOR.

DIANA

What I gotta do?

DOCTOR HIMMLER

You need do nossing, mine deer—except—relax.

(Produces a little BLACK BAG from under the desk and digs into it)

DIANA

What's in there?

DOCTOR HIMMLER

You are a curious kleine schwarze shotsie, ja, little liebschen? You know vat curiosity did to ze little kitty, little liebschen?

(Extracting from the little black bag a VIAL and a HYPODERMIC SYRINGE)

DIANA

You ain't gonna stick *me* with that.

(DOCTOR HIMMLER sticks NEEDLE into VIAL and withdraws FLUID)


DIANA

(Backing off)

You ain't gonna stick me with that thing, no way, no how.

DOCTOR HIMMLER

(Steadily advancing upon her with the needle)

By ze vay, heff you hurt off pseecheeatree?


DIANA

(Steadily backing away)

I didn't hurt nothin', I don't even know what that is, this tree.

DOCTOR HIMMLER

Vat tree?

DIANA

This sike tree. How could I hurt it if'n I don't know what it is?

DOCTOR HIMMLER

(Continuing the advance so it becomes almost like a choreographed movement)

Not hurt as in "giff pain." Hurt, hurt as in "listen," "heer."

(Puts his free hand to his ear as if listening)

DIANA

(Still backing away, the dance continuing)

Oh, heard.

DOCTOR HIMMLER

Ja, hurt. So—*Heff* you hurt off psycheeatree?

DIANA

Not really.

DOCTOR HIMMLER

Vat ist zet, not really? Eezer you heff or you heffn't.

DIANA

I heffn't—I mean, I haven't.

DOCTOR HIMMLER

Are you makink fun off me?

DIANA

It was kind of a slip, doctor. I mean, DOKtor.

DOCTOR HIMMLER

A *kint* of slip, meine kleine shotsie?

DIANA

Ja—I mean, yes.

DOCTOR HIMMLER

I am getting very suspicious off you, meine kleine, schwarze liebschen.

DIANA

Why, doctor? I mean DOKtor.

DOCTOR HIMMLER

I sink maybe you know more zen you pretend you know. I hurt zere vass a girl in zis here institution zet likes to read—books. I sink maybe you are zet girl. You say it vass a *kint* off a slip. Vat kint slip vass you talkink about?

DIANA

Oh—you know.

DOCTOR HIMMLER

A—Freudian slip?

DIANA

That's the one.

DOCTOR HIMMLER

Ach—zo—you do know about pseecheeatree!

(DIANA sings the Peggy Lee hit, "I Don't Know Enough About You")

DOCTOR HIMMLER

Meine country—*meine* country—started it all.

DIANA

Started what?

DOCTOR HIMMLER

Vat heff ve been talkink about? Work vis me, liebschen, vork vis me. Pseecheeatree—Chermany—ve started it all! Ze best sings—ze best sings in life—all—all—Chermany!

(Sings "Ze Best Sings in Life come fon Chermany." Upon finishing, to the Audience)

You vill now ALL sing. Repeat after me.

(Conducts a sing-along, singing each line, then conducting the audience as they repeat the line after him. When it's over, he does a recitative)

*Pseecheeatree—Ze V rockets zet rained on London—World Var Van—Vorld Var Two—Ze Holocaust—*

(Singing)

*Ze best sings in life—come fon Chermany*

(Squirting some of the liquid from the syringe into the air and turning to DIANA)

Now, my little liebschen—you are concerned zis needle vill hurt you?

DIANA

You bet your fat—yeah, I'm concerned. You ain't gonna stick *me* with that needle.

DOCTOR HIMMLER

You know, zet ist a goot idea.


DIANA

What?


DOCTOR HIMMLER

Let us bet. If you feel zis needle, you vin ze bet unt I giff you fifty DOLLAR. If you do not feel it—I vin ze bet.


DIANA

Not that you'd win but I don't *have* fifty dollars.


DOCTOR HIMMLER

Zis ist not to vorry, liebschen. Sings can alvays be vorked out.


DIANA

What do you mean?


DOCTOR HIMMLER

You can alvays—execute—some VORK for me.

DIANA

You mean like housework? Clean your stuff and things?

DOCTOR HIMMLER

Ja—clean mine stuff—unt SINGS.

DIANA

Let's see the money.

DOCTOR HIMMLER

You do not trust me?

DIANA

In God we trust, everybody else, show me the MONEY.

DOCTOR HIMMLER

Ach, you are such a simpatische junge fraulein, I find myself powerless to resist.

(Reaches into his pocket)


(DOCTOR HIMMLER takes out a ROLL OF BILLS, peels off one and hands it to DIANA)

DIANA

(Snatches the bill, examining it, smelling it)

Man, you eat a lot'a garlic. So you sayin' if'n I feel the shot I get to keep this?

DOCTOR HIMMLER

To do vis ass you vish.

DIANA

All I have to do is feel the needle an' it's mah money?

DOCTOR HIMMLER

Zet ist it exactly.

DIANA

How can I not feel a needle stickin' into me?

DOCTOR HIMMLER

Listen, darlink, you vant to heff a discussion group or you vant ze hart kesh?

DIANA

No *way* I can lose.

DOCTOR HIMMLER

So ve heff a bet?

DIANA

You betcha, sucka; this'll be the easiest fifty I ever made, stick it to me, baby.

(Places the bill on the table)

DOCTOR HIMMLER

First ve must shake hants to make ze bet official.

(He extends his hand and they shake)

Goot! Now go to ze couch unt lie on your tummy.

DIANA

What?

DOCTOR HIMMLER

Again "vat." I do not know how to PRONOUNCE ze Englische? "Vat, vat?"

DIANA

Oh, no, you speak perfect, doc. What I gotta lie on the couch on mah tummy for?

DOCTOR HIMMLER

Ve heff a bet, is zis not so?

DIANA

So?

DOCTOR HIMMLER

So I heff to put ze needle vere you vill not feel it, nicht wahr?

DIANA

What's a "wahr," again?

DOCTOR HIMMLER

True.

DIANA

What?

DOCTOR HIMMLER

Vat, "vat"?

DIANA

What's true?

DOCTOR HIMMLER

"Wahr," mins "true." "Nicht wahr?" mins, "Ist it not true"?

DIANA

Oh. So you sayin' there's parts of the body don't feel the needle goin' in?

DOCTOR HIMMLER

Zere are parts of ze body zet feel it *less* zen *ozer* parts.

DIANA

But you still feel it, right?

DOCTOR HIMMLER

Are ve goink to heff anozer discussion group? Zere ist a bet on ze table.

DIANA

(Pause)

On the couch on mah tummy?

DOCTOR HIMMLER

Zet ist vat I said. Now move zet butt.


DIANA

(Goes to the couch and lies down on it)

Where you gonna stick me?


DOCTOR HIMMLER

Zet ist for me to know unt you to find out.


DIANA

You can't tell me?


DOCTOR HIMMLER

If I told you vere I am goink to put ze needle, you could pretend it hurt you unt you could tell me *vere* it hurt you because I vould heff told you ze spot, nicht wahr?


DIANA

Oh, you foxy, you are.


DOCTOR HIMMLER

(Approaching the couch with the syringe)

Pull down your panties, pliss.

DIANA

(Shooting up to a sitting position)

What?

DOCTOR HIMMLER

Again viss ze "vat." So I can giff you ze injection.

DIANA

Nothin' in the bet 'bout pullin' down mah panties.

DOCTOR HIMMLER

Excuse me, ze injection ist in ze buttocks. How can—

DIANA

Why can't you just move the edge of the panties a little?

DOCTOR HIMMLER

Excuse me, are you now tellink me meine chob?

DIANA

What's a "chob"?

DOCTOR HIMMLER

Vat I am doink, meine vork, meine responsibility.


DIANA

Oh, job.


DOCTOR HIMMLER

Ja, chob, chob. Are you tellink *me*—a DOKTOR—how I am goink to do meine chob?


DIANA

Why *can't* you just move the edge a little?


DOCTOR HIMMLER

Because I heff to give ze injection HERE.

(Touching her butt)


DIANA

Don't be touchin' mah ass.


DOCTOR HIMMLER

Ven I am goink to giff you ze injection, I *heff* to touch it.

DIANA

You wasn't *givin'* me no injection, you was just *touchin'* it.

DOCTOR HIMMLER

To show you *vere* I am goink to giff ze injection. Vy you get so upset about touching?

DIANA

Don't like to be touched.

DOCTOR HIMMLER

Vy not?

DIANA

Don't wanna talk about it.

DOCTOR HIMMLER

Aha! Zet ist proof!

DIANA

Of what?

DOCTOR HIMMLER

Zet you heff—a MONSTER—growink—INSIDE.


DIANA

What?


DOCTOR HIMMLER

Again vis ze "vat." Zet ist vat I said. A monster.


DIANA

You crazy.


DOCTOR HIMMLER

Oh, no! You do not call me—CRAZY! I am a DOKTOR for ze MIND. I cannot be—CRAZY.


DIANA

What you talkin' 'bout, "monster"?


DOCTOR HIMMLER

Oh, ja, ja! You heff sings you don't vant to talk about. SECRETS. Deep—dark—SECRETS. Secrets are—MONSTERS. Unt monsters grow—zey grow unt grow—until zey—EXPLODE.

DIANA

Do you know what you talkin' about?


DOCTOR HIMMLER

I am a DOKTOR. It ist meine business to know vat I am talkink about.


DIANA

A monster?


DOCTOR HIMMLER

Zet ist vy we must do zis in a hurry before ze monster grows too big.


DIANA

You sure?


DOCTOR HIMMLER

Liebschen, I am—


DIANA

A DOKTOR, yeah, I know, I know.

DOCTOR HIMMLER

Ve are nossing if not sure. Now I tell you somesing else. If, after I giff you ze injection, you do not fell *so* goot you feel altogezer like anozer person, I vill giff you one hoondred dollar in your hent—kesh.

DIANA

An' if'n I do feel that good? What I got to give *you*?

DOCTOR HIMMLER

Choost clean out a few more meine sings.

DIANA

So the deal is, if I feel the needle goin' in, you give me fifty bucks an' if I don't feel so good afterwards I feel like another person, you give me a hundred bucks, is that the deal?

DOCTOR HIMMLER

Ach, you are so simpatische, meine liebschen, I could burst.

DIANA

Don't change the subject, is that the deal?

DOCTOR HIMMLER

Zet's ze deal. We shook hents, nicht wahr?

DIANA

Didn't shake hands on the hundred bucks.

DOCTOR HIMMLER

Ach, you drive such a hart bargain; are you Jewish?

(Shaking hands)

DIANA

What's "Jewish"?

DOCTOR HIMMLER

"Vat's 'Jewish'?" How charming.

(Crosses to desk, takes COTTON out of black bag, ALCOHOL BOTTLE, dabs the cotton with it, returns to the couch, holding cotton and syringe)

Pull off ze panties, pliss.

DIANA

Down or off?

DOCTOR HIMMLER

Off, off! Take it all—off.

(The BAND gives us a few bars of STRIP MUSIC)

DIANA

Why can't I keep'em on an' jus' pull'em down a little?

DOCTOR HIMMLER

Again vis ze arguments. Ven vill you learn you cannot argue vis ze DOKTOR?

DIANA

Why I have to pull'em off?

DOCTOR HIMMLER

You vill see in a few moMENTS ven you vill feel besser zen you heff felt in your entire life, liebschen. You must trust me. Now pull zem off, pliss, so ve can KILL ze MONSTER.

DIANA

(Pulling off her panties)

This better be good.

DOCTOR HIMMLER

It vill be so goot it vill be beyond your vildest dreams.

(Sits by her on the COUCH, the back of which faces the audience, obscuring DIANE'S body and allowing us to see only the chest and head of DOCTOR HIMMLER as he tends to her. HE rubs the cotton on DIANE'S buttock with his left hand, then, slaps the buttock—all of which is blocked from the audience by the back of the couch)

DIANA

Ouch!

DOCTOR HIMMLER

Somesink wronk?

DIANA

You slapped me on the butt.

DOCTOR HIMMLER

Oh, you felt ze slap?

DIANA

What kind of a question is that, yeah, I felt it. What'd you do it for?

DOCTOR HIMMLER

To get ze flesh ready for ze injection. Zo—are you ready?

DIANA

There gonna be any more slappin'?

DOCTOR HIMMLER

No more slappink. Ready?

DIANA

Ready.

DOCTOR HIMMLER

Goot! You lose ze bet.

DIANA

What?

DOCTOR HIMMLER

I gafe you ze injection unt you did not feel it. You lose ze bet.

DIANA

When? When'd you give me the injection?

DOCTOR HIMMLER

Ven I giff you ze slap. You lose ze bet.

DIANA

You know—I *thought* I felt a sting there that was a little different from the slap.

DOCTOR HIMMLER

"Sought" does not count. Ze bet vas zet you vould *feel* it, not *sink* zet you *might* heff felt it. You lose ze bet.

DIANA

Will you stop saying that? You slapped me so hard.

DOCTOR HIMMLER

Ah, but you did not feel ze needle, did you?

DIANA

You tricked me.

DOCTOR HIMMLER

Ah, liebschen, liebschen—everybody tricks *everybody*. Zet ist vat life *ist*—van big TRICK! Also—I am *supposed* to slap ven I giff ze injection—choost perhaps not *kvite* zo hart.

DIANA

(The injection is beginning to make its presence known)

So you really gave me the shot?

DOCTOR HIMMLER

Really.

DIANA

(Becoming amenable)

So how'm I supposed to pay off my debt now?

DOCTOR HIMMLER

Ve vill find a vay, mine dear. For now it ist important zet ze injection does its vork unt zet ve prevent ze monster inside fon growink.

DIANA

(Beginning to float)

How does it do that?

DOCTOR HIMMLER

Magic, meine dear—magic.

(Looks at his watch)

It should begin any moMENT.

DIANA

What should?

DOCTOR HIMMLER

Vat are you feeling—at zis moMENT?

DIANA

Feelin' funny. My body—my head—getting' light—like they hardly have no weight. Everythin' gettin' light—funny. Feel like laughin'—singin'—dancin'.

(The BAND strikes up a tango)

DIANA

(Sings)

*The story I'm about to tell you*
*You've heard a thousand times before*
*The only reason I feel blue*
*Is that it happened once more*

*I met him first when we were dancing*

(DOCTOR HIMMLER places a ROSE between his lips and comes up behind her)

*He whispered sweetly in my ear*

(DOCTOR HIMMLER whispers in her ear)

*And then we went into the moonlight*

(DOCTOR HIMMLER leads her by the hand)

*That's where he held me near*

(DOCTOR HIMMLER stands behind her, holding her around the waist)

*I was contented*

(DOCTOR HIMMLER places his cheek against hers)

*Because he held me near*
*Said he was born only to love me*

(DOCTOR HIMMLER goes down to one knee at her side, holding her hand)

*He swore I'd never be alone*

(Holding her hand in one of his, DOCTOR HIMMLER grasps the area of his heart with the other)

*And then he left me for another*

(DOCTOR HIMMLER crawls away on all fours behind the couch)

*And now you know my song*
*I sing it sadly*

(Throwing her face upward and placing the upper side of her hand against her forehead in the manner of the old time tragediennes)

*And now you know my song*

(Returning from behind the couch, DOCTOR HIMMLER grabs DIANA. They do the tango, at the end of which he leads her to the COUCH)

DIANA

(In a druggy haze)

You gonna give me another shot?


DOCTOR HIMMLER

(Sitting DIANA on the couch, then slowly guiding her body to a reclining position)

No, meine deer. I am goink to giff you a MASSage.

(Begins to massage her back)


DIANA

(The drug has taken over to the extent she's willing to go along with just about anything)

That part of the treatment?


DOCTOR HIMMLER

Everysing—I do—ist part of ze TREATMENT.


DIANA

Dancin' part of the treatment?

DOCTOR HIMMLER

(Massaging away)

Of course.


DIANA

How come?


DOCTOR HIMMLER

Ze movement helps to circulate ze medicine sroughout ze body. Unt so does zis MASSage. Unt zen—zet ist how ve kill ze MONSTER.

(Continuing the massage as she emits soft sounds of satisfaction)


DIANA

Hey—what you touchin' there?


DOCTOR HIMMLER

(Continuing the massage)

It ist all part off ze treatment, all part off ze treatment.


DIANA

(Lazily, giddily, not really objecting)

But you touchin' mah—

DOCTOR HIMMLER

(Intensifying the massage)

It ist all right, it ist all right, you must remember—I am a DOKTOR! Unt zere are no private parts vis a DOKTOR. Everysing— everysing—ist part—off ze TREATMENT.


DIANA

Wow, what'd you just touch there, that felt *real* good. Whoa, there it goes again; MAMA!


DOCTOR HIMMLER

(Really into the massage now)

Ja, goot, zet means ve are KILLINK ze monster. Goot, goot!


DIANA

There it goes again! That's it, that's it—oh, baby—this is the best treatment I ever got.


(As DIANA begins to get in the throes, the LIGHTS slowly start to DIM)


DIANA

What's—what're you—oh—oh—oh, God, oh—ooooooooh!

(Uttering loud orgasmic sounds)

DOCTOR HIMMLER

(Covering her mouth with his free hand)

Not so loud, liebschen, not so loud, I beg off you.


(As the orgasmic sounds rise in volume, the BAND strikes up the martial air played at the beginning when DOCTOR HIMMLER first appeared, the LIGHTS going all the way DOWN)

# CHAPTER FORTY~FIVE

**W**riting this play, I realized something I knew would stay with me forever. I had known it instinctively when I'd played with a stick as a child but now I knew it in a kind of an official way, so I would never forget it. Creating enables you to experience a state of well being that cannot be equaled by any other means. I haven't taken drugs and I haven't done many things a lot of people are doing, so who am I to judge?

There are things you just know without having had to experience them.

I felt certain about other things making me feel good too. Helping people—witnessing glorious, altruistic deeds of courage and sacrifice. The end of *A Tale of Two Cities*, in which one man sacrifices his life for another moved me to a level of ecstasy, that all by itself answered the question for me of why we live. And whenever I see a noble act I experience the same kind of ecstasy.

I don't really know why such things make me feel so good. Of course, the mechanics of it are easy—endorphins are created and get released into your system, acting as an opiate and making you feel good—it's what happens when you run and do various other things. It can also be induced through drink and drugs—those coming with a hell of a price tag.

None of these ways can equal the joy of creating.

Sex is pleasure. But what is it really if it isn't looked at and performed as the ultimate creative act?

Still, I don't have the answer to the question of why either the creative act or the witnessing of a noble, courageous deed would move me or anyone to the point of producing these endorphins.

Does the execution and/or the witnessing of evil deeds cause such a release of endorphins, making those who perform evil deeds and those who watch them feel as good as the witnessing of noble and unselfish deeds?

Did Hitler get pleasure out of the Holocaust or Dracula (the original and real 15th century Prince Dracula who was the inspiration for the fictional vampire) out of impaling people on sharpened staffs? I'm sure they got *some* kind of pleasure—the kind of pleasure one experiences perhaps when, after living with horrible pain, one gets a momentary respite by causing others to experience even greater pain. A revenge of sorts—on whomever it may fall?

But those are the pleasures of the insane. Why, then, are the rest of us so moved and inspired by creativity and noble deeds?

Could it have something to do with the fact that creativity and creation are God's work and we are all fundamentally made out of the stuff of gods?

I think we are made of the stuff of gods—but have accumulated so much crap from the Beginning that the good stuff in us, being buried in so much crap, resonates only when we witness something noble and wonderful or when we're lucky enough to create. And so you get a plethora of people wanting to create or obtain money or fame or power and they all tell themselves and others it is for practical reasons—but, in the meantime, they create and create because that is what gods do, and we keep doing it even when we don't know the real reason we're doing it, no more than an ant knows why it's carrying the crumb to its lair or why thousands of ants will walk into a river and drown to form a bridge so other ants can cross over their dead bodies to get to the other side.

*De Lord is waitin' to take yo hand*

So now I had found something that would make me happy and that I could keep doing for the rest of my life, I had enough money so the interest from it, if invested wisely, would last a long, long time. Just past twenty, I had arrived at a point most people never get to their entire lives.

But then, the running theme of mine and everyone else's life— there's always the unexpected. Listening to WINS while brushing my teeth, I caught the news item that Luis Gonzales had expired—and it all came crashing down on me. I had killed a human being.

I thought of how high and mighty I'd felt expounding to myself about creating being the work of gods and all that—but snuffing out a human life, well, that, too, could be called the work of gods. He giveth life and He taketh it away. That part I wanted no part of.

And how had it come about?

*The man in sheets with the knife.*

That illusion had caused me to become rich and famous, enabling me to do what I felt like doing for the rest of my life—but it had also caused the end of someone else's life.

I was a murderer.

Not in the legal sense, but a murderer nevertheless.

The man with the knife had caused me to produce a weapon that was lethal. It had put people in the hospital and, knowing how potentially lethal it was, I'd continued using it for the sole purpose of my own aggrandizement.

Undergoing the process that Bill and Sandy had recommended, I never mentioned the man in sheets with the knife. I'd simply gone on to enjoy life and squeeze whatever pleasure it could bring me. And here was Luis Gonzales dying to remind me there was something in me that needed to be resolved before I could go on to enjoy the fruits of my life, fame, and money.

I called Bill Johnson and we got together and I told him about the man in sheets with the knife. He didn't seem surprised. He simply acknowledged what I was telling him.

"Okay," I said, "you're acknowledging me and I know that's what this technology says you're supposed to do. You're not supposed to evaluate or judge, just acknowledge. But let me tell you—you're going too far. I've just revealed something that most people would regard as absolutely out of the realm of reality—yet you sit there as if I'd just said I went to the grocery store and bought some bread."

"I don't mean to minimize what you've just told me," Bill said, "but the fact is we come across such things in this technology all the time and it's not nearly as fantastic as most people would think. Oh, I'll grant you, if you made this public, they might lock you up. But what you've experienced is not an unusual occurrence."

"What do you mean, you come across such things all the time? A man in sheets, holding a knife who appears as real to me as you are at this moment?"

"Not that exact image but—look—I don't want to say any more at this time because one of the guidelines of this technology is that you impart information to people according to what they are able to take in at any given time, what happens to be real for them at that moment. If you give them something that is not real to them, it's going to be a problem for them to accept it. In fact, one is, then, causing more damage than good because it's going to cause a chasm between you. What you need to do is partake in some more of this technology and your phenomenon will become clear to you, it'll be resolved easily and you'll have the answer to all your questions."

Trouble is everybody who believes in any kind of system or religion or any such thing always tells you what they've discovered will resolve all your problems. The media, our mail boxes, the internet all flood us with money-back guarantees that some new drug or potion or vitamin or mineral or herb or homeopathic preparation or a diet or a car or a beer or a perfume or an exercise system or a dish-washing liquid can solve all your problems and make you supremely happy, healthy, exciting, beautiful, glamorous and now they're even telling you that you don't have to age and can live forever.

I believe all that stuff.

I believe all of these things can come true—but not necessarily from the products they're trying to sell you. And that's where the trouble comes in. Consumers read testimonials from hundreds of people who swear the product being advertised caused them to miraculously enter the land of joy, ecstasy, beauty, sexual excitement, and glamour. These people giving testimonials are not glorified whores like the ones who have been paid to sell the product; they're folks—like you and me—and they swear we won't be sorry we purchased the product. Besides, the company tells you, "What in God's name can you lose, we're offering you a refund, no questions asked."

Ah, but how many people go to the trouble of mailing the unused portion back and asking for a refund? Some do, true, but most don't. No, they add another failure to their repertoire, suck it in, and continue on their downward spiral. Those in the upper echelons, from our President down the line, have convinced us they're mostly liars and so most of us don't believe anything any more. Yet, we would love it if it were otherwise. That we *could* believe.

Wasn't it P.T. Barnum who said, "There's a sucker born every minute?" Or was it W.C. Fields? No, W.C. Fields had said his gravestone should read, "All things considered, I'd rather be in Philadelphia." (Philadelphia used to have the reputation of being the dullest city in the nation. With multiple TV channels, the internet, video games, and shopping malls, no town can any longer lay claim to that honor).

*Is* it that most of us *want* to believe so much that every once in a while we get suckered into trying something, much like a woman who's been fucked over time and again still believes there's a good guy out there somewhere who will turn out to be the man of her dreams?

So here I was, having partaken of this applied religious philosophy, after which I felt good but, like most people, believed so little in promises that I did not attribute my improvement to the process I'd undergone, choosing instead to think it was all due to my simply feeling better, nothing to do with anything.

And now here was Bill telling me the very core of the mystery regarding the genie in the bottle who, with his knife had given me riches and fame, but also made me a murderer, could be resolved one, two, three. And now it was time for me to put up or shut up. Either I believed what I had decided about this applied philosophy and the man who founded it—or I didn't.

In having undergone a process in this technology with the decision to believe and then acting as if I didn't really believe it, I'd tried to sit on two chairs and had fallen through the cracks between. Now it was time to either believe or get off the chairs.

I decided there was yet a third choice.

I would do what Bill had suggested; I would "partake" in more of this technology and see what transpired. What could I lose? It was not nearly as expensive as psychiatry. And psychiatry was a joke anyway.

Lori Jacoby, whom I met the first time I'd gone there with Bill, was the one who helped me. I saw her in her office in that same building five times week. She would ask questions and I would answer them, then she would ask more questions and I would answer those. But it was nothing like what psychiatrists did. It was a completely different system of operation.

When I got into it, I understood why people undertook to explore, make new discoveries, become champions, stars, make wars, explore space, perform daredevil stunts, and do all those things that raised them above where they'd been when they started out.

This was why they did it, to find that place in themselves that made them feel they'd reached the $n$th degree in terms of ecstasy, power, serenity—god-dom—this place I was reaching during this process, this was what they'd been after all the time.

It was not an easy path. You sat there, answering question after question and, because of the nature of the questions, the way they were being asked, and the state-of-the art apparatus used to process the answers, you knew you had to answer them truthfully. You had to LOOK at things—really LOOK at them. And very often you didn't like what you saw because you didn't think you were what the answers to those questions indicated you were—and then you saw that you were. Like, for instance, one of the answers led me to realize I was a snob. That I felt myself to be in a superior place and kind of looked down on people. I had always prided myself on being friendly to everyone but I found that, friendly though I might have been, I still looked upon other people from a pedestal.

That's a good thing to discover. Not pleasant but, if you wanted to improve, beneficial. I also realized I had no compunctions about the idea of making love to another man's wife or girlfriend and that, if I ever got married, I would probably have no compunctions about cheating. I also realized I looked at many things from my mother's point of view and my mother had a tendency to condemn a lot of things on a general basis due to prejudice. That was something I'd had no inkling of.

What was wrong with the characteristics I'd discovered? George Bernard Shaw was one of the biggest snobs in history and so were many other geniuses (you understand this doesn't mean I think I'm a genius) but that didn't stop them from accomplishing great things and being admired through the ages. Presidents from Roosevelt to Eisenhower, to Kennedy to Clinton have cheated on their wives with very likely the same consideration about the matter that I'd had. To wit, "It's my body, my emotions, my spirit I can do with them what I want, share them with whom I want, it is my God-given right."

That's where this philosophy differed from all other philosophies and spiritual movements. The other philosophies and religions told you what you should or should not do. It was up to you to find out why you should or should not do those things and how to go about achieving the state of desiring or not desiring the doing of those things.

This technology went about its goals in a different way. It did not say, "Thou shalt not commit adultery." It did not say, "Thou shalt not steal" or "Do unto others as you would have them do unto you," it didn't tell you what you should or should not do. It did tell you, however, what phenomena took place in you when you did things *you* considered wrong—and then it went on to tell you what *you* would do to make yourself the effect of their consequences.

Equally important, it didn't ask you to believe it or not believe it any more than Newton asked you to believe in the Law of Gravity. It was there for you to test and see whether it worked, just like all Newton asked you to do was toss an apple into the air and see if it fell and hit you on the head.

It even instructed you to test it. It told you specifically at the very beginning and as its very foundation that *what is true is what is true for you*. Nothing else is true—for you. It can be true for other people; it does not have to be true for you.

So here I was with all these things I was finding out about myself and being asked to take a look at. Most people, I realized, never placed themselves in a position where they had the opportunity to objectively look at what they felt and were. We always managed to make ourselves right even if we didn't always manage to make ourselves look good. Do you ever see somebody in one of those court shows on TV who has lost a case say afterwards, "Gee, the judge was right, I *am* wrong," even when it is obvious to the millions of viewers watching that the person is as wrong as wrong could be? Nope. Never. The loser *always* maintains he/she is right. It is always the other person and the judge and anybody who sides with them that are wrong. It is not for nothing that one's own farts never smell. Or, at least, they don't smell bad.

The good news is, when you have the opportunity to *really* take a look through the viewing of your manifestations at what you do and what you are, you, then, also have the opportunity to make a conscious decision as to whether you want to keep a certain characteristic or attribute, or whether you want to choose another one from a whole available array of characteristics. Almost no one has consciously chosen the characteristics or attributes he or she possesses. At various points in your life all these things sneaked up on you and became part of you just like that sly or bitter or angry or sarcastic or mean or blank look people carry on their faces without realizing it.

So I took a look at all these items that sprang up—and I'm not going to tell you it wasn't at times like nails scratching across a blackboard or drilling into cement or as shaky and destructive as the collapse of the World Trade Center—it was all of these things. But I got to choose between what I was being—and what I wanted to be.

The difference between spending my life justifying actions—and getting to a position where I would objectively be able to choose what I wanted to be without a whole lot of buttons that would cause me to be angry when I didn't want to be nor was it appropriate and rational to be, and the same thing for being annoyed or frightened or disproportionately selfish or anxious or jealous or petty or any number of things that prevented me from being the kind of person I wanted to be—was like the difference between dwelling in Dante's Hell—and Irving Berlin's "My Blue Heaven."

And in the end, getting to that place turned out to be a greater adventure than all the continents discovered, all the mountains climbed, all the championships won, all the nations conquered, all the daredevil stunts pulled off, all the money made and all the stardom achieved.

What were some of the changes taking place in me? Well, being annoyed at certain things, for one. People are doing things all the time that annoy one; it could be littering, it could be not washing their hands after they use the toilet, picking their noses in public, driving slow on a highway fast lane, being uncommunicative, unfriendly, downright rude—well, there are oodles of annoying things that people do. I was finding these no longer irritated me. And when I discovered they no longer irritated me—people around me stopped doing them. How do you figure that?

Other things happened. I was no longer getting angry, as I had been in the past. My entire attitude began to change. I found myself liking people and being able to look at things from their viewpoint. I had not realized before how much I and everyone else seem to look at everything that happens purely from the viewpoint of our prejudices, how it affects us personally and specifically and then we go ahead and judge people and their actions based on that viewpoint.

It may seem like a silly thing to say but once you conceive of how pervasive it is, it doesn't seem silly any more. Think, for instance, of being in a very crowded space and, suddenly, you are pushed by someone behind you. You are naturally annoyed. Something primordial is touched off when somebody does anything aggressive or threatens us with any kind of loss. Take this example of being pushed. You are annoyed. Extend that example to anything in life. Somebody does something to you that you don't consider a friendly act and you're annoyed, ready to dispute.

But now think, in regard to the example of being pushed, how you would feel if you were able to discover the person who pushed you was himself pushed by someone else and so in no way pushed you willingly but was rather pushed into pushing you. Right away your annoyance toward the person dissipates. Of course, you might get annoyed at the person who pushed *him* but then you realized somebody else pushed *that* person and it's things like that that hold for everything. Somebody or something is always pushing someone to do something that may not be to your liking. If these things are not good and should not be done, it can be dealt with but, if you understand what is behind them, if you can see it from the other person's viewpoint, it can be handled in a much more positive and constructive manner without ill feelings. And it can be handled in terms of the greatest good for the greatest number, not solely on the basis of what you perceive suits you to the exclusion of what is good for anyone or anything else. Because *that*, as it turns out, ultimately winds up being the best thing for *you* as well.

Now, the most fascinating thing about these changes was that neither Lori Jacoby nor anyone else ever mentioned these were the things that should or were going to happen. All that happened was I was asked questions, the result of which was my being able to look at certain things about myself I'd never looked at before, the beauty of it that I could look at them *objectively*. Think of what a challenge it is to come up with hundreds upon hundreds of questions that could put you in a place where you had the *capacity* to smell your own farts.

My idea of falling in love changed too. I began to realize my intense desire to fall in love was a way of creating something that would make me feel good. So I would fall in love, then find a way of falling out, and then fall into it again with someone else.

Stella had seemed like the one and then Sandy and there was the notion maybe Hagit might be or Rachel, then it was Morshia Ellis. But they had all drifted away and that was probably Destiny. Perhaps my path was to keep enjoying the process. I was recognizing all this and now I was thinking in terms of what the truth of a person was rather than what I conjured up about the person that would suit my purposes.

I saw and dealt with people who were on staff of this applied philosophy and they had dedicated their lives to getting everybody in the world to partake of this technology and I found this to be a great goal and they certainly seemed happy and kept trying to get me to join staff, asking me did I not want others to have the benefit of this technology?

I wanted everyone to get the benefit because I knew it worked and, if one was open to it, there would be no one it would not work on. For myself, though, I envisioned another role. I wanted to inspire through my creations and through my emanations and I wanted to be on my own.

But then—then it occurred to me—I still had not gotten to unravel the mystery of the man with the knife. And that was what I had gone into the process for in the first place.

# CHAPTER FORTY-SIX

I continued to absorb this technology. I noticed I was feeling lighter and everything around me seemed brighter. Like car headlights, for instance. They became festive, dancing bright stars coming toward me. And when each one passed, another began its own dance. My feeling toward people and things in general continued to change. I began to like them more, they got friendlier toward me. New Yorkers, for God's sake. I was becoming more benevolent. I began to be interested more and more in what people did and said and my liking for them continued to grow.

I noticed my improved sense of well-being wasn't temporary like the feel-good things I'd done in the past. Even the act of creating or falling in love, which sent you to Cloud Nine, made you feel good as long as the newness of it lasted. When it ended, you snapped back to your usual state like a rubber band. I realized suddenly that everything people did to make themselves feel good worked only as long as the shelf life for any given item lasted; if one kept doing it and doing it, it eventually backfired. It was that way with love, drinking, drugs, adventure, stardom, sex, power. Everything that made you feel good got old and turned on you.

The stuff I was getting here, on the other hand, kept moving me forward and allowed me to keep the gains I got in terms of feeling happier, abler, and more intelligent.

It was the most amazing phenomenon I'd experienced. As if I'd been walking around, carrying heavy weights and looking "through a glass darkly." Now everything was turning bright and clean and I continued to feel lighter and lighter. Oh, baby. I walked around, smiling, bursting with cheerfulness.

At one point during our work together, Lori Jacoby asked me whether I'd had a certain kind of experience in the past. Knowing I hadn't, I said no.

She said very gently, "Take a look—see if there's something there."

"I have," I said. "There's nothing there."

"Take another look," she said. "See if anything appears."

She had these clear blue eyes with the cleanliness and sparkle to them. Together with the intensity, there was happiness and a joy in them too that seemed independent of anything that had happened to her or anything anyone could do to her. Nothing in her seemed dependent on anything that was external.

I had a strong feeling of affection for her. Bill said it was not unusual. Unlike in other self-improvement practices, where those who are doing the helping often form sexual relationships with the helpee, in this movement everyone was highly aware that any improvement and progress had as its fundamental ingredient ethical behavior which adhered to a written code.

So, though I had strong feelings of affection for Lori and sensed she felt the same for me, there was never even a hint of anything that could be interpreted by anyone as improper.

There was something in the way she asked me to keep looking for this particular incident in my past that made me feel something significant was taking place. As if I were about to step into uncharted territory. Except I remembered watching and listening to the founder of this movement on tape and I had the feeling there *was* no uncharted territory for him.

"I know nothing like that ever happened to me," I said.

I'm not being specific about the incident itself because there is a rule when you're undergoing these processes that neither you nor the person you're working with should talk to anyone about the specifics of what is happening in the sessions. The reason is these are delicate processes and if they're invalidated by other people with so much as a word or glance, it can do a great deal of damage.

Even revealing as much as I am may be going too far but, if what

I've written so far is going to do any good, I need to take you all the way to the magic door, open it, and let you look at what is there. Besides, I'm writing this, not talking to you and, unless you write me, I won't know if you're being invalidative.

"I don't mean necessarily in this lifetime," Lori said. "Look even further back. See if you come across anything."

"Are you talking about previous lifetimes?"

"Just look and see if there *is* anything."

Okay. We had come to a crossroads.

The idea of former lifetimes—well, there was the Bridey Murphy affair decades ago and other things that dealt with former lives and a lot of people believed in them. In my view these people were all pretty much flakes. I didn't want to say there *was* no such thing as former lifetimes because, "There is more in this universe, Horatio, than your philosophies can encompass," but who *cared* whether there were former lifetimes? How was it relevant to anything?

Yet, here was Lori asking me to go back to something I didn't give a damn about and felt only flakes indulged in.

I experienced a strong urge to get up and leave.

When in fundamental disagreement with something, I believed in getting up and leaving. If I didn't like a book, a movie, a play, or a person, I walked out. There was never a moment's consideration regarding the fact I might've invested money, effort, or time into the thing or that I might hurt someone's feelings. If I felt it was not worthy of my attention, I was gone.

The only exception was in small theatres. When something I considered awful was taking place on stage, I did not have the heart to walk out, causing the actors to notice me. I allowed myself to be tortured till intermission. Because I know how delicate those actors' hearts are and I cannot bear to break them—although, often, I felt they deserved to be broken—for putting me through such torture.

There were other considerations. Everything I'd found out about this philosophy was on the money and the changes in me were tangible and fundamental. Should I break off with it on the strength of my feeling that belief in former lifetimes was the province of flakes? Or should I give it the benefit of doubt? I remembered both Sandy and Bill telling me to keep an open mind.

Lori, meanwhile, was giving me that intense gaze of hers. No one had ever gazed at me the way she did.

"Just look," she said.

*Give me a break!*

"See what comes up," she said.

There was some kind of a signal in the way she said it. As if she knew something ineffable—that I could discover if I would only take the step into this unknown territory.

So I looked—and looked—and looked—and then—something—something—something—began to form. It was slow—and came in as if someone were throwing tiny pebbles at the window—and then these little pebbles began to form something—something akin to a picture—a moving—picture.

And the feeling it gave me was so thrilling I couldn't believe it was possible to sit in a room and create within yourself something that could excite you this much.

Was that what Christ had meant when he said the Kingdom of God was within you? That you could create—anything—within you? Even such a thrill as I was feeling at the moment?

*I was flying. Over France. It was World War I. How did I know it was World war I? I don't know. I just knew. I was flying a plane. And they were shooting at me from the ground.*

I had to rush back to the present—to this room. I took a deep breath.

Looking at me, Lori asked, "What happened?"

I stared at her. Had I—in my desire to do what she'd asked—concocted the scene of flying a plane the way I did when I wrote a play or a story?

It didn't feel like that. When I wrote a play or a story, I was aware of making things up, I knew they came from my imagination. This was different. This was—*remembering*. I was remembering something that had happened in World War I. More than that. I was actually back there. I was experiencing something that had happened to me—before I was born. So it was not me in the sense it was the same body I had now.

But it was *me*.

"What happened?" Lori asked.

I told her.

"All right," she said. "All right. Good. Good."

And I realized at that moment why it was of the utmost importance not to talk to others about what happens inside that room. One look from somebody after they'd heard what I'd just experienced and everything that was forming in me, happening to me, would shatter into a zillion pieces. How could you talk to people about this and not have them think you're cuckoo?

But I knew what I knew — and I was talking to someone who had obviously heard such things before and also knew it was true. You *could* remember.

Why is it relevant?

Because it gives you the most important epiphany you could possibly have. Knowing you've lived different lifetimes, could you ever bring yourself to look at things in this lifetime the way you'd looked at them *before*? Could you ever be petty again? Or annoyed? Could you be anxious about things you now saw were comparatively insignificant? Could you be selfish? Could you have the same viewpoint on your fellow beings' welfare and doings? Could you have the same goals?

How could I have thought former lifetimes were irrelevant?


*Nothing — nothing — would ever be — the same — again.*


I continued working with Lori. I continued feeling better and better. About people, about life, about what I was doing.

I was writing every day and it made me feel wonderful. But in a different way. There was a wider spectrum to it, a different goal. I wanted to accomplish things with it that would benefit everyone everywhere.

I would see Bill and Sandy and we'd have dinner or lunch. There'd be these events, via-satellite telecasts, of what was happening in regard to this philosophy and how it was doing in the rest of the country and the world. Neither Sandy nor I felt like getting together sexually again; we had both moved on. We were now friends and not in a frame of mind where we wanted to have a future together.

Since I was no longer boxing or training for boxing, I decided to take up another sport. I wanted the exercise and I wanted it in the form of a skill. I picked fencing. There had been a time when actors took up as part of their training either fencing or ballet. Generally, the women took ballet and men took up fencing. The idea was to have more control over one's body and be more graceful. Nowadays, very few actors give that aspect much credence.

But I didn't really take up fencing for the sake of acting. I didn't do speech exercises for the sake of acting either. I don't like doing things for specific, practical reasons. Like working in order to make money or being friendly to people in order to get something from them. I liked doing things because I had decided they were good and fun things to do—for me and for others.

So I did not take up fencing in order to be more effective as an actor nor did I exercise in order for my heart to function better or so I would stay slim. I exercised because it made me feel better, made me a more fit person physically and emotionally, and enabled me to express physically about life what I felt spiritually, just as I did speech exercises because it made me communicate better and made the communication more understandable and pleasing to anyone who listened to it, and it made me feel good to speak beautifully with a pleasant sounding voice.

And then something suddenly occurred to me. There was a question I needed to ask. It was a question that, for a writer who was writing anything, was mandatory and now it occurred to me it was even more vital for that question to be asked by me of me as a person living in this world at this time—at any time.

What was my goal? For me, for the world.

I had already determined, when you asked this question of other people, they acted like students getting a surprise question on their final. And they had a hell of a time answering it.

And I'd never asked that question of myself. But the surprise for me was that I didn't have a hard time answering it.

Joy was the answer. Joy for me, joy for the world. The ability to create things the whole world could utilize to feel and be better. I wanted to feel wonder, joy, and ecstasy in everything. I wanted the entire world to feel that.

Was it possible?

What about the idea that people love to read and watch violence, bloodshed, pornography, perversion, gossip?

That was what they liked *now* but *now* they were also miserable and many were insane and others were slowly going insane, clutching at straws—drugs, alcohol, screwing other people, rationalizations, justifications, excuses, invalidations—to save themselves, to find temporary relief. Was it possible that all these unhealthy diversions were the straws and if people were no longer drowning, they would no longer need the straws?

It was my goal to make that happen.

And if I couldn't?

What do I lose?

Meanwhile, I have a goal I like and feel is worthy.

But I couldn't do any of that until—until I solved the mystery of the guy in sheets, sporting a knife and trying to kill me.

He was my personal poltergeist and as long as he was around, that knife would be hanging over my head.

I would continue doing all the things I was doing and I would be absorbing this technology. If I could find myself in a plane over France during World War I, then—anything—anything—was possible.

# CHAPTER FORTY-SEVEN

The Christmas holiday season in New York is probably one of the most interesting phenomena you can experience. New Yorkers, you know, are very guarded people. Just as the media find themselves in a position where they communicate to a common denominator of society, so New Yorkers have set their attitudes to suit a common denominator in terms of whom they'll run into on the street and subways. People from out of town will often come to New York and tell you, "Oh, I get along just fine with New Yorkers, they're pretty friendly people."

It's true. When you exhibit evidence you're from out of town, mean no harm, and are communicative, New Yorkers will let down their guards and communicate with you. But if you're a New Yorker yourself, you will have your guard up as a matter of course and so will your fellow New Yorkers; you won't be going around with a cheerful, communicative, friendly attitude the way an out-of-towner will; both you and the other New Yorkers will have their guards up, always ready for the weirdos, panhandlers, and muggers you're going to encounter in New York.

That's why the Christmas holiday season is such a phenomenon. You take millions of people who all year round walk and ride around the city, not communicating with anyone; when they buy something, there is the barest, minimal communication conceivable and often you won't get even that. People will go to a store, bring to the counter stuff they picked off a shelf, the amount of money they owe will show on the register, the consumer will put the money or a credit card on the counter and the exchange will be made without a word uttered. People don't even look at each other. They live in the same apartment building and pass each other for years and it will be rare they will say hello.

Sad thing. But fact. People have been saying this about New Yorkers for years and it gets worse. And the rest of the world is following suit. It's become *au courant*. As goes New York so goes America; as goes America, so goes the world.

*What reason is there for being friendly?* has become the prevailing attitude.

But ultimately it's because people need each other less and less. Their opinion of others is lower, except for individuals who are famous.

Yet, somewhere deep inside there is a sense it's wrong. You look at kids and delight in how naturally friendly they are—and you are saddened that in time they will all, like the adults they emulate, learn to be just as unfriendly.

And somehow it's hard to imagine myself living anywhere *but* New York. I can think of a number of places in the world that would be a paradise to live in but I know, after a while, I would start missing this city, thinking about the infinity of people and things happening in it. I would start wondering why I was living away from the center of the world.

Is it egotistical for New Yorkers to think of their city being the center of the world? Probably, but there is no other city anywhere in the world to the denizens of which it would even *occur* to think of as the center of the world. And there is probably no one in the entire world who does *not* think of New York as the center of the world. I read in the book *Megatrends* how Los Angeles was growing to become the most important and powerful city in the world and how important Tokyo is and how the ten largest banks in the world are Japanese and all that other stuff about how Asia is catching up and becoming the most important part of the world in terms of economics, which is the only thing that counts, yet, "Oh, Beautiful for Spacious Skies" still leads the way and is far above any other land in any area you choose. Other countries train their people in athletics, education, and other stuff like that but 99 out of a 100 of those people would give twenty years of their lives to come live here, America the beautiful.

New York. New York. The Christmas season. Living proof you can take millions of people who are unfriendly and uncommunicative and for several weeks each year it can all turn around and they can be cheerful, friendly, communicative, benevolent—excited about life—experiencing the pure joy of it. How is that done? Well, who cares? The question is—if it can be done for a few weeks, could it be done for fifty-two?

I have tried to keep it up after January one. Doesn't work. Everybody, by general agreement, drops after that date, they get gloomier and unfriendlier than the rest of the year. Almost as if they were trying to make up for the weeks they'd been so cheerful and friendly so it would balance out to some kind of yearly average of unfriendliness and uncommunicativeness.

But the fact it can be done for a few weeks is proof it *can* be done. And if it can be done in New York, it can be done throughout the world. People can feel great, they can feel and be friendly, they can feel life is wonderful, and they can be benevolent.

And to somehow get them to be that way was my goal. And I was convinced this applied philosophy/religion was the tool that would do it.

I felt myself getting closer and closer to the capability of doing it. After all, didn't the Beatles change the world? Didn't Elvis? Didn't Abraham Lincoln? Didn't John Kennedy? One could be an entertainer or one could be something else but it could be done.

The key for me was finding out who the man in the sheets was and why he had come to me. If I could solve that, I would give all of myself to making the world a joyful, thrilling, and benevolent place.

The New Year was approaching. It's a time when you want to have someone you can spend New Year's Eve with. Bill asked me to come to the event that this applied philosophy movement was going to hold. It would be telecast from its headquarters in Florida via satellite to all the branches in the nation.

"I don't see myself sitting in a large hall on New Year's Eve and watching on a big screen how well the movement is doing around the globe."

"Why not?" he asked.

"I see myself either being with the woman I love, sipping

champagne, or being by myself, watching Times Square on TV."

"Have you thought how good it might feel to be with a group of people who want what you want for the world and to see there's actual headway being made toward improving the world?"

"Haven't thought about that."

"Why don't you think about it?"

"I'll think about it."

"Sandy'll be there — lots of nice people. We'll get a table together — be fun."

"I'll think about it."

He knew better than to push.

Sandy also asked me to come but didn't push either. A lot of staff members called, leaving numerous messages, inviting me to the event.

I decided I wasn't going to go. The day of the New Year's Eve I would be going in for my session with Lori and as great as it made me feel, it also made me tired. You were digging into some heavy stuff during these processes. In many ways, fight training was easier. While you were undergoing this process, they recommended you take lots of B-1 and E but I took several B-complex tablets during the day and figured it would do me fine.

Spending New Year's Eve alone, feeling the celebration that was going on everywhere around me was a way of celebrating too. I was not one of those people who have a button on being alone, whether for special occasions or no occasion at all. I enjoy being alone and never have the feeling I would rather be with almost anyone than alone. I think it must come from the time I was a kid and with my stick acted out all those stories I made up. Feeling I could people my space with my own world.

"There's always the unexpected," was the point made in *The Bridge on the River Qwai.* And that day, during my session with Lori, it happened.

It happened in a very quiet, unassuming way. Lori asked me to go back — tap into a former lifetime.

I traveled back. And back. And back. Eyes closed — telling Lori everything that was happening as it was happening.

A fascinating process. They talk about time machines and

Crichton came out with a book, *Timeline*, that talks about a technical capacity where they'll be able to transport people into the past in the same way you can send a fax over almost unlimited distances.

But there was no machine took me back. I took myself back. And it's a fantastic feeling. Happens in a flash.

*I found myself in Roman times. How did I know they were Roman? I just —knew. Knew with the same certainty I had of being in that room.*

*Where I went back to was a large room —much larger than the one I was sitting in. I was dressed in a toga.*

*Sheets?*

*There was a circle of friends around me. They were looking to me as —the man.*

*It was March.*

*Before I'd left the house —palace —my wife had—*

*Wife —?*

*Said something about the Ides of March.*

*I shrugged and waved my hand, almost as if she were there, in dismissal of her comment.*

*In the middle of the wave, something stung me in the back. A bee must have somehow gotten inside the room. I changed the direction of my hand toward my back to remove the bee, which must have killed itself in the process of stinging me, when I felt another sting, this one in the soft of my stomach. And then a whole series of stings all over the upper part of my body. I felt my legs giving way as an animal's do when it's received an array of spears and arrows.*

*I willed myself to remain on my feet, though my body was slowly descending. My best friend was in the group and whatever had happened that had caused me so much weakness, I could count on him to set it aright.*

*Indeed, I saw him approach. He would help me.*

*When he was very near, he pulled his right hand from under his toga. The hand held a massive knife with many decorations etched in the part of the handle I could see between his fingers that were holding it. I wondered how he had managed to conceal such a large object but, of course, those togas are quite loose, one can conceal a great deal under them.*

*After all, they were —sheets?*

*He held the knife high —then plunged it into my chest.*

*I said, "You—ugly one."*

*Why did I call him ugly, I wondered. He was not ugly at all. Had a fine Roman nose, a good face, grace, fine bearing—a thoroughly honorable man. What had possessed me to call him ugly?*

*Then I remembered. I would have been speaking—Latin. Latin for "ugly" was—Brutus.*

# CHAPTER FORTY-EIGHT

I walked—from 46<sup>th</sup> Street—down to the Village and then uptown on the West Side to Columbia University on 116<sup>th</sup> and back to 77<sup>th</sup>, to my apartment.

What could I find difficult again? And what could be anything but fun—for the rest of eternity?

I would finish the play, I would do the screenplay for Brad Pitt, and I would make the world into what I envisioned it could be.

*We're goin' to the promised land*

I would go to the New Year's Eve event with Bill and Sandy. Yes, Bill was right, these were the people who wanted for the world what I wanted. I *should* be with them, who else should I be with?

We would fight hand in hand together to bring power, glory and ecstasy to the world.

*Start me with ten—and I'll give you ten million more!*

I called Bill and told him I was coming.

He had reserved a table for us and a few other people he introduced me to when I got there. One was Larry MacDonald, a tall, slim, sturdy man in his thirties with light brown hair and sparkling, smiling blue eyes. You looked at him and felt you could see forever in those eyes, that all was wonderful with the world and it didn't matter there were bad people in it, *this* was what a person was supposed to be like and your heart immediately went out to him and I thought even if I didn't know anything about this applied philosophy, any movement that had this man in it had to be a right-thinking, right-doing movement. Larry was there with his wife Mireya and her three children from a previous marriage. Another man Bill introduced me to was Tom Rainford. Tom Rainford looked like a clone of Charles Laughton, if you can picture that, and he was in his sixties, yet you thought of him as a *young* Charles Laughton.

Tom was irrepressibly bubbly, communicative and articulate. He looked to be one of those individuals who were in perpetually high spirits. He was with a beautiful young woman who seemed very much in love with him and was not in the least bit hesitant about showing it.

Before the start of the satellite telecast on the big screen, Bill filled me in on both Larry and Tom.

"Tom," he said, "is a writer. Years ago he wrote a play that was produced off-Broadway and he was hailed by a number of critics as the next Eugene O'Neill."

"What happened?"

"Well, if you want to be the next Eugene O'Neill or the next anything, you've got to be obsessively single-minded about it. For Tom, life is a cornucopia of desserts and he has to taste them all. The woman he's with is also in the movement, on quite a high level, as a matter of fact; I don't know exactly what she does but I do know she's made a hell of a lot of money doing it and though, as you can see, she could probably get just about any handsome young man she set her sights on, she's chosen Tom, who's more than thirty-five years her senior and whom, as you can see, no one would readily call handsome, though there is an undeniable charm that evidently more than makes up for it in many people's eyes. She has a great big ranch out in the California mountains where she keeps a bunch of riding horses and such things. Tom lives there with her, taking trips to L.A. where he gets involved in movie projects and whatnot. As you can see, he's happy as a sow in mud. On the other hand, Tom, I suspect, is always happy. Before he went out to California to live with that beautiful young woman, he helped Larry write a screenplay called *The Secret Wars*. It's based on a true happening which very few people are aware of. A factual occurrence that's been taking place in this country over the past few years. It has to do with a movement to change the Constitution. You need 37 states to ratify a National Convention, which has the right and power to change the Constitution. There are forces in this nation interested in doing that very thing. At the moment, thirty-four states have ratified the National Convention. Three more and — surprise — we all are going to have a new Constitution. The time limit for this has been removed so anytime they can get three more states — it's going to be done."

"What kinds of changes are being planned for this new Constitution?"

"The trillion-dollar question. Larry's screenplay deals with a young man on a white horse who tries to prevent that."

"Have you read it?"

"Oh, yes. It's the kind of thing Frank Capra would've loved — today's answer to *Mister Smith Goes to Washington* — only with guns and bombs and the rockets' red glare."

Seizing a moment when Larry was not engaged in listening to Tom and was at the point of turning to say something to Mireya, I said across the table, "Larry?"

His sparkling blue smiling eyes turned to gaze at me as if to say, *What fun thing is going to happen next?*

"Could I read your screenplay?"

"Give me your address and I'll deliver it to your doorstep in the morning."

I pulled out one of my cards and tossed it to him.

Just then, the lights began to dim, as the event was about to start.

I got up to go to the bathroom. On the way to the bathroom I passed a table at which my peripheral vision spotted a slim young black woman in a red dress and it felt as if she were smiling at me. I thought it must be someone I'd passed on the stairway or hallway on the way to or from one of the processing sessions or someone who recognized me from having seen me in the ring or on one of the talk shows and, as it was getting dark and hard to see, I simply smiled back and moved on.

On the way back from the bathroom, my peripheral caught her again and the same thing happened. Well, the antennae went up. I had been focusing on the technology and writing for weeks and my mind hadn't particularly been on those kinds of antennae but now they were up. The event, however, had begun and I couldn't very well go over to her table and start a conversation. So I sat and watched the screening, hoping she would be there after the screening was over and I could go talk to her.

The screening lasted a long time—over three hours. Three hours is a long time to watch how well an organization is doing. Though it was interesting, there is an unwritten and an unbreakable rule about how long you can keep an audience watching anything that is not *Gone with the Wind* or *Lawrence of Arabia*.

My eyelids were heavy and I was sure that anyone who was not completely dedicated to the movement would have gone long ago. Also, the end of the telecast coincided with the witching hour and there were probably people who wanted to be someplace else for the midnight kiss. I was sure the woman who had smiled at me was gone by now. Ah, well, destiny.

At midnight Larry kissed Mireya and Tom kissed his girlfriend and Sandy leaned over and kissed me on the lips and kissed Bill on the cheek.

I was worried the woman in the red dress had seen it and would assume Sandy was my girlfriend. I turned around to see if she was there.

Miracle of miracles, she was. I went over.

On the stage the members of the band were gathering with their instruments.

When I was about six feet from her, I stopped suddenly as if my soles were Krazy-Glued to the floor.

No.

"Morshia?"

She gave out that wonderful smile of hers.

I practically leaped at her, threw my arms around her, and hugged her for all I was worth.

And she hugged me in return.

Then she pulled her head back to look at me.

"I hear you're not fightin' any more," she said with that melodic Jamaican lilt.

"No," I said. "I'm lovin'."

"Good," she said. "Good."

The band began to play.

Couples started converging toward the dance floor.

"Come on," Morshia said, taking my hand and leading me to the floor, "I'll teach you how to do it—Jamaican style."

"Hand in hand, baby," the vocalist sang, "and feel all right."

Printed in the United States
24181LVS00002BA/67-198